Blood Rites

Rachel Lynch grew up in Cumbria and the lakes and fells are never far away from her. London pulled her away to teach History and marry an Army Officer, whom she followed around the globe for thirteen years. A change of career after children led to personal training and sports therapy, but writing was always the overwhelming force driving the future. The human capacity for compassion as well as its descent into the brutal and murky world of crime are fundamental to her work.

Also by Rachel Lynch

The Rift

Detective Kelly Porter

Dark Game
Deep Fear
Dead End
Bitter Edge
Bold Lies
Blood Rites
Little Doubt
Lost Cause

BLOOD RITES

RACHEL LYNCH

First published in the United Kingdom in 2019 by Canelo

This edition published in the United Kingdom in 2019 by

Canelo Digital Publishing Limited
31 Helen Road
Oxford OX2 0DF
United Kingdom

Copyright © Rachel Lynch, 2019

The moral right of Rachel Lynch to be identified as the author of this work has been asserted in accordance with the Copyright, Designs and Patents Act, 1988.

All rights reserved. No part of this publication may be reproduced or transmitted in any form or by any means, electronic or mechanical, including photocopy, recording, or any information storage and retrieval system, without permission in writing from the publisher.

A CIP catalogue record for this book is available from the British Library.

Print ISBN 978 1 78863 555 4
Ebook ISBN 978 1 78863 269 0

This book is a work of fiction. Names, characters, businesses, organizations, places and events are either the product of the author's imagination or are used fictitiously. Any resemblance to actual persons, living or dead, events or locales is entirely coincidental.

Look for more great books at www.canelo.co

Printed and bound in Great Britain by Clays Ltd, Elcograf S.p.A.

Chapter 1

When the alarm pierced the darkness, Joe Spencer rolled over and flopped his arm out from under the duvet to silence the damn thing. He sighed loudly. Had he really been that stupid? To think that he could haul his kids out of bed – as well as his wife – before dawn, to get into a freezing car, all to witness the sunrise over a pile of stones?

He sighed heavily again. Annie, his wife, groaned and pulled her pillow over her head.

'You seriously set the alarm?' she asked. He fumbled around the floor, under the bed frame, and found his phone. He switched off the beeping siren and slumped back to his sleeping position. As a National Park Ranger, he was supposed to be used to early mornings, but he was off work, and he'd drunk too many beers last night.

'I've got a headache,' Annie announced.

'You drank too much wine.'

'That's rich, coming from you.' She squeezed one eye open affectionately.

'Come on, we'll regret it if we don't go,' he said, sitting upright, galvanised suddenly by his original excitement from when he'd first planned the crazy idea. The boys had been up to Castlerigg before but never at sunrise. Every time he made an early morning visit to check the site for litter, miscreants and misdeeds he took photos of the captivating dawn and swore that he'd show his family one day.

Castlerigg stone circle was some five thousand years old, though no one knew for sure, and its true history was shrouded in mystery. Funding had never been forthcoming to excavate it, and the circle had sat for centuries, guarding her secrets, in solitude, surrounded by an amphitheatre of rock and fell. The huge glacial boulders originated in Neolithic Borrowdale, some nine miles away, and how they were lugged to Keswick, through such precipitous terrain, was anyone's guess.

'Come on, it'll be worth it, I promise,' he said to Annie. She'd never been. Annie was originally from Cornwall and the whole experience of the Lakes to her had been a revelation. Joe had romanced her with a thousand views of mountain and lake. Now she couldn't imagine living anywhere else. Joe wasn't a local either, but he'd lived here for most of his life.

Annie scowled at him from under her pillow, the only light still was the blue glare from his phone.

'I'll wake the boys.'

Joe flicked on the hall light and went into the boys' room. He quietly opened the door and found them both fast asleep, which he'd expected. He gently nudged the older boy first.

'Callum,' he whispered quietly, and then louder. The boy roused and shielded his eyes from light pouring in from the hallway. His son shot daggers at him and Joe smiled his best convincing grin. He went to Connor's bed and did the same, getting the same response.

'Come on, guys, this will be amazing, I can see the sky is clear and we don't want to miss it.'

Callum swung his legs over the side of the bed and pulled on his trousers, followed by a sweater and a snood. He stretched and leant over to poke his brother.

'Come on, Connor,' he said to his brother, who finally did the same, and in under a minute, both boys were ready and upright.

'Where's Mum?'

'She's coming. Bags are packed, let's go.'

Callum and Connor went out into the hall and towards the kitchen, grabbing protein bars on the way, with Joe following them before going outside to get the car started. It wasn't a long drive to the stone circle, and they'd be there in ten minutes. As part of his contract with English Heritage, Joe was given a house deep in the Lakes, on farmland, in the middle of nowhere, between Keswick and Penrith. There was no noise in the yard; not a neighbour's dog or cockerel stirred. Joe threw coats at the boys, who'd followed him outside, and they took them happily, shocked by the temperature.

'Why is it so cold?' asked Connor. It was only September after all.

'Summer's over. It's winter's turn now. Death cometh to the land and feasts upon the remnants of life...' Joe did his best impression of a menacing stranger, preaching Pagan babble. The boys rolled their eyes. Joe winked at them and went to the car, getting in and starting the engine, flicking on every heating switch there was. The boys bundled into the back and Annie came out of the cottage.

'Keys?' she asked. Joe nodded. She closed the cottage door and got in the car.

'Right, let's go!' He swung the car out of the yard, along the dark track towards the main road. Joe scoured the sky and was happy: it had yet to show signs of the blackness turning to charcoal and then to grey and purple. They were still ahead of time.

The dual carriageway was deserted. Joe could have driven blindfolded. This was his backyard. A small sign, covered almost completely by bushes, said 'Castlerigg Stone Circle', and they turned off another road, which was even narrower. They went uphill and Joe looked to his left.

'Almost there.' His wife said nothing. The boys grunted acknowledgement, accustomed to their father's enthusiasm for outings at odd hours.

'Here!' Joe pointed to a gate leading to a field, though they couldn't see the stones just yet, and parked further up the lane. There were no other cars there and Joe felt a thrill of exclusivity grab him: they might have it all to themselves. He parked and turned off the engine. 'Right, team, come on!' he said.

'Can we stay in the car, Dad?'

'Nope. Denied. You know that new Xbox game you want?' The boys looked at one another and knew what was coming. 'Yeah, well, you have to earn it.'

'By sightseeing in the dark!' Callum thought himself clever and Annie laughed.

Joe got out of the car and went across the road. His eyes adjusted and out of the oily blackness, one, then two, then more mysterious, tall, dark grey structures appeared in the distant field before him. He heard the car door slam, and Annie and the boys approached.

He pointed across the field and the others followed his gesture. Behind the ghoulish formations, a faint glow emerged from the horizon and, in seconds, the stones were silhouetted gently by a purple hue. Joe led them into the field.

'Watch out for the sheep crap,' he warned.

'I can smell them,' said Callum. In the distance, an animal bleated, as if in answer to Joe's insolence. As the forthcoming light materialised, they spotted scores, if not hundreds, of white blobs, moving nonchalantly between the huge stones, chewing and occasionally looking up at their visitors.

They walked closer to the structure and Joe could tell by the silence that it had been a good idea: he looked at his boys, who were staring at the boulders before them. They reached the outer circle and Connor put out his hand to touch the rock.

'How old did you say these were, Dad?'

'About five thousand years. It's estimated that they're Neolithic because of some axes that were found here. The stones have never been properly dated.'

'Why not?'

'Money, mainly. If it was under threat from erosion or farming, I suppose somebody would step in, but English Heritage isn't made of money.'

'That's wrong,' Connor said. 'Who knows what's under there?'

'I agree, but at least it's left in peace and not overrun by tourists.'

Their words merged into the silence around them and dissipated on the wind. It was an odd sensation, and somehow, the absence of other human beings made their voices resonate further. They walked around the stones and came to where it was believed the entrance stood: guarded by two huge monoliths, each perhaps weighing sixteen tonnes. Just inside that, there was a strange arrangement of stones that seemed to indicate an inner chamber.

'What was this for?' It was Connor who asked again. His favourite subject was history. Callum's was maths. Joe reckoned that the stone circle would satisfy both minds.

'No one knows. It could have been an inner chamber. There was a small dig undertaken in the nineteenth century, apparently ruling out a burial. What do you think, Connor?'

'I think it was an altar.'

'How did they mark it out?' Callum wondered at the regularity of the circle and Joe smiled.

'The sun and moon both align to some of the stones at certain times of the year too,' he said.

'Like Stonehenge?'

'Yes.'

The dark turned from purple to grey and Joe pointed to the horizon. The night had been crisp and clear, and the sky turned quickly from purple to red. The sun was coming. The outline of the mountains surrounding them became clearer and they tried to name the peaks they'd climbed. They picked out Helvellyn, which was clear on top. Joe wasn't a spiritual man, as such, but he believed in ancient souls, and he could feel the allure and the magic of the place. He tried to imagine how Neolithic man might have felt trading or praying here, or perhaps even offering sacrifices.

A cry startled them, and they turned to the west.

'What was that?' Annie asked.

'A sheep?'

They heard it again. Callum strode to a stone that was leaning to one side, after thousands of years of abuse from the weather.

'Did you hear something, Callum?' Annie shouted after her son.

Callum stopped and turned around, and yelled with a breaking voice.

'Mum! Dad! Come here now!'

Annie recognised the cry as one of a child in distress and, before Joe reacted, she was sprinting to her son. She arrived by his side, breathless and wide eyed, and almost crashed into him to break her speed.

'Oh my God! Joe! Come here. Callum! Stay back!'

Annie bent over and Callum watched his mother. Behind the great stone, shining ghoulish in the early dawn light, a girl crouched and shivered, naked and terrified. Callum couldn't take his eyes off her skin. It glowed blue-white and appeared like some phantom before him. Annie took her jacket off and covered the girl, speaking to her, soothing her and asking a thousand questions. She barked orders.

'Callum, go to the car and find blankets, food, water, anything that might warm someone up. Callum? Go!'

Callum finally responded to his mother's orders and turned and ran to the parked vehicle, taking his brother with him. Connor babbled questions at his older sibling and tried to keep up. Behind them, they saw their parents' tenderness towards the stranger.

Joe reached his wife and immediately took his phone out of his pocket to dial 999.

'Damn! No signal! Wait, I'll stand on a stone.' In the circumstances, it might seem to an outsider an odd statement, but Annie knew it was their only chance, apart from driving around in the car. Joe wafted his phone in the air and straddled two huge monoliths. Annie comforted the girl.

'You're freezing! What happened? Are you hurt? What is your name?'

The girl didn't respond.

'Joe, I think she's hypothermic. She's not responding.'

'Got it!'

Annie returned her attention to the girl as she listened to her husband detailing their predicament to the emergency services.

Her sons returned across the field and brought a thick picnic blanket, a chocolate bar and an umbrella.

'To shelter her from the wind, Mum,' Callum said.

Annie smiled at her son. 'Thank you.'

The wind whistled around them and the girl still said nothing. She sat cossetted, huddled between the strangers, but showed no emotion or any semblance of cognisance. Seconds seemed like minutes and minutes, hours, but finally, they heard a heavy vehicle and spotted blue lights in the distance. Its sirens were quiet as it drove quickly up the dark lane.

'I'll go,' said Joe. He sprinted across the field, aware that he was running in sheep shit, and reached the vehicle. Two paramedics got out and he gave them as lucid and sensible a report as he could. After all, he didn't know much, apart from they'd found a naked girl shivering behind a stone in the middle of nowhere.

The ambulance personnel retrieved a stretcher from the vehicle and ran across the field. The sun was peeking over the horizon, behind the mountains, and Joe could see his family, huddled behind the stone. A police car drove up the lane and parked behind the ambulance and two uniformed officers got out. They were greeted by the remaining medic in the ambulance and exchanged words, then turning their attention to Joe. He told them what he knew and they nodded, peering towards the field.

'Do you know the woman?'

'No. I came up here with my family to see the sun rise.'

'So you don't know how she got here?'

'No.'

They took his personal details and made their way to the field, where the woman was being treated.

'She's freezing half to death!' He followed them. The two policemen said nothing. When they reached the scene, the girl was shaking and the paramedics were sticking needles into her and loading her onto the stretcher. Joe put his arm around Annie and told the boys they should go back to the car.

'Can we go home, officer?' he asked.

'We'll take statements from you first, if that's all right, sir. Go and get warm in your car and we'll be with you shortly.'

Joe led his family away and they climbed into the car. Callum kept looking back.

'Don't worry, Callum, she's just cold. She'll be all right,' Annie soothed. When they reached the car, Joe started the engine and put the heating on full. They sat in silence.

Chapter 2

Detective Inspector Kelly Porter felt a mixture of relief and dread when she received the notification on her Toughpad. The call had come from the pod in Keswick, and it gave her a reason to get out of bed and stop pondering her paranoia. She kept the iPad, safe in its police issue cover, by her bed, and reached over for it, flipping it open and reading the details they had so far. Johnny, her boyfriend of three years, slept soundly beside her. He always did now.

Unlike herself, who'd taken to dreaming again. It was no coincidence. She'd lain awake since three a.m. trying to be as still as she could so as not to disturb Johnny. She'd occupied herself with various tricks: watching his back rise and fall, listening to the coming dawn chorus from the birds getting ready to migrate at the end of a long, beautiful summer in the fells; and her cases – old and new – that whizzed around her head occasionally, churning questions, as if accusing her of falling short.

Johnny must have become aware of her fiddling, because he rolled over and put his arm across her.

'Have you been awake for hours?' he asked.

'How do you know?'

'I can tell because you're wide awake. You're not grumpy like you are after a good night's sleep.'

He felt good and she held onto him and snuggled down into her pillow, dropping her Toughpad back on the floor. Suddenly she was drowsy. It was always the way when one finally had cause to be awake.

'The letter?' he asked.

'I guess so.'

The letter she'd received two weeks ago had got under her skin. It hadn't been the first and, she suspected, it wouldn't be the last; but it was the increasing level of familiarity that bugged her. She felt indignant and angry, and the negative energy was pissing her off. The first had been posted before the death of her mother, Wendy, and Kelly had wanted to vomit. That was almost a year ago. The sentiment had evoked a guttural response in her and she'd thrown the letter into a drawer, feeling dirty having handled it.

Next came the sympathy card and flowers, after Wendy's funeral. Inside the card was a poem dedicated to everlasting beauty, and how the afterlife protected one from further tainting by human hands, or some such crap that Kelly could barely fathom. It went into the same drawer.

They'd become more regular after that, until Kelly had sought the advice of the National Offender Management Service (NOMS) which handled such harassment from prisoners, past and present. The letters were coming from Amy Richmond, a serial killer put away by one of Kelly's former investigations. She'd been menacingly dubbed 'The Teacher' by the press at the time and it still made Kelly shiver. However, they'd yet to figure out how she was getting the letters out of Broadmoor, the high security loony bin which held such dangerous prisoners. Neither Kelly, nor her team, ever judged Amy as insane: she knew what she was doing and why.

Somebody must be mailing the letters on her behalf, but who? Correspondence from Broadmoor was heavily vetted, unless there was a bent guard – always a possibility. The postcode was a local Bagshot one, near the hospital, on the Surrey/Berkshire border.

At that point, around six months ago, something else had struck Kelly. Instead of launching a formal investigation into the correspondence, Kelly toyed with the idea of using them to her advantage. The letters themselves could hold the key to the psyche of the writer, and could be potentially important in the future study of psychopaths. They could also possibly lead them to a copycat killer. It had been done before. Psychopaths like Amy Richmond often studied the work of their heroes: other killers.

HQ had suggested a positive mindfulness course for her and her team in reaction to Kelly's suggestion. She'd initially turned up her nose. Mindfulness – or the conscious awareness of the energy surrounding all living things – was a *thing* in workforces now, apparently. But within a police force? When crime was the manifestation of the opposite of such drivel? Kelly was a staunch cynic when it came to sending her officers on courses that concentrated on feeling empathy. Not that she was opposed to relating to human emotions in others – far from it – but, as law enforcers, they dealt with the damaged, the ruined, the damned and the downright sadistic. A bit of tree hugging and meditation wouldn't cure them.

HQ got their way, and she and her team had endured five sessions so far. They'd taken place at Eden House and a budget had been arranged to provide biscuits, coffee and juice. Kelly had said to Johnny she'd rather put the money towards catching bastards, but she didn't know how to put that in writing.

During one session, each participant had to identify three instances where they'd actively implemented a self-care plan. They'd joked and suggested examples such as taking a subsidised holiday to Jamaica. The course provider hadn't seen the funny side. Kelly had asked how they were supposed to heighten their awareness of the human side of crime when they dealt with losers who insisted on actively opting *out* of humanity to commit crime. They weren't just dealing with children from broken homes going on to fall foul of the law, they had to consider the career criminal; devoid of empathy and hell bent on causing pain to others.

Nature versus nurture. The course provider said that was a debate for another course, presumably with the same refreshments.

Johnny agreed with her – the army had begun implementing such awareness courses too – and many elite training programmes had been cancelled as too offensive. How the hell they were to train soldiers to go to war when they were encouraged to refocus on feelings was anyone's guess.

Deep breath.

Meanwhile, the letters continued to arrive and Kelly was in discussion to implement a diversion postal address. But her curiosity delayed the process. Part of her wanted to read what the letters said. It was a morbid game. Not only did each correspondence take Kelly back to one of the worst cases she'd ever worked on, they also reminded her of her sister. It seemed a lifetime ago now, to think that because of Kelly's job, her only sibling had almost become The Teacher's final victim. And Nikki had never forgiven her. Theirs was a strained relationship at the best of times and she hadn't seen her blood relative in months.

'I can feel your head whirring, slow down and give me a kiss, Kelly Porter. Have you got a long day?' Johnny brought her out of her wandering musings. She stopped twitching and looked at him. She kissed him and felt safe. It was one of the first things that had attracted her to him: despite his appearance of the wild mountain man in flip-flops, with the intense smile and bright blue all-seeing eyes, she'd been drawn in by his relaxed dominance. It reminded her of her own sense of self. They'd ended up in his bed that first night and she remembered the next morning when they'd stayed there for far too long and she'd had to get to work. It had been the early days of her Cumbria Constabulary journey back then, recently returned from the London Met.

Now, when she looked at him, she felt the familiar calm he allowed her and she wished she could stay in bed again.

'I need to go to Castlerigg. A young woman – well, a girl really – has been found naked and freezing half to death, near the stones.'

'Jesus. Is she hurt?'

'Apparently not. Close to catatonic and very cold, but unhurt evidently. No sign of her belongings and no ID. The officers who attended have had a cursory look and sealed off the area, but there's no indication of where she came from.'

'Naked women don't just fall from the sky.'

'Precisely, which is why it's landed on my desk. I need to get ready and go. It's no emergency but it'll focus my mind.'

'Coffee?' He got out of bed reluctantly, and grabbed his shorts, pulling them on. He was athletic and muscular. She was glad that he wasn't taking on any crazy challenges this year. He'd put bulk back on and they were busy planning their sailing trip to the Florida Keys. Her own body, strong from being back in the fells for three years, and graced with the absence of carrying babies, felt tired and she ached.

She nodded.

'Have you thought about going ahead with NOMS? You really shouldn't have her in your head. That's why it's appearing in your dreams, it's a kind of PTSD. Anything that brings back a trauma as a direct memory or emotion is going to get into your head and stay there. It's invading your place of safety – your home. Could the letters at least be intercepted?' Johnny had worked with hundreds of soldiers who suffered from PTSD.

'I don't know how the hell she got my home address in the first place.'

'Oh, come on, that's the easy part.'

She agreed and stretched.

'Do I look as though I've been boxing all night?'

'It was only the last ten minutes.'

'I've got a bad feeling about this. It's escalating. Letters, poems, theories. It'll be my active investigations next. Do you believe in mind control?'

'You know I do. To what extent?' Johnny asked.

'Someone like that, possessing remote power over a victim or an accomplice? If she's writing to me, who else is she in contact with? If it's really her.'

'I'm sure it's not the first time. I do think it's possible to exert that sort of control remotely. Hell, it's the same as grooming terrorists in a way. Maybe it's time to put her under surveillance and have a team investigate the true origins of the letters?'

She nodded. 'It's under my skin.'

'I know it is. Let's go for a run.'

'I've got to be in the office by nine to brief the team.'

'Come on then, the summer business has gone, it'll be gorgeous up there. How about Steel Knotts? The sun is fully up and over the fells, the colours are incredible. You won't even give The Teacher a second thought when we get up there.'

He was right. She did a quick calculation in her head: the drive to Martindale would take about fifteen minutes and it would take them an hour to get up to the summit of Steel Knotts and back down. She acquiesced. It was only half past seven. It was just a matter of months since she'd travelled to London for a case and spent a week in her old stomping ground. Johnny told her that he'd thought that she might be swayed to go back: lured by the thrill of working with a murder squad – fifty strong – darting around the capital. But nothing was further from the truth. She'd spent ten years in London, slogging her guts out, to be stitched up in the end by a man she trusted. The return home, to Cumbria, had come at a price, but that was behind her now. Three years into her new role, she was putting down roots. She looked at Johnny's bottom as he hopped up and down, trying to get his running kit on: it wasn't just her job that kept her in the Lakes.

'Hold the coffee.'

Kelly got out of bed and went to her cupboard, looking for her running kit. She felt Johnny's eyes on her and turned around. Her long auburn hair fell about her face and she knew that her body was strong from three years hiking the fells: the hills and peaks she'd so long ignored when she'd been obsessed with promotion in the Met. He turned away and shook his head. They didn't have time to run *and* make love.

The sunshine flowed through the curtains and she knew that the south shore of Ullswater would be quiet. They went downstairs and Johnny grabbed their water bottles and his car keys. As she slammed the door behind them and walked to the car, Kelly left the darkness of her nightmares behind her, where they belonged.

There was plenty of time to deal with The Teacher: a killer who'd walked into her head and screwed up the rule book. And who still wanted to be part of her life. Amy Richmond wasn't the type of killer to stop. She enjoyed it too much.

Chapter 3

Kelly scrawled two words on to her notepad. She used capital letters. She'd been doing it for the last hour, and was in the process of what could only be termed as faffing. She had jobs to do, but none of them jumped out to excite her, and, as a result, she didn't know which one to start on first. She'd been at work for two hours. The run with Johnny had been exhilarating and they'd seen not a soul as they pounded the paths up to the top of Steel Knotts. The tiny valley, which protected the medieval Church of St Martin, sat like a giant cradle, and they'd parked by the church gate. Tourists often got married there.

She daydreamt about the smell of the late summer flowers and the nip in the air making the run slightly less taxing than it was in hotter weather. But The Teacher kept jumping into her head, unwelcome and jarring.

She'd already walked around the office, nosing over the shoulders of her colleagues. She'd made coffee for everyone and caught up with paperwork. When active crime was quiet, a rare luxury, they all caught up on admin jobs and minor visits. She was in danger of becoming a micro-managing mindful HR hero of the year. Not that any member of her team needed it. DS Kate Umshaw, in between cigarette breaks, possessed the tenacity of a squirrel building a winter home and ploughed through reports. With three teenage girls to get ready in the morning, she always arrived a little unkempt herself, was always on a diet and starting a new gym membership but tucked into sausage rolls and pastries at her desk. DS Will Phillips was pristine in comparison. Newly married and promoted, his suit was immaculately pressed by a loving wife and he smelled of Ralph Lauren cologne. DC Rob Shawcross was Phillips' right hand nerd, though he looked more like a champion athlete in training. He had keen eyes and stood erect, with his hands in his pockets, ready for whatever Kelly might throw at him. Then there was DC Emma Hide, who'd accompanied her to London earlier in the year on a case. She was wide eyed and deceptively brilliant for her age and experience. She usually wore running kit, cleverly disguised as casual trousers and jacket, poised for anything and always on hand to provide Kelly with expert briefs in record time. Her brain was like a processor and Kelly remembered few like it, across her career. It was Emma Hide's knowledge of poetry that had changed the investigation into The Teacher.

Her team was tight.

Kelly spent more than a few minutes glowing in the pride of the squad she'd built from scratch. Three years ago, the idea of a unit so varied but harmonious was something she'd dreamt of, as she limped back home to Cumbria from the Met, professionally embarrassed and personally damaged. Now, they threw her the odd questioning glance as she prowled around the incident room for the tenth time, looking for something to do. The young woman was in hospital being assessed, Rob was to accompany her to Castlerigg after the initial report by the first responders was collated. Until then, he worked on other cases and she doodled 'The Teacher' on her notepad, circling it and stabbing it with her pen, as if she could obliterate her from her life.

There was other stuff to be doing, like shifting her attention to more senior tasks such as cold cases, missing persons, admin, staff management and reviews. She stared at the two words on her pad and considered making everyone another coffee, or going out for cakes.

THE TEACHER

Kelly had to admit that she was tempted to make contact. Her inquisitive brain wanted to question the psychopath. She could learn so much. Thousands of books had been written on the topic: what motivates a murderer? What negates risk and consequence? But to have a bone fide lunatic at one's bidding was tantalisingly alluring. She knew she'd be able to talk HQ round. It would only take a train ticket to Bagshot. Emma Hide would jump at the chance to accompany her; any of them would.

DS Kate Umshaw walked into Kelly's office and broke her intense musings. It was a welcome diversion. Kate sat on a swivel chair and gave her an update on the woman who'd been found naked and disorientated at Castlerigg stone circle early this morning.

The Teacher was forgotten for the moment.

It was an odd case. Kelly knew the stone circle well; it was beautiful in the dawn light, or at sunset, covered in snow on a winter solstice. They'd already run through normal procedure for missing persons, though this was, admittedly, slightly different. The ambulance crew reported the woman as initially unresponsive and confused to the point of zero communication. Now the hospital had completed its health assessment and she could be questioned this afternoon.

'They said good luck. She's gone mute,' Kate said. 'They can't even get her name out of her.'

'Age?' Kelly asked.

'Not sure, she could be a minor.'

It had been assumed that the woman was an adult, but they couldn't be entirely sure. It was also unclear if a crime had been committed.

'She won't agree to an intimate examination.'

'So we have no idea if sexual violence has taken place. Or if other parties were involved.'

'Exactly.'

Kelly sketched out the stone circle on her notepad and clicked open the email to the report. She marked where the woman had been found, and from where the family who'd found her had approached. Kelly knew the ancient monument well, as did Kate Umshaw, who peered over her shoulder. Kelly and Johnny often ran past the circle or around it, and it could also be seen from a few vantage points in the fells. She hadn't visited as a tourist as such in years. What she did know was that it was pretty tough to get to on foot. She looked at the list of items gathered from the scene. A perimeter had been set up around the circle, and anything remotely not linked to an ancient stone monument in the middle of nowhere had been bagged for examination. Tyre tracks had been set in casts from the only access point by car: the adjacent lane where the family had parked. The woman must have been in the field before the family, and so if she'd been taken there by car, the tracks could have been fresh anytime in the couple of hours before they arrived. Or she had walked, but from where?

Kelly had already appointed DS Will Phillips in charge of organising a trawl for witnesses in the area, though they were unlikely to find any, given the early hour, and Rob Shawcross had been given the task of finding out who the hell the woman was. But with no clothes, no ID, and no communication, his job was almost impossible. No one in the area had been reported missing. Kate said that the hospital was sure that the woman was being selectively mute, because there were no physical signs of trauma to the head, mouth or throat. 'So, she's either unable to talk because she has been so traumatised, or unwilling to talk because she has something to hide?' Kate said. Kelly nodded. She stood up and they both went to the incident room where they found Rob hunched over his computer.

'Any clues for Jane Doe?' Kelly asked.

Rob shook his head. 'I'm trawling through the missing persons' database now. Did you know that more than three thousand people were reported missing in Cumbria last year – about one per cent of the annual UK total?' Rob asked.

Kelly raised her eyebrows; it was an eye-watering figure and she thought of all the families represented by the absent names.

'That's a lot,' Kate said.

'Is she even British?' Kelly asked. The Lakes was a hub for tourists and wanderers. Transients had a habit of taking up home here in tents, vans and lorry parks. It was the perfect venue from which to disappear.

'No idea, she hasn't uttered a sound according to the hospital.'

'I've been through about five thousand pictures so far.'

Kelly brought the mugshot of the woman, taken hastily upon her admission to hospital, up on her iPad. She looked like a frightened little bird, dishevelled and disorientated, as well she might. The photo was utterly unflattering, but it was all they had. At least they had eye and hair colour, face and ear shape, as well as a few expressions, which was more than they had on other cases. Kelly stared at it. Despite the grime and the fear, the young woman was stunning. Her bright blue eyes were hauntingly piercing and her mouth fell slightly open, framed by full lips and perfectly round features. It was an unforgettable face.

'She's physically healthy, right?' Kelly asked.

'She's being assessed still.'

'No, what I mean is, she wasn't obviously hurt, or malnourished or at death's door. In other words, she'd been looked after. She wasn't starving or destitute.'

'That would appear to be the case.' Rob looked at the photo of the woman, who'd been given a blouse and some joggers in hospital, and her face had been washed. She looked terrified and vacant at the same time. Kelly studied her.

'I reckon she's about twenty, what do you think?'

'I'm useless at things like that, guv. I thought you were twenty.'

'Oh, piss off! Look at her eyes: they're plump and open. Look: her skin is thick and fleshy – a classic sign of youth. She hasn't got a wrinkle. Head injury?'

'Don't think so.'

'Gross and fine motor skills?'

'Under investigation.'

'Come on, Rob, you need a break. Kate can you take over for a bit? Rob, get your coat. Let's pay the hospital a visit. Where are the others?'

'Will's coordinating a perimeter of about five miles, setting up requests for sightings, unusual activity, and reports of vehicles on that part of the A66 in the early hours of Saturday, up to around first light. The items from the scene have been inputted into the lab system so analysis can start straight away.'

'How many objects were pulled from the scene?'

'Around a hundred. Mainly litter, I think, as well as the tyre tracks.'

'Good work. Come on, let's go.'

Chapter 4

Fred O'Reilly placed the ornate golden cloth lovingly on the table and lit the candles. The colour of the fabric changed with the seasons. Autumn was celebrated with a wealth of oranges, gold and rich browns. He welcomed the final meeting before the next quarter day: Mabon, when the sun would begin its journey south and away from the northern hemisphere, and thanks would be given for the fruits of summer. He laid out the traditional offerings for the season of nuts, apples, barley and pumpkins, amongst the ritual consecrating tools, which would form the basis of the meeting once he'd marked out the circle. The paten was a golden plate that Fred had acquired from a dear friend and High Priest of the Surrey coven that he'd left when he'd started his own, before they moved to Shap, and then here. On it was inscribed a pentagram within a circle, and at each point the symbol for one of the five elements was engraved: spirit, air, earth, fire and water. It was a thing of beauty and Fred's most treasured of all the tools. He placed it with the spirit symbol at the head because spirit brought together all the other elements.

He looked towards the door and wondered where Mary had got to: she was often late, and Fred didn't mind this so much. What he did mind was her lackadaisical attitude when she finally appeared. He had on numerous occasions considered the wisdom of his choice of High Priestess, but she possessed other strengths that were vital for their group. Mary was the air to his fire, and they worked well together. He reached for the athame, or ritual dagger. It had been a gift from his predecessor and it had its origins in northern Germany. It was simply a tool of magic and not to be confused with weaponry, though it gave the appearance of being more than capable of inflicting serious wounding. As he continued to unwrap the items used in ceremony – an ebony wand, a curved boline knife (like a scythe) and a brass chalice – this was exactly what was on Fred's mind. A local journalist (a girl barely out of nappies, no doubt desperate for attention) had written a newspaper article. It was heinous. It showed no understanding of Pagan practice, used spurious links to a smattering of inflammatory articles about modern witchcraft, and promptly proceeded to damn all those practices outside of organised religion. Fred's blood boiled.

'Evening, Fred.' Finally, Mary appeared and Fred relaxed a little.

'You're almost done.' She nodded to the objects. They would leave the drawing and the consecrating of the circle until their members arrived. The rituals were undertaken at the beginning of every meeting, then they would celebrate with harvest foods and drinks, until it was time to return to their families. Some members tried to remain as part of the group even if their partners were laymen or affiliated to one of the organised religions, but they rarely lasted. It was always preferable if couples and families joined together because, after all, theirs was a way of life and not simply a nod to a nominal god every once in a while. They had deities, but theirs were visions of the seasons, witnessed on the breath of night and day. Rather like other forgotten indigenous practices all over the world, their rhythms were dictated by nature and her laws, and not those that suited man.

'Did you see the article in the *Gazette*?' Fred couldn't hide his irritation from Mary. They were not a couple. It was forbidden for the High Priest and High Priestess to conjoin. Fred was married to Sandra, but Mary lived on her own after her husband had got himself into a spot of trouble with debt and left her high and dry years ago. She'd never remarried, coming close only once.

Fred was married in English civil law, but that meant little to them: what did matter was their hand-fasting in June, during the feast of the solstice; this was their true marriage, not recognised by English law, but the most important denotation of coupling for the group.

Mary nodded. 'Typical naysayers. Ignoramuses, Fred. Don't get your cingulum in a twist about it.'

'Mary!'

The cingulum was a nine-foot belt and they each possessed one. They were used to measure out the magic circle. As High Priest, Fred's was gold, and Mary's was silver. Fred laughed and held his up to show Mary that it was untwisted, though inside, he continued to reel. 'Articles like the one written by Carry Tomlin damage our reputation, Mary. She makes us sound like heathens practising devil worship.'

Mary nodded. She knew how passionate Fred was, and it was true: the occult was misunderstood. 'She actually said that we sacrifice animals,' Fred said, as he shook out his robes and laid out his cingulum.

'Are you surprised? Look at the witch trials. We'll always be on the back foot. The Church had us done for when they stole our festivals and burned our wisdom.'

Fred agreed.

'Ah, Fred. Come on, we've got a lovely night of celebration ahead of us, give thanks for our small family. I've brought a pumpkin pie. Is Sandra coming along?'

'Later. The pumpkin pie with marshmallows?'

'The same.'

'Jock said he was making mulled cider.'

'Sometimes I think we're just an excuse to get pissed.' Mary laughed at her own observation.

'Isn't every communion?'

'I guess so. Jock's cider is the best I've ever tasted so I reckon I'll be rolling home tonight.'

The first members arrived and placed their offerings on a table laid out in the hall, where they'd make merry later. They were a group of twelve; the youngest was twenty-three and the oldest was Jock, who was eighty-three, followed by Fred, who was sixty-seven. They fell into easy conversation about everyday life and it was clear that Jock commanded a great deal of respect. Age was seen as a symbol of wisdom in the group and he'd lived a long and eventful life, remembering the blitz and serving in the Korean War. He'd turned to nature after watching war after war unfolding before his eyes, with politicians on the sidelines, barking their suspect morality and judgemental hypocrisy. He'd had a stomach full. But for Fred stepping in, Jock would have made an excellent High Priest, but he'd rather it went to Fred who, he said, suited the role. Jock said he was happy to support in the background like he'd always done. Jock was the longest current serving member of the group and had seen lots of souls come and go. His cheeks were ruddy, and he still hiked the fells every weekend. He lived alone, and found pleasure in talking about fishing to Fred, swapping gardening tips with Sandra, and visiting his grandchildren, of which he had eight, with others adopted along the way.

One by one, after shaking hands and kissing cheeks, they waited for Fred and Mary to begin. The High Priest and Priestess appealed for silence and began preparing the circle. Everybody held hands. Jock was the only one seated. Once the circle was formed, the tools could be consecrated from all four directions of the elements on the paten, to purify them and remove negative energy. Fred and Mary chanted to all points of the circle and called on the north for the earth, the east for the air, the south for fire, and the west for water. The younger ranks watched in awe as Fred and Mary worked together to create the circle and sanctify the tools. Incense filled the small space and the candles flickered. They sang songs and moved rhythmically from side to side, sharing love with their neighbours to each side. When it was done, Fred read verses aloud and Mary helped with the adherents' replies.

Tonight was not a festival date, as such. There were eight in all during the year, but they liked to meet more frequently and in between festival dates – like tonight – they affirmed their beliefs and shared food, drink and love. Each meeting had a different seasonal significance, and this time of year, they gave thanks in the form of food, newly harvested after a long summer of effort, in order to placate the divine beings and secure their blessing for the coming months of harshness. The autumn equinox – expected soon – was one of the most important festivals of the year, and it preceded the most important of all: Samhain, the death of the year. For now, though, the year was still alive, and summer was still generous.

Mary brought the ceremony to a close and they broke hands. People began sharing the stories of their week and helped to prepare the seating in the outer hall for their meal. A guitar was on hand and a young man picked it up and began playing. Fred let the incense continue to burn but packed away the tools with Mary's help. There was a healing, feminine energy in the room, he noted. He wondered if one of their group was pregnant. Two of the couples were actively trying to expand their families and he noticed that both of the women looked flushed, and one refused the mulled cider.

Fred was happy: theirs was a merry group. It was balanced and warm. Only once had he experienced a dark energy within their number. It was an unhappy memory, and one that he pushed aside. The muscles in his neck and back tightened and he took a deep breath to banish the unwelcome thoughts. All notions, he reminded himself, were mere chemical reactions, and this is what he taught his students. The chain of physical events inside the mind were designed to drive action from the brain to the body. Like animals compelled to kill and provide for their young, so humans were directed by minute responses deep within DNA passed on from species to species. But the mind was the one thing that could bend those ancient urges. Fred had seen just how powerfully the intellect could be used against the body and it was something that was as awesome as it was terrifying.

He sipped his cider and placed the cup on a table while he folded his cingulum carefully and placed it into its box. They rented the space behind the village hall, and had to pack up their belongings after each meeting. It wasn't ideal and Fred was on the lookout for something permanent. He had thought of his own office that he'd had built in the garden, but one of the most important rules of their denomination was that the meeting place should be on neutral ground. Compromises of the orders were rare, and the hierarchical structure, along with the length of time it took to progress between ranks, ensured a smooth and safe environment. But, occasionally, it had been known for an outsider to penetrate their sanctity, and when that happened, one did not want it to be on one's own soil.

Chapter 5

The Lakes air had a nip in it, and Kelly realised miserably that
August was but a memory. Even the sky looked darker earlier
now. Someone said the longest day was in June, but Kelly swore
that it was sometime in August – just before the lights were
abruptly turned out in September. Rob fastened the buttons
on his suit. Kelly closed her grey Burberry mac around her.
Today was the first day she'd worn trousers for weeks. The wind
caught her long auburn hair, which was still tinged with gold
from the summer sun. Rob towered over her with his six-foot
frame and they shuffled to her waiting car. They slammed the
doors once inside and Kelly put the heating on full.

'I don't know how she survived up there. Have you been to
the circle, Rob?'

'No.'

'You'll love it; it's wild. The nakedness bothers me. Did she
strip herself because she was in the latter stages of hypothermia?
Or was she dumped?'

'She's potentially an adult, responsible for herself.'

'Exactly, that's what bothers me, because she's not behaving
like an adult, by all accounts.'

They set off for the hospital across town. Kelly had been
inside the Penrith and Lakes Hospital more times than she'd
care to remember. The last had been with her mother as she
slipped away. The memory jarred her senses but she pushed it
aside. In any given day, there were a thousand moments that
reminded her of her mother: it could be a shop, a view of the
mountains, a telephone call, or someone's perfume. It never

left. The boxes of her possessions still filled Kelly's spare room, as well as a few of Ted's rooms too. Her mother and Ted had reignited their romance too late, and now she made sure that she kept the connection alive.

She didn't need the space. Johnny had virtually moved in – though not fully, because of his daughter Josie – but he'd deposited the stuff he needed in Kelly's bedroom and her bathroom. The image that she'd once had of a beautiful tidy new bathroom stocked with female products placed in order, with fluffy white towels, had disappeared quickly after Johnny left his stuff everywhere. She didn't mind.

They spent more and more time on the boat, the *Wendy*, as he'd christened her, after her mother. He'd repainted the name on the side of the vessel only this summer, and they'd taken her to the Peaks Bay to moor up and sit, staring into the crystal waters of Ullswater and remembering. No words were needed. They'd spent the whole summer practising their sailing skills on Derwent Water, and had been signed off as competent crew, and Johnny had passed his coastal skipper course, ready for their holiday of a lifetime to the Florida Keys. It wasn't something that felt real at the moment, and neither of them had turned their thoughts to packing. The end of November seemed too far away to necessitate preparation.

Traffic in the town was steady and light rain began to fall.

'Goodbye summer,' she said.

'My favourite time of year,' said Rob.

'Really?' she turned to him. He filled the passenger seat and held on to a ceiling strap with one hand. She'd noticed a few crow's feet creeping into the creases at the sides of his eyes: he'd shown his mettle and was becoming a seasoned detective. He ran his fingers though his mousy blonde hair – kissed by the mountain sun – and he peered out of the window, as if looking for something. She'd reminded him of what he liked to do out of work: adrenaline junkie sports.

'It's perfect for gliding and jumping. The tourists have all but gone home but the sun still comes out, and it's lower, so it sheds a light across the fells like no other time of year.'

'That's poetic, Rob.'

'I know. I amaze myself, boss. What about you?'

'My favourite time of year in the Lakes?'

He nodded, still holding on to the strap, as if she were racing with blues blaring, which she clearly wasn't. 'Winter. The crisp blue sky and the fact that you can walk all week without seeing a soul.'

'Nice.' He stared ahead. They were nearly there. The rain became heavier and she flicked her windscreen wipers on.

'Can I ask you something, boss?'

'Go ahead.'

'What's the difference between a lead that you chase and something you pass on?'

'No difference really. I give everything equal airtime. This one won't be settled in my head until we know who she is.'

'I came into this job expecting crime to be clear cut.'

'They're more often than not a shade of grey,' she said. 'This one is a classic question mark. There doesn't seem to have been a crime committed but I work backwards, discounting theories rather than creating them. I suppose you expected every crime to have a degree attached too, so each job is easily dished out? I get it. I won't be able to tell unless I meet her.'

'Do you ever just find something odd?' he asked.

'All the time! Nothing is ever straightforward. A smoking gun would be lovely, wouldn't it? There's something about this woman who just fancied a naked walk into a field at dawn.'

'Running from something?'

'Maybe. Always keep an open mind.'

She parked undercover and they got out. The woman was being evaluated on the female medical ward, and she'd been removed to a private room because she was disturbing the other patients with her bizarre behaviour: apparently she'd taken to pacing up and down the corridors, grabbing on to people and scaring them. She'd even done it to visitors. She'd also taken to drawing with her finger on the floor, but no one could make out what she was trying to produce: a picture or words. She'd been given paper but had refused it.

They reached the ward and two nurses blushed and stared at Rob. Kelly was used to it; he was a good looking young man, as well as tall and strong. If he noticed, he didn't show it. Kelly showed her badge and they were asked to wait to speak to the ward sister. Kelly hated hospitals but this one held a special place of loathing in her heart. It wasn't just where her mother had died, it was also where Amy Richmond worked as a nurse, giving her direct access to her unsuspecting victims. She shivered as she recalled the day she knew that the killer had been in her mother's room, and made them tea. It was also the site of some spectacular fallouts with her sister, Nikki.

A stocky woman in her fifties came towards them with glasses perched on the end of her nose; she looked over them towards the detectives and outstretched her hand. 'Sister Cane.' Kelly hesitated momentarily.

Kelly took her hand and shook it, looking to Rob to copy. Even the middle-aged senior nurse looked a little coy when she took Rob's hand. Kelly rolled her eyes.

'Any news on the mystery woman?' Kelly asked.

'Carla Rigg?'

'Nice, who thought that up?' asked Kelly. It was common for unidentified victims to be given pet names.

'One of the consultants, he's a bit of a walking encyclopaedia and he said that Carles Rigg was the ancient Celtic name for the circle. Who knew?'

'Who has *time* to know?' Rob said.

'Well, she's pretty much the same as she came in, though cleaner: she let us wash her this morning. None of us can tell if she's English. She's had an EEG, an ECG, and a general check-up, nothing wrong with her really. It's a miracle given that Saturday morning at dawn was two degrees above freezing.'

'Any distinguishable marks?'

'Well, that's the problem, she won't let us complete a detailed examination. I told the staff who bathed her to look out but they saw nothing. She keeps herself all coiled up, like a spring.'

'Sexual assault?'

'She won't let us anywhere near *that*.'

'Right. Not surprising really is it? She must be terrified. Psychiatry?'

'They haven't been, you might just catch them; they're due at one o'clock.'

Kelly looked at her watch. Her stomach had been grumbling but she'd ignored it, now she knew why. They had plenty of time to meet the woman and grab a coffee. 'Right, can we go in?'

Sister Cane nodded. 'Follow me.'

They were led down the corridor, past shared wards and private rooms, and came to room number eighteen. In washable marker on a white sign outside the room was written 'Carla Rigg'. Droll, the consultant must think himself a clever dick.

Sister Cane took them inside.

'You have visitors!' she announced breezily. They stood at the foot of the bed looking at a lump of sheets. The blinds were fully open but the bleak, rain-filled sky outside afforded little light. Sister Cane switched on a bedside light. 'There we go, that's better. How are we feeling? Have we got a name? A "hello" would be nice for these folks.'

'Hi there. I'm Detective Inspector Kelly Porter and this is Detective Constable Rob Shawcross. We're with Cumbria police. You do understand that you've been found in Cumbria, wandering about in the small hours? You must have been terrified.' Kelly eased in.

The bundle of sheets shifted and the woman looked over her shoulder.

'So, you can hear me? That's a good start,' Kelly carried on. The woman slumped back to her position.

'Can I sit you up?' Kelly went to the head of the bed to take a pillow and help the woman up. Suddenly her arm was grabbed by a hand emerging from the sheets and Kelly gasped in surprise, but soon recovered, allowing the woman to hold on to her, whilst assessing danger. Her hand was freezing cold.

'Now, now!' Sister Cane waded in, but Kelly held up her free hand.

'You check me out, I don't mind. I'm not here to hurt you. I just want to find out where you've come from. Perhaps a name?'

The woman squeezed and Kelly felt a nail go into her skin. She was aware that she had no idea about the medical history of this stranger, and so she tried to get from her grasp. She used her free hand to aid her. Rob came to her help and the whole time they grappled with the woman's hand, she made no sound, and didn't blink. Finally, Kelly's arm came free and she rubbed it. Her skin wasn't broken. She caught the woman's eye and tried to hold her gaze. Up close she gave the appearance of being around the twenty mark. Her face was plump and innocent: she could even be a juvenile. They hadn't found any ID or personal items on the field and so they still didn't know. The woman sat back and stared into the distance.

Kelly sat in the chair next to the bed and Rob remained stood. The woman glanced at him and Kelly observed her eyes linger: she had feelings. Kelly guessed that she was sexually mature. 'Can I show you this book?' Kelly asked, taking a book out of her bag. It was a baby naming book and had thousands of names on its pages. The woman didn't respond.

'Let's see,' Kelly said. 'You look like a Charlotte, or Emily. My stepdaughter is called Josie and I've got a niece called Ria. They're lovely names. Haven't you got somebody who misses you? A sister perhaps? A mum and dad?'

At the mention of family, the woman – or girl – flicked her vision squarely to Kelly's face and stared at her as if she was offended.

'So, perhaps you can't remember Mum and Dad?'

The girl's lips curled in a grimace and Kelly realised that the muteness was a choice, not a cerebral outcome. The girl was hiding something, and she was terrified of it. And it was something to do with her mother and father.

Chapter 6

'If she's run away from an abusive relationship, then there won't be a missing person's report.' Rob followed Kelly to the canteen and listened to her fire off her thoughts.

'Abusive parental relationship?' he asked.

'Same. They won't want her found.'

'Agree, guv.'

'She could stay anonymous forever, we've got to find a way in.'

They reached the café and ordered coffee and pastries. Having spent a mere week on location in London investigating a case in June, Kelly had become partial to the odd city snack containing caffeine and sugar.

'There's a criminal psychologist I used to work with in the Met, I'm going to try and get hold of her. She broke a few of our cases back in the day.'

'When do we go public with a photograph of her?' Rob asked. They were in a long queue and Kelly looked around at the clientele. It was depressing; people were usually in the café because they were visiting someone sick or were ill themselves. It was a desperate place to be and the memories of her mother and the nurse who showed such warmth towards her crowded her head. She almost expected Nikki to come prancing down the hall in heels, demanding something. To think she'd been so focused on being embarrassed by her sister's behaviour that a killer carried on unnoticed under all their noses.

'We don't have to.'

'Why?'

'It's at our discretion. If we think she's in danger – and that hasn't been determined yet – then it's best not to.'

'Isn't that the only way to find out who she is?'

'It might be the quickest way, but not the best. She might not want to be the person she was.'

They paid for their snacks and drinks and found a table. 'The thing about amnesia is that it's rarely medical in a healthy young woman; it's more likely to be psychological, and I want to know why.'

'But we could be finding her family...'

'You saw her reaction to that, Rob. I'm not convinced she wants to see them.'

'When does it stop being about what she wants and about doing the right thing?'

'We don't know what that is yet.' They sat down. 'How's Mia?' Kelly changed the subject. It caught Rob off guard, which was her intention, she was tired of explaining herself.

'She's found a new job and I think... erm... well...'

Kelly had never seen Rob flustered, but now he didn't know what to say.

'You broke up?'

'No!'

'She's pregnant?'

'How did you know?'

'I didn't, you just told me.'

'But I'm not allowed!'

'Don't worry, I won't tell. That's amazing, you'll be an incredible dad, Rob. Don't expect any time off, though.'

'Mia will understand.'

'I was joking.'

Kelly's mobile rang and it was Kate Umshaw.

'I'm nosing around the Penrith and Lakes, my favourite place to be, what are you doing?' Kelly asked.

Rob looked at her and she nodded to him that they had some new information. He bit into his croissant and waited until his boss hung up. After a sip of coffee, she raised her brow and told him.

'They've found clothes in an adjacent field to Castlerigg. It appears that they have blood on them.' She bit into a Danish pastry.

'Women's clothes?'

They both spoke in between bites of sugary succour and sips of eye-openingly strong coffee.

'Yes. They're been photographed and bagged. Kate's emailing the photos to me, let's see if the hospital psychologist can get anything out of Carla Rigg.'

They finished their refreshments and piled their rubbish onto a tray, dropping it into the waste bin as they left.

'I never know which one to put the bloody things into,' Kelly said, confused by the recycling instructions on four waste bins.

They made their way back to the ward and were welcomed by the staff without question this time, though the two female nurses still stared at Rob. An official looking man in his late thirties, small in build, with a clip board and pen, and studiously revising notes, approached the desk. He had a name badge and Kelly quickly surmised that this was the psychologist. Kelly glanced at his badge and saw the acronym NLMH (North Lakes Mental Health). Carla Rigg would also be assessed by a psychiatrist, but Kelly was convinced that they weren't looking at a mental illness as such, possibly a trauma or personality disorder. The young woman was withdrawn and childlike. Maybe she'd be proven wrong.

She interrupted him and introduced herself. The small man looked baffled and so Kelly showed him her badge.

'It's a police matter?' he asked.

'Until we know who she is and we've ruled out a crime,' Kelly said.

'Ah, right. I never know the rules, I'm just here to evaluate a young woman with potential amnesia.'

'We'll accompany you.'

He remained uncertain as he walked towards room eighteen. They bumped into Sister Cane, who informed them that Carla Rigg was comfortably sat up in bed and ready for them.

When they knocked and went in, the blinds had been pulled down and flapped in the wind. The windows were large and Kelly thought it odd that one was left open. A sinking feeling hit her gut and she pulled back the bed sheets. There was no one under them. She checked the bathroom and the door was unlocked, but when she went inside, Carla wasn't there. She rushed to the window and looked out: they were only on the first floor and an outbuilding was positioned a few feet away from the window; it would be easy to jump on to it and then to the ground.

'She's gone.'

'I beg your pardon?' the psychologist asked.

'She's gone. Whoever she is, she has no desire to be identified or evaluated. She's sick of being examined.'

Sister Cane entered the room. 'It's freezing in here!' She stopped and looked at the bed, then to Kelly, who looked at Rob.

'Maybe it's time to go public now.'

Chapter 7

At Eden House, DS Kate Umshaw led the brief, and pointed to the map projected onto the whiteboard. She was a confident leader, Kelly noted, and it came as a surprise. DS Umshaw had always shrunk to the back of the room, beavering away in dark corners coming up with gems from hours of solid police work, but she wasn't one to push herself to the front of the crowd and put herself on display. She was physically awkward, though wholly capable. Now, she spoke with determination and drive. Kelly sat back with the others and listened.

Castlerigg was marked with a red circle, and where the clothes had been found was marked with a blue circle with a green line showing the direction of her supposed route to the monument. Kate informed them that confirmation that the clothes belonged to Carla had been found inside the jacket: a wallet containing a single photograph of herself with an older man. It was a lead. The clothes had been left in a pile directly to the south of the ancient site, indicating that the girl had come from either the main road or several campsites in the area. She could have walked or been driven. There was no ID.

'Who's the guy?'

'Don't know, guv. He's not recognised by us and there's no name on the photo.'

Kelly noted the same dead eyes on Carla Rigg that she'd witnessed in the hospital. Also the same striking beauty and vulnerability, mixed with something else.

'She's clearly younger, guv. I'd say, compared to my girls, that she's about fifteen or sixteen in this photo.' Kate moved on. 'Dentals were on their way to take moulds when she disappeared on us,' she said.

The mystery girl intrigued them all. As far as workload went, the team had enough hours to dedicate to the case for now; should something more serious come up, then they'd have to redirect resources, but the office was quiet. The vast majority of missing persons reported in Cumbria each year turned up safe and well. As for the others, it was never clear if the person in question was missing inside the National Park or simply last seen there. They faced a bigger problem, though – it would appear that Carla Rigg did not want to be found. If so, she'd be relegated to the depths of cold and inactive cases in the bowels of the constabulary, and looked at every five years or so. Without ID, they didn't really have a case. Kelly wanted to know why, if the young woman didn't want to be found, she had stripped and wandered into a tourist destination? The psychology report would have helped her answer that question, because they still didn't know if Carla Rigg was nuts. Kelly didn't think she was, but nutters came in all shapes and guises. It was her turn to speak and she thanked DS Umshaw.

'We now go public with the photograph. If she wants to come forward, she will, and if she doesn't and someone reports her whereabouts, then at least we can check on her welfare. I didn't want to release an image until we got to know her better, but we're left with no choice. We'll sit on the photograph of the mystery man for now.'

They swiftly moved on to other business, though none of them could get the young woman out of their heads. Kelly walked back to her office and stared at the pile of files on her desk. She resigned herself to an afternoon of trawling, and sat down heavily. When she needed a break, she'd offer to take Rob to Castlerigg; it wasn't far.

The review cases within the files had been selected on a broad remit: length of time inactive, seriousness and simply falling into the treadmill of assessment deadlines. She picked out a brown folder – it was fairly thick – and began reading.

The case was an unsolved missing person: a minor who went missing from her back garden in 2005. Kelly examined the photograph supplied by the parents at the time and wondered why she hadn't heard the case on the news, but she was in London in 2005, a rookie with her nose to the grindstone. A missing thirteen-year-old in Cumbria wouldn't have made her radar. The address of the girl at the time was noted as Embleton, west of Bassenthwaite Lake. It was in the middle of nowhere and as Kelly read on, she found that the investigating officers at the time surmised, after exhausting all leads, that the girl had been seen at the campsite at the northern edge of the lake, acting strangely. Further enquires revealed that the girl had argued with her parents and stormed off in search of some way of funding her growing weed habit. The parents admitted that all was not well with the troublesome teenager, and they'd washed their hands of her. She'd begun drinking alcohol at the age of eleven, fallen in with an unsavoury crowd and often hung about the many campsites dotted around, looking for older men to hook up with.

It was a sorry tale, and Kelly felt a pang of helplessness. She could feel the animosity towards the girl from her parents jump off the pages, and she wondered what the hell they were doing, while their daughter was wandering around looking for drugs and men. It was all too clear that the girl was being sexually exploited by those older men and put herself in regular danger.

No shit, thought Kelly. The girl clearly had no self-worth, and Kelly wondered what the parents had to say about that. A thirteen-year-old girl should be at home, safe and warm, reading a goddamn book about romance and vampires, not smoking weed and allowing her body to be abused. Why?

In her experience of working child cases, Kelly had come to the conclusion that kids were pushed away from childhood, they didn't suddenly wake up one morning and say to themselves 'today I'm going to fuck and get high': a period of nosediving self-esteem came first, usually at the hands of parents or bullies, or both. She examined the history further and found that the teenager had liaised with various lowlifes linked to campsites, but all leads were thoroughly investigated and became dead ends, until there were none left and the parents accepted that she'd probably waded into Bassenthwaite Lake, disoriented and drunk, and drowned.

The lake had never been dredged.

Kelly wondered idly how many bodies might lay undiscovered in the National Park's deep lakes, and if that girl's was among them. She picked up a photograph of her and examined her face. She'd seen it before: dead eyes, lost promises, crushing expectations, and innocence raped. She closed the file and moved on.

The next enquiry was an animal cruelty case. She flipped the folder closed and looked at the date: 2005. She briefly browsed some of the other files and realised that a lot of them were from the same year. Somebody had decided to dig up cold cases year by year, and today she'd landed 2005. She ploughed on. The animal cruelty incident concerned a travelling community camping illegally at Birkett Mire, near Threlkeld, just east of Keswick. They'd been reported for various offences against dogs, sheep and birds. In the end, the charges were dropped through lack of evidence. No doubt the CPS didn't want to become embroiled in a case that involved transient suspects who had a habit of disappearing, as well as non-human victims. It was sad, but reality.

She studied the photographs of the animals and screwed up her nose. One showed a trail of birds' wings, with blood spattered along a track, with the bodies of the animals arranged in a pile, half burned. Another showed a dog with its back legs hacked off. Kelly felt herself becoming indignant and hungry for justice for the animals, but had to remind herself that this was thirteen years ago, and sometimes the police struggled to find justice for people, let alone a few dogs and birds.

She read the statements from the travelling family and noticed a recurring theme: they all stated that the animals had

42

been hunted and trapped to order. A stranger – whose name they didn't know – had approached them to deliver the said animals, but had vanished after maiming them. It was a tall story and Kelly rolled her eyes. Charges hadn't been forthcoming and the travellers moved on. From the testimonials, Kelly worked out that the prominent figure in the small travelling community at the time was a man called Harry O'Connor. There was always a staunch hierarchy in such colonies, and there was usually a man at the top.

She stretched and rubbed her neck.

There were five more cases from 2005, then Kelly turned to a few more recent ones. She leapt to 2010, and a missing boy. He'd been on holiday with his parents in the Ullswater area and vanished one afternoon from their campsite. The family had been camping south of Pooley Bridge in the extremely popular south shore of Ullswater. Kelly had plenty of knowledge of the area. Not only had she pursued police work there, she'd been on plenty of runs up there too, and the last time had been this morning with Johnny. The road was hell during peak season, and it would be quite easy for a young boy to be whisked away from such a busy camping area, she thought, and that's what the officers investigating had concluded too after all leads had been investigated and dismissed. The family was left with the awful realisation their twelve-year-old son had probably got into a vehicle and left the county by sunset the same day. Other police forces had become involved in the case, making it a national enquiry, but again, Kelly hadn't heard of it. She was saddened but not surprised at how many missing children's cases didn't get resolved.

She leant back and stretched. Nothing had jumped out at her so far. She'd read eight files back to back, and found no discrepancies. One thing, though, that she noticed hadn't been done, was a timeline. It was always possible that any number of cases around the same area, from around the same time, were connected, and she began sketching a drawing of dates and locations. What she came up with was a pretty, colour coded map of random events and random locations. She threw her pen down. This was more frustrating than a live case. Her emotions had gone from elation and excitement to desperate sadness and back again, in the space of a few hours.

DS Umshaw knocked and peered around her door.

'Coffee?' she asked Kelly.

'Ah, you read my mind. I need to stretch my legs.'

'I'll get it.'

'No, I need a walk. Seriously, Kate, I'm going to get fat if I vegetate any further reading case files from fourteen years ago.'

'What are you doing?' Umshaw asked.

'Cold cases. Any news on Carla Rigg?'

'Not yet. I've released the photo to the press department and it should be in the local evening news tonight. I've dedicated a helpline based at HQ and they've put three people on it.'

'Well done, Kate.'

They walked to the coffee machine. Kelly wasn't convinced that they'd seen the last of their Ms Rigg.

Chapter 8

'Ah, to what do I owe this pleasure, Joe?' Fred asked. He opened the door wider for the ranger. He'd known Joe Spencer for almost ten years now, getting to know him through his passion for the environment and concern for the National Park. People assumed that the National Trust land would always be there: standing as it had for millions of years, arms open, and welcoming millions of visitors, year upon year, but actually the upkeep was a round-the-clock business. Sheep grazing, weather erosion and the hammering of paths by too many walking boots were the main enemies of rangers and lakes lovers.

'Thought I'd drop in, Fred. I was passing.' The younger man looked agitated, Fred noted, but he let it pass. Fred's house was almost inside Whinlatter Forest, isolated and difficult to stumble across. Joe lived with his charming family on English Heritage land, on the edge of a working farm, near Troutbeck, on the A66 between Penrith and Keswick. Fred very much doubted that Joe was just passing. It had been a while since he'd seen his old friend, and Fred suspected that Annie didn't know he was here.

'Come in, can I get you a warm drink? The air has a bite, does it not? It'll be soon Mabon, and we'll be gathering the harvest. I can't believe where the summer has gone. It seems only yesterday that we were celebrating May Day!'

'I second that!' Joe said, entering the house and taking off his boots.

'Ah, leave those on, Joe. We don't stand on ceremony here, not with these old flagstones. If there's anything of interest on the bottom of your shoe, Bertha will get it.' Bertha was Fred's black Labrador, and she was as sharp as a whippet when a morsel dropped in front of her nose.

'I can hear her,' Joe said. Fred nodded and led the way to the kitchen. As soon as he opened the door, the warmth from the range leaked out into the corridor and caressed them, and Bertha affectionately thrust her nose into Joe's crotch.

'Bertha!' Fred shooed her away but Joe welcomed and petted her. The dog's tail swished to and fro and Fred negotiated his way around her to put the kettle on the fire.

'It's been a while, Fred. How are the grandkids?'

'Ah, we're all good. It's good to see you. You must bring Annie and the boys for Sunday lunch, how about this weekend?'

Joe hesitated, but only for a second. 'I'll have to check with Annie. I think I have an early shift but I'll be done by around two, will that do?'

'Of course! I'll have to confirm with her indoors, but I'll stick my neck out and say it's grand. I'll have a quiet word with you-know-who and get a fresh hind of venison.'

Fred's contact was a farming friend with too many acres and not enough demand for his wild deer. He also let him fish in his trout pond with no charge. Fred watched as Joe warmed his hands by the range fire and didn't take off his coat. He sensed a shadow in his friend's energy. It wasn't uncommon for Fred to read people in this way: he'd been doing it all his life, until finally he'd found a way to harness it and control it, by welcoming Mother Nature to his soul. She'd shown him that he possessed a gift: an endowment from the extra dimension, and a talent that was easily wasted and ignored in today's skin-deep modern world.

He waited. His friend would offload in his own time. Meanwhile, Bertha settled in her basket and the kettle began to whistle. Joe sat in an armchair and Fred busied himself with getting some ham out of the fridge and slicing some home-made bread. He lashed yellow butter on to each piece and topped it with a generous helping of ham. Joe hadn't been asked if he'd like one: it was simply put in front of him. Like many of the ancient traditions, feeding and sharing was one of the more important methods of welcome, and so it was in Fred's kitchen. Two steaming mugs of coffee were placed on the oak table and Fred finally sat down. He didn't say anything. They munched their snack happily and sipped their hot drinks. They discussed the weather.

'Farm tying up for equinox?' Fred asked.

Joe had told Fred on a few occasions that he'd been tempted to join the group, and he'd come close. He had much in common with those who worshipped the seasons. Indeed, his life was ruled by the sun and the moon. But the idea of organised religion, no matter how small and discreet, put him off. Fred assured him that it wasn't a religion, more of a way of life, a belief system by which to guide one's own path through from birth to death. Just like the years, one grew and rested and bloomed and died, many times over until the final chapter. But with the earth, there was no final chapter, and that's why it was so important to take advantage of the opportunity to unite with the earth, before expiry took hold and snuffed out the chance.

'Callum's studying for his GCSEs this year. It's a scary prospect nowadays. They no longer have the luxury of an apprenticeship and then employment for life. It's all about money.'

Fred nodded acknowledgement and lament at the same time. 'What is he looking to do?'

'A-Levels. I think he wants to be an accountant.'

Fred almost spat his coffee. 'Christ alive, Joe! How did you produce such a capitalist?'

'I know! Connor is the historian.'

'He's an old soul, that one.'

'Indeed.'

'You should bring him to a meeting.'

'I don't know. Annie thinks it's all heebie jeebies.'

'I won't take offence at that! Most people do. Did you read the article in the *Gazette* about the occult? It maddens me to the core.'

'No, I didn't. Was it utterly fair and unbiased? I'm sensing serenity in your voice,' Joe mocked.

'I'll give her serenity all right! Young thing doesn't know nothing about nothing, trying no doubt to finish her dissertation for her journalism degree. It had us all down as devil worshippers, sacrificing animals and using magic.'

'Oh dear. How did Mary take it?' Joe knew the group well, and he accepted the odd invitation for social gatherings, Annie just wanted him to avoid anything formal that involved chanting or praying.

'Nonplussed. You know what she's like.'

'And Jock?'

'Ah, he dismissed her as a little lost girl who hasn't yet found her sixth element. Like all youngsters, eh?'

Joe nodded.

'Mary won't judge but I know she was fuming. Mary and Jock are too accepting, that's why Sandra likes them so much, because they calm me down.' He laughed.

Joe sipped his coffee and paused. Fred waited.

'You remember Kirk Junker?' Joe broke the silence.

Fred stopped wiping the crumbs away from his plate. Bertha had enjoyed the odd nibble of bread and even fat from the meat under his feet, but now the trickle stopped. Fred finished his mouthful and picked up his coffee cup, bringing it to his mouth. He took his time and spoke when he'd finished.

'I do.'

'Remember the girl?'

'His daughter?'

Joe nodded. Fred pushed his plate to one side and drained his mug. He looked out of the window, which was misty with condensation, water dripping down the pane. It created a streaky vision and it held Fred's gaze for a minute. Bertha

48

pricked her ears up and placed her snout on Fred's knee. He petted her and reassured her. A clock ticked and it was the first time that Fred had noticed it since Joe arriving.

'I haven't seen them in years. I can't help you with all that, Joe.'

'I'm not asking for help, Fred, just advice. I don't ever forget faces. It's been, what – five years? She hasn't changed a bit: she's still got those piercing blue eyes and the freckles. She must be seventeen or eighteen now. It's the look that I can't get out of my head: you know, the look of wisdom and experience that a young girl shouldn't have? She hasn't changed at all.'

'You mean you've seen her? Did you see Kirk?'

'No.'

'Good. Stay away.'

'I have no intention of getting involved. I only saw her, and she needed help.'

'What do you mean? Was she in some sort of trouble?'

'Have you heard the news? The young woman found wandering at Castlerigg?'

'Yes. Are you telling me that's her?' Fred had heard the story on the local radio. He'd discussed it with Sandra. They'd said how awful and wretched the girl must feel. He went across to the radio and flicked it on. The news was halfway through but, at the end, they mentioned the girl. The announcer said that a photograph had been released by the police. Joe got out his iPhone and googled the story. The photo of the girl flashed on his screen.

'I hate those things. They're everywhere.'

'They come in handy sometimes. Look.'

Fred looked at the dog, who scuttled back to bed and peered upwards towards the two men, doubtful of what to make of their exchange. Fred didn't want to look at his friend's phone. He didn't want to welcome the vision into the sanctity of his home.

'I found her, Fred – well, Callum found her. But I didn't tell the police that I knew her, and she didn't know me. She definitely didn't recognise me.'

'You're mistaken there, boy. Of course she recognised you.'

Chapter 9

Fred made a point of watching the TV report closely that night. Sandra came home with wild boar sausages from the same farmer friend based near Keswick, and she cooked them on the fire with a berry sauce and some chard from late summer offerings in their garden. They'd invited Jock, as often happened. Freshly pulled potatoes smothered in butter and salt finished the fayre and they were all satisfied. Sandra tidied the dishes, leaving the men to watch the news. Fred didn't tell Jock about Joe's visit but he watched him carefully as the police photo came on screen

'Police are appealing for a woman who was found wandering around the stone circle at Castlerigg on Saturday morning to come forward. The Cumbria Constabulary has issued a statement seeking confirmation that the woman is safe. She left the Penrith and Lakes Hospital at around two p.m. on Monday afternoon in clothes similar to these in the photograph, given to her by hospital staff. The woman, who is said to be around twenty years of age, is said to be suffering from amnesia and may not be capable of looking after herself. Police are eager to establish her wellbeing. Anybody with information should contact the help desk number shown on the screen now, or email us, message us on Twitter, using the hashtag #cumbriaconstabulary, or use our Facebook page. It is unknown whether the woman is local to the area or just visiting. As the cold nights draw *in, folks, keep a lookout for the woman shown in the photograph.'*

Jock looked at Fred, who nodded and stared back at the TV. Fred noticed his friend pale and swallow hard. Silence sat heavily between them.

Sandra came back into the room and showed no interest in the TV. She took up her knitting. Another grandchild was due in December. Sandra always knitted in neutral colours before they knew the sex. She chose either white, yellow or mint, not wanting to use pink or blue for fear of bad luck. Their children had been raised in the natural way, but had wandered to different leanings, what with the pressures and allure of modern life. It was their choice. They'd enjoyed a wonderfully free childhood, attending gatherings and pursuing organic pastimes, but partners, jobs and universities had caught up with them and pulled them away. All three lived in or around London.

Fred didn't draw any more attention to the news, and Jock coughed, as if embarrassed in front of Sandra. Sandra looked up but once to smile at her guest. Jock Harris was a gentle giant who'd seen much of the world and the evil within and, for some, he was difficult to read. The old man remained silent and Fred switched channels. Joe was right. There was no mistake. In the photo, she had the look of an innocent, despite Fred knowing the opposite to be true of the poor girl. Fred's heart ached and he wished he wasn't such an empath. It burdened him from time to time but that, he supposed, was the whole point. He felt what others did not. He saw pain, despair, hunger, malice and desolation, often before those who were struck down saw it. His life in general was a peaceful one but, occasionally, somebody would walk into his private space – wittingly or not – and present him with a dilemma.

Kirk Junker was one of them.

Kirk had styled himself as a guru type figure, higher even than a High Priest, and created his own coven, away from the central group that they'd been members of for years. He unsettled the nest. Kirk thought he knew better, even than Mother Nature herself. He was a loose cannon, and the High Priest knew it. If Kirk hadn't left the roost when he had done, he would've been shortly expelled. That was essentially what had put Joe's wife off joining them. It was bloody bad timing. No matter how many times Fred had tried to explain to the lovely Annie that Kirk was the poorest example of their beautiful faith, it didn't matter: she'd made up her mind. It was saddening. She wouldn't let their boys anywhere near him. Fred and Sandra were an exception, obviously, and Joe continued to bring his family to visit often. The calls and drop-ins tailed off though, until they went months, and then almost a year without contact. Having Joe pop in unannounced was heart-warming and he'd told Sandra with enthusiasm. She too was thrilled, and began planning Sunday dinner early, looking around the garden and deciding what she might have to buy in. They were essentially self-sufficient, but, occasionally, they craved food from the supermarket like everyone else, and, of course, their group needed factory processed treats from time to time. Sandra made her own ice cream, pancakes, pastries, cakes and biscuits, but even she couldn't replicate a packet of pink-covered donuts or takeaway pizza. They weren't puritans.

Bertha sat in front of the fire at Jock's feet and looked up to watch Fred, as he pondered what Joe had told him. Fred didn't notice his faithful hound staring at him. He'd advised Joe not to approach the police with the information about the girl. Joe had been indignant and a little scared, but Fred was adamant. It was welcoming unknown forces into their lives, and the girl must have been at Castlerigg for a reason. What it didn't make clear was if Kirk Junker was still in the area. Perhaps the girl had left his clutches and gone it alone. But, whatever Joe Spencer said, Fred didn't believe him that the girl was amnesiac and failed to recognise him. There was always something other-worldly about the youngster, and that was why she'd created such a stir for Kirk.

Seventeen? Eighteen? Maybe she'd run away because legally she could.

It pained him to recall how the girl had been treated, but there was nothing any of them could have done. Besides, there was no evidence. The girl simply seemed withdrawn and uneasy most of the time. She wore long garments and a scarf covering her hair, so no sign of abuse was ever discussed. Though they all suspected Kirk had taken the child as his own partner. It was the way she looked, the way she walked, and the way she flinched from touch.

Fred settled on a channel discussing deforestation and replanting in Cumbria. Jock looked at his friend and at Sandra.

'Another cider, Jock?'

'Aye.' It was all they said.

After Jock had gone home, Fred couldn't get the girl out of his mind. She'd been given the temporary name of Carla Rigg by hospital staff, but Fred knew her real name, or at least what Kirk Junker told them.

Her face burned inside his skull and a memory came searing into his mind. He sat back in his favourite chair and closed his eyes. He had no choice but to allow it, despite the pain it caused. He knew from his conscious memory of self that if he denied access to his spatial wanderings then they would only revisit stronger than the last time, until they haunted his every waking thought. He glanced across at Sandra, who was happy clicking her needles across one another. The noise soothed him and became the only thing he heard as his mind opened and he fell into the abyss.

–

Kirk Junker stood by a tree. He was an accomplished carpenter. It was what they'd found charming in the man: a trade of godliness. Any man who used his hands to create such beauty was a divinity in himself. Though Kirk looked defiant with a scowl and a jutting chin.

A carving on the tree caught Fred's attention and he witnessed the engraving move. The figures depicted danced and cavorted inside the bark, making the tree move in grotesque ways. Fred kept still. The click-click of Sandra's needles enchanted him.

Kirk touched the tree and Fred was impelled to go forwards towards the etchings. They still moved and now Fred looked at Kirk's face, which was set in a lurid smirk. The images were of nymph-like creatures, svelte and feminine, gyrating in positions Fred had never seen before, but found it difficult to tear his eyes away from. He felt Kirk take his hand and force it towards the tree trunk. He felt the movement of the tiny beings and a throbbing radiating from the trunk. His heart beat faster and matched the pulsing of the life of the tree. It was an animal, alive and vital.

Kirk placed Fred's hand on the jagged edge of the wood and Fred flinched away. He realised that the tree was in fact a real person and what he had seen as twigs, branches and foliage, was now the garments and skin of a beautiful woman – no, a girl He tried to back away, but Kirk was stronger than him and the girl offered herself, revealing her pure, cream coloured back to him. She peered over her shoulder and smiled enticingly. Her eyes shone the purest blue but Fred could sense that her heart was not so.

With an electric jolt, Fred broke free of the shackles of Kirk's hands and untangled himself from a thousand fingers, wrapped around him in bondage. The girl sank back inside the tree and looked away: rejected and forlorn. But not before Fred noticed a single basic tattoo on her flesh. It was so tiny that it could have passed for a group of freckles, moles or spots. But it wasn't any of those. It was the symbol of the Moon Goddess with the three moons: waxing, waning and full, and it was near her neck. As quickly as she had come, the girl disappeared and her long hair hid the vision. The tree became petrified and Kirk disappeared, along with his daughter, but not before Fred had witnessed her eyes pleading with him to set her free. The image stayed with him and his heart pounded in his chest until he opened his eyes.

–

Fred looked around the room: he was back home, in the sitting room, in front of the fire with Sandra. Her needles click-clicked and Bertha watched him from her bed. The fire crackled and he realised that a fresh log was required.

He shivered, despite the room being stiflingly hot. Bertha sauntered over to him and rested her muzzle on his lap.

'It's all right, girl. There, there.' The dog's eyes grew less droopy and the corners of her mouth turned up. Fred knew that the presence had gone.

For now.

Chapter 10

Kelly drove along the A66 and turned off south. It was days like this that she wished she could just take her team up a mountain for some squad bonding. Bollocks to the mindfulness: fresh air and Mother Nature was all anyone required. Will, Emma and Rob would be takers, but perhaps Kate would have an issue, given her twenty-a-day habit. Kelly glanced towards the Helvellyn range and it was shrouded in cloud. Even throughout the autumn and winter, they got days that shone blue and crystal clear all day long; they were the days the locals came out in force and posted their findings on Facebook. Kelly and Johnny were members of several pages supporting the National Park and people shared their pictures from all over the world. Tourists came from as far away as Fiji and Siberia, and none failed to be lured by the magic of the hills and dales.

'I see what you mean about being out of the way,' Rob said, holding on to a ceiling strap.

'Have we had any results on the clothes yet?'

'We can't exactly justify an urgent request on this one, however, the stains elevate it a little, at least the ambulance crew had the foresight to get DNA from her, we should have a result in the next couple of days. If they are hers, and so is the blood, then what does that prove?'

'Nothing really, it's just helpful to know which direction she came from. If she stripped – or was stripped – where the clothes were dumped, then we can follow that up. We could also go public with them. Somebody out there must know her.'

'Unless she is foreign after all.'

'I know. There is that. I've sent her photograph to Interpol, following regular procedure, but it'll just be filed along with millions of others. You never know, there might be a hit one day. I'll submit her DNA too. Meanwhile, I've got a mountain of paperwork on my desk.'

'You shouldn't have brought me, guv.'

'Ah nonsense. You've got to see it. It'll give you a feel of how she felt if that ever becomes important. If I didn't bring you, there's no way you'd pootle up here on your own, like some kind of homework project at the weekend. We've all got stuff to do. Sometimes we need a break and we're fortunate to have all this.' She cast her hand across the dash, indicating the whole National Park. 'And right on our doorstep.'

They turned on to an even narrower road and Kelly pulled up and slowed down opposite a farmer's field. They could see sheep milling about inside.

'It's farm land?'

'Of course, what did you expect? It's not an exclusive site like the pyramids.'

'Oh. That's…'

'Disappointing? I know. One day, it'll crumble and disappear, but sheep are more valuable than a pile of five-thousand-year-old stones in these parts.'

They walked through the gate, taking care to avoid sheep shit, and, as they cornered around a series of bushes, Rob stopped.

'Fucking hell, boss!'

'I know, it's amazing isn't it?'

'Do they charge entry?'

'Who? English Heritage? No, it's free. Anyone can come up here, anytime. Even before dawn.'

'What the hell was she thinking?' Rob meant Carla Rigg.

'I have no idea, but I'd love to know if she was alone.'

They walked towards the impressive site and took their time. It was that kind of place: one where time had to be paused and enjoyed. Kelly reached a stone first and put out her hand to touch it. Of course it was cold, as she expected, but it was also soft and feminine somehow.

'How the hell did they haul these up here, five thousand years ago?' Rob asked.

'From Borrowdale Valley as well. God knows, rollers? Cattle and carts? No idea. There's no official history of the place. It makes it a magnet for hair-brained theories and Pagan loonies. Especially around the solstices.'

'Solstices?'

'Oh, come on, Rob. Longest day and shortest day? Don't you watch the news in June when hippies camp at Stonehenge and dance and chant, praying to the sun and moon?'

'Oh, *that* solstice.'

'There are two. One in summer for the longest day, and one in winter – the shortest day. Apparently, the stones align on those days with various points astrologically.'

'Really? Like the Incas and stuff?'

'Yeah, and stuff,' Kelly replied, rolling her eyes. Rob knew much of maths and technology but little of the ancients, and why should he? It was her non-biological father who'd taught her the history of much of the fells. Ironically, Ted, her real father, had taught her the rest.

'Is it important?' Rob asked.

'Not really, we're nowhere near solstice and there's no evidence of symbolism. It could be that it was the nearest structure to where she took off her clothes. It might have been shelter.' She turned around. 'She came from over there.' Kelly pointed to where the clothes had been found. She walked to the centre of the circle and realised that the potential route taken by the girl lined up with the two main stones of the circle. She made a mental note.

'It's incredible,' Rob said. 'I can't believe it was an accidental find. It's too important a site, isn't it?'

Kelly could tell that Rob was mesmerised by the place. It was the same for most people when they first saw it. He was having difficulty separating his own reaction to the stones from the case, and Carla Rigg's motivation. It was easily done. That's why she'd brought him here, to witness the power of the place, even though it might have nothing to do with their investigation, if there was one. If Carla Rigg didn't turn up and they had no forensic match on her, then she'd stay disappeared. 'You see that peak over there?' she asked.

'Blencathra?' Rob asked. The majestic ridge of Blencathra sat on the northern edge of the National Park and looked like a sleeping feline. Just below that was the ancient settlement of Threlkeld. Opposite that, on the other side of the valley, now occupied by the A66, the Helvellyn range of mountains began, and the first and smallest of those was Threlkeld Knotts.

'During autumn, at a specific time every year, the sun rises directly over the Threlkeld Knotts, it's pretty stunning, you should see it.'

'How do you know that?' Rob asked.

'My dad used to bring me. He did tell me when it was but I forgot a long time ago.' Kelly stopped and looked away towards the west. The man she'd thought of as her father, John Porter, was the person responsible for her love of the fells and her mastery of the sport of conquering them. Her breath caught in her throat and she coughed. She loved him like a father, because that's what he'd been. She'd only found out about her biological father recently. It took nothing away from John Porter, who'd never known that Kelly wasn't his. He'd raised her, sat with her when she had a temperature in the night, put calamine lotion on her chicken pox, taken her to watch rugby matches on his moped, taught her how to gut a fish properly, and kissed her before her prom.

The fact that an illicit affair had produced a set of cells not of John Porter wasn't her concern. But the future was different to what she expected. She now had another man in her life, who also didn't know that he had a third daughter until last year. She turned back to Rob.

'That's not all. On the summer solstice, this stone,' she paused and walked to the tallest stone in the circle. It was probably eleven feet tall and weighed fifteen tonnes. 'This casts a shadow a half a mile long.'

'It's like a big clock,' Rob said.

'Indeed. That's what all these circles do: tell the time along ancient and astrological parameters.'

'Did your dad teach you that too?' Rob asked. Kelly nodded. She hadn't come up here to reconnect with John Porter. She'd forgotten the times he'd brought her here and taught her what he knew of the history of the place, which was relatively little. Lacking real knowledge, he'd made up stories and filled her head with witches and wizards to make her squeal and laugh. The memories, along with the stories, came flooding back now.

'So, what's under here?' Rob asked.

'No one knows.'

'What? Why not?'

'It's not a pressing matter.'

'You mean no one has the money to invest?'

'Quite.'

'What a crying shame. There could be ancient kings and queens under here.'

Kelly laughed. The romantic notion was an attractive one and that's why so many poets and writers had made stories up about Castlerigg over the centuries. Tragedies and dramas had unfolded in fiction alongside the stones, but still no one came up with funding to excavate them, and perhaps that was a good thing: it might ruin the illusion.

'Do you think she had some kind of connection with this place then?' Kelly asked Rob.

'It's a pretty specific place to "happen upon". Not knowing it before, it seems glaringly obvious to me that you'd need to know it well to find it.'

'Good point.'

She knew there was a good reason to bring him up here.

Chapter 11

Kelly sought permission from HQ to have the belongings found in the field adjacent to the stone circle examined, despite not having established if a crime had been committed. She'd been given a tentative green light but was told to be mindful of budget. As if she could ever ignore budget. Lab results were expensive but the longer one was willing to wait, the lower the price. They had time, oodles of it. There was no rush, and so the evidence was sent away along with thousands of other inquiries filed around the county. There was a safeguarding element to the missing woman, and so she was able to tick at least one box.

It was agreed that the clothes left were about the right size for the young woman, and suitably fashionable for someone around her age: jeans, crop top, a puffer jacket from Topshop and a pair of Air Force Nike trainers. No socks. There was no jewellery found with the pile of garments and nothing else in the wallet apart from the photo. Kelly requested that a picture of the Topshop jacket be released along with the story about the missing woman. The nearest Topshop was either in Carlisle or Cockermouth. The photograph taken of Carla Rigg in hospital was sent to the two retailers.

Kelly's desk phone alerted her to an incoming call and she hoped that it would be the psychologist with whom she'd worked in London. It was. Dr Demi Cramer had worked on criminal profiles for the Met for close to twenty-five years. Kelly had already emailed her the information they had and she was hoping that Dr Cramer had chewed it over. If nothing else, it was an excuse to catch up.

'In forty-eight hours, the case will be downgraded. She looks over eighteen and she left the hospital of her own free will,' Kelly said.

'Why get caught in the first place? And you say she's mute and amnesic?'

'The hospital didn't have time to make a full assessment but initial evaluation diagnosed her with Transient Global Amnesia,' Kelly read from her screen.

'Bullshit,' Demi Cramer said.

Kelly was used to Demi's style and the brusqueness didn't bother her. 'Why do you say that?' she asked.

'They didn't even do an MRI. Transient Global Amnesia is almost unheard of outside textbooks in a young healthy girl. Certainly not one who stops to take her clothes off and leave them in a rather neat pile, then enjoys a comfortable and lengthy stay in a hospital bed. She is the last candidate for the condition, which is temporary. Also somebody with a bout of TGA usually can't shut up: they're confused and jabbering and a general pain in the arse.'

'Great.'

'What were her eyes like? I presume you met her?'

'Briefly. They were scared.'

'Someone with TGA doesn't show emotion. She was in control. Did she have an MRI?'

'Don't be silly, too expensive.'

'EEG? ECG? CAT scan?'

'Normal.'

'And she never uttered a word?'

'Nope. Nothing coherent.'

'But she reacted when touched?'

'Yes, she wouldn't allow a body check or a rape kit.'

'Control. She wanted to be found.'

'But why?'

'I don't know, Kelly, that's your job. How's things up there in the valleys?' Demi put on a terrible Welsh accent.

'I'm in Cumbria, Demi.'

'Is there a difference?'

'Let's get back to Carla Rigg, shall we? What about the location and time of day?'

'Is she a witch?'

'What?'

'A white witch. I've come across it before, in Kent.'

'They take their clothes off at dawn?'

'Generally, yes. And in places of significance, such as forests, caves and natural landmarks.'

'But Castlerigg isn't natural, it's man-made.'

'Yes, but it celebrates nature, doesn't it? The sun and the moon? I've been reading about it. I'd like to take a trip up there, Kelly. I'm writing a book and this Carla Rigg is someone I'd like to interview.'

'We don't even know who she is or where she is, Demi.'

'Yes, but I know you'll find her. And when you do, give me a call.'

Demi Cramer hung up. Kelly smiled. It was always the same with the doctor: she said about as much as she needed to; nothing more and nothing less. If she thought of anything else, Kelly knew that she'd be on the phone, no matter what time of the day or night.

Kelly googled 'White Witch'. *A person who practises magic for altruistic purposes.* The definition jarred Kelly, because when she'd looked into Carla Rigg's eyes, all she'd seen was fear and terror, not some benevolent and noble power, capable of healing and deep empathy. The young woman struck Kelly as somebody running away from power, not embracing it.

She dismissed the notion and went to find DS Will Phillips. There were no sightings recorded of a young woman alone around the area of the main roads in and out of Castlerigg for Monday morning. He'd had officers visit the campsites around the Thirlmere valley all the way down to the tip of the reservoir and to the north, all the way up to Threlkeld. None of the guesthouses, farmhouses, log cabin owners or English Heritage patrols had seen anything unusual.

The woman had vanished.

Kelly looked at her photograph again and compared it to the one found in her wallet. She studied the man: he looked around seventy-ish, thinning hair, kind eyes, broad smile and – yes – happy. Whatever Carla Rigg had been doing with him that day, she'd been contented and joyful. Perhaps it was her loving grandfather.

Her head filled with what-ifs. It was something that every detective dreaded: she had to close the file and move on. DS Kate Umshaw would alert her immediately should there be any developments to get excited about. Kelly doubted that the photograph of the young woman would make national news, but at least it had made the North West bulletin. It might be enough.

A thought took hold and she called Ted Wallis. It was half an excuse to talk to her father and half business. Semi-retired, Ted rarely visited the office in Carlisle nowadays, unless there was a post-mortem that posed a particular set of problems for the new pathologist. He was still the chief coroner for the North West, and, as such, had the final say on controversial death certificates. It was a long shot, but Ted's memory was as sharp as any twenty-five-year-old trainee surgeon she knew.

'I'm in a wonderful little shop in Keswick, Kelly, I thought you might need a new jacket, the sales are fabulous. There's a Jack Wolfskin – just your colour – it's green, and it's reduced from almost two hundred pounds to seventy.'

'No, really, Ted, I don't...'

'I bought it for you. It will suit you, I'm sure. What about these new walking trainers? They have grips like boots but are open in places up top – they're rather fantastic I should think If I could get away with them, then I would.'

'No, Ted, honestly, I have too many pairs of walking boots anyway.'

'Well, that's my point: they're trainers, not boots, so your feet don't get too hot. The man in here has told me that they're for mid-season, before it gets too cold. And I've picked up a few things for Josie. Johnny tells me that she's taking rock climbing lessons.'

'Really?' It was news to Kelly that Johnny's now fifteen-year-old daughter was interested in the outdoor life. She figured that Instagram and *Love Island* were about the limit of Josie's 'outside' interests, in the loosest terms.

'Yes. She's going to Rock of Ages right here in Keswick.'

'Rock of what?'

'Rock of Ages. It's new. It has the second highest climbing wall in England, after that one in Kendal. She joined last month, and already she's on track to take her first climbing award next month.'

'You know a lot about what she's up to, Ted.'

'I take an interest. She is like my granddaughter.'

Kelly had to concede this one. Kelly had begun to refer to Josie as her stepdaughter a while ago and Ted had picked up on it. Josie was independent, but then in Cumbria, a teenager perhaps had more freedoms than one who grew up in a large city. The streets were relatively safe, crime was low on average, and life possessed a rhythm more suited to fifty years ago than the hectic pressures of somewhere like London or Manchester. At first, when Josie moved in with her father, there'd been problems settling in. Josie found Cumbria dull and boring. But Kelly had to admit that more recently, she'd seen a change in the youngster. She was less critical of her father, for a start. She kept better company, and now she was partaking in activities that took her into the fresh air and away from screens. She no longer wanted to spend lengthy amounts of time with her mother. That posed its own problems because Kelly and Johnny were away sailing for three weeks in November in Florida. As quick as the idea came to her, Ted filled the space.

'I've spoken to Johnny about your little dilemma, and Josie is happy to stay with me while you're in Florida.'

It touched Kelly. Not just that Ted was showing an interest in distant relatives, but it also reminded her of how Josie had connected with her own mother. Wendy and Josie had enjoyed a banter that Kelly had certainly never had with her parents.

'And Josie agreed?'

'Of course.'

'Thank you, Ted, that's brilliant. I'm sure she'll keep you on the straight and narrow. I was actually calling for something else.'

'Are you at work?'

'Of course I'm at work.'

'Do you need a new briefcase? The market has a leather stall, they're very smart. I'll get you one.'

'Ted... I don't even use a briefcase. Never mind. Look, I wanted to ask you if you recall any instances of married couples dying together in the last couple of years.'

'What do you mean?'

'I mean a road traffic accident or a house fire or something of that nature: dramatic and tragic. I've got a missing person – a young woman – who baulked at the mention of her parents, and I was just wondering if she lost them together. She refused to speak and I've evidence to suggest that she's suffering from acute trauma.'

Kelly heard rustling on the other end of the phone and Ted thank a market stall holder.

'Not off the top of my head, but I could do some digging. RTAs don't always come to me. Particularly if they're on the M6, sometimes they go to a big university hospital in Liverpool or Manchester.'

'Thanks, Ted.'

'Kelly, before you go, now I've got you cornered, would you and Johnny like to bring Josie over for dinner this week? She's got mock exams coming up in the winter and she's thinking of using her sciences. Criminology. I wonder who inspired her.'

Kelly was lost for words. If Ted was right, and Johnny's daughter was thinking of studying criminology, then Kelly couldn't remember a time when she'd had a conversation with her about it. She doubted that she was her inspiration. Her relationship with Josie had always been fraught, for want of a better description. Josie was like a tidal current between her and Johnny; pulling first one way then the other, drifting between two poles, but never finding common ground. If Kelly had missed Josie's transformation then she only had herself to blame.

She looked at her watch: it was time to wrap up the day and let her team go home. No further leads were jumping out at them over the strange woman, and the minor cases that were live, could wait until the morning to pursue. Rob Shawcross had a court appearance tomorrow, at Carlisle Crown Court, giving evidence for an assault, Kate was visiting a school to discuss career options in the police force, and Kelly had more cold cases to review. It was a lull like this that allowed them all the opportunity to get home at a reasonable hour, and pretend that they were normal.

Chapter 12

Joe kept sociable hours for the most part. At times he was able to see the boys off to school and be home for their dinner. Both boys were at crucial stages in their education. At fourteen, Connor had just chosen his GCSE options and, at that age, it seemed like those few momentary decisions would dictate the rest of his life.

'Nothing is set in stone,' Joe reassured his son, but it fell on deaf ears. Connor was a worrier.

'But what if history clashes with art?'

Everything with Connor was fatalistic and he was the family's pessimist. On the other hand, Callum, who was embarking on his first year of A levels, was the family's horizontal barometer. His was the 'slide and see' method of future planning and preparation. He'd chosen design and science based topics for GCSE and now he was trying his hand at business. Not that he was business minded. Indeed the opposite was true: Callum was a philanthropist (albeit an armchair one) and the cut-throat world of economics and world corporatism was a millions miles away from his altruistic ideals. Still, he understood the importance of earning, and every company in the world needed an accountant.

Joe let it go. It was Annie who was constantly on their backs. Joe's wasn't a grand wage, and Annie essentially paid the bills. She was a HR boss at the Penrith and Lakes Hospital and it was her income that supported them. As Joe rolled out of bed, pulled on a sweater and jogging pants and cooked himself eggs, Annie had already made sure that the boys knew their schedule for the day, fixed her packed lunch, made breakfast, cleared away, put a load of washing on, and left on time for work. Connor had revision sessions at school until gone five this evening, and Callum was trying a taster session at the new climbing wall in Keswick. Both boys went to school in the town and Annie dropped them off each morning, at the end of the long farm track, to catch the one school bus.

Annie's seniority at the hospital meant that she could take advantage of her position and enquire about the woman they'd found at Castlerigg. It was the main topic of gossip at the Penrith and Lakes this week. The woman – who seemed more like a child – had vanished, and concerns for her wellbeing were mounting. Annie knew before the press and had called Joe to tell him. Her husband seemed still to be in shock and she put it down to his gentle nature.

Everybody at the Penrith and Lakes had their own theories. She was a runaway, a hitcher, a foreign illegal, a drug addict, and she was a nobody. To Annie, the girl was a lost soul, she'd told Joe: she'd looked into her eyes. She'd seen the torment. But, at Castlerigg, she'd also seen the way the girl looked at Callum.

A shiver went down her back as she dropped the boys at the end of the track that morning, the start of a new autumn term, and then made her way to the A66 and on to Penrith. She looked in her rear-view mirror and watched them stand at the side of the road, hands in pockets, occasionally speaking to one another, waiting for the bus. It wouldn't be long before snow started to fall, around November time, and the buses would struggle to make it on time. But that was a source of excitement and anticipation for all the school children in Keswick in the winter: snow days. Annie reflected that when she was a child, snow days weren't a thing. It seemed that suddenly nowadays, teachers found it difficult to negotiate a little snow drift in their four-by-fours, whereas when she was at school, a tiny Ford with a screaming engine and flimsy tyres fared better against the elements.

Character was everything.

The memory of the girl in the field at Castlerigg came back to her as she found a gap in the traffic and pulled on to the busy A road. She'd ushered her boys away from the sight of the naked woman. Joe had taken over and his survival instincts had kicked in. They couldn't get her to the car because every time they tried she'd struggle and cause a fuss, so they threw clothes and blankets over her, with Annie insisting that the boys go and wait in the vehicle. They refused. Understandably they were scared to leave their parents, but it had come as a surprise to witness the boys' vulnerability.

The young woman was all Callum had talked about since they'd found her. He'd bombarded his mother with question after question: did she know anything? Was she all right? Who was she? Had the police made sure she was safe? What was being said at the hospital?

He'd had nightmares. She knew he had because she'd peeked in the bedroom after hearing him thrashing about in bed, though he denied it. This morning, he'd been quiet. It had been on the news last night, that the police were looking for her, and Callum wasn't stupid. He was a mature sixteen, as were many of the children who lived in the outlying villages, and had to be self-sufficient at an early age. He worked out that she was no longer at the hospital. He'd also seen her picture online and on TV. He knew, also, that the police were concerned because they'd released photos of her clothes. Annie saw, as the days passed, that his frown deepened and shadows cursed his eyes.

'Do you know what, Callum? She's probably got herself drunk at a party and is now safe at home, burning with embarrassment at the trouble she's caused.' She'd tried to reassure her son but knew that Callum hadn't fallen for her theory, but it sounded comforting anyway.

The cottage was their warmth and succour, and she hated leaving it every morning at this time of the year, when the cool air seemed sharper and the sun dropped further in the sky. She looked forward to getting home every night and had no more ambitions than to provide for her boys and care for her family. She envied Joe his casual hours and outdoor existence; though when the snow hit, she'd rather be tucked away in her office in the bowels of the hospital any day.

She spotted the school bus travelling in the other direction as it made its pick-ups in the villages between Penrith and its final destination. Callum was talking of attending sixth form in Kendal: that would present a fresh transport headache. His other option was Penrith or Workington, or even Barrow-in-Furness. Annie had an aunt in the large town on the south coast of the Furness peninsula but she'd rather Callum came home every night. It was a conversation for next year.

For now, she was keen to find out if anyone knew if the girl had been found yet.

Chapter 13

The girl at Castlerigg was big news in school, simply because everybody knew that Callum and Connor had been there. They were minor celebrities as a result. Connor embellished the events on the school bus in front of a captive audience, and Callum rolled his eyes. His mind was on other more pressing matters, such as the girl's back and her perfect skin. All he'd seen was the creamy arch of her flesh, bending over behind one of the stones, before sanity returned and he called for his parents to help. He'd locked his eyes on the crease of her buttocks and the way her hair fell down to her waist. She was slender and delicate, and Callum had wanted to reach out and take her into his coat, to warm her and comfort her. He hadn't seen her full face, just a glance at her eyes. They were blue and wide, and he'd ached to hold her, to make her feel safe, but his dad had waded in and taken over, making the stranger scared and rigid. He'd offered to help, but the expression of assistance had been brushed away, as Mum and Dad made a drama out of the whole thing. And now she was gone. It was no surprise really. If it had been handled differently, maybe they could have taken care of her and found out what was wrong.

She'd haunted his dreams and he'd imagined picking her up, wrapping his coat around her and carrying her to safety. He'd laid her gently on a smooth stone and she'd wanted him to lie on top of her and

Callum blushed and looked out of the window at the passing hills. One day he'd leave this place and make his own decisions. It wasn't that he didn't like it here; far from it, he loved climbing with his dad and his brother. He enjoyed wild swimming in summer and going out with his dad to rescue trapped sheep high on deserted, rugged plateaus. He had no idea how the dumb animals got themselves trapped on precarious shelves, but his dad was just about the only person who knew how to get them down. He'd take his ropes and climb to where the idiot balls of white fluff had ended up, tie them off and winch them down to safety, to the immense relief of the farmer. Sheep were like gold up here. A dead one was lost profits.

His dad had told him that he could easily do what he did, but Callum wanted to travel. He didn't have the heart to tell his dad that being a ranger for English Heritage and rescuing the odd sheep wasn't enough. He didn't want to let his parents down, and he respected what his dad did, but he wanted more. They left the Lake District rarely, and this year, again, his parents had explained that they couldn't afford to go on a proper holiday; it hurt keenly. He was ashamed. His friends went to Greece and Croatia on all-inclusive getaways. Several of them flaunted their tanned skin on the first day of term, attracting the girls. His pale white skin was a source of embarrassment. Then he remembered the girl's skin: it was like porcelain and he wanted to touch it. Some of the girls in his year were tanned and it didn't compare.

As soon as he had his A-Levels, he'd have to break it to his parents that he was off: out of Cumbria, wherever the road took him; he was gone. The bus stopped behind traffic and he gazed out of the window at the great peak of Blencathra. He'd seen it a thousand times before. This morning, though, he couldn't help searching the countryside for the girl. She could be anywhere. She could be dead from exposure. If she left the hospital because she wanted to, then she could also be at home, cosy and warm and safe. He hoped she was.

His mind turned to another girl. He'd seen her at the climbing wall. It was brief, but enough to grab his attention. She didn't look like any of the other girls that he was friendly with at school: they were like a tribe; all wearing the same kit, all sporting the same look, all talking in the same urban accent learned from YouTube. She was different, and she stood out. She hadn't learned her style from Instagram.

He'd stared at her and been reluctant to climb in front of her, then he'd realised that she was a beginner too. As his session ended, he'd decided there and then that he wanted to join the club. His mother was thrilled: another hobby! How active her children were! *Whatever.*

He hadn't had the courage to ask her name or where she went to school, but he definitely saw her looking at him. There was a taster session on tonight for beginners, after school, and he'd overheard her signing up for it too.

Chapter 14

Sometimes, children grow up seemingly unaffected by the events around them. It's rare, of course: children are barometers of their environments. However, at times, occasionally, when no one expects it, the child learns a parallel way of life, alongside the standard one that everyone sees.

Or so the girl had read in a book somewhere.

Theories about the mind and what motivates human behaviour had always fascinated her father. He could talk for hours and hours about psychological experiments on human beings. That was, if anyone would listen. Most people grew bored by his long explanations and didactic lectures. But she never did.

He told her about all the important human behavioural trials that had been conducted over the course of the last few hundred years, or as long as psychology had been something to study. She sat in awe as he narrated the experiments. He told her about Stanley Milgram and how, in 1971, he conducted an investigation that showed, when in the presence of an authority figure, volunteers willingly turned up a dial applying a fake electric shock to actors, even going beyond what they were told was a level of pain so great that the subject might die. It went some way to understanding why Hitler was able to become so powerful, despite the brutality of his regime.

Her father also told her about Little Albert in the 1950s: a nine-month-old baby who was taught to develop irrational fears in a laboratory environment. He was gradually manipulated into being scared to death of rats: perhaps the most controversial of all of tests.

She knew Bobo's Doll inside out and found that experiment particularly funny: the idea that behaviour – mean or kind – is copied from adults was obvious to her. In the experiment, children were shown adults treating the doll in varying ways: from kind to pure nasty. The children copied.

One that she wished she could have taken part in was the Stanford University prison experiment in 1961. She would have loved to have been both a prisoner and a guard.

It would seem that the general public had more backbone for such inquiries back then, and she wished she'd lived through such an era where whinging and moaning about rights and conduct was less prevalent. She loved listening to her father talk of it. There were no longer experiments of the same calibre; scientists and doctors simply could no longer get away with it. She knew that her views were controversial. The majority of ordinary folk simply couldn't stomach it.

She acknowledged that she hadn't been raised in a standard way, or one that could be termed as normal or conformist, but that's why she liked it. It satisfied her need to understand, and that's why she took the pain. Pain was a mere stepping stone to salvation, and once that fine lesson was learned, then all the others fell into place. No test is ever easy, because if it was, then it wouldn't be a test: there'd be no progression.

But her father had grown quiet, of late.

The farmhouse, their home for now, was situated on the edge of a small lake (they called them tarns in Cumbria) and it hadn't changed for hundreds of years. It was where she'd gone after leaving the hospital. She hadn't meant to cause trouble. She'd had an incident, a moment; a shadow had fallen across her mind and she'd forgotten where – and who – she was. It was becoming more frequent as her learning progressed, and her father had known it would be the way. He'd told her that he'd been waiting for it; watching out for it to occur, knowing that with a mind such as hers, it was bound to happen.

'Am I your experiment, Daddy?' She'd been six years old when she'd asked that question.

'Not at all, my darling! I don't need to conduct an investigation into you to discover how you behave: I already know. It's only the weak who need to be constantly appraised in case they make a mistake and no one spots it. They have to continually analyse and judge test cases of people who they call criminals, simply because they're scared of them, when in actual fact, violence, aggression, hate, revenge and rage are all quite natural. Take the lioness...'

This was his favourite story. The one where the lioness fought to the death to save her cubs from an aggressive male. All involved knew she stood no chance, and that all the cubs would die as challengers to his authority, but the lioness still defended them.

'Why do you think she did that?' Her father asked.

'Because she loved them?'

'No, my dear, because it's her instinct. She has no power whatsoever over her behaviour because it is hardwired through her DNA. Humans are different. We know nothing when we're born – it's pathetic – we have to learn everything, and that's where mothers and fathers come in.'

'But you said that my instinct is strong.'

'And I was right, Daphne. But you had to be shown where to find it.'

Her father had become an old man, and she missed his smile and his praise. They'd moved into the farmhouse when Mother was left it by an old relative of hers who passed away with no family. It was worth nothing. The farm had been run down years ago, leaving no livestock to manage and the money dried up, but the bricks and mortar stayed. Built of Lakeland slate, a metre thick, the structure was sound, if cold and bleak. The land was handsome and Father had plans to develop it. Before he and Mother grew sick.

They sowed seeds and planted potatoes.

And they took donations from visitors.

The first time she'd understood what visiting was for, she'd been afraid. Father had explained to her that some people – like themselves – acquire the knowledge of the true meaning of the world and worship that instead of what those ignorant fools revere and champion in today's godless world. The girl knew she was different, and that her family was different, and that if anyone ever found out about their visitors and their prayers, then Mother and Father would be taken away.

It remained a secret.

It was a huge burden but one she got used to. In hospital it wasn't that she'd lost her ability to speak; it simply had been that she hadn't wanted to. She'd lost the need to use words a long time ago: they were not required. She still made sounds when she was alone. She read poetry and she sang songs, but she no longer used the common language; or very rarely. The noise that people created was excruciatingly painful to her, and that was the main reason that she'd jumped out of the window – because she couldn't stand the din. The nurses cackled and the trolleys scraped. The farm was silent and calm, and it was home. Father and Mother had stopped asking where she went.

Her room was cold and she went to her small wardrobe for another blanket. She rarely heard sounds at the farm and it was a comfort. If Mother or Father wanted her, they'd come to her room for her. But they no longer did. She sat on her bed and opened a book. It was her diary that she wrote in every day, and she also drew pictures in it. Today she worked on an image that she'd committed to memory not so long ago.

It was a boy. His face was soft and round and he had deep eyes. When they looked at one another, they'd connected. No one had noticed but them. It had felt like a thousand knives going into her: a mere moment in time, but she knew that she came to him in his dreams too. She closed her eyes and imagined them clinging to the rock, the wind billowing her hair away from her neck. His eyes fell onto her hungrily, and he sank to his knees in the mud of the field, where the ancient stones stood proud.

She wanted to touch him so badly that it caused her physical pain. It was an experience that she had never had before now. She didn't understand it and she felt melancholy, as if coming down off a potion that she'd never taken before. It left her with a hangover-like state that was ugly and maddening. The only thing that would make it better would be to see him again.

She lay back on the bed and felt the breeze coming in from the window. There wasn't a sound outside in the empty fields but she could smell life. Soon, the day and night would be equal and the spirits would command superiority. The year was dying, but inside, she was emerging with life anew, and a fire that she dreamed of lighting every time she thought of him.

A single fly landed on her blanket. It looked fat and about to pop. The place needed a good clean, it had begun to smell. She reached her hand under the bed covers and slid it into her underwear, where it was soft and warm.

The boy's eyes filled her head, and she began to feel hot. Her skin tingled, and she moved her hand back and forth.

'Callum,' she whispered. 'I know your father.'

Chapter 15

September was the month of colour in the Lake District. The trees turned various shades of orange and red, and the mountainside revealed scars of brown and grey as the lush greenery disappeared. Kelly and Johnny discussed their holiday plans as they ran. Running together was an impromptu way to meet and chew over whatever needed thrashing out. It could be Johnny letting off steam about an injured child on the mountainside, whose parents were unceremoniously unapologetic for taking them up there. It could be a case – as was recently – of a deceased teenager trying to traverse the Striding Edge route on Helvellyn while taking a selfie. He lost his footing and fell eight hundred feet with no protective gear. His head injuries killed him. His dad watched him fall.

For Kelly's part, it was mostly frustrations involving injustice. Often with domestics in particular, she found herself sitting in court, giving evidence about bruising or witness testimony, only to have the victim change her plea, or an expert challenge the definition of 'force', and her case, so lovingly prepared over hundreds of man hours, unceremoniously kicked out. She'd been thrown side glances by criminals getting away with it more times than she cared to remember as she left Carlisle Crown Court. Kelly hated court appearances. They were never certain, and in her line of work, certainty was key. She dealt in black and white: nothing grey in court was getting past the jury

They both needed to get away. Johnny had worked non-stop for months now, volunteering to be on call, as the mountain rescue found itself increasingly short staffed. Kelly hadn't taken a proper break since her mother's death in January.

They'd arranged to meet Josie at Ted's for dinner tonight, and they'd decided to fit in a run after work. Josie was at the climbing wall in Keswick and would make her way directly to Ted's small cottage afterwards. They both marvelled at the closeness between the pensioner and the teenager. Kelly was sure that it had something to do with the fact that Ted doted on her and spoiled her but she also couldn't deny that there was a genuine mutual joy they shared. Kelly felt a pang of jealousy when she imagined Josie staying with him when she and Johnny went to Florida together in November for their birthdays. Josie would enjoy something that she'd never had with Ted herself. Sailing in Florida had come about as a result of a mixture of factors: Kelly coming into money from her mother's house was one; another was that, next year, Johnny would turn fifty, and she forty, and they wanted to make something of it. It was a rebellion, in a way.

Her thoughts turned to Carla Rigg again. It was Thursday afternoon, but she still had the mystery woman on her mind. The team had begun to forget the strange woman at Castlerigg, but she plagued Kelly and she discussed it with Johnny. No new leads had been forthcoming and her only other option was to release the photo of the man in the picture with her. But it was difficult to justify more resources.

The woman had gone.

For their run, they'd chosen a longer, more challenging route than usual because they both had time. The case of the mystery woman would now take its own course. There had been prank calls as always, and some interesting ones, and of course they all needed chasing, which used valuable man hours. The lab in Carlisle had come up with a DNA profile from the swab taken by the ambulance crew but it didn't match any on their databases. Kelly tried to put it out of her head.

'Do you mind Josie staying with Ted?' she asked.

'No, why should I? He's like a grandad to her.'

'I know, it's sweet.'

'You're jealous!'

'I am.' She blushed and ran on.

They'd parked at Scales and were trekking up the gruelling pathway up the east side of Blencathra. It was known as the dullest route up the beautiful mountain, but when one was fell running, the path underneath was irrelevant; getting one's breath was the only thing of vital importance. The track was a brown scar in the hillside, not visible from the road due to its savage gradient. It led upwards through bracken, zig zagging from the base, right up to where the summit could be viewed from the first rest point. Rest was a relative word, given that the 'run' was vertical in places and their feet barely scraped one in front of the other as their hearts beat out of their chests.

The late afternoon sun beat down on their backs and they wore few layers. Kelly wore shorts and a T-shirt, knowing that her skin would boil and her pulse would pound until they reached a let-up in the terrain, perhaps two thousand feet up. Johnny was the fitter of the two, having done the Lakeland 100 earlier in the year – a hundred-mile fell race with a total of about four thousand feet elevation. He kept a steady pace and looked as though he was bounding up the hill with ease. Kelly knew he wasn't but let him go ahead anyway. Ease wasn't something that was possible with geographical features such as mountains. She concentrated on placing one foot in front of the other and staying just ahead of a walking pace. It was more like a trot. She felt her body respond well but it also gasped for air and her thighs screamed.

Finally, they reached a plateau and Johnny stopped ahead of her, taking a water bottle out of his bag. She reached him and took her bag off her back and looked at the view below. The sky was deep blue and the sun was just dipping over the Irish Sea. Her chest heaved and she gulped water gratefully. She wiped her brow and looked at Johnny, who beamed back at her. There was nothing like it: pheromones made you grin.

'So, what's with the climbing wall?' she asked.

'I reckon she fancies a guy there. There's no other explanation.'

'Oh, those were the days. It was all so simple. No mortgage, no bills, no family woes. Just lust. Bliss.'

'Hang on,' Johnny put up his hand.

'Oh, come on, Johnny. She's almost sixteen. Have you had "the talk"?'

'No!' He screwed his face up.

'You have to!' Kelly said.

'Can you do it?'

She thought about his request. She guessed that Josie was the closest she'd get to having a daughter and she had no hang-ups about sex. It might be quite fun.

'All right.'

'Good luck,' Johnny said.

'Lightweight.'

They looked upwards and reckoned they had another forty minutes to go. Johnny rifled around his bag and handed her a dense chewy nut bar. She devoured it and gulped some more water. Refreshed, they set off again and didn't speak until they reached the next false summit, a hundred metres from the top. They could no longer see the car park and everything below looked like a collection of miniature dolls and toy pieces in an intricate game. The cars on the A66 looked tiny and the town of Keswick looked like a small village. Derwent Water in the distance shone in the late sun and they were silent as they took in the view. There were no sounds and they imbibed the peace, only on offer in such a place.

'Look, Castlerigg,' Johnny said, pointing far away in the distance. He knew the fells like he knew the way to every pub in Pooley Bridge – with his eyes closed. But then he had to. Being a mountain rescue volunteer in Cumbria was like being a cabbie in London. She followed his hand and was just about able to make out the ancient stone circle. From their vantage point, it was easy to see why the ancients had chosen the site and she wondered if Neolithic people hiked up here, or if they thought it magical and threatening: something to admire from afar and even worship. No one knew.

She could even just about make out the shadows cast by the stones, making it look as though it was on fire.

Another twenty minutes and they were stood on top of the mountain, at the trig point, looking across the whole of the National Park. Skiddaw sat silently next to them and no one else was around. They took out warmer clothes and sat down together, huddled and satisfied. Johnny took out more food from his bag and she accepted it greedily. After a hike like this, they both knew that whatever Ted produced, they'd have no problem devouring. Ted enjoyed cooking for guests and he made a mean casserole.

'So, Josie's been at the climbing centre how many times this week?'

'This is her third night.'

'Definitely a boy.'

Eventually, their decreasing body temperatures drove them off the mountain and back down to their descent. It was much quicker on the way down, though tougher on their thigh muscles, and they came within sight of the car park after only half an hour. Across the busy road, Kelly could see the Birkett Mire campsite and she thought of the animal cruelty case from 2005. The animals were reported missing from various owners and farmers from homes and farms as far away as twenty miles. The birds belonged to nobody. Some of the cats were strays. To be honest, more fuss was created by farmers losing valuable sheep than the public response to finding tortured pets.

She made a mental note to look into it. She wanted to know if it was an isolated case or something that had happened before or since. The name Harry O'Connor meant nothing to her, and a quick input into the national police computer had flagged up zero. The O'Connor family, and those like them, were used to moving on; it was their way of life, and it made tracking them down virtually impossible.

'What's on your mind?' Johnny brought her out of her musings. They were almost back to sea level and Kelly's body felt drained, but it had been worth it.

'Animal cruelty case. I don't understand how anyone can do it. It's like kids. I don't get it.'

'Recent?'

'No, ages ago. But still...'

'I heard of that. I hadn't been here long, I thought you were all savages. Was it the one over High Rigg farm? Birds and dogs?'

'High Rigg farm? When was that?' Kelly asked. The one she'd been given was definitely Birkett Mire.

'I've been here five years, so 2013.'

'No, this was 2005,' Kelly said. She began to walk with her hands on her hips, brow creased, staring at her boyfriend.

'Oh, popular sport round here, then?' he asked.

Chapter 16

Ted's cottage smelled homely and full of cooking. Kelly's stomach ached for food, despite her and Johnny devouring several chocolate bars and a slice of cake each after their run. Showered and changed, they'd stopped off for a few bottles of wine on their way back to Keswick. Kelly drove. She could have one glass of red with her dinner.

Josie and Ted were in animated conversation in the lounge and Ted wore a pinafore. They both heard Josie laugh out loud and remained in the kitchen. The teenager hadn't seemed as free from crippling self-awareness the whole time she'd been living with her dad. The girl was growing up. They got crockery out of a cupboard and went into the lounge to see Ted and Josie setting the table.

'Josie was showing me how to floss.'

'What?' Johnny asked. Kelly raised her eyebrows. She only knew what the dance term was because of her attachment to several foster homes around the area. She'd spent many evenings watching teenagers display their talents as she waited to speak to their carers regarding domestic cases. She smiled. They watched as Ted attempted the manoeuvre for his new audience. He was terrible at it.

'Hungry?' he asked his visitors, unfazed by his inability, but a little breathless.

'Starving.'

Kelly and Johnny sank into a large sofa and Johnny accepted a beer.

'How was climbing tonight? That's three times in a row. Must be good. Do I need to start thinking about getting shares in Snow and Rock?' Johnny asked his daughter.

'I got halfway up without needing the harness and the angle is like this, Dad.' The girl enthused and used her elbow to depict the steepness of the plastic wall. Johnny was happy to fund such pastimes, having in the past worried for his daughter spending too much time hanging about the park in Keswick or the centre of town in Penrith: neither were ideal for a girl on the cusp of sexual awakening. He was willing to hand out cash for most things that didn't involve the opportunity to take drugs or drink.

Kids in Josie's year at school threw wild parties and Kelly and Johnny both knew the prevalence of illegal drugs in the area; they'd both come across it at work. It appeared to be endemic. However, neither wanted to come across as bores. Too much conservatism, and the girl would be pushed the other way. Johnny regularly worried about how much pressure to apply, and, as a dad of a young girl, he relied heavily on Kelly's intuition.

They heard banging in the kitchen and a whistle of steam.

'Everything all right?' Kelly shouted.

'Yes! All under control,' Ted replied.

Kelly knew from her conversations with her father that when he was with his ex-wife, she did everything around the house. He'd only began cooking properly since he left her. It was a shame, because he was good at it. Her stomach rumbled. Getting out onto the mountain had been the right thing to do. She and Johnny both felt irritable when they hadn't been out together. She sank into the sofa next to him and he put his arm around her. Kelly barely caught Josie's face before she turned away from them. It had been a look of approval and something else. Love? Not for a cool teenager surely. Like? Maybe. That would do.

'So, you think you'll keep it up, then, Josie? The climbing? Who else goes?'

'Yes! It's brilliant. I'm in a small group. There's another girl and four guys. Callum is a beginner too.'

It was out. Kelly nudged Johnny as he went to say something and he stopped. Kelly smiled and Josie went to help Ted in the kitchen.

'We have a name.'

'Are you going to follow her?' Johnny asked.

'Why?'

'You know? *The talk.*'

'Not in front of Ted! That would embarrass the hell out of her.'

'I didn't mean in front of him. Maybe you could send him in here to set the table or something.'

Kelly saw that Johnny was nervous. She sighed and got up off the sofa. In the kitchen, Ted had his head in the oven, and almost banged it bringing out an enormous pot.

'Smells delicious,' Kelly said.

'I'll just take it through,' he said. Kelly closed the door.

'So, how much climbing have you and Callum done, then?' Kelly got straight to the point. Josie stared at her, her mouth open.

'Don't worry, your dad hasn't got a clue, it was me who thought there might be a handsome young man involved. You like him a lot, I can tell.'

'How... do you know?' It was a sweet question and one that Kelly assumed a lot of teenagers asked, safe in the watertight knowledge that no generation before them ever felt the same.

'Because, believe it or not, I quite like your dad. In that way.'

'Ugh!' Josie recoiled, but Kelly knew that the girl was desperate to share her secret.

'You're old enough to know how to stay safe. Do you talk to your mum about boys?'

'No!'

Josie blushed.

'I just want to say that I'm here. I won't judge. I know a lot of stuff. Come to me anytime. And I won't tell your dad.'

Josie smiled tentatively, then spoke in almost a whisper.

'I feel this thing in my tummy when I see him. It makes me feel sick. I haven't ever had it before. I guess it makes me look stupid. I don't even think he likes me.'

'Well then he's a fool. Does he avoid looking at you directly?'

'Yes.'

'Does he make stupid jokes around you?'

'Yes.'

'He adores you. Have you kissed?'

'Kelly!'

'Sorry. Is he nice to you?'

'Super nice.'

'Good. Because if he's not, I want to know.' Josie smiled at her.

They went back to the living room and witnessed Ted moving to music unconsciously. Josie had sown a seed and Kelly winked at her. Kelly helped him set the final things on the table and they found themselves in the kitchen alone.

'How's your sister, Kelly? Do you see much of her?'

The question caught her off guard.

'No, I don't actually. We are very different, you know.'

'Oh, I know. Wendy told me. Sometimes, you know, difference is inevitable. But everyone needs family. Could you patch it up? For your mother's sake?'

Kelly didn't answer. She felt how Josie must have felt five minutes ago receiving a pep talk from an elder who should mind their own business.

'She knows where I am, Ted.'

They went to the table.

Chapter 17

By Friday, Kelly thought she might make it to the weekend without a major incident at work, and she settled back in her chair to review the details of the cold cases that still bugged her. She imagined Friday afternoons elsewhere to be full of anticipation of a lie in and a weekend ahead full of lazy lunches and leisure activities. Not so in police work. A five o'clock finish on a Friday was something to aspire to.

It was four thirty in the afternoon.

Her eyes were tired and she opened her office window to revive her senses. She couldn't get twelve-year-old Kevin Good out of her head. He was the boy who'd gone missing from the Ullswater campsite in 2005. He'd be a man now. Most children who disappear around that age, never to be seen again, end up dead within twelve hours of abduction. The family appeared ordinary: caring and without secrets. Police investigations into something as serious as a missing child unearth every skeleton in a family, and at times dig up buried gems that no one wants to resurface. Not so with the family of Kevin Good. He gained positive reports at school, he was a helpful boy around the house, hadn't rebelled before, and was an innocent twelve years, by all accounts. His older sister had blamed herself, and she probably still did fifteen years later, thought Kelly. The witness statement from her said that they'd gone to swim in the lake at dusk. She'd admitted being more interested in the boys who joined them from the campsite at some time after six p.m. She was sixteen at the time and under pressure to have her younger, annoying sibling tag along, when she was trying to impress. She'd taken her eye off him and couldn't account for his presence for over an hour before she raised the alarm. The lake had been searched by divers but Kelly noticed that they only covered a hundred square feet off shore, where the kids had been swimming.

It was a sour taste to finish on for the week, and she went into the incident room to see if her team could provide a little light relief. She was overly optimistic.

'Any good news?'

'You've come to the wrong place, guv.' Rob Shawcross had his head buried in paperwork, investigating a domestic abuse case. She looked at the rota for the weekend. Kate Umshaw was on call and Rob was on shift tomorrow.

'Wrap up and go home everyone. It looks like we have a Friday night to ourselves.'

Her announcement was met with smiles and relief, but some of them had more loose ends to tie up than others. As for Kelly, she'd read as much as she wanted to about missing children and bereft families. She looked forward to a glass of wine and thought she might build a fire. She waited for her team to finish off their reports and log off their iPads and computers. The sun hadn't quite dipped behind the horizon and half-light hung over the offices, but they left the lights on for the cleaners. With everything closed down, Kelly said goodbye and they discussed their plans for the evening.

A telephone inside the office rang and Kelly gazed towards where it was coming from: her office.

'Go on, I'll see everybody on Monday.' She let her team disperse and went back inside the office. The phone stopped ringing but she checked the number anyway. Her heart sank as she realised that the call was from the central switchboard for Cumbria Police. All 999 calls went to three pods in the county: Kendal, Penrith and Carlisle. This one had come in to Penrith and she noticed that the code required a detective on scene. She waited, knowing that the phone would ring again.

It did.

The operator briefed her on an incident at a domestic property on the outskirts of Keswick, in Braithwaite. Kelly's gut turned over and she calculated if she had time to drive home to Pooley Bridge and grab something to eat. The crime scene was stable and secure, and a forensic team had been dispatched to process the address.

Kelly didn't call back any member of her team. An initial assessment would tell her if she needed a partner. She was loath to disturb anyone after telling them they could enjoy their Friday. Hers was about to be screwed, but not as much as the poor woman who lay in a pile of cat litter. Kelly had been given a cursory description of the main characteristics of the crime. A CSI had mapped out the floorplan of the property and Kelly was emailed the initial report from the uniformed responders to the 999 call. The original 999 call had been made from a payphone in the middle of nowhere. Red telephone boxes still existed in parts of Cumbria and this one was at a cross roads near Whitehaven: miles away from the property where the crime had occurred. It was curious.

The woman in question was pronounced life deceased at the scene by medics, who'd packed up and gone home. The forensic team had quickly concluded that the death was a homicide.

She called Johnny.

She put him on speaker phone as she drove. 'I'm pulling into mine now. I won't make it No go ahead, eat without me, I'm going to be late. I need to process a murder scene. I know – on a Friday – I'm sorry, there'll be loads of paperwork if nothing else. If there are leads to chase tonight, it'll be really late,' she said to him. They were to eat as a threesome for once. Kelly was looking forward to continuing her new found conspiratorial companionship with her stepdaughter. She thought back to her own parents and how they handled the taboo. It was simple really: they didn't. Kelly was given a book by the library and giggled with her friends at the school disco or in the woods.

Kelly's first fumble taught her little, and the second was no better. Full penetration came as a shock and she wasn't ready, but the boy at the time had been just as scared as she was and they tried again. It was all right, she supposed. She'd learned about the clitoris when she was twenty-three years old. From what she'd seen through her work with local youth, which was extensive, youngsters today knew much more about sex from porn and it was worryingly damaging plenty of kids who thought that rough sex was normal. Violence, it seemed, was on trend.

She parked and went into her house quickly, finding a chicken tortilla wrap in the fridge and a packet of Twiglets. She didn't even take off her coat, grabbed a bottle of water and went back to her car, heading for the address.

The body hadn't been moved.

Chapter 18

The house was a pretty cottage on the outskirts of Braithwaite village, on the edge of Whinlatter Forest. Leaving the village to drive up the hill to the Whinlatter pass, it was easy to miss, had it not been for the police presence and flashing blue lights, and she pulled into a secluded driveway to see several patrol cars, police tape and a forensic van. The most pressing quandary on her mind wasn't what she'd find inside, or if forensics had lifted much, it was why the hell had the call come from a phone box near Whitehaven, thirty miles away? There was only one rational answer: the caller knew what had happened.

She parked her car, away from the police tape, and slipped on a pair of gloves. She'd cover her shoes once she was inside the property. She'd been informed that it was a shocking scene, and messy. She steeled herself. It wasn't that she wasn't used to brutality, it was the unknown that got her heart racing. Cause of death had yet to be established.

She was shown in by a uniform and thanked him. Lights flashed and she heard a camera going off. She smelled the familiar, acrid stench of burning and accelerant in the air.

'Serious Crime Unit,' the uniform announced. A forensic officer, covered head to toe in white plastic, emerged from one of the reception rooms and greeted her, removing his mask.

'Ugly stuff, Kelly.' They'd worked together before.

She took a deep breath, slipped plastic socks over her shoes, and followed him inside. The property was a bungalow. There was a kitchen on the right and a living room on the left, with a toilet behind the front door. The cool evening air lowered the temperature of the house, creating a breeze, which carried the smell of the dead, as well as fire. The main sitting room was dimly lit, but forensics had set up lamps over the body and above various important points of interest. She noted that the CSI had placed number cards on the floor and a trail led off to another entrance to the kitchen.

'Overkill,' said the forensic officer. Kelly nodded.

The woman lay face up with a large knife still sticking out of her chest. Cat litter was strewn across the floor.

'Seventy-three stab wounds. We haven't turned her over. I thought this one should be bagged entirely without too much disturbance.'

'Good call. The pathologist can examine the posterior,' Kelly suggested. After all, forensics and the CSI were there to process the scene, not the deceased: that was the coroner's job.

'Fine, if that's what you want.' The forensic officer was happy to take Kelly's lead. She suspected he'd also like to get back to his wife and kids at a good hour.

'I don't think there's any doubt as to cause of death here,' Kelly said. The forensic officer nodded, but it would still have to be signed off by the coroner. Kelly had worked with the coroner countless times before but now she had a personal relationship with Ted Wallis, she felt protective towards him, as if she had the power to prevent him seeing what she saw right now. The enactment of total rage and the vision of what could be done to human flesh never got easier for Kelly. She walked around the body and was brought up to speed by the CSI about what had already been bagged.

'Fire accelerant here. Blood spatter here, and here. Trauma occurred here, after burning outside.'

'Burning outside? I thought I smelled smoke and chemicals.'

'You did. She had quite the menagerie. The bird aviary is totalled. She had kennels as well, they're still smoking.'

'Show me.'

Kelly followed him out into the garden through the kitchen, and it seemed that everywhere she put her foot, she had to avoid a number tag.

'It was quite a frenzy,' she said.

'Sustained work. It started in the garden and then ended in there. They fought in the kitchen – as you saw as we went past – there's shit everywhere.'

'It doesn't strike me as the tidiest of houses.' Kelly wondered where the mess stopped and the murder began. 'Overkill suggests she knew her attacker. Only one, you think?' Kelly asked.

'We've only photographed one set of footprints found smeared in the blood in the kitchen area. It looks like a common wellington boot.'

'I see what you mean by work.'

'It's methodical. Clinical. Planned. Despite the mess.'

'Except the final blows: they were out of control.'

'Agreed.'

'Thanks. I'll walk around. Do we have a name?'

'Mary Hales. Fifty-nine. Lived here a long time according to neighbours.' The CSI left her and carried on logging the scene on his iPad. CSI was done along the lines of CAD kitchen design nowadays, and it struck Kelly as disturbingly businesslike. For her part, she'd never be able to give up just standing there, in the middle of the carnage, watching, absorbing and imagining what went on. She faced the back of the garden and looked towards the destroyed animal shelters. The wooden structures still smoked. When animals were hurt in a crime, they called a local trusted vet to clear up. Animal carcasses were autopsied just the same as humans and their remains could throw up a whole story of evidence.

Temporary spotlights illuminated the garden, and Kelly imagined the intruder entering from the field beyond, which backed on to the forest. She walked to the end of the garden, peering over the fence. There was a track. It was big enough for a small car or van. She climbed over the fence and walked along the trail to see where it went. After about twenty metres, it turned a corner and emerged on to a bigger dirt track that lead to the main road through Braithwaite. Walking back, she shone a torch to the ground and spotted several vehicle tyre marks. They'd all need to be filed and processed.

Back in the garden, she peered through the cages, where she presumed birds had once lived happily. All she could see was black soot covering the floor and piles of feathers in the corners, with some stuck in the wire. The fire had been intense. As she peered closer, her eyes began to make out tiny skeletons in amongst the carnage and she covered her mouth. There must have been about thirty little carcasses in there. To the side of the aviary, two large kennels were burned out and almost destroyed. Four long chains were attached to each structure and ended with a charred collar. She could make out the remains of six or so animals that she figured were once dogs. The corpses still smouldered and Kelly knew that she was looking at a crime scene that had been active only hours ago. She made her way back inside and spoke to the forensic officer. The coroner's van had arrived and they were ready to move the body.

'Time of death?' she asked.

'She's still warm.'

Chapter 19

Dr Demi Cramer looked at her phone and decided that she wanted to take the call from Kelly Porter. The case in the Lake District had stoked her interest. Genuine nutters were on the decline and a good old fashioned inquiry into a darkly disturbed mind was something that didn't come along enough. She was sure that the facts she'd been given so far were enough to question the diagnosis of amnesia, but she'd love to meet the young woman they'd named Carla Rigg. In fact, she'd begun a case file on her, despite her enigmatic status. It was something to do other than profile rapists and sadists who were two-a-penny in the capital.

She excused herself and left the bar, where she was enjoying an after work drink with colleagues. The conversation was always the same: nature vs nurture: which fucked a kid more? It had grown tedious. Police work for the criminologist was never dull, but lately, it had become repetitive. She answered her mobile and squeezed through the crowds pressed into the basement pop-up restaurant. It was a coffin waiting to happen anyway and Demi wondered how on earth the Straw Captain, in Kings Cross, had got its fire license passed. As far as she could see, there was one way in and one way out, and that was the single staircase.

'Hello?' she shouted above the racket. City workers turned into another species on a Friday night: clamouring for trendy food, packing new bars and staying out late spending hard-earned cash on overpriced entertainment. She shouldn't complain. It was nobody's fault but her own that she was single and frustrated. Jealousy pricked her consciousness when she saw couples kissing and holding one another or enjoying a private meal. Cynicism told her that they were illicit affairs, not marriages, otherwise they'd be arguing.

Her marriage had ended acrimoniously but at least there were no kids involved. She'd continued her contraception despite telling Ivan that she wanted to start a family. In reality, it was the last thing on her mind: her career was flying, she loved her body, and she didn't want to share her cash just yet. He'd found her stash of pills and given her an ultimatum. She'd agreed to acquiesce if he gave up his career to raise the kids, after all, she earned the higher wage. He refused. The marriage was dead in the water after that. Her mother said it was her fault for marrying a Turk. Her friends got her pissed. Her brother told her kids were over-rated anyhow.

She moved on.

She struggled to hear a voice on the other end of the line and almost hung up, but, as she got outside into the fresh air, away from the din, she heard Kelly Porter's voice clearly. It was late on a Friday: the detective must have some news, she thought.

'Demi? Can you hear me?'

'I can now. Christ, Kelly, it's heaving in there. Thank you for rescuing me, I was contemplating an early night. What have you got?'

Demi was always straight to the point and that's why she and Kelly Porter got on: neither were bullshitters.

'Murder. Fifty-nine-year-old female. Odd. Overkill. Arson, stabbing, confidence, control, hate...'

'Comprehensive, why are you calling me? I thought you'd have something on Carla Rigg for me. Now you're telling me you have a murder?'

'Yes. This is new. Forget Carla Rigg. That has gone cold. I thought you might be interested in this, it was good to talk the other day. I thought of you. Will you take a look? It's right up your alley.'

'Of course. Send it over now, I'm going home anyway. So you think the victim knew their assailant?'

'It was passionate. There were animals involved too. They were burned alive; they couldn't escape. The birds were in an aviary and the dogs were chained up.'

'Cruel bastard.'

'Exactly.'

'Victimology?'

'Hardly started. She lived alone with her pets, divorced, no kids...'

'That's a start, I'm sure my ex would love to see me in pain.'

'He's dead. There were no boyfriends according to the neighbours.'

'Wise.'

'Oh, Demi, if only we could share a bottle, I miss you.'

'The way you're going, I'll be able to get funding to drop in your way very soon. Don't you have a reliable psych up there?'

'Of course, but you're the best.'

'Stop it. I'll raise a glass tonight. Tell me, was the woman killed first, or the animals?'

'Good point, I reckon the pets were burning as she was murdered. What are you thinking?'

'It's worth finding out which was the main target: her or her pets. When is she being examined?'

'I need to speak to the coroner. I know him so I'll see if I can get him to come in over the weekend.'

'Cosy up there is it?'

'You could say that. He's my father.'

'Well, well. Keep it in the family. Let me know and I'll get back to you first thing with my initial thoughts.'

'Thanks, Demi. You're a diamond.'

'Bye, Kelly.'

They hung up.

Kelly had made the call on her way home. She would have loved to have joined Johnny and Josie but she feared that Josie might read something from her face, and even perhaps see the gruesome brutality that she'd witnessed only an hour before. She headed home and poured herself a large glass of red wine. Johnny understood her need to be alone.

On her terrace, the night air rushed from the cold lake beyond through the gaps in the wooden plinths, and she pulled a blanket over herself to examine the images from the crime scene on her Toughpad.

There was nothing more she could do tonight to move the investigation forward. That was, apart from *think* about it. Uniforms were swarming around Braithwaite scouring for information, and at this stage, that was all they had. It was a punishment killing; that much was clear. Appearances always deceive, thought Kelly, but this woman was the epitome of gentleness and compassion. Animals, garden, home, her books and even her bedroom: everything shouted care and love. Maybe that was the problem. She needed to find out who this woman had wronged, and how.

Chapter 20

'It's an excuse to spend some time with you, Kelly.'

Ted spoke quietly as Kelly drove. They left the mountains behind them as they approached the M6 and one could just have easily been driving around the north circular as anywhere. Kelly gripped the wheel and bit her lip. Images of the woman's body hadn't left her all night: her face, her chest, and her animals.

'I'm glad we get to do this,' Kelly responded, looking in her mirrors. 'Even if it's under grim circumstances.'

'I'm not having a trainee carry out a murder case. It's not fair. I don't think it's grim. It's only work.'

'If you say so.'

Ted had agreed to perform the post-mortem operation on Mary Hales on Saturday morning as Kelly's team held an emergency briefing at Eden House. She'd dragged them back in from their weekend and left DS Kate Umshaw in charge. Kate's recent display of leadership had impressed her boss. Umshaw was more than capable. It was all about due process and Kate was by-the-book. Besides, Kelly could join the meeting at any time, should she need to. At this stage, a murder inquiry was all about dishing out jobs and gathering information. It was the most tense but also, potentially, the most rewarding time, but, Jesus, it was busy.

Kelly drove them both to the university hospital in Carlisle, where the murder victim awaited them in the mortuary fridge. She'd already begun the process of considering her victim, and immediate family was something she always started with. Time with family was precious to most people, including Kelly, and it wasn't lost on her that Mary Hales appeared to have none. There was nothing in her private papers that they'd found so far inside her house that would indicate that she had any children, siblings or parents left alive or contactable. Everything in the home of the victim spoke to the investigators of a singular life. There were single portions of frozen meals in the freezer, frumpy female middle-aged clothes hanging in the single wardrobe in the bedroom and they saw no photographs in frames of smiling faces beaming back at the camera suggestive of familial ties. The house was ordered in such a way that it was configured for a person living alone. There was little cutlery in the kitchen drawers, only a couple of plates too, few toiletries in the bathrooms, and a single pair of walking boots by the back door.

They'd found a diary. It was bohemian and pretty, covered in golden feathers and ancient symbols of what the inspectors first thought to be good luck signs. Things such as the yin and yang, as well as stars and moons: all associated with somebody interested in the world of the spirit, an empath of sorts, perhaps. The diary had been submitted as evidence and Kelly had paused upon the last entry and communicated it to DS Umshaw this morning. It had been the CSI at the scene who'd pointed it out. Mary's last entry had been written in on Thursday evening, the day before she died. It read:

There are demons out there, and they look like people.

Every investigator knew that when it came to piecing together a profile of a victim, diaries were notoriously misleading. However, Mary had been a vital, middle-aged, intelligent and bright woman, not some teenager given to writing about her angst, hormones and love life gone sour. It didn't fit, thus they took it seriously. Often, murder victims were targets of abuse prior to the climactic event ending their life. Mary could have been scared of something. The fact that she vocalised her fears in the parameters of dramatic satanic language was mere background.

Everyone thought their tormentors demons, including Kelly. She shivered as she thought of Amy Richmond's correspondence to her. The Teacher was demonic, but looked like a regular person.

Carlisle was busy but she managed to fight through the traffic and park in the coroner's spot underneath the multi-storey car park.

'I remember the first time I worked with you, Kelly.'

She locked the car and smiled at him, waiting for a nostalgic tale. Despite her apprehension – always felt when she was about to see a cold, dead body on a slab of metal – he unfailingly managed to calm her worry.

'You were concentrating as hard as you are now, desperate to get justice for the poor woman laid out on my table. You bring a lot of good into this world, you know.'

Kelly smiled. Only a man of Ted's generation spoke like that. People her age were too busy bemoaning fatalistic gloom. There was no room for simple compliments. Her hair whipped in the wind and she ran her fingers through it.

Once inside, her hair settled and so did her nerves. The wait was over. Now they could get down to the serious business of finding clues. They fell into an easy silence and took the winding route through the bowels of the hospital to the mortuary. Familiar noises welcomed them and Ted handed his jacket to his assistant. His staff greeted him with affection and respect. Once scrubbed up and adorned with gowns, they entered the examination room.

'Right, let's have a look,' Ted said.

Kelly watched him settle in to what was now a familiar routine. The way he moved, the instruments he laid out, his choice of saw, and scales to weigh organs; they all told a story of his method and practice learned from years of post-mortem operations. It soothed her further. He fixed his microphone and Kelly rubbed her nose under her nostrils, spreading the perfumed oil she'd applied when they'd entered. The body lay inside a thick black rubber bag. The contents were gruesome and Kelly had warned Ted that the murder was a particularly brutal one. The rage exacted upon the victim was something Kelly hadn't seen for a long time, and it indicated passion. Passion came in different guises, and hate was the strongest of them all, closely followed by love.

She couldn't shake the nagging presence of Amy Richmond in her head: this is what she used to do to her victims. Frenzied rage left her targets humiliated and dehumanised. She shivered and Ted noticed. She smiled reassuringly and tried to concentrate.

The noise of the zip jarred Kelly's senses.

The familiar knot under her stomach made adrenaline pump into her body and make her feel nauseous. Apart from the discolouration, facially, Mary looked asleep. However, her body told a different story. It was bruised and swollen from the violence exacted upon it, and the only difference from when Kelly had seen her in situ was the colour of the blood: it had turned almost black. Her clothes were torn to shreds where the knife had penetrated and Kelly had no idea how Ted knew where to start and how he might count the wounds or log their shape.

Ted stood back as an assistant finished opening the bag. A search of the contents would be carried out first. Post-mortems often took a few hours to complete on, say, an eighty-year-old woman who'd fallen over in a nursing home. However, the autopsy of a murder victim was the final opportunity for the dead to speak, and so Ted took his time. Kelly knew that he'd work straight until he was satisfied, and he'd be here for as long as it took. Everything was recorded methodically into the microphone almost touching his mouth, and secured around his head. Kelly found a chair and sat down. Mary was in the best hands, and Ted would flag up anything unusual. Kelly watched as he walked around the body, noting anything that stood out to him. He peered up close and stood back intermittently, curious and serious at the same time.

'It looks like she was restrained.' He pointed to contusions around her wrists. 'There's bruising around her mouth too, look: it sweeps up each side like the force of a gag. Remember I told you that bruises go on developing after death?'

Kelly nodded. It made her wretched with pity for the woman.

'There might be some usable DNA in those cheek scratches,' Ted said, nodding at the victim's face. Deep welts penetrated the delicate skin. He examined them with a magnifying lens and removed some tissue with tweezers.

An assistant photographed the numerous wounds on her torso and Ted took a pair of scissors and snipped off Mary's blouse. He stood back and put down the scissors.

'I don't think there was just one weapon.'

'Really?' Kelly went over to the table and tried not to look directly at the deep lacerations into the flesh, but she caught sight of the damage and winced. She'd seen stab wounds plenty of times before and it never got easier.

'This one is slightly different in shape to, say, this one,' he said, pointing to two vicious slashes in the victim's chest.

'I can't see properly,' said Kelly.

'You see this one is nice and neat? It looks like a perfect shard of glass, like a fish's mouth: it is larger in the middle and symmetrical.'

Kelly nodded. Her heart pounded.

'Whereas this one is larger at one side and has left rather a hole shape here, then tapers off upwards.'

'Oh, yes.' Kelly did see now, but her head felt hot. 'And what does it mean?'

'Until I measure them and track the direction I can't say, but what I can say is that two weapons were used. My technician said that a weapon remained in her chest when she was bagged. I had it removed.'

'It was a standard kitchen knife.'

'Agreed. It looks like it made these wounds: the ones tapering off to one side, like most kitchen knives are designed to do.'

'Two killers?'

'Or plenty of time and opportunity to use two weapons.'

'This one isn't like the kitchen knife found in her chest, it's more like a sporting or ornamental type.'

Kelly made notes. She figured that anyone in such a rage, and focused intently on harm to this extent, would grab anything to hand. Or they could have brought their own weapon, making the death significantly more ritualistic and exciting. 'Did you say ornamental?'

Ted looked up. 'Yes, why?'

'Wait a minute.' Kelly tapped on her iPad and brought up an image of a table in Mary's living room. It was an occasional table with bits and bobs on it, including an oddly shaped knife.

'What about this?'

Ted studied it through glasses perched on his nose as he held his hands away from the screen, not wanting to contaminate it with cadaver fluid.

'That's got quite a curve on it, these smaller wounds look straight. Was it sent to a lab for examination?'

'Yes.'

'Good, I can tell you for sure when I get to see it.'

Ted's instruments clinked and pulled on the victim's clothes and limbs, and he announced that he wanted her turned over. In an hour, he'd logged, measured and photographed every injury on her anterior side; now he wanted to see her back.

'Did you say she'd been dragged?' he asked.

Kelly sat up straight. 'Yes. The initial crime scene investigation report said she'd been set upon after the animals had begun making a riot of noise when they were attacked. The pursuit went through the house and the victim was attacked fatally in the kitchen, but blood smears suggest that she was placed into a different position post-mortem, or as she was dying: some fine blood spatter at the scene would indicate that she was still breathing when she was moved.'

'And was there anything obviously significant about the position of the body where it was moved? Was it aligned to a room, or a doorway perhaps?'

'We looked at all the photographs in detail and we think that she was placed facing her animals with her head to the south. Some of her personal items, such as underwear and handbag, were then thrown into the fire in the yard, with her animals, but didn't burn fully.'

'Rage, again.'

'Indeed.'

'She has no injuries to her back, so she was disabled then stabbed, face to face.'

'Personal.'

'Of course.'

'Defence wounds?'

'Quite extensive for someone who was overwhelmed and eventually bound.'

Ted nodded to the assistant, who began removing the rest of the victim's clothes with a large pair of scissors. Ted indicated that he was ready for the body to be put back down on the slab in preparation for evisceration. Kelly peered at Mary's face and tried to marry the image with one she'd seen in one of the few in photo frames in the woman's living room: a smiling woman, hugging one of her dogs, taken by an unknown acquaintance by a gate, at the foot of a fell. It was always difficult meeting the dead and imagining them alive, but she had to, so that Mary could live on long enough for her to piece together not only what had happened but why.

The sound of the saw made Kelly turn away and she fiddled with her phone. Glances towards Ted, and his blood covered apron, confirmed that the autopsy was now in full swing.

'Just as I thought,' said Ted.

'What?' Kelly asked.

'She died from an air embolus.'

'What's that?' she asked.

'The stab wounds didn't hit any major organs — as miracle would have it — however, they hit her liver, sending blood into her abdomen and many veins, too many to count, sending an air pocket to her heart: that's what killed her.'

'Caused by a knife going through her a few times,' Kelly added.

'Sorry, of course, you know I have to be specific, I didn't mean to denigrate the manner of her passing.'

'I know, Ted, don't be sorry, I didn't mean it to sound like an admonishment, it's just the technicality of it can override what it must have been like for her in those final few moments.'

They fell silent.

'I reckon she fought before she was bound. Her desire to live was admirable.'

Kelly looked at the lacerations up the victim's arms and she marvelled at how Mary Hales had fought for her life, facing a ten-inch kitchen knife and acrid smoke from the torture of her beloved pets, not to mention their howls.

Chapter 21

Neither Ted nor Kelly had any problem eating a late lunch after being surrounded by death all morning. Kelly had kept a close eye on Eden House. HQ approved her request for extra uniforms and they were sent straight to work interviewing as many residents of Braithwaite as possible. It took time and people were generally enjoying their leisure time on a Saturday in the Lakes. They didn't mind being disturbed, however – a murder inquiry, unusual in most people's lives, brought a certain extra willingness to take part and help.

Forensics still worked at the home of Mary Hales, which had been turned into a lair of tragedy and ferocity, leaving behind a trail of hundreds of pieces of evidence, some large and some invisible to the naked eye. Only chemicals and trace experts could figure out where hints and clues might be hiding.

Kelly's phone was glued to her ear all day. No one wanted answers more than she did but HQ barking down the phone at her wouldn't make anything go faster. Murder had a funny way of producing budgets and she could send what she liked to the lab, but results took time, even when they paid extra.

The relative tranquillity of the morning vanished the minute she left Ted in Carlisle.

Eden House had woken up. From the lull late yesterday afternoon, it was now consumed with the buzzing activity of bodies running from room to room with printouts, uniforms gathering kit to attend witness interviews, phones going off and a hundred emails into Kelly's inbox.

It felt good. When the team was required to step up, it did. HQ would have to wait, like the rest of them. The extent of violence inflicted upon Mary Hales was, at least, somewhat encouraging. Such attacks were rare and Kelly had briefed the team on the personal nature of the injuries, as well as Ted's finding of two weapon patterns. No other knife matching the type of blade had been found at the property. This begged the question: why did the killer leave one knife but take the other?

Kelly yawned. She couldn't help herself. Watching autopsies was emotionally draining. She took the stairs up to her office because it was quicker than waiting for the lift. She found DS Umshaw on the phone to the Highways Agency discussing CCTV. Kelly made them both a coffee and noticed that the incident room was fairly quiet. The activity was on the ground, outside and around the village of Braithwaite where Mary had been assaulted. It was situated west of Keswick and was a favourite start point to the walks around Whinlatter Forest. Kelly couldn't think of a more peaceful existence than living under the shadow of a great mountain range, Derwent Water not too far away, and the smiles of strangers come to tackle a physical challenge and share a pint at the end of it.

Braithwaite folk were used to strangers but they were a close bunch too. It was emerging that Mary Hales was a private resident and didn't socialise much with locals. They swapped words in the local shop, and exchanged pleasantries when the weather changed, but none of her close neighbours seemed to have a significant relationship with her. All said the same: they wished they had.

Kelly was able to use the opportunity of her team being out on the ground to soak up the scene on the incident board. DS Umshaw had done an excellent job. Kelly worked the old fashioned way. Sure, modern technology was a godsend and HOLMES did the work of a hundred officers, with no emotional baggage and no breaks. However, to Kelly, nothing beat photos, notes, string and a marker pen.

The whiteboard was half-full already, and she studied it. A photograph of the victim was posted in the middle, just how Kelly liked it. Around the edge were, to be expected at this stage, mostly questions. A photograph of the kitchen knife caught Kelly's attention. Knife attacks always made her uneasy. The ability to plunge a blade that big into someone over and over again suggested to her a complete absence of empathy. And they were the most difficult bastards to catch.

But also the most arrogant. Amy Richmond had thought herself untouchable when she tortured and punished four women a few years back before she was caught. But she was caught. And this one could be stopped too.

Kelly paused and caught her breath.

In black pen, under a copy of the initial crime scene report and diagram of the body, someone had written 'face up? = punishment?'

Kelly felt her skin go quite cold.

Amy Richmond's first victim had been a woman in her fifties and she'd been horrifically brutalised and subjected to what was no doubt a long and harrowing experience.

Kelly tried to push the thought out of her head. She couldn't jump to wild conclusions because she was being harassed by a lunatic. She reminded herself that all psychopathic killers lacked empathy and this one was no different. They didn't have to be linked, at all.

But the timing of it.

She went back to her office and DS Umshaw put the phone down and began to speak to her, but Kelly opened a drawer and re-read the correspondence. She called a number hastily scribbled onto a piece of paper attached and asked the sergeant on the other end if any progress had been made into finding out where the post was being sent from.

She was told that the investigation into the origin had temporarily been suspended as the department moved offices, as well as the lack of direction from Cumbria Constabulary HQ.

'It says here, ma'am, that the case is pending further instruction from yourself.'

Kelly closed her eyes.

'Look into it, will you? It's part of a live case now.'

It was a white lie.

'You look as though we've had a new victim,' DS Umshaw said dryly.

Chapter 22

Sandra hoovered through the downstairs and wiped the surfaces with a mixture of olive oil, organic white vinegar and essential lemon oil. It was her own recipe and it left no stains or streaks on natural wood. It also left the house smelling fresh and light. Their guests were expected at two, after Joe finished work, and she wondered where Fred had got to. She peered through the back window in the kitchen and spotted him pottering about in the garden. The wrens had not yet abandoned their nests for warmer climates across the Atlantic, and she watched them playfully squeezing in and out of the crevices behind the sheds that they used year on year to nest and breed. It had been a bumper year for them and Sandra's cabbages and cauliflowers were almost twice the size of last year's harvest thanks to the tiny birds feeding on the fat caterpillars and bugs.

Spring was the most satisfying time to watch them as the male competed for mates to lure to admire his nest-building skills. Quite the noisy engineers. Sandra sat for hours listening to them shout tunefully at one another, as if arguing like married couples. Their return each season warmed Sandra and reassured her that their souls were pure: wrens didn't nest in the midst of dark hearts.

She watched her husband and fiddled with her pinafore. She was nervous. It was simply because her only dealings with Annie had been mired with gossip and misunderstanding, and she'd never had the chance to put it right. She almost didn't believe Fred when he'd told her that Joe was bringing his family to Sunday lunch. She'd kept it fairly light and dismissed Fred's idea of a whole venison roast: she'd seared fillets from a fallow deer and sliced them thinly, alongside a ham, potatoes, salads, home-made quiche, and cheese. Puddings were her speciality and she figured that any teenaged boys would love chocolate cake, late season strawberries and cream.

Fred came in from the garden with mucky hands and went to wash them in the newly rinsed sink.

'Go in the bathroom, Fred!' she admonished him. 'And take off those boots!'

He smiled casually and did as he was told. She knew she was being crotchety. And he knew why. The knock on the door startled them and Sandra looked at her clock: their guests were a little early.

But it wasn't the Spencer family at the door. It was the police.

'Oh, hello. Can I help you?' Sandra said, peering over their shoulder. House-to-house calls and just the very presence of the law on her doorstep was about the last thing she wanted to present to Annie Spencer: it looked as though they were in trouble.

'Good morning. My name is...' The uniformed officer began speaking and Sandra zoned him out, perturbed in the midst of her anxiety.

'Sorry?'

'We'd like to ask you a few questions, ma'am. Is your husband in?'

'My husband?'

'Yes. Mr Frederick O'Reilly?'

They now had her attention.

'Erm. Yes. What is this about?'

'We'd appreciate it if you'd get your husband, Mrs O'Reilly. It's important. Perhaps we could come in?'

'Well, I'm expecting guests. It's not really ideal.'

'I'm sorry, ma'am, but it is very important.'

'What's it regarding?'

'Could we see your husband?'

Sandra rolled her eyes and shut the door. 'Fred!'

Fred came out of the downstairs toilet with a towel and responded to his wife's hollering. He looked behind her, expecting to see the Spencers, but no one was there and the door was closed.

'Who was that?'

'The police.'

'Really? I wonder if there have been some burglaries in the area again. They came in the gardens last time.'

'I know. Can you hurry them along? I don't think it will look good if Annie sees—'

'You're paranoid, Sandra. Let me see what they want.'

'They want to come in.'

'Well, they're on our side. We've got nothing to worry about.'

Sandra was unsure and fiddled further with her garments. 'I'll go and check the cakes.' She disappeared into the kitchen and Fred went to get the door. As he opened it, he saw Joe pull up in his car. Fred waved but he could see that Joe's face was concerned when he saw the police at the door.

'Can I help?' Fred asked the officers.

'Are you Frederick O'Reilly, sir?'

'Yes.'

'May we come in?'

'I'm about to have guests. Look, they're behind you. Is this to do with the burglaries last year?'

'No, sir.'

Fred didn't move. Joe came through the gate and Annie followed behind him, staring at the police officers. Their boys looked as though they'd grown a full foot each, thought Fred.

'Joe! Annie! Boys! My goodness, you've shot up!' He gestured to the police officers. 'House calls. Go in, I won't be long.'

Fred moved aside and shouted Sandra. He went back to the two officers, who – he noted – looked a little impatient, and waited.

'Sir, do you know Mary Hales?'

'Of course I do. She's a dear friend. Is she all right?'

Something in the officers' faces made Fred stop and pay more attention to the Sunday house call.

'What?' he asked, looking from one to the other.

'We can see you're busy, sir. We would have preferred to come in. Mary Hales was found dead in her home on Friday evening, sir. We have reason to believe that you might have been one of the last people to see her alive.'

Fred stopped breathing. A loud ringing noise entered his head and made his vision blurry. He stumbled and held on to the door, vaguely aware that the two uniformed officers were grabbing him. He allowed himself to be held up, because he was able to do little else. Sandra gasped when he was half carried by the two strapping young men in black and white into their sitting room and plonked onto a sofa.

'Fred?' Sandra fussed about and Joe and his family stood by helplessly trying to work out what on earth was going on.

'Sandra? Is everything all right?' Joe asked.

'What happened?' Sandra asked one of the officers.

'I'm afraid we just delivered some bad news, ma'am. He might need some water. We'll take the liberty of waiting to see if he's all right.' It wasn't a request. Sandra knew her rights, and she was fully aware that the police couldn't insist on entering or snooping around one's abode, but they didn't seem to have any such agenda. She wondered what the bad news was.

'It's Mary, Sandra,' was all Fred could say.

'Mary? What?' She looked at the police officers.

'I'm sorry, ma'am, Mary Hales was found dead in her home on Friday evening.'

Sandra put her hand to her mouth and sat down heavily.

'Sandra, maybe it's a bad time. We should go.' Annie spoke and looked worryingly towards her boys.

'Perhaps the family could do with your support right now? It seems you know one another well?' One of the officers spoke to Joe and left him little choice.

'Annie, take the boys home, I'll stay here.'

'But all the food,' Sandra said. 'Let me pack some up for the boys.'

'No, really, Sandra. Thank you. Maybe we'll stay a while. Boys, can you come with me into the kitchen?' The boys did as their mother bid them. Annie found the kitchen and closed the door behind the boys. She put the kettle on and turned off the oven.

'Christ!'

'What is it, Mum? Who's Mary?' Callum asked.

'A friend of Fred and Sandra's. It's a huge shock. I think Dad will stay. I feel torn. I should help but I don't want you two getting involved.'

'We're all right, Mum.'

'I'm starving,' said Connor. Annie smiled. She allowed them to fix a plate of food each and told them to sit at the kitchen table while she took some tea through for everybody. She put the kettle on and laid out some things on a tray, finding her way easily around Sandra's kitchen, and took it into the sitting room. The two police officers were sat down and had removed their hats and coats. One took notes and they were asking questions about Mary. Joe sat silently. The police radios crackled.

'What happened?' Sandra asked.

'The details of the investigation are being analysed.'

'Investigation?'

'I'm sorry, sir. Your friend was murdered.'

Sandra hadn't seen Fred cry for about ten years. It was when his sister died from cancer. He put his hands over his face and rubbed his eyes. Suddenly he looked old and Sandra went to him. Joe shook his head.

'When was the last time you saw her?' the officer asked.

'At group. On Monday.'

'Group?'

'We're members of a meeting group – a social group – we read books and play music.' Joe looked oddly at Fred, and Sandra looked oddly at Joe.

'So that would be the day marked in Mary's diary. That's how we found your name, sir. She had several meetings arranged with you.'

'Of course. We ran the group together. Oh my, I can't…'

'Sorry, sir. We can arrange for someone to visit from the family support unit. I appreciate that Mary appears to have no immediate family, but it looks to me as though your group was very important to you both?'

Fred nodded. Joe looked at his feet. Sandra looked at Joe. The police looked at Sandra.

'Where does the group meet?'

'Behind the village hall in Braithwaite.'

'How often?'

'It varied.'

'We'll need a list of the members.'

Fred nodded.

'Tea?' Sandra asked.

Chapter 23

Kelly agreed to meet Ted and Johnny in Pooley Bridge for a quick lunch. She'd barely seen Ted yesterday, and over a dead body, and she hadn't seen Johnny since early Friday.

In the end, the autopsy had taken Ted just under five hours: it was a long one, but not bad considering the gravity of the crime. She'd read of autopsies taking two or three days. However, she was beginning to see signs of fatigue when he finished an operation. Though he would never admit it.

The journey from Eden House in Penrith was a short one and she parked outside the Rose and Crown. News of the murder had travelled and she saw headlines on Sunday papers, and tourists pointing and discussing it. She moved around them and entered the pub, anonymous and nonchalant. Everybody deserved a bloody break and she needed to take her eyes off her computer screen for an hour otherwise she'd go mad. She insisted her team take regular breaks too, but it was sometimes impossible to implement when new information came in or things moved quicker than expected. With this in mind she'd been able to get away and once in her car, she folded the cover over her iPad and looked forward to seeing Ullswater in the distance and sitting by the lake for a short while.

For a moment, she was able to push the small village of Braithwaite to the back of her mind. The small community was in shock. It had emerged, though, that perhaps Mary wasn't as accepted a member of the village as was once intimated. Fear had begun to set in, especially with the older residents of nearby streets who also lived alone. Gossip spread fast and the word on the street was that a mob had robbed Mary's house and turned angry: youths likely. Another theory was that it was somebody who was sick and tired of her animals.

It had emerged that the local sentiment was that the dead woman kept too many pets: the property had a distinct whiff of the four-legged lodgers, and neighbours often complained about the noise of the cats worrying the birds. For the most part, this seemed to be exaggerated, but the uniformed police performing house calls had to log every detail, and as a result, had recorded a dozen or so incidents where neighbours were upset with the growing menagerie. According to the way their statements read Mary Hales was in fact more unpopular than had at first been reported.

During initial inquiries on such a sensitive and brutal case, conjecture always crept in to witness accounts. The police presence provided by head office was large, and it reflected the local panic resonant in the pubs and streets of the surrounding areas. The height of the summer season was virtually over, but tourism still brought in wages during the glorious autumn months when people flocked to the Lakes to enjoy the majesty of the autumn colours: bronzes, golds and oranges tinged every corner of the hills and framed award winning photography. The press was also out in sizeable force. Reporters from Manchester and London had been seen outside the victim's house, and had been asking questions in the surrounding villages. Some wacky stories had circulated, including reports from one local journalist, Carry Tomlin, about the case being linked to witchcraft.

The news had caught Kelly's attention.

Carry Tomlin was a young reporter, fresh out of university, trying to make her mark, and she'd already recently published an inflammatory article about the practice of worshipping sun and moon deities in the Lake District going back thousands of years. It was DC Emma Hide who'd marked the journalist as one to watch. Anything with cruelty to animals as a background canvas always raised a flicker of a concern about ritual, and gossip had to be contained. Kelly had asked Emma to look into any possibilities, and had also given her the file on the Birkett Mire cruelty case: it was a line of inquiry, nothing more at this stage. After Johnny's revelation, she'd also found the file on the High Rigg case from 2013 and, without looking at it herself, passed that to DC Hide also.

Several statements from Mary's closest neighbours reported the noise of animals in distress on Friday evening; however, it had taken the fire itself for anybody to raise the alarm. Acrid smoke had drifted through an open window, and the neighbour had called the police to report illegal rubbish burning, until she noticed an unusual smell.

What Kelly really wanted to piece together was who came and went at the property, and who saw Mary regularly. A few neighbours reported that Mary could often be seen driving her car (she rarely walked), and the gates and bushes at the property prevented further prying, giving them very little to go on regarding her behaviour. Nobody reported seeing visitors. The houses around the village were scattered fairly well and they enjoyed privacy. Kelly had seen the lane out of the back of Mary's property for herself: it was isolated and private, and somebody familiar with it could easily arrive and depart undetected. The only other entrance and exit was the front, and that was shrouded in trees and bushes. The gates were always closed.

The name of Frederick O'Reilly had popped up routinely and that was all it was, or so they thought. Initial interview notes coming from the O'Reillys were encouraging and perhaps Mr O'Reilly knew her better than anyone. That left them with only one strong lead into Mary's routine: her social group led by Fred O'Reilly. It was something.

The Rose and Crown was thronged with tourists and locals, enjoying the last of the carvery on offer since midday. The owner provided four cuts of meat each weekend, and when they were gone, he closed the kitchen. It provided a roaring trade and the place was always packed. However, Kelly rarely chose the roast option, and the bar menu was just as good, with the staples offered in smaller portions, providing ample sustenance for their small party. Kelly had managed to convince Ted to sleep at her house tonight, and save him the journey to his cottage in Keswick. It also meant that he could enjoy a pint and let his hair down a little after yesterday's gruelling work. His preliminary report had been in her inbox first thing this morning and she knew he must have stayed up half the night to complete it.

She felt a tap on her shoulder and Ted smiled broadly. She hugged him. They went in together and Johnny waved at them from the crowded bar. He chatted easily to people she didn't know. That was his way: the opposite of hers. Johnny was well known in the area, not just for his mountain rescue work, but because he was damn good company and easy to talk to. His old army stories were popular with the locals and he rarely paid for beer.

Ted strode over to Johnny to take his hand, and Kelly watched them together. It was times like this when she felt a pang of heartache that her mother couldn't see it. Johnny had been a regular feature around Pooley Bridge longer than she had, and he knew more people. But this afternoon, their mood was more serious. Kelly was less likely to pass time with local drinkers, and it could be said that she actively avoided getting herself into situations where she might be drawn into long conversations about where she'd been all these years, or her job. It was a topic that she didn't care to delve into and she was known for her privacy.

She ordered a coke, needing the calories, but wishing she could order a large white wine, in the mood for booze after seeing, first hand, what Mary Hales had been subjected to. There was something shatteringly hopeless about a murdered body. In London, their antidote to death as a murder squad had often been fuelled by alcohol and late nights in the local pub. It softened the edges.

'I think the carvery's finished already, I'll grab some bar menus,' said Johnny, after he'd kissed Kelly.

'I'm starving,' Kelly said.

'They'll still serve us something light,' Johnny said. For most punters, when the Sunday carvery had gone, the food was finished, but for familiar faces, the kitchen was always open.

'How's it going?' Johnny asked before moving to the bar.

'Pretty shit what happened to her,' she whispered.

Johnny half smiled in sympathy and squeezed her arm. 'I don't know how you do it.'

She looked over to Ted.

'I do nothing, Ted does it all. I just watch,' she said. They found a table.

'I'm not taking any credit when you finally solve this one, it's nasty, that's for sure,' Ted said. Johnny shook his head and went to get the menus. When he came back, Ted changed the subject.

'How is Josie getting on with her climbing?'

'I can't keep her away. We think there's a boy involved, and she mentioned the name Callum, but she says she goes for the exercise, and it gets her away from "fake" people at school. Her words, not mine.'

'Well anything that gets them active is good, I say,' Ted said. 'What exactly is "fake" these days? I'm not familiar with their jargon, I can't keep up.'

'I don't think it means anything different to what it meant to us: being in competition with other teenagers is the toughest part of growing up, I think,' Kelly said.

They gave their food orders to Johnny, who went to the kitchen.

'I'm glad you're staying at mine tonight. It reminds me of when you would visit with Mum,' Kelly said to Ted.

Ted nodded his head and smiled. 'Me too.' He took a long swig of his pint.

'Sorry, I shouldn't just blurt that sort of stuff out. It just happened.'

'I'm getting used to it, no need to apologise. June and Amber said they very much enjoy your company and your candour. They'd like to meet again.'

He spoke of his other daughters, from his marriage, with affection. It was true, their meeting had been enjoyable. She'd been nervous about usurping their positions but she needn't have worried, both daughters seemed pleased for their father. Kelly smiled. 'The feeling is mutual. They're confident women, I like them. What's their mother like?'

'She's an alcoholic. I haven't seen her in about three years now. The girls keep me updated but it's usually the same every time: *she had a fall, she was admitted to A&E, she hit her head*, etcetera, etcetera.'

'I'm sorry.'

'So am I. I used to blame myself. I told myself that it was my job to stay with her because it was my job that isolated her.'

'How?'

'Well, I worked crazy hours and she was shy. All she did all day was stay in and run the girls around.'

'It must be hard for them seeing their mother like that.'

'It's crucifying, but they love her. Every now and again she'll promise to stop but she's back on it within the week.'

'Can't she be treated?'

'It isn't something that is diagnosed and treated. It's psychological. Addiction like that has one purpose and one purpose only: to drink more.'

'Surely it will kill her.'

'Yes, it will.'

'Does she live on her own?'

'Yes, I walked out of the family home and wanted none of it. The girls say it's like a prison. She lives in a few rooms and the others get cleaned by my daughters when they have time.'

'It's not your fault. You didn't cause it. She could have gone out and made friends, she could have got a job.'

'No, not a job. I was the man, the provider, the bread winner.'

'God, I'd go mad being kept like that.'

'It was the way then.'

'I suppose you're right. My mother gave up work to raise my sister and me.'

'I wish I'd known, Kelly.'

When Johnny came back to the table, Ted's hand was on Kelly's.

'I've been invited to speak at a PTSD conference later in the month.'

'Johnny, that's amazing, where is it? Could I come with you?'

'It's in Manchester. Suicide rates among veterans are going through the roof.'

'I know, I read about it most weeks,' Ted said.

'They just don't get the support they need when they come back to normal life after what they've seen.'

'I suppose that's why it's called traumatic stress: stress that we're not designed to deal with.'

'Exactly.'

'That's well deserved, Johnny, and I know you'll do a marvellous job. Now where's our food, I'm ravenous.'

'You two amaze me, with what you do for a living, I think I'd rather skip dinner.'

'It's a job like any other. I couldn't do what you did. I'd be a useless soldier. What about you, Kelly?'

'Me? A soldier? My God, I'd want a solid argument presented on moving forward before I agreed to anything.'

Johnny laughed. 'It's true, you'd be a liability. I can just imagine it: being briefed on a dawn raid and you questioning some brigadier and his tactics. I'd pay to see it, though.'

'Theirs is not to reason why...' Ted quoted Tennyson.

'So, can you talk about the case? I don't mind if you do,' Johnny said.

'It's ugly. There are no clear pointers to a love interest or a burglary or the usual first set of theories that come to you when you first examine a scene. It was so staged,' Kelly said.

'I agree,' said Ted.

'You see, that's the interesting bit: when you two put your heads together and postulate and chew over your vast experience. It's the fallout I couldn't handle. You know, the families, when kids are involved, and people doing that stuff to each other when they're not even at war. It makes no sense.'

'Does war make sense? Who was it that said war was just organised murder?' Ted asked.

'Ian Brady, the Moors murderer.'

'That's a whole other debate, I think I might go and see where our food is and get another drink.' Johnny left the table.

'He's not proud of being ordered to kill,' Kelly said.

'I understand that, and I see it in him. I've no experience of war, and I have no desire to. Conscription had ended when I was old enough. I feel for these men who are given a rifle and told where to aim it. It's inherently wrong. But I like Johnny immensely and I know your mother did too.'

Later, when Kelly was walked to her car, needing to get back to work, she put her arm through Ted's on one side, and Johnny's on the other. It was only after they'd walked five metres that she realised the intimacy of what she'd done and that it had happened so naturally. It had felt the most unpretentious thing to do and she glanced sideways to see if Ted had reacted at all. He tightened his arm and they strode on.

Chapter 24

When Kelly went to leave the house the next morning, she didn't disturb Ted. She'd got in late. But she was glad she'd taken the time out to meet him and Johnny. The spare room door was shut tight and she crept downstairs, made a coffee and checked her emails. The fire department had got back to her and she flicked through the report. It was detailed and lengthy – as she'd expected – and she closed it to read in more detail later. The post dropped through her door and she went to pick it off the mat.

The sun shone through the windows and lit up her hallway all the way from the back, where it overlooked the river, to the front. She lived in a quiet part of Pooley Bridge, away from the tiny central square where all the tourist shops and cafés plied their trade. The odd ice cream seller parked up outside her house in summer, because it was along the route to the steamer that took day trippers to Glenridding and Howtown.

She bent to pick up the post and flicked through it, stopping at a handwritten letter with a Surrey postcode. She recognised the writing. She sighed and lowered the envelope, tempted to throw it straight into the waste bin. She looked at the letter and couldn't help but be a little intrigued by what might be inside. The mind of a psychopath was something that the most eminent psychologists all over the world would give their life savings to unpick, and here she was, being contacted by one of the sickest. After the Amy Richmond case, she'd had letters, emails and phone calls from professors from Beijing to Canada asking for her opinion on what motivated the series of gruesome killings that gripped the Lake District.

She'd ignored them all. She couldn't begin to explain what she thought motivated such cold and calculated actions. It was all she could do to manage the grief of the families and stretch resources so that they had enough liaison officers attending them. The money didn't last forever, and at some point, the support was withdrawn. But crimes such as those perpetrated by The Teacher never went away. They weren't just murders; they were *lessons*. Amy had played God for a while and got away with it.

She threw the letter into her bag and packed the rest of the stuff she'd need for the day: her water bottle, her running kit – just in case she got the chance – and a few packs of food she'd prepared to eat at her desk. On her way out, she grabbed an apple.

Her drive to Eden House was uneventful and she drove in peace, listening to the radio. It was only when she arrived at her office that a chaotic buzz assaulted her. If she was looking for an early direction in which to take the investigation into the death of Mary Hales, then she'd have to work fast. The first forty-eight hours had passed. This was what any detective considered as the golden hours: the time when vital clues and evidence are either gathered or lost. After that time frame, the investigation becomes trickier. She'd worked them hard over the weekend and now they were entering another investigative phase where things slowed and chances waned. Her whole team was gathered for an early brief, but first she had to read the fire report. She glanced into the incident room and nodded her greetings.

'Guv, the vet has got back to us with the reports on the animal carcasses. It's an interesting read.' DS Kate Umshaw followed Kelly into her office.

'Did you manage to get some rest?' Kelly asked.

'Not really, a sixteen-year-old who is sexting her boyfriend, a fourteen-year-old who thinks she's fat and a twelve-year-old who still wants to sleep with me. It's quieter here, frankly.'

'I'm sure your passion for parental duties is rubbing off on the others; it certainly has on me. Though I have to say that my stepdaughter is remarkably mature and trouble free at the moment.'

'Calm before the storm, guv. Give it time.'

Kelly nodded. It was true: Josie had rarely displayed such tranquillity in the few years she'd been living with Johnny. There was always some argument, angst, or tension surrounding her that Kelly waded in on, unannounced and regretful of later. She'd found herself chatting to the teenager about boys, image and the dangers of online dating before she could even consider herself anything like a parent, but it had happened, and she'd survived. The climbing club seemed to be taking most of the strain lately, even though it was early days.

'I'll read the fire report too and we'll get together in an hour,' Kelly said.

'Oh, the shoe print people got back: the wellington boot was a generic plastic mould produced in hundreds of factories all over the world. Size eight. Coffee?' Kate asked.

'Go on then.'

Kate left and Kelly turned to her main computer and began to read. She opened the attached file sent to her by the chief fire inspector for north Cumbria. The case had been passed from the regular fire department due to the nature of the crime, and Kelly was expected to present the findings as part of her inquiry. She read that the fire had been started with an accelerant in the backyard and had spread rapidly through the animal pens and crates, which had been locked. The fire was intense and brief, but hot enough to produce enough smoke to kill the animals, and heat and flame to finish them off, if they survived the smoke. The report stated that it appeared this act of arson was a sadistically motivated crime and one which was deliberate and destructive. The animals stood no chance of escape. Traces of the chemical accelerant had been sent to the lab, as well as the remains of a few rags used to start the blaze. The results showed that the accelerant was a standard product purchasable anywhere in the country, and the rags were towels probably already in the animals' shelters, given the amount of hair and mud on them. In short, whoever started the fire had reached into the cages and coops and removed the towels without disturbing the animals, indicating that either the person was known to the animals or they gave off a calm demeanour, which was unusual. Kelly read that deliberate fires involving the death of animals are rare, given the fact that Britain was a nation of animal lovers, but also because animals have an acute sense of danger and often escape under such circumstances. In this case, the animals trusted their killer enough to allow themselves to be locked away. The state of the yard indicated that the animals were free to roam, if not all the time, then most of the time.

Kelly tapped her chin and moved on to the vet's report. The photographs were graphic and sickening. She'd seen victims of intense fires before, but this fire hadn't been particularly long lasting, and yet it had still caused hideous damage. The vet had concluded from the autopsies she'd carried out that the animals were mostly conscious at the time of burning.

In summary, it was the vet's belief that whoever did this was hoping to harm the owner of the pets, not just the pets. Her premise was that those who keep pets have a love for them, in most cases, akin to that towards a child, and the animals were all in excellent condition ante-mortem. They were well looked after. Loved. Thus, the pain and terror caused to the animals was apparently deliberately aimed at the owner. Kelly knew that Mary died after the fire and so perhaps she watched her animals die. She certainly witnessed their pain. She remembered what Demi said about who the attack was aimed at: it seemed that it was Mary. The vet's report continued to say that burning was a particular method of cleansing evidence from the scene. The fire officer had said the same, and Kelly had seen it in other cases.

Animals can't be witnesses and so it left Kelly with the glaring fact that whoever killed Mary killed her animals because they wanted to hurt Mary with such vehemence that they chose the thing she loved most.

But another attachment caught her eye. It was a photograph of some of the animals' remaining pieces of flesh. Most of the bodies of the animals had been badly charred and left little fur or skin, however, a few of them had patches remaining and, on three of them, a triangle had been cut with a sharp instrument. The vet confirmed that the cuts were fresh and inflicted before they had time to heal, meaning they were scored into the skin on Friday evening. Possibly by the person who killed them. Kelly stared at the photos. The triangles were neat, small and deliberate. The vet had attached an appendix. She'd noted that she'd never seen any farming branding made in such a manner. She'd also proven, by the way the animal had bled and the blood coagulated, that they were alive when cut. The vet had done some research on the use of any forms of triangle symbolism and learned that alchemic tradition marks the element of sulphur – strongly associated with fire – the symbol of an upward-pointing triangle.

The final attachment was about the dead birds. They were all wrens. The vet, again, had done her homework and had commented that keeping wrens in cages was highly unusual; they were migratory. However, they did come back to the same breeding nests year on year and it was possible that Mary Hales' garden was a firm favourite, and so the birds would feel comfortable there. She'd handwritten a note next to a photograph of a common wren. 'Such a shame to see this bird treated in this way. The wren is the king of all birds.'

It was a heartfelt statement from someone who worked with animals all day long. Vets had a special relationship with animals; one that ordinary people couldn't begin to fathom or replicate. The death of these animals had touched this one and Kelly could tell that she wanted justice. She could also tell from the level of technical detail that she'd included in her report that the vet didn't think that it was the work of some local thugs messing around. The animals were tricked and tortured.

She went into the incident room feeling depressed. Her team was gathered and she nodded to some familiar faces who'd joined them to aid the investigation. She shared what she had so far and the room remained silent. She took questions and listened to reports on the subjects of traffic, house-to-house questioning, CCTV and a detailed labour-intensive search of the area around Mary's house.

There was a decisive sense of gloom in the room, but Kelly knew that the worst was over. The details had been hard to listen to, now they could look ahead to doing their real jobs. A photograph of Mary Hales was pinned to the whiteboard and Kelly stared at it. They hadn't found many images of the woman; this one had been in a drawer in her bedroom. It showed a slightly younger Mary, vibrant and smiling. It was portrait-like and Kelly wondered why it had been taken. And by whom. An image of Mary laying on Ted's slab popped into her head and she felt a tightness in her chest. The two visions fought for attention. She could almost hear the woman speak. But more than that, the savagery involved in extinguishing a life like this one pestered her. And she knew why.

Chapter 25

Fred O'Reilly stared ahead but saw nothing.

'I made you an egg sandwich, just how you like it, Fred. The eggs were laid just this afternoon.'

Sandra tried her best to pluck her husband from his depression. It was a melancholy that he'd sunk into as soon as the last of the police had left on Sunday afternoon: only yesterday in fact. It felt like a month, not a day, since they'd been told what happened to Mary.

Nobody could believe it.

It wasn't that Sandra knew Mary as well as Fred, it was the manner in which she'd been killed. The *fact* she'd been killed. *Murdered.* It was a word for books, for thrillers on the BBC, not Braithwaite. Sandra had met Mary lots of times, more than she could remember, and she found her mild mannered, charming and quiet. She'd been a woman who would cause harm to no one and, as such, deserved no harm in return. And then there were her animals. Whoever did it was sick in the head: that was for sure. And that's what they'd told the police.

Sandra didn't like the way the police had looked at her husband. She felt they suspected him when they asked him difficult questions about their friendship, calling it a 'relationship'. Sandra would have laughed had it not been such dire circumstances. Though she did notice that Fred held back on telling the police the exact nature of their group. She understood: ordinary folk saw what they did as nothing short of black magic. Nothing could be further from the truth, but to those who didn't have the luxury of wisdom it was a dark art to be mistrusted. Fred was right to protect them, and her loyalty, too, was to her husband, not the police. And Mary would agree. Would *have* agreed.

'Love. Eat the sandwich. I made the bread.'

Fred continued to gaze into space. Occasionally he would sigh and run his hand through his silver hair, shaking his head, as though if he did so, things would return to normal. Then, upon realising that they wouldn't, he'd shake his head, close his eyes and settle back into his sorrow.

'Why, Sandra? I can't...'

It was the first he'd spoken all day. She knew he hadn't slept last night. He'd been up, reading his books and notepads, saying blessings and mantras all night, hoping to protect her soul from the underworld. Autumn was the most active of seasons for the spirits, as daylight gave way to darkness. It was almost the autumn equinox, and after that, the days would get shorter and shorter, until winter solstice. Until then, they were vulnerable to the most active of the spirits, and with a bereavement hanging over them, they were weakened with an imbalance of auras and thus less armed if attacked. It made them exposed.

Sandra had never shown interest in becoming a High Priestess: she was happier to follow the way rather than organise it. That was Fred's job, and he found a willing and able collaborator in Mary. Mary had been the ultimate fixer, arranger, coordinator and regulator, and the group was held together by her. Her passion for what she did drove them all forward and they'd relied on her: Sandra realised this now. Without Mary they were lost, and with Fred in the pit of despair, she didn't know who to turn to. She thought about calling a meeting so they could at least mourn together. The police said they'd be interviewing everyone who was a member of their social group. She'd called all of them last night to deliver the awful news before the police. And to warn them.

'Fred, can I call someone? Perhaps Jock? Or Joe maybe?' she asked.

It had been a lovely surprise to see Joe and his family again. Sandra knew, that secretly, Fred was hoping to woo Annie into recognising that their group was not hocus pocus or weird, just peaceful and beautiful. If it was Fred's wish to change her mind, he stood little chance of that now.

Of course, Joe had been kind, but Annie had been horrified, and in front of her children too. She'd spoken to her in the kitchen when the police were there, and out of earshot of the boys, and it was clear that Annie suspected the group was involved in some way.

'If you get yourself caught up in something you don't understand then it's bound to come back on you. What was Mary doing that you don't know about?' Annie had asked her. Right here, in her own kitchen. Sandra hadn't known what to say. What could she say? Annie was talking utter nonsense.

Because they were in the house when the police came, Annie and Joe were questioned too. They'd both said they knew Mary through Fred, but they hadn't seen her for a few years. Sandra supposed it was true enough. The boys were ushered back to the car, once they'd been fed, and Annie took them home, but Joe had stayed. He was a good man and Sandra could tell that Fred wanted him there. He'd been like a son to him at one point.

Jock had come round and it had been like old times, of a sort. Until every other minute they remembered why they were gathered. Joe left first, after a handful of phone calls from Annie. Sandra had fed him, and then Jock. Nothing could put Jock off his food and he fired questions aimlessly at anyone listening as his head whirred in search of answers that no one had.

'Are you sure you can't think of anyone who had something against her? Someone who tried to join the group? Someone who despised her animals? We all know that she was seen as the local cat lady, and their whining and pissing everywhere drove her neighbours nuts.' Jock was a doer. He was the last person to be caught wallowing and wailing. Sandra felt his frustration.

'But you don't kill someone because their cat shits in your garden,' Sandra said.

'But you heard what they said: the animals were all killed as well, don't you think that's odd?'

Sandra agreed. It had to have something to do with Mary's pets.

'She was so innocent, such a good person that she was. It's tough on you, Fred, most of all. I can't believe it.' Jock's eyes were pink at the edges and Sandra's heart ached at the pain caused by the violence of Mary's death.

'I know, Jock, but people get angry, and anger makes them do stupid things. Sometimes, people simply don't like anyone who's different, and Mary was different all right. Like we all are.' Sandra's words were unsettling.

'What?' It was Fred who spoke.

'Oh, I know they say I'm odd for growing everything myself. They call us "do-gooders" and "hippies". I got called a gypsy in town once. It was a young boy; can you believe the cheek of it?'

They were different; there was no getting away from it. They wore old fashioned clothes, they grew their own food, they were private and they smiled a lot. Like the witches of Salem they were anomalies, and they knew full well that anything that deviates from what society deems to be standard or normal is treated with suspicion. It was human nature, and they knew that when they took their oaths. So did Mary. Jock had finally left in the early hours and she'd listened to Fred wandering the house all night.

Sandra sat down next to him and reached her hand out to his lap. He slowly turned his head and looked at his wife.

'Oh, Fred,' she said, taking him into her arms. He allowed himself to be held and his shoulders heaved with the agony of what had happened. He didn't need to speak.

Chapter 26

Kelly drove towards Keswick and went beyond the town to Braithwaite, which sat nestled at the foot of the Whinlatter Forest. It was a hub of bed and breakfasts for walkers, who started the fine routes to the fells beyond Grizedale Pike and the Hobcarton Horseshoe. The largest peak in the area was Grasmoor, and the views from the summit were staggering on a bright day, such as it was today.

The O'Reillys lived in a small cottage, off the beaten path, outside of the village where Mary had resided. They weren't a family on her radar, and they hadn't flagged up on regular police checks. Fred and Sandra O'Reilly seemed like law-abiding citizens who'd had a shock; that was all. Kelly was on her way to visit them to gain her own impression, though. And she'd brought Rob along with her.

'She was a bit of a hermit as far as we can make out, and yet she had this friendship circle – and quite a close one – meeting regularly in the village hall. Have we tracked down the other people who attended yet?'

Fred had supplied the police with a list of names, and they were being contacted simultaneously. Mary's killer could be one of them.

'Uniforms have been sent to every contact given to us by Fred O'Reilly. There are currently twelve active members who meet in the village hall. I have a list and their statements taken late last night. All twelve members were interviewed and all pretty much said the same to the uniforms conducting the inquiries.'

'What sort of a group is it?'

'They said they meet to play cards, paint, birdwatch and make crafts.'

'Cute. Demographics?'

'Oldest: eighty-six-year-old male, youngest is a twenty-three-year-old female. No anomalies reported, no red flags. All dates corroborated and all have alibis that checked out.'

'Good. Right. Here we are. Let's go and meet Fred and Sandra, and see if we can get to know Mary a bit better, shall we?'

Kelly parked on the quiet lane outside the stone cottage, flanked by tall bushes on all sides. Birds flitted between branches and late summer flowers bloomed unashamedly in the pretty garden. The house looked as though it had been lived in and loved for many years. The paths were well tended and clean, and the fences freshly painted. Kelly noticed also that the windows were not sparkling clean, something her mother always told her to look out for: *never fully trust a woman with an immaculate house.* Since Wendy had died, Kelly found herself thinking more about the snippets of wisdom that her mother had passed down, only to be ignored at the time and consigned to a forgotten chamber of irrelevance, until she was gone and could no longer speak.

They knocked on the door and a woman answered. Her face held a look of concern as well as wariness. Kelly figured that the woman was Sandra O'Reilly.

'Good morning. Is it Mrs O'Reilly?' Kelly spoke first.

The woman didn't answer straight away. She looked between the two strangers and held on to her door, contemplating closing it.

'Are you from the paper?' the woman spoke.

'No. We're police detectives, Mrs O'Reilly. We're here to see your husband. I believe the preliminary responders told you we'd be coming? We need to ask you both some questions about Mary Hales. I know you've been over so much already. If we could come in, I can explain.' She showed her ID tag and Rob did the same.

'This is Detective Constable Shawcross, and I'm Detective Inspector Porter,' Kelly said.

The woman appeared relieved and Kelly took this as a good sign. She let go her grip of the door slightly and a faint smile appeared at the corners of her mouth.

'I am Sandra O'Reilly. I thought it was the paper. We've had a few journalists around here. One young woman was very pushy. I think they've gone now: bored with it all. I have no idea where they got the information from that Mary was our friend. I suppose they can get hold of anything now.'

'They can.' Kelly smiled, waiting to be let in.

'Oh, I'm sorry, come in. I'll make tea.' The elixir of all British ills awaited them as it did in most homes friendly to a police presence: and that wasn't all of them. It was a good start. They went in and Sandra closed the door behind them. She shuffled past them and led them down the hall. She stopped outside a closed door and turned to them both.

'He's taken it badly. He just sits and chews it over and over.' Sandra looked pained and Kelly understood. It was completely normal behaviour and she hoped they'd get something out of him. For now, anyone who knew Mary was a suspect who had to be ruled out.

'Of course. It's only to be expected.'

Sandra nodded again, then opened the door. 'Love, it's the police. They're detectives, don't worry, I know you've told them all before, but they're not in uniform.'

Kelly and Rob waited to be shown in. As they were ushered into the room by Sandra, they were met with a pleasant aroma: incense. It took Kelly back to university and her grubby room on campus. Incense was used to mask the scent of body odour or drugs, but she doubted this was the case here. A window was open and so the smell mingled with fresh air and it was invigorating. Soft music played gently in the background. The room was a haven of calm.

Fred O'Reilly stood with effort. His face bore the strain of somebody grieving. He looked older than his sixty-seven years written in her notes, but then the bereaved always aged rapidly. They must have been close, was her first thought. She extended her hand and Fred took it, shaking it firmly.

'Detective Inspector Kelly Porter.'

Rob did the same.

'Is this your bodyguard?' Fred showed a little humour and Kelly smiled.

'Absolutely. He's also Detective Constable Rob Shawcross.'

'What did your mother feed you? Home grown I'll bet. We grow all our own.' Fred extended his hand to the window and Kelly presumed he meant their back garden. They sat down.

'Absolutely, sir, everything cooked the old fashioned way,' Rob answered and Kelly saw Fred O'Reilly relax a little.

Kelly gave Fred a few minutes to gather himself. Sometimes, witnesses liked to begin their own narrative. Some didn't. Fred clasped his hands together and began talking.

'She was a fine woman. I can't think who'd want to hurt her. She had no enemies. None at all. Her animals were noisy, I believe, but that's not reason enough is it? She bothered no one. She helped anyone who came to her.'

'Who came to her for help?' Kelly asked.

'All sorts, I suppose.'

'Members of your group?'

'Yes. She gave advice to the younger ones and did a spot of home help for a few of them, like gardening and the like – she was green fingered sure enough.'

'I've seen her garden. It was beautiful.'

'Was? Burned eh? Dreadful. Who'd do that? Have you caught anyone yet?'

'No, I'm afraid not. We're looking at all angles. It would seem that Mary had no family. Can you comment on that?'

'She was married, but they parted before any children came along, though she would have made a wonderful mother. I never heard her speak of sisters or brothers. Her parents are long gone I think; in fact, I seem to recall that was their house she lived in.'

'Yes, we've found that from the deeds. So, the group was important to her? It seems it was her main social outlet. How often did you meet?'

'It wasn't set in stone. We tried to get together once a month but it didn't always happen. Erm, sometimes it would be a handful of us and other times, we'd have all of us.'

'What was the nature of the group?'

'Birdwatching.'

'Really? That's interesting. Who created it?'

'I did. I advertised in the local area and Mary was the first to respond. We ran it.'

'There's quite an age range. I never knew birdwatching was so popular.'

'You'd be surprised. We live in an area so rich with birds that people come from as far away as the USA to spot rare migrations and even eagles.'

Kelly knew that a pair of golden eagles nested around Haweswater reservoir, but they were notoriously private and difficult to spot; they could easily be myth

'That explains why Mary kept so many wrens. I can hear birds in your garden too, do you keep them in cages?'

'We like to call them aviaries. *Cages* sounds so barbaric.'

'Of course. I apologise. What birds do you keep?'

'Keep is an anomalous word. One never keeps a bird unless it is in captivity. A true lover of birds never locks them in. Our birds are all migratory and they come back here every spring. They're getting ready to leave now, I can hear them chattering. They'll fly to Central and South America, and return in March. The loudest ones are wrens.'

'That's quite a journey.'

'They're more gifted than us.'

'The king of birds.'

'Quite.'

'I believe Mary attracted wrens to her garden too.'

Fred nodded.

'Mr O'Reilly – Fred – can I be blunt? Mary's pets were destroyed in the attack, which you know. They were all locked away. How would anyone manage that?'

'Isn't that your job? They were barbarians like I said. They either came in a pack, drugged them, or knew animals the way Mary did.'

'You mean *tricked* them into their pens?'

'Yes.'

'How would they do that?'

'If you know animals it's easy to communicate with them.'

'Surely someone who you're describing would be an animal lover?'

'Maybe. Maybe not.'

'Did you see Mary outside of the birdwatching group?'

'Occasionally.'

'Did she mention other friends? Fallings out? Problems or anxieties?'

'No.'

'Were you aware of any other close acquaintances? What about her neighbours?'

'She kept herself to herself. She trusted animals more than people, and I tend to agree with her.'

'It says in the report that when the initial responders came to visit you to inform you of Mary's death, you had Mr Joe Spencer and his family around for lunch, is that correct?'

'Yes, why?'

'How do you know Mr Spencer?'

'I can't remember how we met. He works for English Heritage and I volunteer a lot. We have a love of the fells in common, and nature in general. We both like peace and quiet.'

'Did he know Mary?'

'Not really.'

'Can you be more specific?'

'He's known me a long time and so he's heard a lot about Mary.'

'It says in his statement that he met her.'

The door opened and Sandra came in with a tray of tea and biscuits.

'They're home-made with my churned butter.' She set the tray down and Rob took a biscuit. Sandra poured tea. Kelly watched Fred.

'Mrs O'Reilly. Which bird is it making all that racket in your garden?'

'Oh, they're the loudest birds on earth. They're wrens. They've been coming to our garden for ten years or more.'

'The king of birds,' Kelly said.

'Yes, they are. People think it's the eagle but legend has it that when the eagle dared the smaller birds to fly the highest the wren hid under his wing and tricked him, flying out at the last minute to fly the highest and gaining the regal epithet. They act like it too.' Sandra smiled. 'They strut round and shout their desires like any small dictator would. But they eat my bugs and protect my cauliflowers so they're welcome here every year.'

'Mary had wrens too. Did you talk about them at the bird-watching group?'

'What birdwatching group?' Sandra looked at Fred. His face barely changed, but it was enough.

'The group that Fred and Mary ran together, it was a bird-watching group?'

'Ah, of course! I thought you meant some sort of rambling group who went and hid in bushes spotting new species. You mean the group where we painted them, and talked about their habitats and how to protect them? I call it more of a conservation group, that's why I'm confused.'

Sandra stood, spoon and sugar in hand, waiting for Kelly to respond. Fred's face was set and still. Kelly noticed that Sandra's décolletage had turned pink.

'The biscuits are lovely, Sandra, thank you,' Rob broke the silence.

'How well did you know Mary?' Kelly asked Sandra.

'Only through the group, and she came here for tea once or twice. She was a lovely woman, very peaceful and good natured. She loved her animals.'

'Can you think of anything she mentioned about making enemies or being in conflict with anyone?'

'No, never. Well, her neighbours complained about her animals, the cats mainly. But it was never aggressive or threatening. It's terrible.'

'We've interviewed the other members of your… conservation group. Would you say that you had the same casual relationship with all of them?'

'I'd describe us all as friends.' Sandra was tentative and glanced at her husband, who nodded.

'How long have you known Joe Spencer?'

'Joe?' Sandra looked at Fred and Kelly noticed fear behind her eyes. 'Has Joe got something to do with this? He was with us on Sunday.'

'Of course he hasn't, Sandra! He was here, that's all, he could have known Mary,' Fred corrected his wife.

'Oh. How long have we known Joe and Annie, Fred? Five or six years? I don't rightly know. They're a lovely family. I'm not sure he ever met Mary properly.'

'Properly?' Kelly asked. Again there was a slight shift in atmosphere and the incense mingled with the draft became irritatingly sweet rather than soothing.

Sandra fiddled with her apron and began to fill up Fred's tea cup.

'Sorry?' she asked Kelly.

'You said you didn't think he met her *properly*, that implies that he met her but perhaps not to get to know, can you clarify what you meant?' Kelly asked.

'It must have been here. A long time ago. They must have met over tea. Joe likes wildlife.'

'Right. Of course he does, he works for English Heritage. Well, if you think of anything else we might consider. It's vitally important that we piece together Mary's life, so that we can spot anything unusual. There's our cards, call us anytime. Thank you for the tea.'

They stood up and said pleasant goodbyes. Sandra saw them to the door. As they left, they could hear frenzied chirping from the back garden.

'They're noisy aren't they?' Kelly asked.

Sandra opened the door. 'They're deceptive. They have the loudest voices but the smallest demeanours. Often the strongest punch comes from the underdog.' Sandra was back in safe territory, talking about her birds.

'Do wrens have special significance for your birdwatching group, Sandra?' Kelly asked as they were shown out.

Sandra made a noise that was akin to a cross between a grunt and a laugh. Kelly had heard it thousands of times before: it was the classic sign of nerves. 'They're considered to be the most ancient of birds and really were once people. Druids in fact. That's why they like nests that resemble caves. They're cheeky because they have to trick the winter.'

'Are they that clever?'

'Oh, yes.'

'What would it take to trick them?'

'It couldn't be done.'

'You don't know anyone capable of it?'

Sandra faltered. She looked down and back inside the house as if looking for Fred to rescue her.

'Only Mary.'

'Thank you, Sandra.' Kelly gave the woman a card and they said goodbye.

On their way back to Kelly's car, Rob munched on a biscuit he'd taken as they left. 'These are incredible. I was waiting for cake; I could smell something baking in the oven.'

'What were you doing in there?' Kelly had spotted him taking profuse notes.

'Sketching.'

'What?'

'Behind Fred, in front of the window, there was a table. It was where he was burning his incense.'

'Yes, I saw it.'

'It was exactly the same as a table set up in Mary Hales' front room. It was just about the only thing that wasn't destroyed. It was a small desk-sized table, covered in a cloth, with what looked like ornaments on top. Fred's table reminded me of it, so I'm going to have a look when we get back.'

'What's on your mind?' Kelly asked.

'Fred and Sandra's garden is south-facing.'

'Yes?'

'So the table faced west.'

Kelly unlocked the car and they got in. She sat behind the wheel and started the engine. Rob slammed his door.

'And you're going to tell me that so did Mary's.'

'Yes.'

'And does this mean something?'

Kelly put her belt on and checked her mirrors, pulling away from the home of Sandra and Fred O'Reilly.

'I don't know, but they looked the same. I'm sure – in my limited knowledge – that birdwatching groups don't have tables facing compass points containing trinkets like candles, pots and shells, which look as though they've come straight out of a magic potion book.'

Kelly stopped at a junction.

'You think they're running some sort of magic ritual cult? Like that young journalist accuses?'

'I'll tell you later.'

Chapter 27

Kelly studied the photos of the animals found dead in the forests surrounding Birkett Mire back in 2005. DC Emma Hide had been busy and had flagged up several curious factors not seen as significant on the original investigation. It was over fifteen years ago and yet something about the veterinary report on the animals found in the forests of Birkett Mire reminded her about the remains of the animals in Mary's yard. It wasn't long before she found the images she was looking for.

On the sheep, the marks had been put down to farmer branding. It was common amongst sheep farmers in the fells, whose flocks wandered freely, to brand them with either dye (a more modern method) or branding. The sheep were shorn and so no colour identification had been visible, giving rise to disputes between farmers who reported their livestock missing. However, what was visible were arrangements of crude markings on the undersides of the carcasses. The marks had scabbed and so it was clear that they'd been inflicted before the animals died. Some of the cats bore the same emblems etched into their skin. Kelly clicked on the original veterinary reports and looked for any mention of the other wildlife, notably birds.

She came across a photograph of a mound of feathers and, on closer inspection, realised that it was a pile of dead birds. She knew without checking that the birds were wrens. Suddenly she was taking an interest in birding. She could easily tell because of the distinctive golden stripe that could be taken for a ring above their eyes, as well as their razor-sharp tiny beaks, delicately poking above the pile of rotting corpses. It was a tragic pose.

Legend had the golden ring revered as a crown: thus the regal title of king arose. Kelly pondered that such a gathering of birds would have to be caught, just like Mary's wrens. From what Sandra told her, they wouldn't allow themselves to be tricked en masse like that; it would take incredible knowledge, experience and skill. They were quick and agile animals. The same was true of cats; though a few tasty nibbles under a basket would be enough to con the felines. The sheep would be easy to herd.

She studied the marks on the remains. She was sure she was looking at various arrangements of triangles. She compared them to the marks found on Mary Hales' animals and they were similar. Some of the triangles were upside down, and some had lines through them. The vet at the time had noted his findings, but the pressure on the police department then, of cases involving humans, took over, and the animal cruelty investigation took a back seat.

She googled triangular symbols, and the element of sulphur popped up on an alchemic table: just as the vet who wrote the report about Mary Hales' animals had said. Underneath, though, were links to other triangular symbols, and they made up the four characters of the elements: earth, air, water and fire. She compared them to the photographs taken in 2005. She was able to identify all four elements in the photographs and decided to get the same vet who autopsied Mary Hales' animals to go over the case. Emma was still working on the 2013 file from High Rigg. The more Kelly learned the more she became convinced that the animals were key to understanding this case.

She stretched and contemplated getting another coffee. But she was fully aware that, really, she was avoiding one task she'd put off all day. The unopened letter sat on her desk and stared back at her. She reached across to pick it up and tore open the seal.

Broadmoor Rehabilitation Home
Autumn 2018

Hello Kelly,

She stopped reading. Her stomach churned. The familiarity was revolting. Visions of women, maimed and terrified, came into her head and her hands shook. It had been a shitty week: the young woman at Castlerigg who'd disappeared into thin air, the murder of Mary Hales, and now this. She got up from her desk and closed her door. It was a thing that she rarely did, but she did it in an attempt to protect her team from the vileness that was about to spill out of the letter into the clean air of her office: she didn't want to infect them.

> *Hello Kelly,*
> *I have been following the local news up there in Cumbria and you've become quite the superstar, haven't you? I'm allowed an iPad now because I'm so well behaved — only you will appreciate the irony of this.*

She stopped again. She shook her head and the corners of her mouth turned up into a half-smile, half-snarl at The Teacher's arrogance. She noticed that her pulse was racing and, fleetingly, it reminded her of the initial emergency assessment of Carla Rigg at Castlerigg: her pulse was normal, despite her being in a state of trauma.

> *I meant it when I said that you and I have much in common. Your mind thinks like mine. They're very rare, you know, minds like ours. They have a long name here for all of my qualities, and I'm sure you've heard each one. I'm assigned so many head doctors that they lose track of one another, and I have to start all over again. It's super fun.*

Kelly was taken back to a time when she was in The Teacher's car, being driven through the dark streets of Penrith. She remembered the smell, the lurch of her stomach when certain words and phrases jolted her back to her reality, and the way the killer always referred to the two of them as kindred spirits. It made her shiver. That night she knew that if she didn't find Nikki, then she'd be dead by the morning. She'd acted as Amy Richmond's friend, or at least confidante, so she could save her sister. But Nikki never knew that.

> *Did you find the missing girl from the stone circle? I doubt it. One can't find something that burrows away from the light. Don't make the mistake of thinking that you happened upon her by chance; it was all planned. She'll appear again soon, but blink and you might miss her. But hurry, because time is running out. When the day meets the night, and darkness descends across the land, and the Moon Goddess returns to slumber, then only the spirits rule until balance returns.*
>
> *Sloppy slaying in Braithwaite. Amateur. I love animals. That part really made me sick.*
>
> *Namaste x*

Kelly stared at the letter. Her hands began to shake, and she couldn't stop them. Mary's body had been discovered late Friday afternoon, the news hadn't hit until the ten o'clock bulletin. How the hell could anyone get a letter here to Cumbria about it so soon? It was feasible that it had been posted first thing Saturday.

The content was wrong on so many levels – morally, personally, intellectually – and Kelly's initial instinct was to crumple the piece of paper between her hands and throw it into the waste paper bin, but she couldn't. Too many questions remained unanswered. It wasn't *why* a killer had decided to follow her two most recent cases that bothered her so much – any psychopath has to have an obsession, and Kelly had reluctantly accepted a long time ago that she had become The Teacher's fixation. So, it wasn't the personal nature of the letter that bothered her. It was more the tone of the narrative about the crimes themselves. *The girl at Castlerigg... Sloppy slaying at Braithwaite...* She was being taunted, and it angered her. She read over the letter again, this time without emotion: she was looking for what had triggered the uncomfortable feeling in her gut that Amy Richmond might have something more to say about her current cases. *One can't find something that burrows away from the light...*

And who the hell is the Moon Goddess?

Kelly had dabbled in the supernatural at university, as many young people did. Some bright spark bought a Ouija board, and they'd tried to contact somebody's dead grandmother or cat. One joker always pulled the glass around, making the girls scream, and somebody else freaked out, smashed the lights and blew out candles. It was all rite-of-passage stuff.

But to be taken seriously in an investigation, it was a tall order, and one that Kelly was having a hard time processing. She left her desk and went to find Rob. After all, it was he who'd spotted the tables in the homes of Fred and Mary, and likened them to altars. He'd actually used that word, 'altar'. Kelly had done a double take.

The incident room wasn't busy, with most available officers out on jobs, others sat hunched over their computers filling in reports and filing paperwork. She went to Rob's desk and perched on the edge.

'Guv?' he looked up.

'What can you tell me about Pagan worship?'

'I'm glad you asked. Look.' He brought up photos of tables decorated with various bits and pieces. Kelly looked at the one discovered at Mary's house.

'These are altars?' Her voice was sardonic but intrigued, and Rob smiled at her.

'I know what you think about all this stuff.' He wafted his hand around and pointed to the images. 'I'm not saying I'm a convert, or a believer; all I'm saying is that there are too many parallels to ignore here. They're the same connections I'd make on any case.'

Kelly folded her arms. 'Could I get it past HQ?'

'Nope.'

Kelly rolled her eyes. Rob ignored her protestations and carried on with his explanation.

'This is Mary's altar. Hers was a portable one, and she kept it behind a silk curtain. It was a very private thing. It's not as if we think she had many guests, but she still kept it out of view. If you look closely, it's set up for harvest festival.'

'You've been doing your homework.'

Kelly peered at the table in the photograph. It was very attractive. The curtain that was pulled away to reveal it was gold. The table itself was covered with an orange cloth and leaves were scattered around. There was a dried ear of maize, as well as other dried fruits, such as cut apples, and Kelly spotted cloves, thistles and other herbs. A small basket contained a small curved knife (the one she'd shown Ted) with a blade the shape of a crescent moon, and a cup was filled with yellow liquid. She recognised the yin-yang symbol and an incense burner, either side of which was one black and one white candle.

Kelly said nothing, but looked intently at the array of items on display. The thing that touched her most, once she studied the arrangement in detail, was the love and care on display; it wasn't just a few articles scattered here and there, like any messy table in households up and down the country. At first glance, the crime scene investigator, as well as the attending officers, including Kelly when she first saw the photos from the scene, thought it an occasional table full of ordinary household detritus. Except one thing.

'That knife. That could do some damage. But I did check with the coroner, he didn't think it was the right shape, but he hasn't come back to me with a definitive no just yet.'

'It's for cutting herbs, I looked it up. It's called a boline knife.'

'It's beautiful. Did Fred have one?'

'Not that I saw.'

Rob clicked a tab and another photo came on the screen. 'This is what I think is Fred's altar by his window: the one facing west. Mary's faced west, too, I had it confirmed.'

'Why west?'

'It's the direction of autumn.'

'The *direction* of autumn?'

'Every element has a direction and a season. Fire is south.'

Kelly opened her mouth but nothing came out. The tiny hairs on her arms stood up on end. She saw months of investigation before them, stretching out into possibly years, as they chased some spurious nods to witchcraft, ultimately making her look like a prize dickhead in front of HQ.

'Oh, God, Rob. You better make this watertight.'

Rob sat back and allowed Kelly to study the scanned image of his sketch, drawn hastily as she'd spoken to Fred and Sandra in their home. He'd labelled all of the articles and they were drawn in proportion so she could make them out clearly.

He was right. The table wasn't a receptacle for random household objects, forgotten in a hurry and not tidied away. There was order, love and care – just the same as Mary's. Fred's table was covered in a more subtle brown cloth. There weren't any leaves, but he had a small pumpkin, some nuts in their shells, a bowl of what looked like dried herbs, a similar incense burner and two candles: one white and one black.

'I don't know if you remember, but his table was partially covered with another cloth, as if he'd done it as we arrived.'

'He hasn't got as many things on it as Mary.'

'I reckon he tidied some away for our benefit.'

'Like maybe a boline knife?'

'How thoughtful. Rob, does the Moon Goddess mean anything to you?'

'Actually it does. I came across her when I was researching the magic tools.' He looked at her awkwardly.

'Magic tools?'

'The items used for Pagan worship, the boline knife being one of them. She's a Pagan goddess, the ultimate symbol of femininity.'

Kelly felt a sinking feeling in her stomach.

'Are there any other types of knives used as magic tools?'

'Yes, this one.' Rob brought a picture up on his screen and Kelly examined it. Like the boline knife, it was beautiful and lethal. Small and straight and bejewelled. It was called an athame.

Chapter 28

Daphne fitted in easily amongst the people coming and going at the climbing centre. She looked like any other teenager wanting to purchase a chocolate bar from the vending machine, and toying with the idea of joining a new club to meet new friends. The club was large enough to be anonymous, and no one looked oddly at her for wearing sunglasses indoors. The entrance was lit by natural light, gushing in from an atrium above. It was reverent almost, and she squinted as she looked up. It reminded her of a church.

She wore skinny jeans and a cropped top with words emblazoned on the front. Over that she'd casually thrown a fur jacket; it replaced the one she'd left in the field near Castlerigg. The exact details of the visit to the stone circle still hadn't come back to her, and it sat uneasy under her ribcage. She possessed a laptop computer and watched the news, but she kept it from her parents, who were less inclined to partake in modern technology, seeing it as an indulgence. The computer had been bought with her own money and she'd worked out how to connect to the internet via an old cable under the house. It took a phone call and a bank card (stolen) to get the connection working again.

She'd seen her picture online, as well as her clothes, when she'd googled the incident, but the fuss was beginning to die down and no news channels ran the story any more. She figured that with lack of evidence – or a person – the case had fallen flat. She was just a woman wandering round, probably drunk or lost, who'd decided she didn't want to be found. Simple. The police had other more pressing things to investigate, such as the recent murder of that woman.

She approached the notice board and looked at some photographs of kids enjoying themselves climbing. They smiled at the camera and larked about, hanging off ropes and giving thumbs up to the photographer, whoever that might have been. It was an advert for fun. She peered at the facial expressions: they weren't the type that she usually saw. Wide grins, fresh faces and sparkling eyes were alien to her. It unsettled her and she felt vulnerable, and out of her depth. She couldn't imagine being surrounded by such joy. And noise. She searched the faces but Callum wasn't among them. Perhaps he was a new member.

'Hi. You looking for something?' A young man stood next to her wearing the familiar light blue T-shirt of the club with its logo on his breast. She looked at his name badge: David. Her senses jarred at the cordiality.

'Hi. I'm thinking of joining.' She managed to speak convincingly well.

He grinned broadly and asked her if she'd like a tour. She noticed that he stared at her sunglasses but she kept them on. She agreed and tried hard to take great interest in everything David told her. He informed her of upcoming trips, classes for novices, taster sessions and where they climbed. In the end, she agreed to have a half hour taster with him, and he told her he was free now. She signed some paperwork and followed him to a large hall where noise assaulted her. She stopped and held her head. In the entrance, the light flooding from the ceiling had soothed her, but now, with the echo and acoustics of the vast hall, and the shouting from children being taught a physical sport, she had to stop and breathe deeply.

'Are you all right?' David asked.

'Yes. I think I've got a migraine coming. Would you mind if we did this another time? I'm so sorry.'

'That's why you wear sunglasses? I understand now. Of course. My sister gets migraines, they're awful.'

'I'm so sorry.' She left the hall and went through the reception area, back into the car park where she'd parked. She sat on a wall and took deep breaths. Sweat gathered at her temples, and she searched her bag for a bottle of water and gulped it deeply. The noise in her head settled down and she was able to see more clearly. She had what she came for after all: all she needed was dates and times of sessions and events, and she'd find him; she was confident of that. She got up and straightened her jacket, and walked back to her van.

Before she'd driven five minutes down the road, her head began with its analysis: images of people milling about the centre, a man in the coffee shop, the woman buying a helmet, and David, all accosted her. How had they behaved towards her? Were any of them like her? Did she recognise any of them as visitors? Did one of them watch her suspiciously? She went through the series of questions one by one, eliminating them all. She felt like an imposter: a different species in the skin of another. Her mind threw up a cacophony of scenarios – none of them to her liking

All she wanted to do was find that connection that she'd felt so keenly at Castlerigg. It had been both real and unreal, physical and heady, spiritual and elemental. She'd never felt anything like it before, even when her father taught her how to explore it. Connection to things other than oneself was a fundamental part of her learning, and she'd practised so many times in fields and woods with foxes, birds and insects. Sometimes it worked and sometimes it didn't. Most of the time she ended up dismissing it as all a pile of crap and she gave up, stomping home to lie on her bed, branding herself a failure. But at the stones, when he looked at her: she'd felt it then.

She slammed on the brakes. A couple crossed the road, laughing and joking with one another, as if oblivious to the fact that she could have fucking killed them both. She flung her arms up as if to say, 'what the hell were you both thinking?' They stopped giggling and slowly the realisation of what had just occurred hit them. But it wasn't the anger that coursed through Daphne's body that arrested her and made her lower her arms and slowly drive around them. It was the face of the male.

It was Callum. He was with a girl.

She drove away, peering in her rear-view mirror to check that he hadn't recognised her. Of course he wouldn't: recognition is 99 per cent in the eyes, and hers were covered, thank God. She watched, and saw him looking at her vehicle as she pulled away. The girl put her hand in his and pulled him away from the road.

They were close.

Her heart raced as she reached the main road and pulled onto it. As she drove back home to the farm, she remembered the tiny details of what he was wearing, what colour his hair was (she hadn't seen it that clearly at dawn, near the stones), what he wore, how his clothes fell over his body and his hands. Her skin began to tingle again, but this time it was tinged with pain.

She could be a relative.

Unlikely.

She could be a friend.

She'd soon find out.

Chapter 29

'It doesn't necessarily follow that what happened to Mary was directly linked to her lifestyle.'

Joe fended off a thousand questions from his wife.

'I would have thought that was perfectly obvious.'

'You're doing what anyone who reads gossip is doing: jumping to conclusions. There's no evidence whatsoever that Mary had got herself into something that was dangerous or couldn't handle. That's not what it's about, Annie, for God's sake.'

'How can you use that word when you don't even believe in God?'

'It's a generic term for all deities.'

'Don't patronise me!'

Joe was frustrated. He wanted to leave the house. Arguing with any female was always a bad idea, but when it was his wife he never stood a chance, even though he might be right and she in the wrong. She never saw it like that. In her mind, and those of the surrounding areas who were beginning to suspect that Mary was dabbling in some form of dark arts, she'd got herself in too deep and got herself killed.

'Look at this,' Annie waved the local paper in front of his face. She pointed to an article by a local journalist about the prevalence of Paganism in the area and a tenuous link to Mary's death. Joe noticed that it was the same young journalist who'd written the article that upset Fred: Carry Tomlin

'That's enough, Annie. Fred has lost a dear friend, and I'm done with this small town speculation.'

'You always thought yourself too important for simple folk not concerned with the business of saving the goddamn world, starting here with piles of stones and sheep.'

It was a low blow but one he'd heard before. Joe was an outsider. He was born in Nottingham and, as such, was not considered a local in Cumbria, despite the fact that he'd lived there for over twenty years. Occasionally, Annie used it when she was sifting through her arsenal during a heated altercation, overlooking the fact that she was from Cornwall originally. There was truth in it, and that's what hurt; he knew that he overcompensated on the conservation side to show his loyalty to the county. It was a desperate act and it surprised him. He stared at her, not knowing what to say. It was thoroughly juvenile and pointless to argue against. He walked out, and expected the parting shot.

'That's right, walk away. That's what you do best.'

He slammed the door and walked to his car. The boys were out. Connor was at a friend's and Callum had gone to the climbing wall. He'd finally told them about a girl he'd met there. She was called Josie. They'd asked to meet her but Callum had shut down, blushing. They dropped it; he'd introduce them in good time if that's what he wanted. No doubt, like all relationships at their age, it would last two weeks and they'd never know who she was. He tried to remember what it was like meeting a girl when he was sixteen. All he could recall were Tina Galway's breasts. He dreamt about them every night. Soon, their eldest son would be more interested in a girl's breasts than them. Perhaps it had already happened. He'd had 'the talk' with both of his sons, and they'd reacted like he supposed he had at their ages.

'I know, Dad. God, that's disgusting.' Or words to that effect. Annie was better at it. She'd offered to buy Callum some condoms but he'd looked horrified and said he didn't need them, but he'd be sure to let her know when he did. Joe got into the car and drove away with the intention of driving somewhere remote. But as he left the main road, he decided to call on Fred to see how he was holding up. One of the reasons he'd begun arguing with Annie in the first place was that she'd asked him to stay away from Fred and Sandra. He'd said it was a ludicrous suggestion and they would need friends more than ever now.

The sky shone orange and shadows grew longer and longer each day. His journey took him under the canopies of Blencathra and Skiddaw: two of his favourite mountains. It irked him that his own wife called him a foreigner and a fake. He lived and breathed these valleys and fells.

He pulled up outside Fred's house. The pretty cottage exuded charm and contentment. Sandra was the one who answered the door and he noticed her face change dramatically at the surprise. It had been slack, sparkle-less and drained. Now, her eyes flashed with enthusiasm, she stood taller, and her face came alive.

'Joe! What a lovely surprise! Come in!' She was emphatic and warm, and Joe smiled, happy with his decision. She fussed over him and bombarded him with questions. One thing she didn't mention was Mary.

'How's Fred?' he asked. The shadow that had haunted her face earlier returned and she wrung her hands.

'Not good. It's a terrible shock. It'll take time. They were very close, and she was such a gentle spirit.'

Joe knew that Sandra used the word spirit in its purest sense: the essence of a human. It was true. The little he knew of Mary suggested nothing else.

'Can I see him?'

'Of course! Fred! Joe is here to see you.' She led him into the front room and they found Fred going to stand up, and damning his aching knees. He'd clearly been sat for a while. Fred outstretched his hand.

'Joe! It's good to see you. Good heavens, I'm sorry about that business on Sunday. Shocking. I hope Annie and the boys weren't too upset.'

'They'll be fine. I came to see how you both are. I know you were great friends.'

'We were. I still can't believe she's gone. I just can't understand it.'

'Sometimes these things can be random. It could have been an intruder who didn't expect her to be there.'

Fred shook his head. 'Perhaps you're right. Anyone who knew her couldn't have done it.'

'Can I get you some tea?' Sandra fulfilled her role as hostess, Joe accepted gratefully, and she disappeared.

'There's a newspaper article suggesting that Mary's, erm – religion – played a part.'

'Hogwash! Who's saying such things?'

'I brought it.' Joe unfolded the article that he'd removed from the paper and passed it to Fred, who scanned it quietly, tutting at sections and shaking his head.

'My God! Who is this woman? Carry Tomlin! Bloody hell. Well, blow me down! Who does she think she is?'

'She's out to cause trouble, that's for sure,' Joe said. He felt wretched for his old friend.

'She's the one who Mary and I were discussing only last week. It was the last time I saw her – at a meeting. I was ranting on about this young idiot and what she had to say about us.'

'Us?'

'You know, our groups.' Fred wafted his hand around, indicating that the defining edges of meaning surrounding various Pagan groups in Cumbria were blurry.

'Could there be any truth to it?'

'Why?' Fred became agitated.

'I'm sorry. I didn't mean to indicate that I believed it to be true, of course I don't, but the article makes sense. What if Mary did find herself in too deep? You know what happened last time.'

Fred sat back heavily in his armchair and looked away. Joe sat down. 'What do you think?' he asked.

'He's long gone.'

'But I told you I saw his daughter.'

'You were mistaken.'

'No, I wasn't, Fred. I would never misplace those blue eyes. It was her. I'm telling you, he's back. They're back. They might never have left at all for all you know.'

'There was no reason for him to stay. He gave us all a bad name.'

'But what if he is back? Mary rejected him. Not only that, it was very public, in front of everybody there, and he was obviously snubbed. We've all listened to enough crime reports to know that a jilted lover is the prime suspect in the vast majority of crimes. I think we need to tell the police.'

'I'll have nothing to do with it.'

'You'll have to if I tell them.'

Fred looked at Joe.

'You'd do that to me, Joe?' It was a moment that made Joe waver. Fred stared at him with hurt and fear behind his eyes. He tried to work out what Fred was more scared of: the police or Kirk Junker.

'I can't get her out of my head, Fred. She was terrified and probably high on something. We never saved her all those years ago. I feel it's my duty to try now. And what if he did kill Mary? I'd never forgive myself if I didn't try everything to get justice for her.'

'You barely knew her.'

'I know. But I know you, and I know you're suffering. And I could ease that pain, even if it doesn't seem like it today. Surely finding out the truth about Mary would put her spirit to rest? What's stopping you?'

'That if it is him, then I'm guessing I'll be next.'

Chapter 30

Carry Tomlin drove to a remote wooded area south of Keswick, and towards Thirlmere. The address she'd been given was a campsite at the foot of the Helvellyn range. The road on Thirlmere's eastern shoreline was dotted with car parks, and was a popular starting point for those wanting a short, sharp, tough climb to the summit of the majestic Helvellyn. Most walkers used Glenridding as a base, and meandered through the rolling valleys of Birkhouse Moor to get to the iconic peak; fewer used the road next to the Thirlmere Reservoir. She had no idea if her contact was a hiker, a camper or simply using the location because of the sensitivity of the subject. A public place was commonly the preferred site for a clandestine meeting with a nervous informer. It meant that if the volunteer changed his or her mind, then they could walk away without being coerced or making a fuss. She'd had dozens of prank calls about her recent articles, but this one seemed genuine, and the caller appeared to know much about the occult and the prevalence of various groups around north Cumbria. Carry couldn't let the opportunity pass her by, and she gladly agreed to meet the stranger.

It was a perfect Lakes day and she hummed to a pop song on the radio. For her age, her career had begun a startling upward trajectory recently, and she was loving every minute of it. It was a chance conversation with a university lecturer that had got her started on the topic of the occult and its links to crime. She was fully aware that the vast majority of covens (that was the official word for a gathering of Pagans) were peaceful, spiritual and non-threatening entities. However, there was growing evidence to suggest that the dark arts were making a comeback due to the godlessness and chaos of modern life. There was a real feeling that spiritualism was lacking in the world, and a few notable figures had begun looking for alternatives to organised religion. It was estimated that nineteen covens existed in Cumbria alone and her whistleblower had told her that Mary Hales was a member of one of them.

It was the kind of lead that makes one's palms sweaty and the heart race. If true, the news could potentially make for a ground-breaking article of journalistic content in the possession of no one else. She'd tried to interview other members of Mary's coven, without success.

Beyond a stretch of dual carriageway, she spotted a small car park underneath some trees and flicked on her indicator. There was one other car in the clearing. She pulled up next to it and turned off the engine. There was no one in the other vehicle and so she looked around and got out. She checked her phone, aware that she had no idea what her contact looked like. One could guess from a voice but they were often wildly incorrect. Her phone buzzed and made her jump. She had a new text.

'Drive down the Great How Road towards Raven Crag. I'll meet you at the farm gates, about two hundred yards from the main road,' it read.

Carry looked around her and shrugged her shoulders. Maybe her informant had got cold feet and didn't even trust the isolation of a small car park. Though she did usually see National Trust car parks pretty full most of the time in the Lake District. It was worse in summer, of course, but even out of season, it was difficult to find parking along the most popular routes. She walked back to her car and got in, starting the engine. She was torn between excitement at some juicy information for a new article, and concern that she was being wound up. If the meeting was a hoax, she'd be angry and frustrated. She decided to give it one more go and drive to the supposed farm gates, wherever they were. There were no signs indicating a farm, but she kept looking for the gate.

The text was bang on. She waved when she saw a figure standing near the gate and they waved back, opening the wooden structure to allow a car in. She was directed to a vehicle parked behind away from the road, out of sight, and it was made clear to her that she should follow it. There must be some acreage to the farm, Carry thought, as well as some money. They rounded a clearing and she spotted a slate farmhouse, nestled in a natural dip in the countryside. The vehicle pulled up outside and Carry parked beside it. She grabbed her bag containing all of her notes and a dictaphone, as well as a bottle of water. Her stomach was knotty, and it was a familiar feeling when she thought she'd sniffed something valuable. She was excited.

They shook hands and Carry was cordially invited inside.

It was only once they were in the hallway, and Carry looked around, that she realised that the family wasn't perhaps as well off as she'd assumed. The décor was shoddy, the house was freezing and the furniture looked dusty and dirty. There was also a foul smell, and Carry covered her mouth. She heard the buzz of flies and guessed the place was a hovel. 'Can I make you a drink?' she was asked. It was a mild-mannered voice, immature almost, and it touched Carry that perhaps her source was nervous too. She relaxed a little.

'I'm so sorry about the smell. One of the dogs crawled under the house, after a rat, and we didn't find her until it was too late.' As if on cue, Carry heard barking.

'Oh, what a shame!' she said.

'It was the smell that led us to her. We've cleaned and cleaned but it still lingers.'

'The poor thing. I've got water, thank you. Shall we talk about what you told me over the phone?' Carry asked.

'Of course. I wasn't comfortable meeting down at the car park. It felt silly in the end, sitting in the middle of nowhere, as if I've done something wrong, when I could invite you here.'

'Well, thank you. Is anyone else home?' Carry asked.

'Just the dogs. Come on, I'll introduce you.'

'How did you know Mary Hales?' Carry felt as though she might as well dive straight in.

'I recognised her photo in the news. I used to frequent the same kind of groups as she did.'

'Covens?'

'They could be called that, yes. I came to the conclusion that I was perhaps a bit too cynical for the average member, so I stopped attending, but Mary was a High Priestess: very high up in rank. She ran things. When I read your articles, I thought you might like to know. You seem interested in it.'

'Oh, I am. Could you tell me about the coven? Any names? Meeting times? Locations? Rituals?'

'Let's go and sit down shall we?'

'I'm sorry, I'm bombarding you with questions.'

'It's not a problem, I need to feed the dogs, that's all.'

Carry followed into another hall and through two more doors. The interior of the house was dark and lifeless and Carry thought that it must be a depressing existence living here. The smell became stronger and she stopped following.

'In here.'

Carry paused, but she shook away the nagging doubt and went into a large room, where she could hear the dogs. Two hounds bounded over to her and jumped up and she recoiled away when she smelled them. They stank, as if they'd been living with the dead dog for weeks: maybe they had. They slobbered on her and she noticed a brown, foul smelling gunk around their mouths.

Then she saw their bowls.

One contained part of a human hand.

Carry's instinct was to run, but her exit was blocked by her host. She desperately looked around for another way out, but she knew there was none. The dogs barked and licked her hands. She pushed them away and screamed for help.

'We're five miles from our closest neighbour. No one will hear you.'

Carry stopped screaming and breathed deeply. Her chest heaved up and down and she made tiny whimpering noises. Her ears pounded with silence and her host smiled at her. Without thinking, she threw herself forward and hurled her whole weight at the sick fuck that she'd trusted. She had no time to question her foolishness as she charged ahead, but the dogs caught her from behind and felled her with their combined mass. She felt their teeth bearing down on her ankle and calves. Her jeans ripped and she squealed as one of the animals bit into her flesh. She tried to fight them off, but only ended up protecting her face from them. She felt their teeth and their growls as they became more aggressive and bloodthirsty in their attack. She tried to scream but no sound came out. The dogs bit her hands and she curled into a ball.

Then they were called away.

Chapter 31

'I cannot believe that my sister talked to that journalist.'

'Yes you can.'

Kelly and Johnny ran from the climbing centre along to Castlerigg stone circle. Something about visiting the place with Rob had renewed her fascination and it seemed the perfect opportunity as Josie enjoyed a climbing lesson. They climbed a lesser known road up towards the field and entered the gates. Perhaps a dozen tourists walked around the magnificent monoliths and took photos. Some climbed up on to them, as was permitted, and children ran around them. Kelly and Johnny ran around the full circle and stopped to admire the view.

Kelly had been shown the article by Johnny. She'd dismissed the witchcraft stuff as unhelpful and amateur, but the writer – Carry Tomlin – had managed to use the piece referring to Mary Hales' death as a vehicle for also criticising the police. Her sister, Nikki, had been interviewed as part of the piece on police incompetence and Dave Crawley's case was used against them.

Dave Crawley had been released early from a prison sentence earlier in the year and it had been Kelly who put him away. He won his appeal on lack of evidence and Kelly was livid. It happened: she couldn't lose sleep over it, but it just so happened that Nikki was Dave Crawley's wife's best friend and she held her personally responsible for the downturn in her friend's fortunes. The story was laboriously retold by Nikki to Carry Tomlin in glorious technicolour. And now it was in print.

Kelly thought that Dave Crawley's wife might want to reassess her taste in men (Crawley's original conviction had been for people trafficking in his lorries out of Europe), but on this occasion, it was Kelly's judgement that was in question, not that of the criminal. It pushed thousands of Kelly's buttons simultaneously. Only a run could sweat it out, and even then not all of it.

'It's because she knows it will get under your skin,' Johnny said.

'And it has. It's not so much the journalist: her articles might be read by a thousand people and forgotten. It's her criticism of my team.'

'Come on. Focus on the good. You know it's bullshit and that's all that matters. You're not mentioned by name. You can't let her concern you, she knows nothing about your job. No one will associate you two. It hurts because she's your sister. She wouldn't have done it if your mum was still here.'

'I know.' The pain of missing Wendy was still keen. Both her mother and John Porter had been taken too young. Cancer. It was tragically unfair.

'I wish I could ignore her.'

'It's a good excuse to do just that,' Johnny said.

'What?'

'She's betrayed you in a very public forum. It's shitty behaviour. You are fully justified to break off any ties to her. Your mum's house is sold, you don't need to have anything to do with her any more.'

'What about the kids?' Nikki had three daughters.

'Send them gifts and cards. They'll make their own minds up when they're old enough.'

'It's harsh, I still feel responsible.'

'For putting a trafficker away where he belonged?'

'For taking a man away from his family.'

'No. Don't let Nikki win. Dave Crawley is scum and he got what he deserved. What about the girls that died because of him? You'll never find out how many had their lives ruined because of him. Think of the young girls, chained to beds in a stinking flat in Workington, sold to vagrant trade for sex.'

'I know. You're right.'

They stood watching the families and tourists talking about the stones and pointing to various points around the natural amphitheatre. Kelly guessed that's why it had been built there in the first place: because it was in a natural dip surrounded by mountains. It was a dramatic setting. Johnny stretched his calves and Kelly jumped up and down on the spot.

'Ted said to me that I should try and heal the rift for Mum's sake.'

'Really? That surprises me. He doesn't know what's gone on. Do you want me to have a word?'

'No, but thank you.'

'I guess as you get older, you feel mortal and arguments seem pointless. Ready?' he asked.

Kelly nodded.

'What do you think about black magic?'

'What do you mean?' They left the circle and ran north towards the fields separating the ancient monument from the main road. They crossed a tiny single carriageway road and on into more fields.

'Satan worship, ritual sacrifice, symbols and signs... you know, Tarot cards and that sort of thing. The journalist is basically theorising that Mary Hales was into all of that and died as a consequence of it.'

'It's a huge topic. It's not all one thing is it? Was she into it?'

'We think she might have been, but to what extent we just don't know. But do you believe in it?'

'That it happens? Yes. Of course. People always want to believe that spirits exist. It's comforting. But I don't believe that you can conjure them or anything whacky like that. Don't tell me you're being persuaded?' He asked.

'It's just odd that I keep seeing evidence of weird markings and symbols at the crime scenes of a few cold cases, and at Mary Hales' house.'

'I take it that information is unknown to the public?'

'Of course. It's something I don't even understand. Rob reckons she had a Pagan altar, and he's convinced me.'

They didn't speak for a few minutes and she could tell that he was thinking.

'Maybe you shouldn't confuse their beliefs with the case: the two could be unconnected entirely. It's like a murder of a Catholic person or a Jewish person automatically being linked to their faith: it's not more or less likely than any other theory. Keep it in mind and investigate it like you do best. The answers will come.' He smiled reassuringly and she nodded. Their snippets of chat, chewing over sticky elements of her work, were moments of pleasure not because of the subject matter but because they got to spend time together talking, and he always made her feel better. It was a connection that they shared, and it was valuable in a hectic world.

'When does Josie get to climb outdoors?'

'I've paid for her to go to a relatively small test climb near Sharp Edge on Blencathra.'

'Sharp Edge!'

'It's not what it sounds like.'

Sharp Edge was one of the most challenging scrambles in the entire district and cherished by climbers.

'She won't do it all, it's just a section and it's low down. Then on Friday she goes to somewhere called Woden's Face.'

'I've never heard of it.'

'Neither had I. It's down in the Borrowdale valley.'

'And is Callum going?' Johnny had told Kelly what he knew of Josie's mystery love interest who she'd met at the climbing centre.

'He is.'

'Can you remember your first love?' she asked. They continued to follow a low dry-stone wall along a field to the east of the stone circle.

Johnny caught his breath. 'Christ, that's going back a bit. She was called Tracey and she broke my heart.'

'No! Bitch. Mine was called James and he broke mine too.'

'Well, we're both scorned lovers. James was an idiot.'

'So was Tracey.'

They ran on, coming to another road. They paused to check for traffic and ran across. An old sign attached to a fence caught Kelly's eye.

'It's a missing person poster.'

'Recent? Why don't you know about it?'

Kelly stopped running and approached the fence. She leaned closer and read the information. It was laminated but the age of the sign meant the photograph was almost invisible from weathering and the wording was difficult to read.

'Missing boy. 2003. Contact Mrs Edna Beverley.' The name of the boy was faded too much but the phone number wasn't. Kelly got her phone out and took a picture of it. The picture was grainy but she reckoned that the boy was a teenager. She hoped he'd been found.

'I'm going to check that out. I've been sifting through cold cases lately but the name Beverley doesn't ring any bells. Let's hope he was found quickly.'

'The boy could have had a different name to the contact.'

'Sure. Should we make our way back to the car?' she asked. Johnny agreed and they ran back along the road, coming to the main road and heading to the climbing centre car park. Josie came out of the entrance with a boy. She didn't spot her father, or Kelly, and she was holding hands with him. Kelly nudged Johnny.

'Oh God,' he covered his eyes. 'My little girl.'

'Don't scare him away, will you?'

'I've already been given a warning by her. I'm going over.'

Kelly pulled him back. 'Wait. You'll embarrass her.'

'That's the point.' He strode over to the entrance and shouted Josie, who immediately dropped the boy's hand and blushed. Johnny waved manically and Kelly ran up behind him to try to offer the voice of reason, should it be needed.

'I'm Josie's dad,' Johnny said and outstretched his hand for Callum to take.

'Dad!' Josie looked livid. Callum took his hand and shook it.

'And your name?'

'Callum.'

'Hi.' Kelly caught them up. 'Good session?'

The teenagers went mute and Josie's cheeks burned. Kelly felt for her. 'Hi! When are you climbing at Blencathra?' Kelly asked. It worked as a diversion and Josie told her the details and said goodbye to Callum, who walked away quickly.

They went back to Johnny's car.

'Thanks, Dad. That was so embarrassing.'

'I want to know who you're hanging around with.'

Josie sulked all the way home and as soon as Johnny parked outside his house, she got out of the car and slammed the door.

'Well done, I think you handled that beautifully,' Kelly said.

'Will you come in for dinner?'

'You mean for some moral support? I'll go home and get showered first.'

They kissed and she got out of the car. Her cottage was a five-minute walk from Johnny's house. When she got in, she clicked on her iPad for any updates and saw an email from Ted. She opened it and saw that it was an invitation to attend a forensic conference with him at Lancaster University. There were to be several guest speakers and he suggested grabbing dinner with his other daughters, June and Amber. She replied and said she'd check her diary, and if she was able to, then she'd love to. They'd met once before. It had been a success and Kelly liked both of the women. They were like their father: easy going, calm and kind, unless they were bickering. Maybe that's why Ted thought that her relationship with Nikki could be salvaged, because they merely bickered. But he didn't see underneath it. He probably assumed that all sisters squabbled. His daughters both lived in Lancaster with their partners, and so Ted saw them frequently. She hadn't asked why there were no grandchildren; it was none of her business, but she knew that Ted would have loved some. For now, Josie was fulfilling that role.

In his email, Ted also confirmed that the curved knife at Mary's house couldn't have been the second blade; the shape wasn't right. He had yet to comment on the athame. The problem was that all athames were different, precisely because they were ornamental, and they hadn't found an example at Mary's or Fred's.

As she went upstairs to get a shower, she chomped on a cereal bar grabbed in haste from the cupboard. She called Eden House and spoke to the duty officer for the evening, tasking him with finding out what happened to a missing boy in 2003 whose mother was called Edna Beverley. She'd already dialled the number and listened to a dead tone. The phone had obviously gone out of use.

He called back as she stepped out of the shower, soaking wet and ill prepared to take a call. She wrapped a towel around her anyway and answered, trying to dry her hands at least.

'Guv, the boy's name was William Beverley and he was never found, I'm afraid. He was twelve at the time. The case went cold in 2009.'

She hung up with a heavy heart and promised herself she'd look into the case first thing in the morning.

Chapter 32

Joe Spencer's address was a farmhouse in the middle of nowhere, off the A66. By all accounts, it was a perk of his job with English Heritage. The surrounding farm was still actively worked and it looked prosperous to Kelly and Rob, who approached along a concrete single track on Wednesday morning. It had been five days since Mary's death, and they'd cleared pretty much every lead they'd created. The victim hadn't had visitors, there was no CCTV of her near her house, her diary hadn't given them any clues about those present in her life, Fred O'Reilly had given them no reason to treat him as a suspect, and her team had found no holes in the testimony of the other 'birdwatching' group members. It was looking more and more like a random psychotic incident, or even an animal rights activist making a point. It might seem perverse for an animal campaigner to hurt animals but sometimes that's exactly what they did, if it meant making a point. None of it sat easily with Kelly or Rob, and they considered the possibility that Mary had found herself a member of a satanic cult probable: she was lonely, she dabbled in Paganism and she could be classed as vulnerable.

Joe Spencer and his wife Annie had been in attendance at the house of the O'Reillys when they were informed of Mary's death. He'd also been the man who found the woman wandering around Castlerigg. It was a small community; however, with a murderer on the loose – potentially still in the area – Kelly was concerned for the young woman who'd seemed confused and vulnerable. She still wanted to locate her to make sure she was safe. Joe Spencer needed ruling out as a person of interest.

The lane to the farmhouse was long, but finally they arrived and parked outside. It was a stone-built cottage, attached to a wooden annex, which looked as though it had once been a cattle shed or something similar. Kelly noted the peace of the place, though they heard the odd sheep from afar. They approached the door and Rob knocked.

'Winter's almost here,' Rob said, looking at the sky.

'That's cheery,' Kelly said. Rob smiled and spread his hands.

'I'm a summer bloke.'

'I know you are. You're also a northerner, so man up.'

They heard a noise behind the door and a woman answered. She was expecting them. Kelly introduced herself and Rob. The woman welcomed them and said that she was Annie Spencer. She invited them inside and Joe was waiting for them in the kitchen, sat at the table, sipping tea. He stood up.

Kelly hadn't before met the man who'd found Carla Rigg wandering around naked in the early hours of last Monday morning. She'd read his statement, and those of his wife and children, but now she came face to face with him, and she was struck by his calmness: he reminded her of Johnny. The realisation jarred her, but she soon gathered herself and sat down when she was invited, as did Rob. Annie busied herself fixing refreshments.

'We'd like to ask you a few questions about Mary Hales and how you knew her.'

'Still haven't caught anyone, then?' Joe asked. Kelly felt the question to be rhetorical.

'No. Sadly not. Our inquiries are ongoing. We're piecing together movements of the deceased and where she might have been, or who she might have seen before her death.'

'We didn't see her very much. She was Fred's friend, really. I met her a few times at parties, at his house; you know, garden barbecues in the summer, that sort of thing. I thought – we thought – she was a lovely woman.'

'Everybody has said that,' Rob said. Annie put tea in front of them on a small table, as well as some biscuits. Rob took one happily.

'When was the last time you saw her?'

'Probably last year. She looked well and was in good spirits, as she always was.' Joe saw Kelly looking at Annie and added, 'My wife wasn't there.' Annie turned away from her husband and began washing pots at the sink.

'Mrs Spencer? When was the last time you saw Mary?' Kelly asked. The woman stopped washing and took off her gloves. She turned back to face them.

'I really can't recall, I think it was at Fred's, one Sunday a few years back. All the times I saw her she never struck me as down, or worried, or scared; there was no hint of thinking she might be in danger. I really can't get my head around what happened.'

'Thank you. What you're both telling us really echoes everybody else's statements who knew her. It leaves us the question of a random attack. I have another question for you, though. There are rumours, and have been articles in the press, about black magic and Pagan worship. Of course, it's conjecture and might be nothing, but I wondered if you ever saw any evidence of independent religious worship going on with Mary, or indeed Fred. Did they ever talk about a particular kind of gathering where they attended and worshipped spirits, for example?'

Kelly waited. She noticed that Joe shifted in his seat and looked uncomfortable. Kelly felt a damn fool. She was ready to tell the couple to forget her last question when Annie Spencer tutted loudly.

'Oh, come on, Joe! Tell the woman what you know and get it off your chest!' Annie virtually spat out the words. Kelly and Rob stared at Joe. He spread his hands.

'Can I just say: Fred is no black magic worshipper. My wife has a different view of the religion that Fred follows and Mary followed.'

'Religion! It's dangerous, that's what it is,' Annie interrupted again.

'Of course it's not bloody dangerous! Christ, Annie, you're delusional!'

Kelly and Rob stared at one another as the married couple vented. It wasn't the first domestic they had witnessed as police officers, and it wouldn't be the last. They waited patiently for the partners to stop their sparring.

'Perhaps it might be better if we spoke to you both separately?' Kelly suggested.

'Fine, I'll go and bring in some logs.' Annie left the room. Joe looked at the officers. The door banged as Annie left.

'We disagree on Fred's passion for Paganism.'

'Is it an organised form of religion, then? People meet, follow scripture, worship images and pray? I just need to get this clear for myself,' Kelly asked.

'Of course. It's just like any form of group devotion, it's just that most were associated with witchcraft and the dark arts during the ascendancy of the Christian Church, and they died for it. It's had a bad image ever since. You know, the lonely old hag in the forest with a black cat? She used to be seen as the wise woman, who used herbs and nature to heal, but the Church wanted people to believe that only God could heal, and so they destroyed ancient learning and replaced it with their own, burning witches as they went.'

'That's a damn fine history lesson, but why are people so scared of it? Why does my team and I keep reading about spiritual symbols, ritual sacrifice and demons?'

'Because that's the reputation it's been given. Fred doesn't belong to any large organisation; Pagans tend to organise themselves and meet with like-minded people, to basically revere nature. It's all about the rhythms of the seasons and the sun and the moon: just like it was thousands of years ago. You must have heard of the Druids?'

Kelly nodded. 'Of course, they transformed into wrens, right?' Joe stared at her with an odd expression on his face.

'I'm impressed, yes, legend has it that they did.'

Kelly carried on. 'Am I right in thinking that the bird-watching group that Fred and Sandra told us about is perhaps a Pagan group? And am I also right in thinking that perhaps part of what they did involved worshipping a Moon Goddess?'

Joe looked down at his feet and sighed.

'Yes and, yes. It's called a coven, but they don't tend to use the term because covens are associated with witches, thanks to Shakespeare, of course.'

'Quite. So why would Fred be so secretive about something that sounds quite beautiful to me? I like the sound of worshipping nature, isn't that what a lot of peace-loving people around the world still do?'

'Yes, communities have done it for centuries, but have always been victimised for it, which is probably why Fred was less than willing to share the information.'

'Right, so let's get this straight: Mary was part of the group?'

'She was the High Priestess.'

'Run that by me again,' Kelly said. Rob stopped eating.

'Every group has a High Priest and a High Priestess who run it. They shouldn't be a couple themselves – as Mary and Fred weren't. It just means they've had more experience and training than the others.'

'So, Mary was a leader? Did anyone stand to gain from taking that title away from her?'

'I can't think of anyone, and, as you know, everybody respected and admired her. But there is one person that I thought had left the area a long time ago, who Mary upset.'

Kelly glanced at Rob. They both sat up a little taller. Rob put down his half eaten biscuit. 'Go on,' said Kelly.

'It's a long story,' said Joe.

'You have our attention,' Kelly said.

'I was thinking about joining Fred's group. Annie was less convinced but agreed to learn more about it. I work in nature, I see it all about me. I think that the basic mores of what Fred and Mary put across were quite beautiful, and it all makes sense to me. Everything revolves around seasons: light and dark.'

'Light and dark?'

'Yes, the science and awe of the cycle of the year. So, the beginning of the year is in February, when the ewes first lactate for the spring lambs. From then on, the nights get shorter and the days get longer. Life returns to the land.'

Kelly thought that Joe was doing an excellent job of explaining it all. His passion was infectious. It's just she couldn't see how it all might be relevant yet. She listened. Rob started on another biscuit.

'However, there was an old member of the group who created tension, and there was a strong belief that he might not have had the purest of souls. He portrayed himself as a moral rod, the leader in many ways, and it upset Fred and made the group somewhat lopsided, if you know what I mean. He unsettled people. He brought imbalance.'

'So why was he allowed to join?' Kelly asked.

'Because he was in a relationship with Mary. I didn't know the details but they were an odd pairing. He was stern and mysterious, and she was meek and gentle. It turns out that he was actually married and Mary ended the relationship. He was asked to leave the group but said some pretty awful things before he did.'

'Like what?'

'About revenge and ill-will. The ramblings of someone who's been caught out.'

Kelly nodded. 'But you said this was many years ago?'

'Yes. But I thought I should tell you because he is the only person I can think of who bore ill-feeling against her.'

'It's helpful, thank you. What's his name?'

'Kirk Junker.'

'British national?'

'I don't know. It sounds Germanic to me but I'm no expert.'

'Why do you think Fred didn't tell us any of this?'

'I would have thought that was quite obvious. He is protective of his group and Mary's name. He won't want her reputation sullied after death.'

'But you think it was important enough to tell us?'

'Yes.'

'He knows this?'

'Yes.'

'And his reaction?'

'He's worried that you'll disband his group.'

'Why would I do that? It's a free country. Unless they're sacrificing sheep and dogs of course.' Kelly watched for Joe's reaction. He gave none.

'How important is the wren?'

'I was wondering when you'd get back to that. The King of Birds. It's hugely important to the Pagan.'

'Really?'

'Yes. It's migratory and shrouded in traditional folklore about being a talisman of sorts. It tricked the eagle in a contest to see who was the king of birds by hiding under its wing, so when the eagle could fly no higher, the wren came out and won the title.'

'Clever little things.' He told her what Sandra had shared, almost to the letter.

'Treasured by naturalists.'

'Mary kept lots.'

'You don't keep wrens, they migrate every year.'

'The wrens in Mary's yard were locked in cages.'

'But that's impossible.'

'This Kirk Junker, did he have a way with animals?'

Joe looked deep in thought and took a minute to answer.

'His reputation for seduction was more directed towards women, but yes, he had a way with animals, as you put it. They went silent and cowed around him. I saw it with Bertha, Fred's Labrador, as well as birds in the garden.'

'Are you serious?'

'Deadly. Birds didn't sing when he was around.'

Kelly saw an image of Mary's pets falling silent as they saw a figure approach them.

'Can we speak to your wife now?' Kelly asked.

'I'll go and get her.'

Joe left the room and Kelly raised her eyebrows to Rob. 'What do you think?'

'I told you they were altars. I reckon we're on to something.'

'Bloody hell,' Kelly said, looking past him.

'What?' Rob asked.

'I know that boy.' She pointed to a family portrait. It would appear that Josie's boyfriend, Callum, was Joe Spencer's son.

'Important?'

'Not really, he associates with a friend's daughter, that's all.'

'Small world.'

Kelly coughed uncomfortably as Annie Spencer came back into the kitchen and sat down. The woman looked irritable, as well she might. They'd already witnessed her degree of annoyance at her husband's lack of cooperation thus far. Coming between a husband and wife on an investigation was tricky: at the end of the day, their loyalties were to each other, and picking apart what was truth and lies could be treacherous.

'Would you like to tell us your version?' Kelly asked.

'I don't know what Joe told you but I presume he told you about the group. I didn't like them, apart from Fred and Sandra. There was another man, another would-be leader, who worried me. He once made a suggestion to me about similar groups who worship naked. I told Joe, and Fred dealt with it, it was just another item on the long list of ugly reasons why nobody liked him.'

'Kirk Junker?'

'Yes.'

'But Mary did.'

'She seemed to. She certainly never spoke to me about him, but what would I know? I was never comfortable with any of it. But the O'Reillys are good people. I don't mind going over for a barbecue but I don't want to get involved in the Pagan stuff. It gives me the creeps.'

'Fair enough. In your opinion, was Kirk Junker capable of murder, as well as cruelty to animals?'

'One hundred per cent, yes. I know I didn't have much to do with him but there was something so odd about him.'

'Have you any idea where he went? Did anyone see him again?'

'I don't know. I never asked.'

'It's really important that we find out what happened to him. Do you know where he lived?'

'No. I think he stayed with Mary sometimes, and with Fred also. I'm sorry I can't help.'

'He stayed with the O'Reillys?'

'And Jock Harris.' Kelly looked at Rob; she wasn't familiar with every member of the group, she'd just read their statements. Rob nodded, indicating that he'd fill her in later.

'Do you think you could help a police artist come up with a photofit?'

'I could try. I mean, we could try. Between Joe and I, we should be able to, but why don't you ask Fred or Jock?'

'That's exactly what we intend to do. Mrs Spencer, thank you. If you think of anything else...'

Kelly indicated to Rob that it was time to leave and they gathered their things. Annie looked relieved to have them finally going, and they said goodbye. They walked back to the car and got in. Rob started the engine.

'They're still not telling us everything,' Kelly said.

Chapter 33

The Police National Computer had nothing on a man named Kirk Junker, so they checked the passport office and Interpol. The guy didn't exist, at least not on their records. It was another red flag. They contacted the office for census records and got them to run a check. He didn't turn up.

Meanwhile, Kelly arranged to re-interview the members of Fred's group regarding their ex-associate. She also arranged for a police artist to visit Fred and Sandra to get a workable image drawn. Joe had told them that he hadn't seen Kirk Junker for a good five or six years, his appearance could be wildly different now, but it was a chance still.

She had DC Emma Hide compile a list of all families named Junker in the country. There weren't many. Junker was indeed a Germanic surname and its origins referred to a noble man. Without context, it meant nothing.

In her office, Kelly brought up the file on William Beverley, the missing boy from 2003. She recognised his photo from the poster. There was also a picture of his mother, Edna, and somebody had added to the file recently that she was deceased. Kelly read on. It read in much the same format as the case she'd read from 2010 just last week. That had also been a twelve-year-old boy. The Kevin Good case had gone cold, too.

Her telephone rang and it was Ted. She was grateful for the break. Reading about missing twelve-year-old boys was depressing.

'Hi Ted.'

'Good morning, Kelly. I've got some news for you. It's something that niggled me when I did the post–mortem operation on Mary Hales.'

'Go on,' Kelly said.

'I was going over the photographs for my final report. Sometimes I spot something new. In Mary's case, there was a lot to consider.'

'I know. It must have been one of your longest ones, was it?'

'Close. Anyway, I came across a photo of a wound in her chest. Some of the edges of the knife wounds are quite jagged, but on closer inspection, one of the marks caught my eye, because the photographs are enlarged. The mark was the same colour as coagulated arterial blood, that's why I missed it. But I got my assistant to take a look too and it's not just my eyes and age. I had another look at her: her body is still here, until I sign her off.'

'So, do you know what the mark is?'

'Yes, it's a tattoo.'

'Really? And?'

'I looked it up and from what I can see it's likely to be the symbol of a Moon Goddess.'

'Moon Goddess?' Kelly sat upright and the tiny hairs on her arms stood up.

'It's a round, full circle in the middle flanked either side with a waxing and waning symbol that represent the three phases of the moon.'

She googled the symbol with Ted still on the phone and an image came up that fitted what Ted told her. She stared at it. She'd seen it before, but she couldn't place where. She recalled what The Teacher had said in the recent letter. *And the Moon Goddess returns to slumber…*

'Hold on, Ted. Have you seen this mark anywhere, before today?'

'Well, that's why I was calling. I was going to just record it in the report but when I studied the photographs from the crime scene to comment on the direction of the blows on Mary's body, it was actually marked in the floor.'

'What? Which one? Which photo?' Kelly opened the Mary Hales file and flicked through the photographs frantically. She saw nothing, but then she was rushing, and her heart was pounding because she'd realised where she'd seen the sign of the Moon Goddess. It had been written next to Edna Beverley's phone number on her son's missing poster.

'Wait a minute, it's evidence article MH101,' Ted said.

Kelly clicked on the relevant photo. 'Right, I'm on it, where? I can't see it.'

'Spin the photograph once to the left, I only did it myself to check how the blood spatter covered the floor on her left side, absolutely confirming that she was in the supine position when the majority of the wounds were inflicted.'

The detail sent a slight shiver through Kelly's body. Mary Hales looked into her killer's face as she died. They already knew that, but to be reminded of it was unwelcome. Kelly tried to ignore the body on the screen in front of her and search around it, after she'd spun the photograph around.

'Fucking hell. Sorry, Ted.'

'Can you see it?'

'Yes. I'm zooming in. Does it look like it was drawn in blood by a finger to you?' Kelly asked.

'That was my theory exactly.'

'Oh God.'

'What is it, Kelly?'

'It couldn't be a smear as a result of there being so much blood, could it?'

She already knew the answer. But she didn't want it to be true. She didn't want the symbols and altars to be relevant or connected. It reminded her too much of The Teacher, who left signals for her team to find, to join the dots. Everything pointed to a Pagan type of sacrifice or ritual and with this in mind, she'd have to get her team together to work from that as

189

their core motive. The symbols on the animals were convincing, but with this added communication from Mary's killer, it was about as solid a lead as they got. She remembered, as part of the investigation into The Teacher, they'd discovered previous spates of killings dating back decades. Some of the older ones, in Yorkshire, she thought, had been religious in nature and symbolism. Amy Richmond had been killing all her life. Had she taken an apprentice that none of them knew about?

Mary's killer was glorifying his or her work, and enjoying it. She looked back at the screen and to Mary's mutilated body. She heard Dr Demi Cramer's voice in her head. Demi had once given a lecture, which Kelly attended, years ago, when she was studying the forensic paper of her detective exams. She'd thought the woman a legend back then too. The lecture had been called 'Serial Apprentice' and it was Demi's own phrase for how killers developed. Murder had been a commonplace mishap of humankind for thousands of years. Passion, arguments, love, hate, rage, jealousy and sex all collided in the mind, to produce such an alarming wave of violence that murderers often forgot the actual moment of the crime. Occasionally, though, one came across a killer whose Modus Operandi boasted such skill and composure that it was obvious that the planning and preparation was as important as the delivery of the event.

The Teacher was a good example. Kelly couldn't help thinking that this was the reason why she'd had more correspondence of late from the nutcase languishing in Broadmoor at Her Majesty's pleasure. The Teacher had been used by Demi to write a book, with Kelly's blessing, and it was a fine piece of work: a bestseller in fact. Who better to recognise a fellow crazy than Amy Richmond?

'Ted, can I call you back?'

'Of course, but one more thing. When we re-examined Mary Hales this morning after noticing the mark, it was clear to us that it had been made at the same time as the knife wounds.

It wasn't an old tattoo, it was done that night. We're trying to work out what sort of ink or equipment was used but no luck so far.'

Kelly allowed the news to sink in. She hung up and hunted for the letters from the Bagshot postcode in Surrey. Finding the latest, she was thankful that she hadn't torn it up, like she'd wanted to. It was possible they were now evidence, and when she found what she was looking for, she knew that she'd have to officially get Demi on board. She re-read the words that had been playing through her mind.

Did you find the missing girl from the stone circle? I doubt it. One can't find something that burrows away from the light. Don't make the mistake of thinking that you happened upon her by chance; it was all planned. She'll appear again soon, but blink and you might miss her. But hurry, because time is running out. When the day meets the night, and darkness descends across the land, and the Moon Goddess returns to slumber, then only the spirits rule until balance returns.

Sloppy slaying in Braithwaite. Amateur. I love animals. That part really made me sick.

There it was in black and white: the Moon Goddess. It was no accident. The Teacher had worked it out before all of them. But how was that possible? Unless Amy had known all along, and even been party to it. There was one thing that didn't make sense but now began to worry her: the reference to the girl found naked at Castlerigg. It implied that she was somehow involved. She realised, with dread, that she might already be too late. If the girl was something to do with their killer, then the chances were that she was already dead.

She grabbed her coat and bag, and went to the incident room. 'Midday. Briefing in here. Everyone to attend. I'm going out. Emma, I want all the information on the element symbolism. Rob, has the artist been contacted?'

He nodded.

'Good, get him over to the O'Reillys right now, I'll get the necessary diversion of resources to satisfy HQ – don't worry about that. Prepare to present on Kirk Junker. Kate and Will? What are you working on?'

'Witness statements from Braithwaite,' replied DS Kate Umshaw.

'Tyre tracks from behind Mary's house,' replied DS Will Phillips. 'Everything all right, guv?' he asked.

'I can't explain now, let's just say that I think I might be getting the advice of an occult specialist on this one. The ritual aspect seems to be panning out. I'll flesh it out at midday.'

Will whistled and exchanged glances with his colleagues. Hocus pocus theorising was often bandied about during weird murder scene investigations, but they were rarely taken seriously. None of them had worked on one before.

Kelly went to her car and entered the SatNav details for Fred O'Reilly's house.

Chapter 34

As she drove, Kelly put Demi Cramer on speaker phone.

'I knew it!' Demi said.

'What?'

'When Ted Wallis called me to ask if I was lecturing at Lancaster University, he filled me in, and I knew you had a first-class crazy on your hands.'

'Thanks for letting me know,' she said sardonically. 'Are you coming up to Lancaster?'

'I'm there now. I'm only an hour away from you, want me to hop into my car?'

'I certainly do. What do you know about ritual killers?'

'The most famous was Jack the Ripper.'

'Really? What, because of the surgery?'

'Yes. As well as the escalation, number and locations of the bodies. They were in a perfect pentagram across Whitechapel, when the demon Astaroth is invoked.'

'What?'

'Five is a very important number for the occult, it's a symbol of balance. And it's seen across numerous cultures, including Japanese cooking, would you believe? We have five senses, there were five wounds of Christ, five pillars of Islam, five rites of passage, five elements, and it symbolises the Wiccan kiss.'

'Demi, I've got a headache already, where do you learn this kind of stuff?'

'If you're interested, it's everywhere. What I can't wait to find out is why *you* are interested. What have you got? It must be good, Kelly Porter, because you wouldn't be giving it any airtime unless you thought it convincing. I'm intrigued.'

'I'm confused.'

'It's a huge subject, but don't worry, the believer often has a specific set of mores; we just need to find out what they're into. It shouldn't be that hard if you've already got some evidence for me. Which I'm guessing you have, otherwise you wouldn't be calling me.'

'I'm giving a brief to my team at Eden House in Penrith – the main police station – at noon. Can you be there?'

'Plenty of time. I'm packing my things now. I have two lectures to deliver tomorrow. Ted said he was bringing you.'

'I think that might be out of the question now.'

'Sure. Well, I hope I can help.'

They hung up.

When Kelly arrived at Fred's house, there were several parked cars outside, which seemed odd to her for such a quiet area. She drove further along the road and parked, walking back the twenty metres or so to his house. Last time they'd been, they'd parked outside easily. She gathered her notepad and decided to leave her coat in the car. When she got out, she heard the song of birds and the smell of cooking. It was homely and peaceful, and every instinct she had told her that Fred and Sandra were loving, law-abiding people. But she could only work with facts, and if they said anything else, she'd act upon it. She was writing no one out of the story just yet.

Sandra answered the door and beckoned Kelly inside, explaining that the police artist was with Fred. She was shown into the empty sitting room.

'It's a most inconvenient time as we're having a small gathering to remember Mary.'

'Gathering? Like a ceremony?'

'No. Just friends coming together to recall her light.'

'Her light?'

'Her spirit.'

'That's why I'm here, Sandra, to talk to Fred about the occult.'

'Goodness me. Whatever for?'

'Because that's what you practise, isn't it? Along with your birdwatching buddies. My team is coming across signs of ritualistic significance as part of a murder investigation. It doesn't make sense to me and I don't like that. I need to understand exactly who Mary was in order to comprehend why she was punished.'

'Punished?'

'Yes, Sandra. Dying can take some time, and occasionally, that's the whole point.'

Sandra put her hand to her mouth. Kelly felt mean, but it was the reaction she was after. The secrecy had to stop.

'I can caution you and all your pals and we can have a gathering at Penrith police station, or you can help me willingly. I'm on your side. I want to know what happened to Mary, and why, but you've got to be transparent with me or I'll have no choice but to interview you under caution. Take me to Fred. Where are your guests?'

'They're in the back garden.'

'Keep them here, please. I assume they're the members of the "birdwatching" club?'

'Mainly, yes.'

'I'll need to speak to all of them. If they tell you they don't need to, because they've already given statements, then tell them I need another one. Do not let them leave, please.'

'Right.'

The unexpected visitors threw Kelly and she considered calling for a few uniforms to take further statements. However, without context, and if they weren't already working on the inquiry, they wouldn't know the right questions to ask, and explaining that would take more time than just getting on with it herself. She followed Sandra into the hallway again and upstairs.

'Why up here?'

'For privacy. Fred was embarrassed.'

'He shouldn't be, he's helping us.'

'He was embarrassed that we didn't tell you about Kirk.'

'And why didn't you?'

'Because he's long gone. He was horrible, and a stain on our community. He hasn't been seen around here for years, they obviously moved away.'

'They?'

'His wife and daughter.'

'Daughter?'

They got to the top of the stairs and Sandra led Kelly into a bedroom. Fred looked less than impressed to see her.

'Will you people ever leave us alone?' he asked. It wasn't rude, it was more desperate.

'Fred, I have to speak to you. Like I told Sandra, we can do it under caution in Penrith if you like.'

'I am helping! I'm helping your artist.'

'I know. I can talk to you at the same time.' The artist didn't look enamoured with this idea.

'You ask him about a chin shape and I'll nip in while you work. Easy,' Kelly said. They all looked at her. She ploughed on.

'Tell me about the Moon Goddess,' asked Kelly.

'What colour eyes did he have?' asked the artist.

Fred looked frantically between them. It wasn't going to work. Kelly looked at her watch and then at the artist.

'Look, give me ten minutes and I'll leave. I'm the DI who sent for you, could you just work on what he's told you so far and then he's all yours?' she asked. The artist nodded and sighed, turning to his pad.

'Tell me about the Moon Goddess.' Kelly heard the door close and realised that Sandra was back in the room. She hoped she'd done as Kelly asked and made sure no one downstairs left the premises.

'Come here, love,' Fred said to his wife. Sandra went and sat next to him on the bed. Kelly remained standing, waiting.

Fred told her, in his own words, the importance of the Moon Goddess for Pagans. The fact that the deity symbolised the warmth, fertility and vitality of the earth, and that she emerged resplendent in spring and disappeared again for the winter.

'So, when exactly does she sleep off the winter?'

'Mabon. The autumn equinox. It's September twenty-second this year.'

'Soon then? Next week in fact. What *exactly* is an equinox?' Kelly remembered The Teacher's letter again. It left an unwelcome knot under her ribs. *But hurry, because time is running out. When the day meets the night…*

'It's when the day is equal to night. It happens twice a year: once in the spring and once in the autumn. It signals the tipping of the balance of the seasons. It's one of the eight important festivals of the year.'

Kelly pictured John Porter standing in the middle of Castlerigg stone circle pointing to Threlkeld Knotts, telling her about the alignment. That was it, she remembered now. It was the autumn equinox, when sunrise appeared directly over the peak.

'What are the others?'

Fred explained all eight to her. Including the two solstices and two equinoxes, there were also four ancient celebratory dates in between, and all marked by solar or lunar events.

'Why is an alignment so important to you?'

'It's the basis of everything we believe. It's like Christians believing that Jesus was crucified. To us, the seasons are fundamental to connecting to Mother Nature. Civilisations all over the world, for thousands of years, have celebrated alignments.'

'Such as?'

'Chichen Itza in Mexico. During spring equinox, the sun makes a shadow that looks like a serpent slithering across the huge pyramid's steps.'

197

'Is that for real?' Kelly asked. Fred nodded.

'During summer solstice at Stonehenge, the sun rises directly above the Heel stone.'

'The Heel stone?'

'It stands outside the circle and it's not worked like the others. If you stand in the centre of the circle, the sun rises above the Heel stone. It's quite incredible.'

'You've been?'

'Many years ago. I wouldn't go now, it's like a circus. But even more impressive is the Machu Picchu Intihuatana stone, it's like a solar clock of the year.'

'How could they have achieved this all those years ago?'

'I believe that various wars and natural disasters wiped out their civilisations along with their knowledge and we simply don't appreciate how advanced they were.'

Kelly put her hands on her hips and let the information sink in. She fiddled with her ponytail and folded her arms. The artist didn't look up from his pad. If this shit got out before she could understand it fully, she'd be a laughing stock.

'Tell me about the importance of this symbol.' Kelly showed them a picture on her phone of the mark of the Moon Goddess.

'It's the full moon with a waxing and waning moon. She's seen by some as the sun, or Mother Earth, she has many names. It depends on what you believe.'

'And what did Kirk Junker believe?'

Fred blushed, it was Kelly's first mention of the man Fred O'Reilly had failed to tell them about.

'He was more interested in the Horned God.'

'Excuse me?'

'It's the male deity in Paganism – the Moon Goddess being the female – and he's associated with winter, masculinity, hunting and virility.'

'What kind of father was he?'

'Father?' Fred looked at Sandra.

'I told her they moved away,' said Sandra.

'He was stern. I always said he suited puritanism more than Paganism. It was a joke. He didn't find it funny.'

'We're struggling to locate him, and now I know he has a daughter, it's even more imperative. What was her name?'

'Daphne.'

'Daphne Junker?' Kelly asked.

'Just Daphne, we don't take surnames officially.'

'Did she go to school?'

'Probably.'

'Where did they live?'

'They lived in an apartment in Penrith. I never went there. He was very secretive.'

'How did he find your group?'

'He met Mary out walking one day. They struck up a conversation and I believe they found things in common.'

'Would you say that was naïve of Mary?'

Fred blushed. 'Yes. She was vulnerable. He was a predator. She found him… exotic.'

'Predator is a strong word for someone who's missing with a young daughter, how old would she be now? Did he go by any other names? I'll need the name of his wife too.'

'I never heard him call himself anything else. His wife was called Gloria. I think Daphne would be about eighteen now.'

'And they simply vanished?'

'If they were still about, I'm sure somebody would have seen them. He was quite distinctive, as I was explaining to this gentleman.'

Kelly looked at the artist's pad and agreed that, with his dark features and almost black eyes, the man depicted on the page, not yet even fully drawn, was strikingly unconventional.

'Did Kirk ever talk about ritualistic torture or killing?'

'I beg your pardon? Look, that journalist has given us a bad name. You offend us with your ignorant questions.' Fred tightened his arm around Sandra, who stared at the floor.

'She said that Mary took time to die,' Sandra whispered just in earshot of the artist, who stared at Kelly. Fred looked at her, and the colour drained from his face.

'It's a line of inquiry,' Kelly said. 'Her animals were also tortured, they weren't just burned.' She had to hit them hard and make them think about complying with full transparency.

Fred bowed his head. 'Kirk was a potential sadist, that's all I can tell you. I have no idea if he actually was interested in the dark side of the faith. Like any path: there are always two directions.'

'Indeed. Did he show signs of dominance or violence towards his daughter?'

'The girl was always terrified,' Sandra said. Fred shot her a sharp look.

'So why were they invited to stay here occasionally?'

'What?'

'The testimony of Annie Spencer.'

'It was once,' Fred spoke in a whisper. The air in the room was thin suddenly, and nobody else spoke. The artist shifted uncomfortably.

'He made Sandra feel... tense.'

'Could you describe her, Daphne?'

'She was a child when we last saw her. She was very pretty. Blonde hair. He never allowed her to cut it. She also had the most striking bright blue eyes.'

Kelly felt her eyes linger on Sandra for long enough to make the woman look away. Angry, she brought up the image of Carla Rigg released by police to the media.

'Is this her?'

Fred and Sandra clasped their hands tighter and Sandra nodded. Fred sighed and rubbed his eyes.

'You're now going to tell me that you don't watch the news and you haven't seen the police appeal for her?'

Sandra's eyes widened and she looked at her husband, who looked guilty as hell. Now it was Sandra's turn to be angry. Kelly pointed at Fred's face.

'Don't go anywhere. I'll be requesting you visit Eden House in Penrith to be interviewed formally, you might want to contact a lawyer. I'll see myself out after I've spoken to your guests.' She went to the door but stopped.

'Actually, Fred, I'd like you to show me something downstairs. I'm sorry, you'll have to wait a little longer,' she said to the artist. In the short minutes he'd known Kelly Porter, the artist knew better than to argue.

'Now?' Fred asked. Kelly didn't answer. He got up and accompanied her downstairs. She knew her way to the lounge and went in.

'That.' She pointed to the table covered in silk, which had been sketched by Rob. 'Is it an altar?'

Fred looked at his feet. Kelly saw that he was too weary to argue. He nodded. 'It's not what you think.'

'How do you know what I think?' she asked. 'If you'd asked me two weeks ago what someone might want with an altar in their house, I'd have probably written you off as a devil worshipper, but now I don't think that at all. But I *would* like you to explain it to me. The more I know about Mary's lifestyle, the more chance I've got of getting inside the head of who killed her. And you think it was Kirk Junker, don't you? Just like Joe Spencer. I hope, for your sake, that his daughter is safe.'

Fred shuffled to the table and lifted the silk. 'This is symbolic of everything I believe. Those people out there,' he nodded to the garden. 'Everything they believe too. These are our magic tools, as well as emblems of our lives and seasons.'

A voice inside Kelly's head told her to laugh, but another, stronger one, made her pause and not just listen to the man before her, but feel his passion. He was simply stating what meant the most in the world to him, and at the same time, mourning the passing of a dear friend. She could tell by the way he touched the items, and the way he spoke, that he believed that Mary was killed for her faith. Carry Tomlin might have a point after all. She'd already tasked DC Emma Hide with questioning the journalist, but so far they'd failed to contact her.

'What are they?' She pointed to several items on the altar.

'We celebrate the four elements: here, this is a bowl of earth, the candle symbolises fire, incense the air, and this is purified water.'

'I thought there were five elements?'

'You mean spirit? Yes, but it commands the others. It's more ethereal. This is an athame.'

'That's quite a blade, Fred. It's very beautiful. What's its significance?' Kelly noted with interest that Fred was showing her a very ornate and slightly curved knife that had been absent – or covered by cloth – when Rob drew his picture. She particularly noted the shape of the blade.

'It represents fire. It's not for violence at all. The opposite in fact. It's male, as the chalice is female. Everything in our faith is about balance. That's why we have the black and white.'

Kelly took a deep breath. 'Fred. I believe what you're telling me and I believe that all those people out there are gentle and peaceful. But...'

'There's a but? I knew there would be.'

'It's about the knife. I need to take it. We found one at Mary's too but it was fully curved like a crescent moon.'

'Her boline?'

'Yes, I believe that's what Rob called it.'

'But that's for cutting herbs, and this is for worship only. Why would you want to take it?'

'Isn't it obvious, given the way Mary was killed?'

'But this knife...'

'Give it to me.' She found plastic gloves in her handbag and he handed it over. She felt for him, but she couldn't reveal details from the case to reassure him now.

'Wait, I have a sheath for it.' He went under the table and brought out a jewelled leather holster, slipping the knife into it.

'Are there many types of athame and boline, Fred? I'm confused by why such a peace-loving organisation such as yours would put emphasis on knives.'

'It's not an organisation, and they are purely symbolic. It's tradition that goes back to when a knife was the main tool of life, before microwaves and plastic forks. And yes, they're as varied as ornaments. The rarest and most ornate go for thousands at auction. But it's the symbolic value that is important to us. This one was given to me by a friend in Scotland. It was in his family for four generations, dating back to 1792.'

'I'll look after it.' She took a plastic evidence bag out of her handbag and slipped it into it.

'Did Mary have an athame as well as a boline?'

'Of course.'

'Could you describe it?'

'I saw it many times, and I held it. It was more curved than mine, with a dragon at the hilt. It was more pointed than mine too, and had a blue gemstone on the handle. I can see if I can find a picture of something similar? Didn't you find it at her house?'

Kelly shook her head. 'Can you look for a similar one in a picture?'

He nodded, and Kelly knew that he'd worked out what she was thinking: that Mary's athame could have been used on her.

'That would be so helpful. You better go back up.' He did so, slowly and heavily.

She took off her gloves and went out into the garden and was faced with around ten people staring at her. They fell silent.

'Good afternoon, I'm Detective Inspector Porter. I'm going to ask each of you to come into the rear kitchen, one at a time. You'll be formally interviewed again at a later date. Do not leave the premises without my permission.'

Her eyes met those of an elderly gentleman and she stopped speaking.

'What's your name, sir? Can I start with you, please.'

'Jock Harris.' He got up slowly to follow Kelly, who made her way back into the house.

As she did so, she called in a patrol car. The man she was about to interview was the man in the photograph next to Daphne, found in the girl's wallet.

Chapter 35

Before Kelly arrived back at Eden House, news of the body of a dead woman, found on the edge of Thirlmere reservoir near a car park, had made its way to the investigation team. One of the uniforms on site, when called to the spot by a member of the public who'd been preparing to climb Helvellyn, had taped off the area for a search, and noticed wounds to the woman's neck, arms and legs that looked like animal bites. Any such concern was immediately viewed as suspicious and the crime squad involved.

Kelly parked and spoke to DS Umshaw on her phone, Kate told her the few details they knew about the woman, and that Dr Demi Cramer was waiting for her in the incident room. Kelly didn't know what to do first: eat, get a coffee, or punch something. Jock Harris had given her very little. He'd confirmed that the photograph was of him and Daphne, but it was a one-off at a barbecue, hosted by the O'Reillys, years ago, when Kirk was a member of the group. He too hadn't seen the police appeal, because, like most of the others, he didn't possess a TV. He said he had no idea why the young girl would keep his photograph and found it as odd as they did, though she did seem to fixate on people.

She turned her attention to the new case. Life went on, cases didn't stop because they were working on another. Regarding the identity of the dead woman at Thirlmere, there were no current missing person reports, and no ID on the body, but an officer at the scene had tentatively suggested that he knew who she might be. He'd named her as the journalist Carry Tomlin.

'How sure is he?' Kelly spoke into her phone.

'He doesn't need to be sure, guv. We got sent the images taken by the CSI ten minutes ago. It's her. She's been taken to the mortuary in Carlisle and her NOK have been informed; they'll be requested to formally ID the body when the coroner is ready.'

'Ted Wallis?'

'Yes, guv.'

She rang off and entered the building. She couldn't get ahead of herself and assume that the victim of a new murder case had anything to do with Mary Hales, so she took a deep breath and decided to stop at the coffee machine downstairs before she did anything else. After a sip of strong espresso, she felt more human. But the fact that Carry Tomlin had been investigating local Pagans wouldn't go away. Her mind whirred with information and she hoped that Demi would provide some sanity and clarification for her. She caught the lift and entered the incident room, going to Demi to greet her. The two women hugged. Demi looked older than Kelly remembered and she guessed it must be six or seven years since they'd seen one another. She'd always admired her dress sense, and Demi pulled off bright colours where anybody else would have failed. She teamed all hues of the rainbow with scarves and jewellery, and gave the impression of an eccentric art teacher. Her eyes hadn't changed: they were still those of a hawk, intent on the hunt. Her smile was warm and they lingered a moment on the exchange.

'It's good to see you, Kelly Porter. You haven't aged a day. No husband and children to look after, I think?'

Somebody in the team coughed. Kelly wasn't surprised, it was Demi Cramer's bluntness that got her theses published and taken seriously.

'Everybody, this is Dr Cramer, a leading expert on psychotic lunatics.'

'What an introduction! But I admit it's true.' She went around the room and shook hands with the crime team one by one. As she did so, Kelly told her a little about each of them. She spoke proudly and Demi looked interested.

'Deep breaths everyone. Some new information has come to light and Dr Cramer is going to sit in on our brief. I've just come back from Fred O'Reilly's house and he's given the forensic artist a great description of this man.' Everybody sat down and paid attention, as Kelly wrote the name Kirk Junker on the whiteboard. At the moment, the board wasn't full. Leads were crossed off as they were checked and they had few left. Kelly rearranged some photos and a map, and Kirk Junker's name went in the middle. She brought up a photo of the artist's impression so far.

'Rob?' As instructed, Rob gave the team everything he had on the enigmatic character, including a possible motive to murder Mary Hales. It wasn't much.

'We still haven't located anyone matching the description or name. The boss has agreed that only an appeal to the public might give us a chance.' Demi watched and waited. Rob looked at Kelly, who nodded.

'This girl,' Rob added the photo of Carla Rigg to the board, 'has been positively identified as Kirk Junker's daughter, she's called Daphne. It's our strongest indication that he's back in the area, after being told that he moved away some five or six years ago after being jilted by Mary Hales. You might recognise the photo.' A ripple of excitement travelled around the room. Kelly spoke next.

'Fred and Sandra O'Reilly have both informed me that Kirk Junker could be described as a sadist, and that he left the area with a wife and Daphne, his daughter.' Kelly paused and added them to the board. 'Now, rewind five years, and Kirk wants to run the local Pagan worship group his own way. Yes, you heard it from me first. These photos were highlighted to me by the coroner this morning.' She used her laptop to link the files to the whiteboard and pointed out what Ted had told her.

'This is solid evidence of ritual torture and a calling card. Demi, could you give us your interpretation of killers who use calling cards.'

Demi studied the photographs. Kelly hadn't held back. She'd decided to show them the fire symbol found on Mary's animals, as well as the triple moon sign found on Mary, as well as on the floor. She also showed them a picture of the missing poster giving Edna Beverley's contact details.

'A calling card is a message,' Demi began with the basics. She moved closer to the board and pointed to various parts of the photos and asked Kelly for details such as the position of the victim.

'Geographical and anatomical positions. Any of these symbols can be categorised as calling cards. It's overdone, as if the perpetrator thinks the inquirers might miss something.'

'Exhibitionist?' Kelly asked. Demi nodded.

'Huge ego.'

'The coroner said the triple moon was tattooed into her chest on Friday night. He tells me from the coagulation of the blood around the ink, that she was possibly alive when it was done,' Kelly said.

'We're talking about a seriously disturbed individual here. I have never come across one case where a murderer so advanced has not been abused as a child and subsequently continued that behaviour,' Demi added.

'There's apparent abuse in the Junker family, so I'm concerned for the welfare of the wife and daughter. Turning up randomly in the early hours, in a psychotic state, mute and afraid, and refusing to communicate with authority: it's all indicative of victim-like behaviour. She was terrified of her father, perhaps? We re-appeal for the naked girl, with her name, along with her mother, and see what happens. I've got an artist working on what she might have looked like as a little girl too. As far as they recall, the O'Reillys have no photos of them. On to this man.' Kelly brought up the file on Jock Harris' statement, and beside it the photograph found in Carla Rigg's wallet.

'He meant a lot to her. HQ have agreed and I've made arrangements to have both Jock Harris and Fred O'Reilly brought in under caution.' Kelly let everyone finish taking notes and moved on to the knife.

'When Mary Hales was examined, her wounds had been inflicted by two separate knives. One we found at the property: a large kitchen knife taken from the kitchen block. The other was never found. All the knives at the property were examined forensically. The coroner told me that he believed it wasn't a regular kitchen or eating knife, but an ornamental one that could have been curved.' She pulled out the evidence bag and showed it to everyone. She put on gloves and removed the knife from its sheath and held it up. 'This is a ritual knife, called an athame, used in Pagan worship. It belongs to Fred O'Reilly. Now, his prints will be all over it, but I want it tested for human blood, other prints and blade shape. He also told me that you can get different versions. Emma? Could you get a collection of them together for me to show the coroner to see if he can match any of the blades with Mary's wounds? Then at least we'll have an idea of what we're looking for. Rob? Was there an athame on Mary's altar? Fred told me that she had one and it looked a bit like this one.' She showed them the photograph of the athame that Fred had identified, with the dragon and blue gemstone.

'No guv. Definitely not. I itemised everything.'

'So, it is possible that it was used against Mary and taken away. Right, let's move on to the body of Carry Tomlin, shall we?'

Kelly closed her laptop and took a chair. 'What the hell happened?' she asked. DC Emma Hide shared the little knowledge they had so far.

'Can I have the photos up? That was quick moving her to the mortuary wasn't it?' Kelly said.

'The body was fresh, guv, and the scene almost sterile. The forensic officer at the scene was one hundred per cent sure that it had been on the shoreline for less than twelve hours, and that she must have been put there shortly after her death.'

'Interesting. I mean, I know she was snooping around looking for information this week, so we know that's probably the case. It's the last thing any of us needs right now and a new case will stretch us, with Mary's case taking so much time. I'll have to take everyone off non-urgent duties, but I know how much you all love that anyway.' This got an appreciative laugh of support. A series of photos came up on one of the other whiteboards, arranged by DS Umshaw, who'd first received the notice from the initial responders about the body at Thirlmere. Kelly and the team, including Demi Cramer, took a few moments to study the images, and Kelly read a very basic preliminary report.

'Found by a walker heading for the Helvellyn range. Noticed what he thought were large white rubbish bags on the beach of the reservoir, which turned out to be her pale skin.' They stared at the board. The photos were a mixture of close-ups and scenic. The body was face-up and looked like a mannequin.

'Forensics said the wounds looked like bite marks from an animal. There's also deep bruising around her wrists.'

'I don't really need to confirm that this is a homicide investigation,' Kelly said.

'Kelly, can you see those stones?' It was Demi who spoke. The team weren't used to hearing their boss's given name used so casually. They waited.

Demi and Kelly approached the board. Next to the body was an arrangement of stones. It hadn't been noticed because people position stones all the time on walks in the Lake District. Cairns of them denote summits, and passers-by build made shift stoves and games out of them. There wasn't a lakeside beach in the whole of the National Park that didn't have evidence of children setting out stones to pass the time.

'It's a triangle,' Kelly said.

'It's the same as the fire element on the animals found at Mary's.'

'But there's no fire.'

'Guv.' It was Emma Hide, who Kelly had tasked with researching the symbols for the five elements: one of them being fire. 'It's upside down, the opposite of fire. That's the symbol for water.'

Chapter 36

Josie packed her bag, checking off her list for this afternoon's climbing practice. She had butterflies in her stomach, not because of the climb ahead, but because she was to see Callum again. He was like no other boy she'd met. At school, they acted in character and one had no idea who was really underneath it all. The talk was all of knives, weed and alcohol and it bored her. Anyone who carried a knife was an idiot. She knew there were gangs operating in the local area but she also appreciated that they were small time compared to somewhere like Manchester or Liverpool. It was one of the reasons she'd come to live with her dad, though she'd never told him: her best friend had been raped.

Safety was something that never crossed her mind until that night. They were tipsy but not blind drunk. They said goodbye at the corner of the main road like they always did and Josie went home to her mother. The next morning, the police came to their door asking for Josie to give a statement. They visited her friend in hospital and Josie refused to go out of the house for two weeks. Her mother suggested she go and see her father. It was the countryside: it might help heal.

It had. The nightmares subsided and she stopped looking over her shoulder all the time. She lost touch with her one time best buddy, who, she heard, had turned to hard drugs.

And now she'd met Callum. He didn't have the swagger of teenage boys in the city. His dad was a tree hugging type who worked for the National Trust, or English Heritage, she couldn't remember which. His little brother was adorable and said 'hi' to her when they Facetimed. He sent her stupid Snapchat pictures of his wonky eyes, and he commented on her Instagram page with cool emojis and code words they'd agreed. They'd gone from linking to proper dating in the space of days and now they couldn't bear to be apart. He was her best friend. The climbing was something that had started as an excuse to meet but they genuinely wanted to keep going back.

Their first test climb was to be a small rock face at the foot of Blencathra's Sharp Edge. It sounded more daring than it was; she'd seen the pictures. They would be under instruction the whole time. Both she and Callum had applied for the basic level exam, and that would be tested at Woden's Face on Friday. Woden's Face was a rock face in the middle of a forest, supposedly in the Borrowdale Valley, wherever that was. Her dad was thrilled that she was doing something physical. She knew it irritated the hell out of him that he was this super fit guy, but had a daughter who spent her days on social media. She didn't see the point of working out; surely you only did it if you wanted to date someone at the gym. Plenty of her girlfriends did, and had boyfriends with bulky shoulders that made their legs look spindly and stupid. It wasn't her thing.

Callum had told her about the girl at the stone circle and it freaked her out. She knew that Kelly had handled the case but the girl had disappeared. It was weird, but then everything her dad's girlfriend did was weird. But cool too. Kelly was a kick-ass woman and Josie hoped to be as confident and no-bullshit as her one day. Every time she saw Kelly, she watched her father swoon just a little bit more, but it was a good thing because Kelly mellowed him. She remembered arguments at home between her mum and dad and the night he left them. At first, she had hated him for walking out, but since meeting Kelly and living with him, she'd begun to love him like she used to.

Her dad and Kelly were getting pretty old and Josie had told him last weekend that she'd love a baby sister or brother, if that's what they were thinking about. Her dad didn't answer.

'You don't need to get married. I'll babysit, and change nappies, and play with her, or him.'

'Thanks,' he'd said. He'd had an odd look on his face after that and Josie wondered if she'd said something wrong. Maybe Kelly couldn't have kids? That thought had made her regret her words so badly. She decided not to bring it up again.

Her thoughts turned to Ted. He'd promised to buy her a skiing outfit for her birthday. Her dad was paying for her to go on the school trip. She'd asked him when she found out that Callum was going.

'But you don't ski,' he'd said.

'That's why I want to go.'

She liked Ted. He was like a grandfather. She didn't know what a grandfather was supposed to be like but she guessed the job description would have something along the lines of the following: be kind, generous and funny and let them do what their parents say no to. He'd taken her to the pub and let her have a sip of his beer. Her dad knew where they'd been but assumed it was for crisps and a coke, while he and Kelly went running. They were always running. It was tiring just being around them. People their age were obsessed with eating healthily and exercising. It puzzled her.

She thought that Kelly looked amazing anyway and didn't need to bother. Older people always talked about how hard it was to stay in shape as you got older. It was boring.

Satisfied with her rucksack, she went through to the kitchen to see what was in the fridge. Her dad bought all her favourites and kept the cupboards stocked with chocolate biscuits, crisps and fizzy drinks. She'd heard Kelly telling him that it wasn't wise for his daughter to start bad habits at her age, and worried that they'd both pay the consequences later in life. Josie had kicked back at her father for that and – admittedly – made it difficult for Kelly at times to have the access to his time that she wanted.

That all changed last Christmas. It was the first time that Josie had seen Kelly not in complete control and she'd softened towards her. They all missed Wendy. The funeral had been horrendous. Josie knew that Kelly still kept her mum's ashes in a plastic urn on her wooden mantelpiece above the fire. She'd secretly opened it once, when she'd been alone in Kelly's house. She couldn't really explain why: if it was to be close to the lovely older woman who'd been so generous and kind to her; or if it was macabre curiosity to find out if cremation got rid of everything. When she opened the lid, it stuck a little and a cloud of ash had puffed out, settling on her jumper. She'd been mortified and quickly put the lid back on, pushing it firmly. It was the smell she'd never forget: it smelled of musty old concrete and she'd nearly been sick. From then on, she'd remembered Wendy as she was that Christmas Day: funny, loving and protective. It was a good place to be: under Wendy's wing. The absence of it was felt keenly and Josie had asked Kelly for a photograph of her to have in her bedroom.

Kelly had cried and hugged her. They'd hugged each other. From then on, there was little or no tension between them. She also noticed that her father was more relaxed when she was calmer, and they didn't argue as much. Josie had felt overwhelmed when she realised the power she'd held over her dad's relationship and she felt guilty.

She poked her head into the fridge and opened the drawers. Her dad ate too much salad. She smiled to herself. That was the other mystery about adults: the amount of fresh vegetables and fruit they ate. She reached to the back of the shelf where she knew she'd find a strawberry milkshake and a chocolate mousse. She took them to the lounge and looked at her phone. She had three Snapchats from Callum. They'd arranged to meet in Keswick and it meant that Josie had time to go shopping with Ted. It was an INSET training day at school and they had the day off. They were due to meet at midday, outside the outdoor wear shop on the market square.

She scrolled through her notifications and finished her snack: Ted would buy her lunch later. Then she'd see Callum.

A call from her dad came through and she answered brightly. 'Hi Dad.'

'Josie? Where are you?'

'At home, I'm getting the bus to Keswick soon. I'm meeting Ted, remember?'

'Yes, I do. It's just that Kelly called me and told me that there was a woman found dead near Thirlmere this morning.'

'Ugh! And why are you telling me, Dad? That's gross.'

'So you will remember to be careful. Don't take any risks and always tell me where you are.'

'Of course, I always do.'

'What time is your climb?'

'Three p.m.'

'And where is Callum meeting you?'

'At the club.'

'I'll pick you up from there.'

'Dad! I was going to go to Nando's with Callum tonight.'

'I'm sorry, Josie, not at the moment. He can come and have dinner with us. I'd like to meet him properly anyway. I'm sorry for last time. I'll drive him home. With two murders in two weeks, I want to know where you are every second of the day until somebody is caught.'

'Kelly has probably already got him.'

'I'm sure she's close, but until then, you're not going out at night.'

'For God's sake, Dad! I'm not a baby. I can take care of myself!'

'Right. Of course you can. A six foot bloke bundles you into the back of a van and knocks you out, and you reckon you could get out of that situation, what? With your phone?'

She didn't answer him. Her cheeks burned with fury. He was embarrassing her and Callum wasn't even here. She could think of nothing worse than her dad grilling Callum, army-style, about his life. She closed her eyes.

'Josie?'

'Dad.'

'I know you hate this but I love you, that's the only reason I want you to be safe. It's not to annoy you.'

She sighed deeply. 'OK.'

'I'll see you at the climbing centre.'

They hung up.

Chapter 37

Kelly sat with Demi in a small coffee shop round the corner from Eden House. They discussed her cases.

'I can't help thinking that Amy Richmond is more involved than even the letters suggest.' Kelly aired her thoughts.

'What have HQ said?'

'They've approved a visit.'

'Holy crap.'

'Indeed. My boyfriend doesn't want me to go.'

'I'm not surprised, the last time you were in her company, you nearly died. As did your sister.'

'Let's not go there.'

'When do I get to meet him? He sounds wonderful. I bet he's all mountain air and muscle.'

'Demi!' Kelly laughed, but then said quietly, 'Tell you the truth, I'm nervous.'

'Just nervous? I'd say a healthy dose of terror is in order. With good reason. I was granted two visits for research purposes for my book, and I have to say that I've never been so close to somebody like that before. Not someone who harbours no sense of regret, remorse, or emotion at all for what they did.'

'I thought you worked with other murderers in the past.'

'None quite like this. Her composure is quite something. It was a masterclass for me. Did you read my book?'

'I'm sorry, Demi, I didn't have the stomach. I saw all of the victims.'

'Of course you did. For me, it was more academic.'

They finished their drinks.

'The sooner I go the better. My gut is telling me that meeting Amy Richmond face to face is fundamental to unlocking all the puzzles to this case. Why does she know so much? It's just like last time when she toyed with us like puppets for weeks until we finally caught up with her. We all assumed it was a man.'

'Haven't you assumed the same now?' asked Demi.

'Kirk Junker? Are you thinking his wife could be involved too?'

'Of course, if the child was that terrified. Couples who kill. Think Rosemary and Fred West.'

'There has to be a link between Amy Richmond and the Junkers that I've missed. I wonder if Daphne was ever in care. She's far too young to be a peer of Amy's but, as a nurse, the time frame fits: five years ago, she was working at the Penrith and Lakes, and that's when Mary Hales dumped Kirk.'

'But the way The Teacher worked was to punish people like Junker. If Daphne was being abused and Amy Richmond, as a nurse, found out, he would have been a prime target for a victim,' Demi said.

'But she only killed women.'

'You know as well as I do that there are seven other murders linked to Amy Richmond that won't be tried because of lack of evidence, but I saw the files. She'd killed before.'

'The Yorkshire cases?' asked Kelly.

'More than that.'

'There usually are with killers like her. It's been a long time. I can't imagine being in the same room as her.'

'You need a strategy before you go in, because once you're face to face, the last thing you need is Amy taking control.'

'Any tips?' asked Kelly.

'Decide on your questioning and stick to it. Don't get distracted. Take the high ground.'

'There is no high ground with The Teacher.'

'Can you send somebody else?'

'It wouldn't work. She wants to see me. That's what she's wanted all along.'

'Sexual fantasy?'

'I never doubted that, but she knows it's not a possibility in reality.'

'Fantasy can be a powerful world in which to live.'

'Exactly. I've never lived there and so I don't know what to expect. She'll have an agenda and she'll have known all along that it would come to this. There's this sense of inevitability about it all.'

'You can't avoid it.'

'Like *The Bear Hunt*, I've got to go through it.'

'When will you go?'

'HQ have signed it off so I guess this afternoon or maybe tomorrow now, looking at the time. I'll only be gone for the afternoon. I can catch an afternoon train to Reading and be back by one o'clock in the morning. I'm only allowed two hours anyway and I can't see me wanting to be in there for that long. It's important to do it face to face, though.'

'I agree. You can only get a true understanding of what is real and what is fantasy by going head to head. The security is very good. You'll be absolutely fine.'

'It's not my physical health that worries me.'

'Mind manipulation?'

'Exactly.'

They paid their bill and walked back to Eden House.

'What's your instinct? Do you think this is the start of five killings, all replicating one of the elements?' Kelly asked. Her team all agreed that this was the most plausible explanation for the symbolism they had so far unearthed. Finding the water symbol next to Carry Tomlin this morning was a game-changer.

'That's what it appears to be, but sometimes things don't always go to plan. I think it's safe to say, though, that it *is* the plan, and everything points to it being executed quickly.'

'Why now? Mary dumped Kirk Junker years ago.'

'If it's him. Remember, it could be the wife. Jealous lover.'

Kelly's phone buzzed as they entered the building. The initial homicide assessment on the death of Carry Tomlin was on HOLMES. The dynamic reasoning engine was invaluable for complex cases and Kelly feared that this one only threatened to get weirder and weirder.

'We've got Carry Tomlin on CCTV at a petrol station on the A591 travelling south.'

'What time?'

'Yesterday, late morning.'

'Blimey, they didn't hang about. That's odd,' Demi remarked.

'What?' Kelly asked. They took the stairs up to her office.

'A killer so mature in MO, and one so deliberate and precise, not keeping the crimes hidden, is unusual. I've seen cases like this – ritual MOs for example – where the bodies are kept somewhere, or at least hidden for a long period. This is so public that it's brazen.'

'Like The Teacher,' Kelly said. Demi raised her eyebrows. They went into the briefing room and Kelly checked up on the progress of the crime scene processing, the piecing together of Carry Tomlin's last movements and when the autopsy would be performed. Ted had been supposed to meet Josie to take her ski-outfit shopping and for lunch. She wondered if he'd start work on the body today or not. A quick phone call gave her the answer. Ted said that a post-mortem was already underway on an elderly lady who'd fallen down some steps in her residential care home, and the autopsy of Carry Tomlin was scheduled for first thing tomorrow. There was nothing he could do – half her organs were already on the slab. The inquest was something that Ted had passed to a colleague, but he would perform the operation on the murder victim himself.

'I'd rather it was me tomorrow than send her elsewhere this afternoon. I've looked at the photos carefully and I've read the whole report – well, as much as your end was able to send over.'

'I'll keep updating you and I'll talk to you tomorrow, I have to go to Berkshire. Have a good lunch with Josie, give her a kiss from me.'

It was something that Kelly would never have imagined saying a year ago, but now she meant it and it came naturally.

'I will, I'm going to spoil her.'

'Like that is surprising.'

'Why Berkshire?'

'A psychotic murderer in Broadmoor has been sending me letters referencing the recent killings here. I smell a rat and HQ have agreed that I need to clear it up as a lead.'

'Psychotic murderers do like you, don't they? Be careful. Do I know this particular one?'

'You sure do, it's Amy Richmond, The Teacher.'

'Really? Do you have to go? I mean, that was personal, Kelly. I'm not happy at all, what did Johnny say?'

'I'll be behind a screen, don't worry. I don't need a minder.' Inside, she wished she had that option.

They hung up.

Demi looked sympathetically at her and Kelly felt her concern.

'Do you want me to create a profile while you're away?' asked Demi.

'You took the words out of my mouth,' said Kelly.

'We've got air, earth and spirit to go,' Demi said.

'Fred said spirit was in charge of the others and that it's not strictly speaking an element. How would you kill somebody with earth?' Kelly asked.

'Burial? asked Demi.'

'I agree. What about air?'

'That's trickier. Pushing someone off something?'

'Needle in a haystack isn't even close is it?' said Kelly.

'Let me know if The Teacher enlightens you. I wish I could come, but I'm glad I'm not at the same time. It's the kind of meeting that sits in your head.'

'I know. I've spent plenty of time in that head space.'

'Yes, I'm sorry. You must have been terrified.'

'I was never terrified for myself, but for those I knew might still be alive somewhere. My biggest fear was that I might never find them.'

'But you did. And you will again.'

'Try explaining that to my sister. We haven't got much time though. Fred explained to me that next week is the festival of Mabon.' Demi looked oddly at her. 'It's when the equinox happens and day is equal to night. Remember The Teacher's reference to dark and light being equal?'

'Bloody hell. That's next week?'

'Next Thursday. I've checked the trains and I can go this afternoon.'

'Good luck.'

Chapter 38

Daphne shook.

He'd made her watch.

His face told her nothing. Her mother and father were looking older by the day, by the moment, even. He'd always ruled their house with an iron will, and her mother acquiesced every time. It might be something as tiny as how he took his tea, but it could also be something so grave and portentous that it could impact all of their lives. But his power had dimmed. Even his clothes looked shabby now and she found herself repulsed by him.

She dreamt of escape. To run away from this hellhole. At times, the child inside her came skipping back into her life and she forgot, for a moment, how monstrous her existence had become. Other times, the child was forgotten and she sank back into her world of secrets, sacrifice and fear. It was safer that way; there was no room for games.

He said she'd get used to it, like Mother. And she had.

She looked at her parents, sat stern and upright in cold, heartless silence, staring straight ahead. They could be asleep and Daphne wanted to shake them and scream into their faces. To reason with them and plead. But they never listened. Their expressionless faces refused to look at her and she felt more alone than ever.

Daphne considered love, and thought of the boy from the stone circle. She'd read about passion, and hate, and all the emotions that could possibly swim through her body at one time. She knew loathing, and she knew revenge, as well as fear, dread, sorrow and despair. But she didn't know love. She didn't see it, so she couldn't define it. But ever since meeting Callum at the circle, her foundations, and what she'd built them on, had begun to shake.

There were plenty of opportunities for her to vanish from the life Father had created for them. They'd existed on the fringes of society, like gypsies and travellers, in forests, in caravans and tents, for so long now that her disappearance would be irrelevant.

Had that been what she was doing the night she'd found herself naked and wandering around the huge stones? Disappearing? She couldn't remember.

Neither could she remember what brought her back. It was as if some force took her hand and opened the hospital window, made her feet climb out and her legs jump to the electric box and then to the ground, running for her life, towards the old farm. As soon as she'd opened the door, she knew why she'd come back. She saw it now, in her parents, erect and vacant at the same time.

She wanted to shake them and scream. But the house was silent, except for the flies. Father liked it that way. She left them and went to her room to watch TV on her laptop, with the volume on silent. She viewed the characters on screen with odd fascination, and she considered herself lucky to be protected from it. The behaviour of the actors was puzzling. They were all so animated and loud. She could tell this even with no sound. It was a dangerous world out there, that's what her parents told her, and maybe that's why she'd come back.

Her journey to the climbing wall had been risky and reckless. But her parents had not questioned her. They never expected her to become infected by the outside world. They'd educated her about it, of course, teaching her literature, mathematics, science and faith. It was a rich and varied learning and she knew much. But it still surprised her when she watched people interacting with one another, either in the real world, when she dared, or on a screen. She'd had countless opportunities to flee her parents in the last couple of days alone, but she hadn't. Each time, she was pulled back by the invisible hand of what she guessed was loyalty, honour, duty, yes, but never love.

If only she could think of a way to show Callum that her way was more alluring than what he'd been showed in his limited world. He too lived in isolation, on a deserted and windswept farm, just like her. He too looked at his parents as though they provided the biggest obstacle to his spiritual growth, out of all of them. He too had a look of wanting to break free, but lacking the courage to do it.

The girl irked her. Daphne saw no value in her whatsoever and felt disappointed with Callum for giving her his energy. It sapped his aura. She saw his colours fade around him. The girl carried with her an energy of the lost. She was like the personalities Daphne watched on her laptop: plastic, embellished, empty and noisy. Whenever she saw her, her head exploded with the cacophony of an entity so adverse to nature that it must hurt the earth too. If only she could tell her father. She was taking more and more risks, driving around looking for Callum and the girl.

She walked up and down her bedroom, running her fingers along the dusty texts so lovingly gathered here, possibly over a hundred years. There were maps, novels, geography texts, nature tomes, serials, dramatic works and atlases. It was a library of scholarship. An altar of knowledge.

She stopped at the end of the bookshelf and wandered back again.

She looked at a clock on her bedside table, an old antique left in the house, and calculated that she had time to watch the climbers' practice ascent, if she left straight away. She remembered being caught sneaking out, and the severe beating which followed. Her body ached for weeks. The memory of the pain made her fearful of leaving the house. But if she didn't go and watch Callum then she knew she'd lose her mind. She meant no harm. She'd be careful. With binoculars, sat on an adjacent peak, across from the rock face, no one would see her. She could be back before dinner.

She heard an engine and looked out of one of the shutters. It was a Tesco van: they couldn't survive on potatoes and kale all year round. She sighed and got into her uniform: a different hat each time, an overall, a walking stick and the box of dog shit that she opened to make sure they wouldn't want to come in. The dogs barked noisily at the sound of the vehicle and it hurt her head.

By the time she'd watched the van disappear back down the track and brought in the shopping, she realised that she'd need to head off if she had any chance of catching the climbing group. But first, her laptop sounded a notification, and she was glad for once that the volume set itself back to normal when she logged off, because it was a Facetime call that she did not want to miss.

Chapter 39

Ted waited for Josie outside the changing rooms. He'd been skiing once in 1974 and, in those days, everyone wore white all-in-ones with luminous blue sun cream across their noses: it reminded him of the glow of luminol when sprayed on human blood plasma.

Josie had chosen a sophisticated beige two-piece, with fur at the collar. Her figure was slender and strong, and Ted thought she looked like a woman for the first time since he'd met her. He felt a strange sense of pride radiate inside him, and his chest puffed up a little as he'd walked around Keswick with her. People assumed she was his granddaughter. And she was.

She came out of the dressing room and Ted smiled broadly. She looked like a Bond girl, he thought, though Josie probably didn't know the character.

'Have you heard of James Bond?' he asked.

'Are you telling me I look like a man, Ted?' she smirked and winked at him. Her sense of humour was sharp and that was one of the reasons he enjoyed her company. When Kelly and Johnny went to Florida in November, they'd have a hoot.

'Like a Bond girl. You know they're all very beautiful.'

'Ted, you can get arrested for saying stuff like that nowadays. I think the next James Bond should be a woman.'

'But she wouldn't be called James.'

'Jamie Bond, then. Aren't you a feminist?' she asked. He didn't know what to say. She laughed.

'Everybody at my school is a feminist, but I find it a bit confusing. If you're a communist, then you believe communism

228

to be the only way – that's what they said in history – so if you're a feminist then surely you believe that only females have superior qualities. Which isn't fair, is it? Is that controversial?' She fiddled with her zip and Ted admired her intellect, in awe.

'I know you want to study criminology. Have you thought about a profession yet?' he asked.

'What, like a proper job?' she asked, looking at her rear in the mirror.

'I love it. Is it warm?'

'Style over comfort, Ted. It's what it looks like. So?'

'Wonderful. You look fabulous, but I'm a little worried that you might get too much attention.'

'Let's get this one.'

They grinned at each other. 'What's *your* job? I know you work with Kelly sometimes, are you a police doctor or something?' She went back into the small cubicle and he held hangers and odds and ends, waiting for her.

'I'm a pathologist.'

She came out, fastening her jumper and tidying her hair. The ski clothes were on the floor. Ted went to pick them up. None of his girls had children, and he was coming to realise that he wished they had.

'Is that someone who deals with mental health?' she asked.

'No. That's a psychotherapist.'

'Oh.'

'I find out why people die.'

She screwed her face. 'Ugh. That's grim.'

'Not really. As long as you're not offended by that sort of thing. A body is just a bunch of human cells that can work properly or not. It's my job to make sure we understand why things go wrong.'

'So why do you work with Kelly?'

'Because I also find out how people are killed.'

'Like murdered?' Her eyes widened, and her face lit up.

'Yes.'

'That is so cool. Are you the one who cuts them up and saws their chest open?'

'Yes. Shhh, there are other people in here.' He tried to lessen her excitement. It wasn't the kind of conversation one might expect in a climbing shop, especially when there had been two killings reported in the area in as many weeks. People were jumpy. It reminded him of when The Teacher was at large. It changed people's behaviour; they became nervous and careful. He thought briefly of Kelly and hoped she knew what she was doing, going to pay the murderer a visit; he didn't think it wise.

'Can I watch one day? If I study criminology at university that includes a module on Crime Scene Investigation. Do you work with CSI?'

'Yes. They process the scene, along with forensic examiners, and I bring it all together. With Kelly of course.'

'She's so clever.' It was touching to hear Josie's view of his daughter. He couldn't agree more, he just wished Kelly could hear it herself. She'd never believe that this young lady admired her so much. Teenagers were highly underestimated in his opinion: they didn't miss a thing.

'So are we taking these? Don't you need jumpers and gloves and other bits and pieces?' he asked, standing in the waiting area, like Josie's personal assistant. She went to him and put her arms around him, and squeezed.

'Thank you.' It was very simple but Ted felt overcome and had to look away.

'Let's have a look at the helmets,' he said. She followed him.

'Have you worked on the murder victims this week?' she whispered. He stopped and looked at her, pretending to be mad at her impertinence, but he couldn't.

'I could get into a lot of trouble discussing this with you,' he said.

'Just tell me if you learned a lot, and Kelly is going to catch him?'

'Of course she is.'

Chapter 40

Kelly left Penrith on time. She'd indulged in an upgrade to
first class, and reclined in the large comfortable seat, with no
one next to or opposite her. The quiet was luxurious and she
intended to spend the whole journey taking her time to ponder.

Sometimes, the job got in the way of a good investigation, in
the sense that being busy created stress, and stress clouded judgement. To sit and think, to chew things over, was a real treat. She
placed her phone, iPad and laptop beside her, should she need
them, and settled back to reflect. However, the expected relief
never came and, instead, nerves fluttered under her ribcage at
the thought of what she would soon walk into.

She separated each of the two murders and approached
them independently, over time, starting at the beginning. First
she rewound to Mary's house, late on the Friday night, the
distressed animals making a racket outside, and Mary going to
see what the fuss was all about. The neighbours – she surmised
– were used to the commotion, and so turned up their TVs.
Whoever was in Mary's yard gave her very little time to react:
no 999 call, and no reports of screaming. It could mean that she
knew her attacker, and they talked. Or the animals stopped their
noise. The conversation didn't end well and Mary was overpow-
ered, forced to watch the torture of her beloved animals, and set
upon with two weapons. Both she and Rob had checked the
inventory of the home, and the athame was missing. It could
mean that Mary had taken it somewhere, or it could mean that
it was the second murder weapon and had been removed by
the killer. The murderer didn't bother to clean up footprints

around the body and throughout the kitchen because they were wearing standard wellies that could be purchased at a thousand different outlets across the world. They were more concerned with advertising their power and control by tattooing the victim and leaving the sign of the Moon Goddess, much the same as branding the animals with the fire element. They then calmly drove away in a vehicle pre-parked in the private lane behind the garden.

Mary knew them.

Second murder. Carry Tomlin was connected to the first murder through her vocal opinions of the occult being responsible for Mary's death. Had the killer posed as a source and they'd arranged to meet? No rage was evident but this was yet to be confirmed by Ted. That was a difference. The symbol of water arranged above her head connected the two murders further. Kelly made a note of the three other elements, including spirit, and googled all five. The problem with the internet was that once you pursued one search, something else popped up that stoked interest and, before you knew where you were, you had seventeen pages of information open.

She called the office to see if they'd had results for the tyre tracks found behind Mary's garden lane, or any news on who Carry Tomlin had met or spoken to prior to her death. Her newspaper team was in shock, and they were trying to process what had happened. As a result, none of them were very helpful. The reporter hadn't left a journal of daily appointments, she'd told no one where she was going when she left the office on Tuesday lunchtime, and her phone records had still to be sent back from Vodafone. None of her colleagues knew of an appointment that would take Carry south on the A591 late morning yesterday.

It was DS Will Phillips who looked into the tyre tracks taken from the lane, and he reported that the track specialist he'd been working with in a lab in Manchester had narrowed it down to a tyre used on Fiat campervans. It was a Michelin Agilis Camping Green X tyre with a distinct feathered shaped tread.

It was great news because they were so distinctive. However, campervans in the Lake District were like Range Rovers in Hampstead Heath.

Next she re-read the letters from The Teacher, but with a renewed context provided by Fred O'Reilly about seasons, balance and the goddess. She opened the most recent that she'd only read this morning (this time wearing plastic gloves) and it seemed a life time ago.

> *Broadmoor Rehabilitation Home*
> *Autumn 2018*
>
> *Hello Kelly,*
> *Are you ignoring me?*

She stared out of the window and realised that they were passing Crewe already. Her neck ached and she rubbed it. She went back to the rantings of a maniac.

> *Several years ago, a little girl was brought in to the Penrith and Lakes Hospital with extensive injuries to her arms. The mother said she'd been self-harming because of bullying at school. The girl must have been around eleven years old, I guess. She was so scared.*
>
> *You see, I recognised in her a fellow empath. She was hurting so badly but she wouldn't tell me what happened. The records may still exist. It was the eyes that gave it away, Kelly. The way she looked at me: it was as if she was asking me to rescue her. Her big, beautiful, blue eyes.*
>
> *I recognised the marks. They're always the same, the symbols of harm dished out to children from their carers. I should know.*
>
> *They walked out of hospital never to be seen of or heard of again. They gave false names, addresses and histories.*
>
> *Odd, don't you think?*

Kelly put down the letter. She picked up the previous one and went to the last line about Mary's animals and tried to remember when that information was made public. The date stamp on the letter was Saturday 10 September, the day after Mary was murdered, so it was feasible for Amy to know about the girl at Castlerigg: that had been reported the previous week, but the bit about the animals raised a flag. It was impossible for anyone to have learned so much information in that time, but Kelly was unaware if gossip had been posted online by neighbours or those who'd given police interviews. She read on.

> *You know what pain and misery does to a child. It's the same with animals: you can torture them, abandon them and starve them, but they'll keep appealing for your love.*
> *We became friends.*
> *Namaste x*

The tiny hairs on Kelly's arms stood upright and she closed her eyes. She willed herself to calm down. There was little in the correspondence that couldn't be explained by clever manipulation of snippets from online news and gossip. But that's what she was on her way to find out.

Chapter 41

Before leaving Penrith, Kelly had tasked DS Umshaw and DC Shawcross with following up her series of brief interviews at Fred O'Reilly's house this morning. Contrary to Kelly's expectations that the guests would want to flee, Kate and Rob found them mostly still in attendance at the address when they visited shortly after Kelly's departure.

It had been Kate who spotted it first.

They were a mixed bunch, and Sandra O'Reilly was surprised at yet another visit from the police department in the same day. She looked weary when she answered the door. Kate introduced them both and Sandra recognised Rob from the previous interview.

'Something new?' Sandra asked.

'Yes, actually. Could we come in?'

Sandra moved aside and scolded herself for forgetting her manners.

'Who is it, San?' Fred hollered. He came into the hallway and stopped, deflated at the sight of two well-dressed professionals who looked like coppers or lawyers. Kate made introductions again and Fred recognised Rob, whose stature was fairly unmissable. They shook hands.

'Something new?' he asked.

Rob nodded. 'Can we sit down? I see you have guests still here, we didn't put them off?'

Fred sighed. 'I would have organised it another day if I'd known. Besides, you lot made it clear that they were to be interviewed again, which I think has finished.'

'Investigations don't work like that I'm afraid,' Kate said. 'We never know from one hour to the next what might come in, and finding Mary's killer is our absolute priority, now that we have another woman killed in the area.'

'What?' Sandra and Fred said in unison.

'You're not aware? Perhaps you haven't listened to the news? The journalist, Carry Tomlin, was found dead by the shore of Thirlmere this morning. It's a homicide investigation.'

'Oh my goodness, Fred, that's the one who wrote the article about us all! What's going on? What's happening?' Sandra asked. She was visibly upset; her face flushed and she put her hand to her chest.

'Turn the TV on, San,' Fred said. Sandra got up and lifted a tablecloth away from a cupboard and opened the wooden doors, grateful for something to do. She found a remote control and flicked on the machine, searching for a local news channel. It didn't take long. A report showed an area beside Thirlmere reservoir sealed off with police tape and crawling with officers. Images of an older couple (who turned out to be Carry Tomlin's grieving parents) were shown, with photographers hounding them outside their house in Ambleside.

'We're aware that you weren't fond of her views,' Rob asked. Fred looked at his wife and spread his hands.

'I admit it. I was livid when I read the twaddle she'd printed about people like us. I don't know where she got her information from.'

'Do you know anyone else who expressed anger over her work? We believe she might have been meeting someone posing as a potential source of information.'

'Golly. A lot of people I should think,' Fred said. 'I'm sorry, it was poor journalism and a shoddy representation of who we are.'

'We understand. Could you give us a brief summary of your movements between eleven a.m. yesterday and this morning?'

Fred and Sandra looked at one another and shook their heads. Then they nodded. Kate knew they understood. They'd vocalised anger towards the woman, and they'd probably been overheard, so they had to be ruled out. Any evidence of passion towards a victim of homicide had to be properly investigated.

'So, yesterday, about ten in the morning, we shopped at Booths in Keswick for everything we needed for today. We try to stay as self-sufficient as we can, and we manage to an extent, but for a gathering we need extra.'

Kate and Rob waited patiently. Rob was the one tasked with taking notes. Fred carried on, with Sandra nodding. 'We finished in Keswick about three in the afternoon because we stopped for lunch at the new organic place.'

'So there'll be parking and till receipts,' Kate said. It wasn't a question. Rob made a note of the restaurant name. 'Carry on,' said Kate.

'We came home, unpacked the shopping. Then I began making all the bread rolls for today. That took me all afternoon,' Sandra said.

'So you didn't travel south on the A591 towards Great How?'

'No.' The couple looked at one another again.

Kate had already checked CCTV footage for Carry returning north, and she hadn't found any. There'd been no more record of her driving south after the next traffic camera at the Wythburn car park, so she had to have stopped between those two destinations. They'd already entered the number plates of everybody currently on the investigative list on the Mary Hales case, and Fred's car hadn't been down that way. Though it didn't mean that he hadn't driven another vehicle and Sandra was covering for him. It was unlikely, but they weren't off the hook yet.

'We need all the vehicle registration plates of your guests, as well as descriptions of their vehicles. Do any of them own a Fiat campervan?'

Fred and Sandra shook their heads.

'Thank you both. One reason we came back, apart from as part of our inquiry into the death of the young journalist and to warn you of further press interest, was because a name popped up in one of the statements given by a guest here today and it's of interest to us. Have either of you heard of a woman named Edna Beverley?'

'Of course. Edna was a dear friend. She died of a broken heart after her son, William, went missing. They never found him. It was terrible.'

'And that's what the witness told us. They mentioned her because DI Porter was asking about past members of your group, and she specifically asked them about Kirk Junker.'

Fred and Sandra looked puzzled.

'Well, the thing is that this afternoon, we received a phone call from one of your guests, wanting to add information, and that's exactly what DI Porter told them all: if they remembered anything else, get in touch.'

'Right,' said Fred.

'He told us that Edna had an on-off relationship with Kirk Junker too. Is this true?'

'Crikey. I think that might have been before our time. We only came here from Shap ten years ago. Who told you that?'

'Jock Harris.'

'Ah Jock, he's been here as long as the hills, I'm not surprised. So, Edna and Kirk, eh? Before Mary I assume?'

'At the same time, apparently. There were rumours that Edna did Skyclad meetings with him, which I understand means worshipping in the nude.'

Fred bent his head. 'No. I don't believe that for one minute. This is the sort of thing that gets us a bad name. That journalist said we were all into orgies and naked prancing around the forests, chanting nonsense and raping virgins. It's a hate crime, I tell you! That's what you should be investigating! Who told you that?' Fred stood up. His face had gone purple and Sandra soothed him.

'We're not at liberty to say.'

'Edna was a lovely woman. She had nothing in her heart but love for her son when we knew her. Have you news of him? Not that Edna will ever benefit from it.'

'Not at this time, but if Kirk Junker is a suspect in Mary's case, then we have to consider him in the disappearance of Edna's son.'

'My God.' Sandra sat heavily. 'What's he done? He's the devil, so he is.' She put her hands over her eyes and rubbed them. Kate decided that they'd caused enough trauma for one day, and the couple needed to process what they'd discovered in a very short space of time. They had a solid alibi for yesterday, pending receipts, and they still needed to talk to Jock. The boss wanted them both brought to the station, but she'd also told them to get their line of questioning spot on.

'Is Jock in the garden? We'll talk to him and get out of your way, it's been a hard day.'

'Yes, it has.' Fred snapped at them.

'We're just doing our jobs, Mr O'Reilly. DI Porter advised you to speak to a lawyer, how is that going?'

Fred didn't answer. It was time to leave. Sandra showed them into the garden, where a young man played guitar, and others sat around him. It was a lovely late afternoon and the sun had turned golden. There was a nip in the air but it was a scene that warmed the heart, Kate noted. It was unusual for her to feel something approaching pure happiness. More often than not, her life was one long circus train of teenage angst, fights over the shower, endless bills, a lazy husband and bastard criminals. In this garden, she felt at peace, and she didn't want to leave. She smiled at Rob, who looked at her oddly. She noticed that some of the women had flowers in their hair and a few children played in a tree house.

Sandra took them to meet Jock, who sat in a chair with his eyes closed, listening to the music. They'd seen his face before: next to Carla Rigg, real name Daphne, in the photograph found in her wallet. The case was becoming like a game of pick-up

239

sticks, with Kate and Rob trying to keep tabs on which one could be pulled out of the pile next. They had yet to work out how to remove each stick without disturbing the others, but it was impossible. Every time they gathered a new nugget of information, it was as if the whole game changed and more sticks were thrown into the pile.

'Jock,' Sandra pushed his shoulder gently. His eyes flickered open and Kate introduced them. He took their hands firmly and waited for them to sit down. He was a large man with a relaxing charm about him, and a twinkle in his eye. He hadn't changed much since the photo had been taken with Daphne. He sat upright, ready to help the detectives.

'Can you tell us more about Edna Beverley and her son William?'

'He was the sweetest boy. A bit soft, actually. That's why I think he wandered off; he wasn't streetwise like his mother. She tried her best, but he had no father figure around to make him a man.'

It was a stark assessment, but honest to the teller of the tale. Kate and Rob noticed that the guitar had fallen silent and, slowly, people were gathering around them, listening to Jock speak.

'She looked for him for years. The police stopped after six months. They said he'd likely got into a car with a stranger and left the county; they passed it to other counties, who never came up with anything either. Did you know that one hundred and forty thousand children go missing in the UK every year?'

'Yes,' Kate said.

'Of course you do, you're a policewoman. It's not your fault is it? You do your best, with stretched resources, and politicians who care more for their second home in Chelsea than a missing child. Children are twice as likely to disappear as adults. But you know that too, don't you?'

Kate nodded. 'Were you and Edna close, Jock?'

The man looked down. Kate reckoned she'd found the source of his interest in UK statistics regarding missing kids.

Jock looked around the group. The adults were huddled around now, somehow aware of the suffering that their friend faced. Kate watched as they rallied and she felt envy. There was human connection here in this garden, and it was quite beautiful.

'How well did she know Kirk Junker?' she pressed on.

At the mention of his name, the adults tensed and stiffened, forming a barrier of sorts between Jock and the detectives.

'Hang on, it's all right, we're just trying to get some answers, we all want to find out what happened to Mary,' Kate said, holding up her hand. She saw that Rob leant on a wall, keeping an eye on her and watching the dynamic unfold. He had her back. She clocked the two males he was watching: the one with the guitar and another who'd moved behind her. She didn't think they were in danger, but in a situation like this, with emotions running high, tension could escalate quickly.

She turned around and addressed the whole group. 'I know you've told DI Porter what you remember about him, but it's vital that we find him. Did he ever mention a property that he owned or rented? Did he use different names? Even a nickname would be helpful. Did he say where he was going? Did you see him drive a Fiat campervan?'

The members of the group looked at one another and shook their heads. The laughter of the children from the tree house ricocheted around the small walled garden. Sandra came out and sat next to Jock, taking his hand in hers. The nervousness of a few moments ago dissipated.

'We came to the group after he left,' one said. Kate recognised her from taking her statement.

'We didn't like him, we stopped coming until he'd gone,' said another.

'Before Edna died, she told me that she thought Kirk was responsible for William going missing. She fancied he took him.' It was Jock that spoke. Sandra squeezed his hand.

'Why would she think that?' Kate asked. The whole group tensed and Kate thought they wouldn't breathe again. They watched Jock and no one moved. Even Rob was transfixed from his vantage point, and he stood upright, away from the wall.

'He disappeared during the festival of Walpurgis. The thirtieth of April 2003. I will never forget the date. Edna's world ended that night. It's May Eve, the day before May Day: the beginning of summer. You Pagans know it as the night before May Day, it's usually a bank holiday but no one really knows why.'

'I thought you were the Pagans?' Kate asked. The group laughed, and Kate and Rob looked around: the joke was on them.

'That's what the Christian Church would have you believe: they just hijacked all of our festivals and called them their own. Christmas? That's Yule, and we've celebrated it for centuries. Easter? That's Beltane, and your Easter eggs come from our fertility celebrations. You're the Pagans.'

'I'm actually an atheist,' Kate said.

'Good. There's hope for you yet!' The group laughed again.

Kate found herself smiling. 'Tell me about William going missing on May Eve. What did you call it?'

'Walpurgis Night. It's a Christian term but stolen from ancient Germanic culture.'

'Did you say Germanic?'

'Yes, why?'

'Something about Kirk Junker's name: that's Germanic isn't it?'

'Prussian actually, and no, he isn't. He's more Essex I'd say.'

'Really?' Kate got out Fred's photofit of Kirk Junker and held it up. Some of the group recoiled. Jock sat stock still.

'He liked to think that he was exotic. The hair is dyed and he dressed up like some bohemian prince, but he's an Essex boy. The name was made up.'

Kate hung her head in exasperation with this tight-knit bundle of loyalties and secrets. She made a note to contact Essex Police with his artist's impression.

'You could have told us that sooner.'

'You never asked.'

'That's why we can't find him,' Kate said. The group was silent. Rob shook his head and leant back on the wall.

'Carry on.'

'Like I said, we call Easter Beltane. It's when summer emerges and life returns to the land after the spring equinox. Some occultists believe that "bringing in the May" means performing certain sordid rituals. Edna thought Kirk capable of it.'

'Capable of what?'

'Using the innocent to sacrifice in celebration.'

To Kate, the euphemism was clear, but she'd have to get him to be more specific in private and get him on the record.

'Why didn't she tell the police?' she asked.

The group mumbled quietly together. Kate was stunned.

'Wouldn't any of you report a fellow member if *your* child went missing?' Kate looked around the group. To her amazement, they were considering their answers.

'She was scared of him,' Jock said.

'But if the police could have apprehended him and found William…'

'It doesn't work like that, detective. You're missing the point. She feared the *spirit* of Kirk more than the agony of never finding her son.'

Kate looked at the ground, and tears dampened her eyes. She thought about her girls and how tortured Edna must have been.

'I know what you're thinking,' Jock said. 'Edna told me before she died that Kirk had invited her and William to join him for lunch. He took them to a hotel. At the time of William's disappearance, the appeal on TV reminded a hotel worker to come forward and give a description of a man who she'd seen with the boy at the hotel the day before May Eve.'

'And still Edna didn't tell them about Kirk?' Kate asked.

'She believed that William went of his own free will.'

'What? He was twelve! And why didn't you come forward when she confided in you?'

'I did. I wasn't taken seriously.'

'What? When was this?'

'Goodness. Years ago. Edna died in 2012, it was shortly after that, you'll find it in your police records if you look, and if you don't, then it wasn't even logged.'

'I'm sorry. I can only apologise if it wasn't handled well at the time. I'll chase it, I promise.'

'She also told me that Kirk wasn't booked at the hotel under his own name.'

'Did she tell you the name?'

Chapter 42

Kelly caught a cab from Reading station and grew more anxious as the minutes ticked past. Traffic flowed freely through Bracknell. Her stomach knotted and twisted, making her feel queasy and her hands clammy. She'd gone over what she would say to Amy Richmond, but she knew that whatever happened it would be virtually impossible to control the outcome. The best approach would be to allow the psychopath to lead, to calm her ego and, along the way, squeeze as much information as possible from the interview. She remembered what Demi told her.

'It's a game.'

She just needed to hold her nerve.

The Teacher's crimes were sordid, depraved and alongside some of the worst anyone had seen. Every now and again, a serial killer comes along who defies all logic and learning on human behaviour. Their brains are so damaged by twisted and degenerate perversion, that they inflict harrowing injury with impunity.

Perfect for understanding her Lake District ritual killings.

HQ, in granting her permission to interview the patient, had agreed with the emerging theory that some sort of formal rites were involved. In that, she argued, the perpetrator was trying to communicate with them just as The Teacher had. The symbolic evidence was indisputable and HQ accepted that the crimes were linked. They had another serial killer.

This time, though, Kelly did not want a private audience with said nutter, as she'd had, against her will, with The

Teacher; she just wanted to nail him, or her. She switched her phone to silent and gave her ID to the man on the gate.

We became friends.

The vast arrangement of buildings nestled between some of the most expensive real estate in the country, and was a stone's throw away from the Royal Military Academy at Sandhurst, where future war glitterati gained their commissions from Her Majesty, the Queen.

The irony. Legal and illegal mass murder...

Kelly felt frustration at the pressures on the modern force. Too many killers went free. But wading into politics didn't get police work done.

It was a beautiful day, and in Berkshire, the temperature was around ten degrees higher than the Lake District. The hospital was shrouded in trees, and the only way anyone would know it was there was the practice alarm at eleven a.m. every day. It was Britain's maximum security hospital for the worst offenders and psychos to ever have taken a breath.

The cab drove through the gates and up a long winding driveway, towards another series of metal gates.

'Visiting family, love?' The cabbie was prying.

'No. Work related.'

'Christ, you work with this lot? Good luck.'

'Thanks.'

He pulled up outside a guard box and she got out, after paying him.

'Would you wait for me? I need to get back to the station in about an hour or so?'

'Of course, love. If you're paying, I'll wait.'

'Run the meter.'

She nodded at the guard, who found her on his list, checked her ID and let her through. The walk up to the main reception was long and lonely. She wished Demi was beside her, or Johnny. Two voices of reason who she'd trust beyond all others.

Or Ted. She hadn't had the heart to ask him, and pull him away from his afternoon with Josie. Because he'd have said yes.

A man in a suit was waiting for her and walked towards her with an outstretched hand. It was the guy she'd been talking to on the phone about The Teacher. She'd expected him to be reticent, or nervous about the pending meeting, but, in fact he was just as excited about meeting somebody who'd been apprehended by his patient, and survived. He jabbered on, and she barely registered what he said. Her nerves jangled and she tried to breathe. She imagined her letters being penned behind these walls, by The Teacher's hand, and sent to be stamped in an office somewhere. Her stomach turned upside down.

Then they were inside a set of metal doors, each locking in front and behind as they passed through.

'May I go in alone?'

'Of course. I expected you to say that. I'll be watching on the screen.'

'I know. I hope I get something for your research.'

'Here we are. We've finally found the leak in our system, have you been informed?'

'No.' Kelly was puzzled.

'The letters, sent to you I believe?'

'What about them? I just know they were posted in Surrey.'

'They were traced to one post box, near the house of an employee of ours. She has admitted taking financial reward for posting the letters on behalf of our patient. She is being suitably disciplined.'

'That makes sense. Thank you for letting me know.'

Kelly looked along the corridor. It was the isolation unit, where patients were kept alone for their own safety. It was painted white, with a green linoleum floor, and smelled of disinfectant. There wasn't much noise, apart from the odd clang of a trolley or a door elsewhere. A series of doors lined the walls and at the end there was a room, and she saw that Amy Richmond was waiting for her, behind a strengthened screen, sat in a chair, staring at the ceiling. The hairs on Kelly's neck stood up. She turned to the doctor and he told her to wait for the guard to unlock the door, then go through the inner door and sit down in front of the patient.

'Did you agree with the verdict?' she asked.

'Insanity? Of course.'

Kelly nodded. It was what they all said. Except Demi. The Teacher wasn't mentally ill. Just evil, and should be in the worst category A gaffe imaginable, with all the other bastards, not languishing in a hospital, mollycoddled by sycophants and studied by academics.

She walked through. She could hear her breath and feel her heart as she approached the window. All the way down the corridor, Amy gazed at the ceiling in her cell and never looked at Kelly once. Until she stopped in front of her, almost so close she could smell her. She sat on the chair provided.

Kelly stared through the glass at the felon before her: androgynous, chubby and, now, smiling.

'Kelly. I've missed you. I knew you'd come eventually. How's Josie?'

The question completely threw her and The Teacher saw it, and smiled. *Fuck!*

It was not the ideal way to start.

'Leave my family out of this. I'm here to talk about Daphne and Kirk Junker.'

'*Your* family? Things are hotting up between you and Johnny, then? I'm jealous!' More smiling, this time with teeth: stained and wonky.

Kelly felt sick. She was instantly transported back to the night when she'd gone home to Amy's house, held against her will, but fully knowing that Nikki was tied up somewhere, scared and alone and even possibly dead.

'How the hell did you know about the Moon Goddess and Mabon? I thought you were more into Lakeland poets.' It was her turn to take control.

'It's all there, should you choose to open your eyes to it. I was right, wasn't I? I've been reading about Carry Tomlin. I think she was an incidental killing, by the way – not like Mary – who was a victim of hate, along with her animals.'

Breathe.

'Why incidental?'

'Opportunity. She wrote shit articles and your killer was pissed off.'

'When I get pissed off I go for a run.'

'But we're not all like you, are we? You're pure, and noble, and wholesome. You do things because you know they're right, not because you *feel* them.'

'Feel?'

'Yes. Your killer *loves* killing. A bit like me. How I miss it. The sensation of…'

'You made mistakes. You were sloppy.'

'As will yours be. Be patient.'

'I don't want to wait for any more bodies.'

'So, you've at least worked that bit out then? Four or five? What do you think?'

Kelly's heart beat faster and faster as she tried to keep one step ahead of the questions.

'What do *you* think?'

'It doesn't matter what I think. I'm sorry about your mother. Is your sister still a bitch?'

Kelly didn't answer.

'Colluding with journalists isn't dignified is it? Have you told her off yet? I bet you haven't. You don't want to face all that again.'

'Stop psychoanalysing me! I'm not here for this bullshit. Tell me what you know about Kirk Junker and his daughter Daphne. Was she the girl brought into the Penrith and Lakes as a suspected child abuse case? We still haven't found her and I think she's in danger, I'm worried about her.'

'So you should be, poor girl. The mother gave her name as Gloria, but she didn't list paternity. He came to meet her at the hospital but stayed in the car park. I followed them, of course. I bet your artists have got an image by now: he stands out, doesn't he? I thought you coppers were good at spotting oddities?'

'Why didn't you kill him? Didn't you want to save the girl?'

'I was otherwise engaged.'

'You mean you were already mid-kill spree? How inconvenient for the child. I thought you were busy butchering in Yorkshire back then. Forgive me, were there more in the Lake District before Moira?' Moira Tate was who they thought had been The Teacher's first victim.

'Murder takes practice, Kelly.'

The way the words slipped off Amy's tongue and onto her lips, out of her mouth, made Kelly shudder. It was a moment of pure joy for the killer.

'You haven't found any trace of Kirk Junker, have you? Otherwise you wouldn't be here. You want a name from me.'

'I want to know how come you know so much. You must have a pretty close relationship to him or Daphne: what's the deal?'

'Close? No. He's an amateur. We met after the girl came to hospital. I dabbled in the occult for a while but it wasn't for me. Too obvious. Too clandestine and tacky. A bit clichéd. Anyway, I preferred to work alone.'

Kelly felt bile rise in her throat. She'd seen the 'work' first hand.

'Is that why your first lot of murders used religious references.'

'I'm so embarrassed about that.' Kelly noticed the first flicker of humanity: shame. Get a narcissist on to themselves and it usually shows.

'So, is my trip going to be wasted or are you going to level with me?'

'Will you come and see me again?'

'Probably not.'

'But if I think of something else?'

'Think? It just might *occur* to you that you know more than you want to drip feed me today?'

'It's your fortieth next year isn't it? You don't age. But I suppose that's because you've never raised a child. Is it on the cards for you and the delightful Mr Frietze who I had the pleasure of meeting, alone, on a wild mountainside?'

Kelly didn't move. It wasn't working. She realised that the game was an even field. The Teacher was stalling for time: time with her. Broadmoor was a lonely place.

'And all that running. I can see your carotid pulse; you have the heart of an athlete.'

And you have the heart of the devil.

Again, she didn't answer. She felt the balance of power shift to her, and she waited. Amy got up and Kelly saw her in full view. She looked like a normal woman; overweight, ageing and slow, but a woman nonetheless. She looked vulnerable, pathetic almost. She waddled around the room that was her cage and put her hands on her hips. She'd lost muscle and gained fat. It took all of Kelly's strength not to feel empathy, and even sympathy for her.

'Harry O'Connor.'

Kelly didn't flinch. She made no sound and gave away no indication of feeling anything at all. She'd heard the name before.

'Are you sure?'

'Positive. Would I lie to you?'

Kelly slowly got up. She desperately wanted to run but she had to remain in control.

'Leaving so soon?' Amy taunted her.

'You know they won't let me see you for too long in case you turn me into a nutcase.' She began walking away.

She longed for fresh air and to be out of this hellhole. Names, dates, seasons, birds and sheep raced through her mind in a cacophony of chaos. Her palms grew sweaty and she felt slightly faint as she walked away towards the door, which she banged on, ready to be let out.

'Kelly! Come back. You'll have to come back! I'll be here waiting. I'm not going anywhere!'

She left the secure unit with the sound of maniacal cackling in her head. Her hunch was right. She knew it was the right thing to do to come here. She couldn't put her finger on what made her trust The Teacher, and she agreed that it was perverse, but she knew it was the truth. Snippets of cold case files slotted into place. The details of William Beverley's case came back in full technicolour to haunt her, and she felt deep visceral pain for the mothers who'd lost their children across the Lake District at certain times of the year. She wondered how many more?

Eight festivals, Fred told her. Eight per year. Four elements and four directions. Christ it was fucked up shit! But it was beginning to make sense.

The cabbie was surprised to see her so soon, and she jumped in, in silence.

'Go well?' he asked. She ignored him.

'Reading station.'

Chapter 43

Johnny drove his battered Jeep Grand Cherokee to the brand new Rock of Ages climbing wall just outside Keswick. His pulse hadn't dipped below ninety since he last spoke to his daughter. He couldn't explain it. It had been the same since she was born: the intense feeling of protectiveness towards her that overshadowed every other thing in his life. Leaving his ex-wife had been hard for that reason alone: it meant leaving his daughter.

Their relationship had come apart at the edges, as he guessed it would, mainly thanks to his job taking him thousands of miles away, but also due to the woman's bitter nature. Tours of Iraq and Afghanistan weren't conducive to nurturing familial ties. It's why he'd eventually left. But it still took him a long time to work his way back into Josie's life, and by then, she was emerging as a young woman herself.

It threw him. But then he realised that his daughter was a mirror image of himself in temperament, approach and character. She didn't suffer fools and she was driven to go after what she wanted. She was just like Kelly.

The thought of Kelly sat face to face with The Teacher made his skin crawl. The whole investigation was odd. Usually, during a high-profile inquiry, Kelly had forged her direction by now, but this one had thrown her. They talked. What couple didn't? He kept her secrets. It relaxed her to throw snippets at him and listen to his take on a suspect interview or a family dynamic. And for his part, he found it fascinating. He couldn't do what she did – the agony of seeing the victims would kill him, especially kids – but he was in awe of her approach, and how she attacked the job. He had no doubt that she'd catch whoever did those horrible things to those two women, but he could tell that she was wavering uncharacteristically.

He looked up at the sky as it darkened and, by next week, the days would grow shorter until the spring. It was a depressing prospect but he and Kelly were similar in that they loved the winter when it finally came. They adored the sunshine of summer but not the throngs of tourists who choked the roads, or needed to be rescued from the fells. Maybe now that Josie was climbing, she'd want to come along with them as they escaped the crowds finding hidden havens. He'd toyed with the idea of meeting the kids at the foot of the rock face on which they practised, but he knew that it would embarrass his daughter, especially in front of Callum.

He seemed a nice enough boy, but nice *enough* was never going to be adequate for his daughter. It was the first time that he'd thought of Josie's affections in a grown-up way and it made him uncomfortable. He tried to remember what his first girlfriend had been like, and how old she was when they had sex for the first time. He reckoned she was around fifteen. Josie's age exactly. Callum was sixteen and he seemed to remember that was his age when said occasion occurred.

His grip tightened on the wheel and he started to think of locations where the two youngsters could pull it off. His experience had been in the girl's garden shed. Her parents had put a comfy sofa in there for the kids to go in and take their friends to play. And play they did. His grip tightened further. Then he saw her. As he drove into the car park, the minibus was unloading and he saw her beaming and fresh, as if she'd had the time of her life.

Without thought, she spotted him and bounded over to him.

'Dad! That was amazing! We abseiled forwards too! I can't wait till Friday.'

'Can I come this time? I want to watch you.' They hugged. He looked over her shoulder and saw Callum helping with the unloading of the equipment.

'You've got dirt on your nose,' he said, wiping it. She laughed and recoiled at the same time. 'Come on, I'll help you.' They walked to the bus and the instructor, Kev, shook Johnny's hand. He was a part-time mountain rescue colleague, and they'd been up plenty of hairy rock faces together in the past. They chatted about how the kids had done and the arrangements for Woden's Face on Friday. The exam would be as soon after school finish time as possible and so they had to be here ready to go at four p.m. sharp.

'You been on duty recently? I haven't seen you?' Johnny asked Kev.

'It's been quiet, mate. They only call me when you guys are stretched. They keep me busy all winter, which is perfect for me so I can concentrate on this in summer.'

'Good plan. How did she do?'

'Josie? She's a natural, like her old man.'

'Can I come along on Friday? I'm on call but I'd love to see her if that's all right.'

'Course, mate, take a ride with me. Get here by four and we'll sort it, you can help me out and do me a favour by belaying, it'll speed things up.'

They shook hands. Johnny had been climbing for most of his adult life and he could remember when they had to learn to tie a Tarbuck knot; there were no rock boots back then, and harnesses were slung around your waist (and if you fell you knew about it); and ropes were numbered one to four denoting 1000 lb breaking strain and so on.

It was different now as Johnny watched all the kit being unloaded. It was for good reason that technology moved on, of course, especially when his daughter's life was at risk. Climbing to this day was an underestimated sport, and Johnny knew all too well the cost of not taking the dangers seriously. Conceit led to death, and Johnny had pulled enough bodies off the mountainside to witness it first-hand. The advances in equipment saved thousands of lives worldwide, every year. The scores of coloured carabiners (biners) clanked together on the ropes, and an array of other mountaineering kit was hefted out of the back of the bus in hardy bags, tied with the latest kernmantle ropes, all graded by numerous charts and tables.

'Impressive kit. Everest next?'

'They need to learn the kit as much as the skill.'

'Tell me about it. Is there a written exam too?'

'Yup. They have that at the weekend. In no time at all, mate, she'll be belaying you off the top of Bowfell Buttress.'

'I don't doubt that for a second, having seen you in action.'

Johnny turned around to find Josie close up to Callum, apparently saying their goodbyes.

'Hey, you two. I can take Callum home, or are you sorted for a lift?' he asked Callum.

'I was going to get a bus, it's only a couple of miles down the A66.'

'And what time is the bus?' Johnny asked. He noticed Josie bend her head and shake it.

'I don't know.'

'Right. I'll take you, come on. We live in Pooley Bridge so it's on our way.'

Callum shrugged and did as he was told. Josie smiled and Johnny could tell that, despite her protestations, she was chuffed to be spending a little more time in his company.

As they thanked Kev and left the centre, Josie turned up the radio and settled into the front passenger seat, with Callum behind her.

'Cool,' Callum said from the back seat as they pulled out of the car park.

'What?' Josie asked. Johnny strained to listen to their conversation to report back to Kelly later, if she made it back from Broadmoor tonight.

'Did you see that campervan? That's what I want eventually. I'll take it across Europe and down to Greece.'

'Wow,' said Josie in awe.

Johnny looked in his rear-view mirror and spotted an ancient looking Fiat van that looked as though it had seen better days. Callum had a point, though; those old Fiats had tons of character, and with a lick of paint, and tender loving care, one of those things could easily smash Greece in a summer.

Chapter 44

'Ted. Did you look at the images I sent to you?'

Ted was watching the six o'clock news, eating his mashed potato and Cumberland sausages off a tray, sipping a fine glass of Malbec.

'Hello, Kelly. Good trip? Don't you ever breathe?'

'I'm sorry, Ted. This afternoon has presented me with some new angles and I need to bring it all together in my head while it's fresh.'

She'd emailed him the images of Mary's athame (or what Fred had said was a very close replica) once she knew that Josie was at the climbing centre, so not to disturb his time with her.

'Your artist's impression of Kirk Junker is on the national news,' he said.

'Fantastic, let's hope it encourages loads of leads. I'll find him one way or another. I have a possible further alias for him as well: Harry O'Connor. Does that ring any bells?'

'No. I can do some digging though. I had a wonderful afternoon with Josie.'

'Of course, I didn't ask. I'm sorry. I bet you guys had fun, she's a great girl.'

'She is.'

'Did you spoil her?'

'Of course I did. Skiing equipment has come a long way since my day. Let me put my dinner down and I'll go and get my laptop. I worked on those images you sent me for two hours and I think I have some good news for you: well, I'm hoping it's what you want to hear.'

'I'm sorry I'm disturbing your tea, Ted.'

'Not a concern. Though this wine is rather nice. Here we go. So, I used the manufacturer's instructions to get the definitive measurements down to the tenth of a millimetre and I compared it to the gash wounds, and they match.'

'Really? One hundred per cent?'

'In my opinion. This athame knife is what made your second set of punctures, and it's the one that killed her, going through several veins in her upper thorax. The lower stab wounds were consistent with the kitchen knife that was sticking out of her chest, just missing her heart by three hundredths of a millimetre.'

'But in the end it didn't matter because of this other weapon used. But it's not traditionally a weapon, despite what it looks like. It's a magical item of worship, and should never be used physically.'

'Well it was, so whoever used it was a non-believer.'

'Rage. No rage,' said Kelly.

'I beg your pardon?' Ted asked.

'Oh, something The Teacher said to me today. Mary was killed with such rage, and yet Carry's death was almost nonchalant and perfunctory.'

'How did it go?'

'It was awful. I felt undressed and examined, yet at the same time I couldn't tear my eyes away. I played the game and came away with what I wanted.'

'I never doubted that for a second. You sound tired. Have you spoken to Johnny?'

'Not yet. I've got some phone calls to make and then I'll speak to him last, uninterrupted. He should have collected Josie by now.'

She fiddled with some notes and stared out of the window. She had no idea where she was, because it was dark, but the scenery told her she was out of any built-up areas and well on her way home. Her train was due to get in at one o'clock in the morning.

'I was thinking of taking everybody out for dinner to celebrate when Josie gets her competent ascent qualification,' Ted said.

'That's a lovely idea. When? You know what it's like when I'm in the middle of something like this. If you tell me when you're thinking then I can perhaps juggle a few things.'

'Saturday?'

'I'll see what I can do.'

They hung up.

Next, Kelly called Demi and hoped she'd answer. Demi was planning to go back to Lancaster to give her lectures, but return to the Lakes tomorrow to help out.

'Kelly? Are you still down south?'

'No, I'm on my way home.'

'That was quick, but I can't say I'm surprised. How did it go? Did you get anything worth working on?'

Kelly told Demi what The Teacher had told her.

'Did you come up with a profile?'

'It's difficult to be sure when I haven't got the report on Carry Tomlin yet. If you're sure it's the same killer then the MO is all over the place. We've got opportunity versus premeditated, we've got rage versus no rage, and we've got day versus night.'

'Wait a minute.'

'What?'

'That's it! Day and night. It's all about bloody balance! Jesus!'

'Give me a clue?'

'Sorry, let me explain. Mary and Fred's altars are all about balance, that's the whole point about the wheel of Paganism and the eight festivals: dark and light, black and white, winter and summer, Horned God and Moon Goddess. Everything in and of the earth has an equal action and reaction – like goddamn physics. It's the same with the elements; they all balance one another with direction and power. God, do I sound like a lunatic?'

'Yes.'

'Good, I'm on the right path. It's the least crazy thing I've thought for two weeks. So, the next one will be brutally violent and, wait, let me look at my map. Braithwaite… Thirlmere car park, they're directly diagonal to one another… balanced. If I cross the other way, I get… oh Christ, Demi, this train is throwing me about all over the place, I could be anywhere, it's like the needle in the haystack.'

'I never heard of a diagonal cross used in the occult. Sorry to piss on your parade. It's more a Christian thing, you know, like the staff of Christ carrying the lamb: was it Christ carrying the lamb?'

'What? I think it was John the Baptist. My reception is terrible, we must be in the Midlands. I'll speak to you first thing. Have a think about what I've said. I'm with the coroner tomorrow for Carry Tomlin's autopsy. It couldn't be pulled forward because there were complications with another operation apparently.' They hung up.

Finally, she called Johnny, who told her that the climb had been an out and out success. Her shoulders dropped slightly and she breathed fully, taking in the calm of the moment. The night flashed by the large window and, in first class, she was alone again. It was a rare opportunity to sit and be in the present, rather than running to the future all the time. Her job was all about the conclusion and the climax, rather than grounding oneself in today: if she did that, then she might lose vital information and momentum, and the next victim didn't have the luxury of spare time. There was no doubt in her mind that there were at least two more killings coming, and that they'd be found somewhere along the opposite perpendicular to the line she'd drawn from Braithwaite to Thirlmere car park, if she didn't crack the case soon.

'Can you come here tonight?' he asked.

'I was thinking about going to Eden House.'

'Are you crazy? Your team is doing all it can. You're working from the sparrow's fart till you drop. You need to rest.'

'Did you rest when you patrolled in Helmand?'

'Absolutely. If we didn't we'd have lost more men. A tired soldier is an inevitability, but picking the right moment to rest is the job of the officer in charge. Exhaustion is different to weariness. Come here, come and say hi to Josie. I'm cooking.'

'She won't be up.'

'You'll see her in the morning if you stay. She's like you, she wakes up and expects everyone else to do the same.'

She smiled, though Johnny couldn't see it, but she knew he felt it. 'OK. My train gets in around one a.m. I'll get a cab.'

She spent the rest of the journey fixating on the map of the Lake District. She drew axes this way and that, but one person's choice of location could be a millimetre away from the next person's and she still had no solid profile on the elusive Kirk Junker. It had crossed her mind that Fred O'Reilly, along with all of his cronies, was having her on, pulling her leg to cover the fact that Kirk Junker didn't exist and was in fact a smoke screen, behind whom to hide the fact that they were all in on it.

Johnny was right, she was tired. Her mind played tricks on her. She looked at the line she'd drawn on the map again and worried if she had missed the right angle. What if the criss-cross was imperfect? Surely it wouldn't be that obvious? Fire, water, earth, air. Fire, water, air, earth. No matter how much she googled them, no particular order flashed up. Some ancient texts suggested earth first, some water. Then, allegedly, Aristotle decided to add a fifth: aether. Or, in her case, spirit.

Five.

What was it that Demi had said about the number five?

She stretched and took off her shoes, first checking that her carriage was still empty. She slumped forward on her table and put her head in her hands. It was comfortable for about a minute, and then she yawned and settled back into her seat.

Her eyes flashed open and she looked at her watch. She must have nodded off, but she'd only been asleep for five minutes or less. Nevertheless she felt refreshed. Fred's altar came to mind and she returned to his description of all of the magic tools and how he described them.

There was one missing.

She'd added to Rob's sketches and the images they had of Mary's disturbed altar, and all this time, she'd known that something was amiss. None of the altars they'd been shown were complete. They'd seen the honours to the four elements: fire, earth, air and water. They'd been shown the celebration of balance in the candles and the yin and yang, and they'd shared the beautiful items used to purify the group's gathering: the plate that Fred told her was called a paten, which was full of pine, the two ornate knives, sometimes a wand, chalice and even a cauldron. But the most important item of all was the one that had been missing on both altars. It was so important that Mary had chosen to protect hers (or it had been taken along with her athame) and Fred had most definitely hidden his.

She googled pictures of it. It was the most important shape for worship: the circle. The circle had to be blessed before all ceremonies and Kelly couldn't believe that she'd allowed Fred to lead her away from this fundamental fact. The group had sat in a circle in the garden at Fred's house. The magic tools were set out in a circle and the elements all belonged inside a circle.

Inside the circle, there were five main points, with spirit at the top, and that's what turned a pentagram into a pentacle. She kicked herself for not having a paper map on her, but who carried paper maps around? She called Eden House and managed to catch someone on duty at the front desk not dealing with drunks or emergency procedure. They confirmed that a paper map of the Lake District would be waiting for her first thing in the morning, on her desk.

She googled the pentacle and an image of Da Vinci's Vitruvian Man stared back at her. But it was a link underneath that sparked her brain to waken fully, despite the darkness and the hour. The perfectly proportioned man, drawn by Da Vinci in

1490, was encircled by a flawless pentagram. The top of the five-pointed star was above his head, the two arms denoted the right and left points and the outspread legs the bottom two; in all, a geometrically pristine pentagram.

It was Demi who'd told her that Jack the Ripper's five victims were found in a pentagram across the East End of London. Now she looked at the map and the shape of Da Vinci's model. She'd seen it a thousand times at the beginning of *World in Action* on Granada TV, and the evocative theme tune played on the organ jumped into her head. She tried once more to get a map up on her iPad that she could use to impose a five-pointed star. Braithwaite and Thirlmere could be two points and she drew with her finger to see if she could make the other three. It could work, but she'd have to get Rob to do it on a computer properly to find out for sure.

It was with renewed energy that she pulled into Penrith station.

Chapter 45

By the time she arrived at Johnny's, the place was in darkness, apart from a tiny light near the kitchen. She was sure they'd both be asleep. She felt sorry for Josie, having to give the details of her whereabouts and every movement to her father, but Kelly knew that it was vital for his peace of mind. She guessed she'd be the same with a daughter, or son.

The vast majority of the Cumbrian population slept soundly, blissfully unaware of the double murder investigation ongoing under their noses. Homicide was reported in the local press, and occasionally it created panic and uneasiness. Sometimes it made the national news, depending on what was trending in the capital lately. The bizarre nature of Mary's death had caused such a buzz in Braithwaite and beyond to Keswick, but outside the small towns, it had died down. Until the killing of the journalist. In her absence, her team had made excellent progress on piecing together the final movements of the young woman.

Carry Tomlin was known to be a fairly reckless individual who wasn't well liked at work: she was arrogant and given to condescension at times. In other words, no one was interested in who she'd arranged to meet. The initial apparent grief in her office had been just that: apparent. It was shock at the proximity to the crime, and not sentimental. One colleague had told them that the young journalist was desperate to break into a national newspaper and had taken risks before. On a recent fishing story, she'd pleaded with the skipper of a trawler to be allowed to accompany a trip, and had almost disappeared over the side in bad weather. She'd bagged some great photos and produced a sellable story, but it was only after the production of the piece that anyone knew she'd gone.

The 'meeting a stranger' lead was looking more and more promising. So who'd be able to lure a hard-nosed journalist to her death? She'd find out more tomorrow when Carry Tomlin gave Ted Wallis some of her final secrets.

She shivered. Kirk Junker might be contemplating his next killing. Or he might not even exist. Harry O'Connor existed, but so far no one could find him either, except on the case files of two animal cruelty cases eight years apart. Nobody at the time had associated the two brutal cases because they were investigated by two separate teams: one in Penrith, the 2005 case Kelly had looked into, and the other had been passed to Kendal for some reason. The merry cult led by Fred O'Reilly bothered her and she knew they weren't telling her everything they knew. But she had no leverage. She certainly didn't have any of them down as capable of savagery towards animals, but there was something about their ways and habits that reminded Kelly of a band of brothers, willing to risk all to protect the group. In such circumstances it was almost impossible to break the bond and get people talking.

Before she got to the door, Johnny opened it and stood, waiting for her, smiling. He opened his arms and she went to him and they stood together. He kissed her neck and smelled her perfume. His warmth felt like a huge glove of security to her. He smelled of bed and a recent shower and she felt herself aroused. She disliked having sex in the same house as a teenager, but occasionally she couldn't resist, and she knew that tonight would be one of those times. She needed to feel connection and to let go, lying in his arms until she fell asleep, finally allowed to turn her brain off, even if just for a night.

He took her rucksack and handbag off her and shut the door behind her. She walked into the dark lounge and took off her jacket and shoes.

'Let's go straight to bed,' he said. He pulled her towards him and they kissed. Kelly closed her eyes and felt, in that tiny moment, the luckiest woman alive. Not simply because of Johnny, but because she didn't have a kid in the mortuary, she didn't have a brother at the bottom of a lake, and she didn't have a mother hacked to death in her own home. She shivered again and she felt goose bumps form on her skin. She followed him through to his bedroom, passing Josie's.

Johnny's house was a bungalow and she could find her way around in complete darkness. There was no sound in the house at all, and the village of Pooley Bridge was fast asleep. She couldn't even hear the sound of a lone drunk staggering home and kicking an empty beer can. Nothing stirred.

She fell onto the bed and, suddenly cold, wrapped herself in the covers, peeling off her work clothes, eager to rid herself of the association. Johnny had little to take off but he did it quickly. He unwrapped her and she stifled laughter as he tried to find fastens and buttons underneath the fluffy duvet. They fumbled in the dark and to Kelly it felt glorious. They said nothing, and heard only their breath becoming more rapid. Kelly's clothes fell in piles away from the bed as Johnny found them and got rid of them. Kelly noticed a small shard of moonlight across the bed and it illuminated her lover just enough to watch him watching her.

'I love you,' he said. It was a tiny whisper but enough for her to hear, and it was all she needed.

Tomorrow was a day away, and, for now, everything she wanted or needed was here in bed with this man.

Chapter 46

When she woke, her head was heavy and her eyes felt stuck together. She felt Johnny's pillow. He wasn't there. She heard the reassuring hum of father-daughter conversation coming from the kitchen. She put her hands over her eyes and blinked a few times, trying to wake up. Her body ached. She needed a shower and forced herself to the en-suite bathroom to gather the toiletries she needed from the stash she kept at Johnny's. The hot water revitalised her and she took her time, hearing Johnny come into the bedroom and announce that breakfast was ready. She poked her head around the shower curtain and smiled.

'Thank you. God that was a good sleep. I can't even remember moving.'

'I don't think you did. Josie is just about to leave, I'm going to say goodbye, and apparently she's meeting Callum on the bus.'

'It's getting serious?'

'I took him home last night, he seems a nice lad.'

'I've met his father.'

'Really?' Johnny asked.

'Yes, you know the girl who was wandering around Castlerigg?'

'Yes, did you ever find out who she was?'

'We think so. It was Callum's family who found her.'

Johnny went back to the kitchen to say goodbye to his daughter, and Kelly finished up and dried herself vigorously. She kept some clothes at Johnny's house too, and she found something suitable and applied some make-up, found in her bag. She was ready in time to give Josie a hug and wave her off.

'What are you up to today?' Kelly asked Johnny, after Josie had gone.

'I'm going sailing. It's a cracker out there, and we've got our final exams coming up.'

'I know, I hope I can fit in a bit more time before then, this case is taking all my time and energy.' She sat down at the table and Johnny put eggs, toast and mushrooms in front of her.

'I'm ruined,' she said, licking her lips. 'Have you got a large map of the Lakes?'

'How large?' He sat opposite her and began eating. He poured hot coffee and dribbled brown sauce over his eggs.

'About an inch per mile would do.'

He nodded. They ate in silence, each relishing the fayre. She sipped her coffee and pushed her hair behind her ear. She didn't need to dry it, she'd always been lucky in that sense: it fell into place if she left it alone. It was thick and luscious from a long summer, and her tan was still apparent against her white top.

'You look refreshed,' Johnny said.

She nodded, in between mouthfuls. 'I am. I wish I could come on the boat with you today. I fancy a day on the lake.'

'I'll get the map. What's it for?' he asked.

'I'll show you.' She finished her food and cleared the plates away, making room for the map. When he came back with it, she cleared a space on the large oak kitchen table, opened the map and spread it across the table. She pointed to Braithwaite and then to Thirlmere car park, near where Carry had been dumped. The forensic team had ascertained that she hadn't died there, there simply wasn't enough blood or evidence of a scene of crime around the body. It had been pretty obvious to Kelly too, but she figured that it was the bodies that were important marker points. Given the need for their killer to communicate, she settled on Thirlmere being the point of axis.

The two sites formed a perfect axis of a saltire, going from left to right, downwards. Kelly looked around the kitchen and found a packet of spaghetti. She took a few sticks from the bag and placed one from end to end.

'What are you doing?' Johnny asked.

'Wait. I know it looks like I'm going crazy. The pentagram is a five-pointed star, and all of these occultists agree on one thing: it's a magic symbol. The pentacle is a pentagram inside a circle and it's also the sign of the five elements: earth, water, air, fire and spirit.'

She took another stick of dried spaghetti and crossed it the other way, completing the saltire. The axis crossed through plenty of notable places, as well as some more obscure.

'Have you got any string?' she asked.

'Somewhere, probably.'

Johnny rooted through drawers and found some. Kelly got some scissors and placed them on the table, next to the map. She took a roll of string and made a circle, using the axis of the saltire as a guide. She made sure that the edge of the circle touched Braithwaite and Thirlmere car park, and adjusted the spaghetti to pinpoint two locations on the opposite axis.

'It's impossible,' she sighed and sat down heavily. 'I thought I could use the major points of the pentagram to predict where the next victim is in danger.'

'Really? Are you that sure?'

'It makes complete sense, but it's impossible to be accurate. I need to get it on to a computer programme and Rob is the man for the job. I need to go.'

'You said a pentagram is five pointed: what about the fifth point?' he asked.

'It's the top. The head. It's the main element of spirit. Looking at this, it suggests somewhere around Lonscale Fell, which is about as precise as saying "somewhere on Helvellyn". Do you think I'm being ridiculous?' she asked.

'It's not like you to question your instinct. If your gut is telling you this, then I'd go with it. There's nothing more bizarre than what goes on in the human brain. You can't *not* investigate it.'

'I looked into that other animal cruelty case you told me about. You know the one at High Rigg five years ago?'

'Yes, that's right. You said there was another, at Birkett Mire?'

'Yes, and the same name came up in both. I would never have made that connection if it wasn't for that conversation.'

'There you go, that's one more step closer. How was the person involved?'

'I'm not sure, but when the same name pops up in two investigations, it raises suspicion. There's no trace of addresses or phone numbers though. He might as well be a phantom, like Kirk Junker.'

'You still looking for him?'

Kelly nodded, packing her bag.

'Kelly,' Johnny said. She looked at him and saw that he was fiddling with one of the pieces of spaghetti. She went to the table and looked at where he was pointing his finger on the map.

'That's Birkett Mire, and next to it is the Threlkeld Quarry. It fits the circle.'

'It does. And it screams out another element.'

'Earth,' they said together.

Chapter 47

Kelly had agreed to drive Ted to the university hospital in Carlisle, where the autopsy of Carry Tomlin's body was booked for 9.30 a.m.

They were running a little late, as an accident on the northbound carriageway of the M6 slowed them down. It was a common occurrence: by the time lorry drivers from Europe got so far up the dullest motorway in Britain, they tended to fall asleep. One had jack-knifed across the road early that morning, but traffic was now flowing, albeit slowly. The driver wasn't hurt. Kelly had left strict instructions with the office and Rob was briefed to work on a programme that could superimpose a pentacle over a map of Cumbria, taking in the two points they already knew: Braithwaite and Thirlmere. She also told him to factor in Threlkeld Quarry. She'd shared her theory with Demi, who was tasked with delivering it to the team in her absence.

Kelly could hear the excitement in Demi's voice and could see the front cover of a new book, should she be proven correct. But. There was a huge whopping *but* in their way. The accuracy of her predictions were about as reliable as asking a child to draw the circle and guestimate the second axis. They were trying to enter the mind of a deranged killer, where anything could happen. Expectation had to be kept low at all times, because there might not be any plan at all. The murder at Braithwaite and the dump site at Thirlmere car park could be two random dots on a map, and nothing more. She had to stay level headed.

'It's a shame I can't make the conference and have dinner with June and Amber. When will you go?' she said to Ted.

'I wanted to catch some of Demi Cramer's work.'

'She's working with my team at Eden House on these cases for me. Come and meet her.'

'Well, that would be an honour, I do like her work.'

'She was my senior mentor when I was doing my detective exams.'

'Lucky you. What's she like?'

'She's eccentric, loud and colourful.'

'Sounds fun.'

'She is.' Kelly watched the road as the traffic freed up again, and they turned off to enter Carlisle city. The hospital wasn't far from the motorway junction and they could see it in the distance, the mortuary chimney standing ominously on the skyline. Beyond that, on a clear day, they could make out Glasgow and, on the far side of that, the beginning of the Scottish Highlands.

Kelly ran her theory past Ted as they approached the hospital, explaining all the circumstantial evidence they had so far: the athame, the positions of the bodies, the element symbols, the letters from The Teacher, what she'd found out about the importance of the pentacle... The map, and Johnny pointing out the quarry near Birkett Mire.

'You need something solid tying it all together. Otherwise, there's no way of telling if someone is out there plotting still, or it was two single unrelated targets.'

'I don't buy that,' Kelly said.

'Neither do I, but you're talking about investing scarce resources; like any department on a tight budget, you'll have to justify yourself. What did Demi Cramer say?'

'She's on board. She wrote a book on The Teacher, and bagged a few interviews. I never want to experience that again.'

'It sounds awful, I wouldn't want to be in your shoes.'

Ted had never met Amy Richmond but had autopsied all of her victims, or what was left of them. The image of him removing a piece of paper from the thigh of one of the victims had never left her.

'Here we are.'

Kelly parked and they made their way to the mortuary. She'd come prepared and armed with a large, warm jumper to go over her blouse. She'd also brought some scented oil for under her nose. It seemed only hours since she'd been here last time with him. She was now familiar with where the gowns were stored, how many times Ted checked his equipment, as well as his personal routine before he commenced the grim operation. She never tired of watching him, and witnessing his subtle habits of walking around a cadaver and tapping his chin. The photographer was ready, as was Ted's assistant. They all waited until Ted opened the body bag. Kelly had come to associate the slow grating sound of a zip with this very moment, and today was no different. The first glimpse of a corpse always made her catch her breath and she had to fight to keep back tears as she thought of Carry's family. A formal identification had already taken place and Kelly was glad that it wasn't her job to accompany families when they did so. It was hard enough being on the informing party, and she'd done plenty of those. As a SIO, she no longer carried out that heartbreaking task, but she counselled and mentored those who did.

When she looked at the body of Carry Tomlin, what struck her most of all were the bites. It was clear, now they were away from the shores of the reservoir, and in a place of quiet and sterility, where one had no choice but stare at them, that they were caused by an animal.

'Probably canine,' said Ted. They were all over her arms and legs, and there were a few on her face.

'None of them were fatal, they don't go deep enough,' Ted said. He took clippings of her nails and noted the bruising on her fingers and lower arms, indicating a good fight.

'She was aware when she was set upon.'

'She must have been terrified.'

Ted measured the bites carefully.

'There are three different jaw measurements. That's three animals, at least.'

274

'But it wasn't a frenzy, so maybe they were called off.'

Ted agreed.

Kelly avoided looking at the faces of those she saw dead, unless it was the initial crime scene investigation, because here, on the stainless steel slab, with no dignity left, and a trail of bereaved relatives waiting expectantly for the police to catch those responsible, she found it difficult to face them. They were so vulnerable, even in death, on the slab. It also brought home the terror they'd suffered before their last breath.

Ted spent a long time examining her neck and head, considering the statistic that most homicides involved blunt force trauma to the vital physical structures protected therein.

'Come and look at this,' he said, stopping his search. His face told Kelly that he'd found something important. She looked at the side of Carry's neck, behind her ear. Crudely knifed into the skin was a rough tattoo, etched there in a sloppy, amateur fashion. The sides were encrusted and Ted wiped away the scabs to reveal an unskilful but indisputable carving of the Moon Goddess symbol. An untrained eye would have missed it but Ted's experience and knowledge of the largest organ of the body – the skin – gave him the tools necessary to spot discrepancies such as this mark. It was red around the outside and an inky colour had been applied to it.

'Was she alive?'

'By the way the skin has reacted, I'd say yes.'

'Oh God.'

It was photographed from all angles and entered into Ted's oral record via his microphone. He carried on silently, and Kelly could tell that he was thinking about how this young woman suffered. She must have been severely disabled to allow such mutilation. Or scared beyond sanity.

'I can't see any evidence of swelling on the cranial surfaces, and there's no evidence of ligature or other types of strangulation.' Ted returned to his step by step process. That was his anchor. It was how he got through it: a trusty methodical approach that allowed him to concentrate on the evidence before him. Kelly realised that it wasn't glaringly obvious how Carry Tomlin had met her end; just that, so far, she'd been set upon by dogs, and tortured. Whether that horrible experience was linked to her final demise was still unclear. It was also obvious that the young woman had been tied at the wrist. Like the Mary Hales murder, Kelly could see signs that the killer had enjoyed the ritual.

Dozens of photographs were taken before Ted announced that it was time to open her up. Kelly looked at her watch: he'd been at it for over three hours already. It was time to check in with her team. She had hoped that Ted would have given her a cause of death by now, because homicide victims usually show visible signs of their demise on the outside. Apart from the restraining wounds around her wrists, this was not the case for Carry. Ted would only know for sure when he examined her internal organs and that would take countless more hours, which Kelly did not have. There was always the chance that a body found by water would produce evidence of drowning, but there was no evidence that Carry had been for a swim, and she was found on the beach rather than in the water.

She stretched and considered her options. Then, she heard the first slurp of skin being peeled back, and it turned her stomach. Ted reached for his Stryker saw and Kelly knew that Carry's chest was being sawn open so the coroner could get to her organs. She decided that she'd let him finish up with the saw and then excuse herself with a promise that he called her the minute he knew more. She caught sight of Ted grabbing Carry's gullet and rooting around for the base of the tongue; he was trying to eviscerate all of her organ sac – containing gullet to anus – in one. It was no easy task: it weighed as much as a few serious dumbbells in the gym, but Ted was a seasoned professional. However, he realised halfway through pulling it out of the cavity that it was heavier than usual.

'Thought so,' he said.

'What?' Kelly asked.

'There's water in her lungs. You have your cause.'

'Could she have been unconscious?' Kelly asked.

'Yes, it's possible, or she could have been restrained still.'

'In broad daylight, next to Thirlmere? It's highly unlikely.'

'I agree,' he said. 'I still think we'll find evidence that there isn't lake water in there.'

'All right, Ted, I'll wait a little longer, then I really need to be going.'

'I'll examine the lungs first.' He slapped the sac onto a stainless steel slab next to the one holding Carry's body, and it reminded Kelly of a fishing programme, when large specimens were landed after a fight. A fish's body out of water looked just as awkward and bulky, flopping onto any surface it came into contact with, and wobbling until it settled in an ungainly fashion. Carry's organ sac did the same. And it stank. Ted expertly cut away one lung and weighed it. As he did so, the bronchial tubes leaked water all over the gurney.

'Can you smell that?' he asked. Kelly struggled to decipher what exactly he was referring to. There was such a buffet of smells awaiting detection during an autopsy that she didn't know how to answer.

'Soap,' he said. 'It's highly perfumed. Look at the bubbles.' He went to the liquid that had leaked and rubbed it between his gloves fingers. Sure enough, it produced a soapy soup. As Kelly came closer, she also smelled perfume.

'Why the hell would she have soapy water in her lungs?' Kelly asked Ted.

'She drowned in a bath?'

'The dogs were called off and her wounds were cleaned?'

'A trick?'

'Or genuine care, and someone else was involved? It means she was in a home of sorts, or at least somewhere she could wash. But why the restraints? Was it all a sick role play? I need some air, Ted. Will you call me as soon as you're done?'

'Of course. I think I'll be another three hours or so.'

Kelly left the sterile metal environment of the mortuary and ripped off her overalls. She gathered her personal items as quickly as she could and went out into the corridor to get the lift back up to civilisation where murderers didn't play games, or set dogs on terrified women.

Animals.

They were looking for a remote and quiet location, with pets, and a vehicle. Carry could have been driven to Thirlmere in her own car, but that couldn't be the case, because her car wasn't seen again after travelling south on the A591.

That's where they should search. On the way back to her car, she called the office and asked to speak to Rob.

'How're you doing on my pentacle?' she asked. She updated him on Carry's autopsy so he could enter the details on HOLMES.

'Sorted, guv. Piece of cake. You can open the map and impose any shape you want in any size. I've done what you said and inputted Mary's house and where Carry Tomlin was found in Thirlmere, and a perfect circle, with a perfectly mathematically correct pentagram inside, gives us a few options. Threlkeld Quarry isn't an exact match, but then I'm assuming that our killer isn't also a mathematician or an astrologer.'

'I'll be back in under an hour, I'm just leaving Carlisle.'

Ted had already booked into a hotel in Carlisle for the night, knowing that he'd want to put his all into the operation, and be exhausted afterwards. Kelly felt guilty that it was her work that was so demanding of him.

'I want a detailed search of a three-mile radius around where Carry's body was found: fields, woodland, farmhouses, youth hostels, caravans... the lot.'

'Yes, guv. By the way, I called Fred O'Reilly as you asked, to find out if he had a pentacle for his altar.'

'And?'

'It's always been there, right under our noses. It's on the plate. The pentacle is engraved on the plate, but we couldn't see it because it was covered in pine. I sent someone to take it for evidence.'

'Great work, Rob.'

Chapter 48

Harry O'Connor was entered twice into the police national computer as a person of interest in the two animal cruelty cases, and it was Emma Hide's job to revisit the investigations, page by page, and report back to Kelly.

In 2005, his name was logged as living in a caravan on the edge of Birkett Mire campsite, thereby avoiding the site fees. It had caused great annoyance for the site at the time, because the travellers gave the area a bad name. The injured animals had been reported by a tourist, cycling with his family in the area immediately around the site. The first responders took statements from all the residents (legally and illegally camping) and Harry O'Connor was one of them.

The statement informed Emma that Mr O'Connor was parked illegally on National Trust land, but refused to move on, until he was requested to give permission to search his vehicle, which was denied, then he moved on of his own free will.

In 2013, his name popped up again as a witness to another animal cruelty case, this time in the High Rigg area, just barely two miles away from Birkett Mire. Another tourist had reported a pile of sheep and other animals seemingly discarded underneath the packhorse bridge over the beck, next to High Rigg. Mr O'Connor stated that, despite camping overnight on National Trust land, he hadn't been a witness to any maltreatment or discarding of the animals' bodies. No one recognised the name because Kendal handled the second case. Besides, with a gap of eight years, the staff had probably changed too.

She couldn't understand why HOLMES hadn't flagged it up, and assumed it hadn't been inputted correctly.

It was frustrating. They had no usable address, and no photograph of the man. The travelling community was notoriously difficult to trace, but occasionally they held down a job, or even sent their kids to local schools for a while. Sometimes they had criminal records, but Harry O'Connor was clean. She looked at some of the other names linked with the two cases and ran checks on those as well.

She found that there were three Harry O'Connors currently living in Cumbria, and checked their contact details in the phone book: the police still used the ancient tome, and it proved useful for people who were careful to mask their online identities. The general public assumed that the police were in possession of a magic app that could trace anyone in the country. In reality, they based their information on the amount of traffic and CCTV cameras, people's internet search history and iPhone traceability mentioned in high-profile cases. Mixed with a Big Brother style paranoia pedalled by the national press, the fallacy took hold. In fact, the police found it a challenge to trace somebody who didn't want to be found. There were all sorts of ways to stay under the radar, and thousands did. Both Harry O'Connor and Kirk Junker had, but Emma had a few ideas; one of them was patience.

She found addresses for the three and looked them up on a map. One of them was registered to a farm near Thirlmere reservoir. When she'd collated the numbers, she called each one. Two gave convincing enough information to be ruled out. The number for the farm near Thirlmere was out of service. She googled it on the off-chance and got a hit straight away. Some farms, facing hard times, had branched out into children's theme parks, animal feeding or seasonal shows, and a quick search would flag this up. Not so with Great Raven Farm near Thirlmere: it was derelict, and the owner – Harry O'Connor – was dead. The article she'd found was about the demise of stone buildings in the Lakes, and apparently Great Raven Farm was a classic example: the owner ran out of money, mismanaged the estate and failed to save the two-hundred-year-old family business. Harry O'Connor was the freeholder and, as he left no family heirs, the place had been left to ruin.

It was a sad story, and Emma sighed as she went to cross poor Harry off her list. It was another dead end. But she had another idea and found out which officers had been involved in the search around Thirlmere inside the three-mile radius set by DI Porter, and called the desk to see if they were on duty. The search was still ongoing, and she spoke to one pod in the area, and currently making a search of the woodland along the shore of the reservoir.

'Has anyone been down the Great How Road yet?' she asked.

'We were told to concentrate on the eastern shore first.'

Emma tapped her pen. She'd have to get authority from DI Porter to divert already scarce resources.

'Any news?' she asked.

'Nothing but a bunch of litter. It was a dry day so there are no prints on the ground: it's gravel. We've got appeals up and down the A591 for witnesses but we've had no responses that match the time frame yet.'

'Thanks.' Emma hung up. She wheeled her chair towards Rob, who looked up from his desk.

'Social call?' he asked.

'The search around Thirlmere is taking forever because there are about three pods available to search. I've found this.' She showed him the address for the deceased Harry O'Connor.

'Might be worth a visit?'

'But he's dead,' Rob said.

'Kirk Junker might be dead, too. Isn't it just a little too convenient? It's the closest property to where Carry was last seen and the deceased owner was called Harry O'Connor?'

'The boss is driving.'

'She's got speaker phone.'

'Ask Kate.'

DS Kate Umshaw was DI Porter's deputy and so she could make decisions in her absence. Emma scooted her chair back to her desk and left it there. Kate was in DI Porter's office on the phone. Emma waited. It sounded as though she was discussing lab results. She heard DS Umshaw hang up and went across the hall.

'They got usable DNA from the pile of clothes found in the field near Castlerigg: no matches. What's up?'

Emma shared what she'd found.

'The boss would get into a car and head over there. Take somebody else, though. Don't go on your own.'

'Can't I just get a squad car there?'

'I don't think that's justifiable unless one is in the area. You need the boss to agree to that.'

Emma went back to her desk and looked at the pile of jobs she had to plough through. She toyed with what to do. Driving to Thirlmere could take forty minutes or more. She decided to wait and run it past her boss. The farmhouse was going nowhere.

Chapter 49

From the comfort of her car, Kelly got a squad car to have a poke around Threlkeld Quarry, to see if everything was in order. By in order, she expected an abandoned quarry to be empty of people, especially ones up to no good. There shouldn't be any sign of work or life. If there was, she wanted to know about it.

It didn't take long for the uniforms to report back that the quarry was as it should be: deserted, decrepit and unloved. There was no sign of foul play, apart from some old graffiti, smashed beer bottles and discarded cigarette butts.

Kelly was almost at the Penrith turn-off when DC Emma Hide called her. She listened with interest and mulled over her priority list. It was perhaps a five- to ten-minute drive from Threlkeld Quarry to the address given by Emma, and Kelly put in a request for the same squad car to visit the abandoned property called Great Raven Farm.

'Have a snoop around, see if the place is empty.'

She turned off at the Penrith junction and called Emma back. 'Get going on the arrangements for Fred O'Reilly and Jock Harris to come in and make formal statements, will you? And get me the exact dates of those two animal cruelty cases.'

'I can tell you without looking, I've been working on them all morning,' Emma said. 'The 2005 one was February first, and the 2013 case was February second.'

'Thanks, Emma, I'm five minutes away.'

Kelly ended the call and her pulse rate quickened slightly. She knew that she was on to something. Fred had tried to explain to her the eight festivals of the year, and she'd struggled to keep up. The beginning of spring had stuck in her mind because the name was so memorable. Imbolc. It was Gaelic and meant 'lamb's milk'. It was the day of the year when ewes began to lactate in time to feed their spring lambs. It was a hugely important time because it celebrated the end of the dark winter and the beginning of the light.

Light and dark again. Balance.

Each year it changed slightly and lambing could come a week either side of the date. It was usually from the first to the third of February, beginning on the eve of the end of January.

When she parked at Eden House, she went first to the switchboard and asked if any information had come in on the photofit released of their main suspect. The names Harry O'Connor and Kirk Junker had been released alongside the picture.

They'd had several calls, all giving different names, creating more work for her already stretched staff. As usual, the information would take time, and valuable resources, to process.

As she took the lift upstairs, the squad car reported back to her from Great Raven Farm. The place was deserted but some of the buildings were padlocked, with vehicles inside.

'What type of vehicles?'

'Old tractors and the like. We can't see inside all of them, but it looks pretty dead around here.'

'Thanks.'

They hung up.

Chapter 50

She watched Jock drive up the long track, and her heart broke into tiny little pieces.

'Father, I don't want this to happen.' Her voice was a whisper. She rocked back and forth on top of a large chest, pushed up against the window. She'd had to be as quiet as a mouse when the police car came. The place was a rabbit warren, and there were plenty of places to hide, if one knew where to go. She'd been still as the trees out in the fields, silent and strong, until the intruders left. They had no right to be here.

It was another missed opportunity to escape. She could have run into the yard, flailing her arms, waving and begging for salvation, but she was more scared of her father than she was of the law. Even though she knew what was going to happen to Jock. She stayed put and made not a sound. The dogs were muzzled and calm, nestled next to her in her den, above the old scullery.

Two policemen had actually nosed around the place, knocking on doors, banging on windows, pulling on locks and shining torches into outhouses. It had taken an interminable amount of time for them to leave and her heart raced. How Father didn't snap and run at them with a plank of wood was an incredible show of resolve. But then she remembered that he couldn't, and why.

Finally, the police left, and now Jock was here.

She could see his face inside his car, as he peered back and forth, and she could tell that he was wondering if he'd found the right place. She'd made the call. Father and mother made her do it, or at least that's what she told herself. Even now they remained in control. It was easy to find someone's phone number if you knew where to look. He looked worried and she smiled. His face brought back so many memories of warmth and safety. She'd wished for so many years that Jock was her father, instead of her own. She'd punished herself for her deceitful thoughts over and over again.

Father pardoned her.

But she never forgave. Or forgot.

Jock's car bumped up and down on the gravel path and he pulled up to the main house. She understood why he looked unsure. The place looked deserted; even the police had given up and driven off. She watched him look around and lean against his car. He'd aged. She had been a mere girl the last time she'd seen him.

Her heart lurched and she wanted to scream at him to drive away, but her terror prevented her from saving him. He walked towards the door.

She covered her ears and eyes, not wanting to know what was to come next. Jock was here to make peace, to see what he could do to help. Little did he know why he was really called upon. She couldn't trust father to let him go, now he knew where they were. It was a gamble contacting him in the first place. But Jock was loyal. His pride was such that to tell anyone where he was going, he'd have to have good enough reason, and there was none. Yet.

A loud banging on the wooden door made her jump. She shook her head and pushed her face into her knees.

'No, no, no, no, no,' she whispered.

Lovely, gentle, kind, caring Jock.

'Go away. Get in your car and go away!' she willed him to rethink his trust. He'd walked blindly into something he could never predict.

The door opened and she knew that he was inside. The latch had been left off for him.

It was time to leave. It was time to disappear. Again. One police car had given up. There'd be more. It was no coincidence that they'd found this place now. She was tired and she didn't want to move again. She wanted to be Callum's girlfriend: a normal schoolgirl, shopping, chatting to friends and going to climbing classes.

She grimaced into her knees and bit herself hard. None of that would ever happen as long as she remained here.

She felt a hand on her shoulder and looked up into Jock's sweet face.

'What happened to your father?' he asked.

Chapter 51

Kelly pulled her car into her driveway and switched off the engine. Demi had been lecturing all day in Lancaster and had accepted Kelly's invitation for supper. Her involvement on the case had been welcomed by her team and Demi had fitted in well. It was a shame she wasn't local. She'd dismissed her team to get some rest. Fred O'Reilly was booked in to be formally interviewed in the morning. They hadn't managed to speak to Jock Harris, though.

'I hate this stage of investigations. I remember you lecturing us on the tree. "Only when the tree has leaves," you kept saying.'

Demi laughed.

'Where the hell do you get your ideas?' Kelly asked. She got out of the car, and Demi did the same.

'What a lovely house. Which lake is that? I'm afraid my knowledge is sketchy. What a beautiful place to work, I envy you.'

'It's Ullswater. Thank you. It is a beautiful place but my work doesn't exactly get me out sightseeing.'

'I can never understand the names around here, they're all so non-English.'

'That's because it's never really been English. It's more Celtic. Neither the Romans nor the Anglo-Saxons could be bothered to come this far, and when they did, they found tribes of hard nuts willing to fight to the death.'

'Northerners! You're a history teacher all of a sudden?'

'No, I studied biology, but one of my colleagues is a history buff.'

'Which one? I like them all.'

'Ted Wallis, the coroner. He's a fan of yours, in fact he's coming to listen to one of your lectures tomorrow.'

'You're lucky to have such a tight-knit team. It's what most detectives and SIOs dream of. To work with the same coroner all the time must be fabulous. That must make life a lot easier.'

'It's not London.'

'I can see that. It reminds me of a few investigations I worked on in the Isles of Scilly years ago – everyone knew each other, there was no need for CCTV because the islanders bloody knew everything. The perps didn't stand a chance!'

'It's not that cosy here. If only I could find a few key players, I reckon I could get to the bottom of this craziness. I know another one's coming, and soon.'

'I agree.'

Kelly unlocked her front door and they went in.

'Welcome,' Kelly said. Early evening orange sun flooded through the north-facing windows of the house, filling the kitchen with a Mediterranean glow. The back of the house, overlooking the river from its tiny terrace, was darker, but no less captivating; it had the lion's share of the sunshine throughout the day. Demi went through the double doors and peered over the fence to the water below.

'It's so peaceful! So now I know why you were in such a rush to come back home. Where's your man?'

'My man? I love how you speak your mind, Demi. That's one of the things I hated about London: all those egos and pretence. Johnny should be joining us soon.'

'And he's a mountain rescuer? How chivalrous! And sexy as hell.'

'He does that part time when required, the rest of his time he invests his army pension and enters crazy endurance races.'

'I can't wait to meet him.'

'He'll be here soon. You'll like him, he's very casual. He's been sailing all day. He'll make sure his daughter is safe and tucked up at home, and then he'll be over. People are jumpy round here at the moment, and rightly so. The journalist's articles were fairly high profile and the gossip circulating regarding her death hasn't died down yet.'

Demi nodded. 'Has anyone had a sniff of the occult angle yet?'

'Not that I know of. I know that a few national papers have been in touch with the press office, give it time, stuff always leaks.'

'Quite.'

'I'm just quickly going to throw something more comfortable on to wear. I won't be a second, there's wine in the fridge, help yourself. I took the liberty of making up the spare room for you, unless you've booked a hotel? I can always call you a cab,' Kelly said.

'Thanks, I'm booked into a Premier Inn on some motorway junction. It'll do, but thanks for the invite. Next time. I could murder a glass of wine.'

Kelly went upstairs and peeled off her detective uniform: when she wore it, she called it her 'plain clothes shuffle'. She pulled on some jeans and a thin sweater, checked her make-up and slipped on some pumps. When she went back downstairs, Demi had made herself comfortable under one of the blankets on a lounger outside on the terrace. Kelly poured a glass of well-chilled white wine and joined her.

'You know Rob's app — DC Shawcross — he made the pentacle app so we could impose it onto a map at any scale? Yes, well I reckon the seasons have something to do with the killings as well. The two animal cruelty cases were at the start of a spring festival Pagans call Imbolc, and the disappearance of the two boys happened much later in the year during the festival of Samhain. That's the death of the year, and it kicks off with Halloween. Now, before you go all spooked on me, Halloween isn't anywhere near as old as things like the Day of the Dead — which is essentially the same thing — the death of the year, and treating the dead with respect has happened for centuries. The Christian version is much more recent.'

'I'm not spooked at all. I was in Mexico three years ago for the Day of the Dead, it's a fabulous experience if you ever get the chance. You say these crimes are connected, and if that's correct, then it means that over the course of the last, what? Twelve years? They've been happening subtly – carefully even – not brazen or exhibitionist at all, so why now? It's a change of profile, a change of MO. It doesn't fit. Sure, you have escalation, but the finality of what's going on, the public nature of the crimes, is unexpected, given the rest of the information we know.'

'I know.'

'Different perps? An accomplice branching out on their own? An apprentice finally ready?'

'It's all plausible. That's what I find so frustrating. There are so many potential outcomes for this case, and at the moment, catching the bastard isn't one of them.'

'Or bastards.'

'No. It's a lone operator. I've seen it before.'

'The Teacher?'

Kelly nodded, sipping her wine and covering herself with a blanket. They'd used Rob's newly created app to predict the next locations from the points of the pentagram, but it was impossible to predict inside the mind of a killer. Like she'd found with the spaghetti, it was anyone's guess. One degree to the right or left on the map, and it changed the location by miles. Birkett Mire made sense but she had no evidence. Likewise with Threlkeld Quarry, but the squad car was checking the place every couple of hours, and so far they'd witnessed no behaviour or presence out of the norm. Similarly, further south, at the point that could match up with one of the bottom points of the star, it could be anywhere. Then, as Demi had reminded her, it could be a reverse pentagram, with two points at the top and only one below. It was an attractive theory because an upside-down pentagram was used in devil worship, with the two points at the top representing Satan's horns. The Horned God. That's what Fred had said Kirk Junker was more into, not the Moon Goddess.

'Any news from Broadmoor on her behaviour?'

'She's tried to bribe two more prison officers to smuggle mail out, unsuccessfully. She's been under surveillance but we've been told nothing irregular. If she was in contact with anyone regularly – say, an apprentice of sorts – we'd know. She did say that she'd "made friends" with Daphne. I still have no idea what that means. It could be role play as usual.'

The front door bell rang and Kelly went to answer it. It was Johnny. 'I forgot my key,' he said.

'Come and meet Demi,' she said, kissing him. 'Wine?'

'Beer?'

'Sure. How was the lake? I'm so jealous.'

'You would have loved it, it was perfect. Flat all the way down to Lodore. I stopped for a pasty and a swim.'

They went out on to the terrace and Kelly introduced him to her old friend.

Demi stood up and placed her blanket on the lounger. She looked him up and down and went to him with her arms outstretched. Johnny kissed her on both cheeks and Kelly swore that the psychologist was flirting. She could tell that Demi liked him.

'I'm not interrupting?' Johnny said.

'Not at all, Kelly tells me that she bounces ideas off you all the time. I taught her that.'

Kelly rolled her eyes, though it was true. She thought she'd leave them to thrash out the medals while she switched the oven on and threw some vegetable tarts on oven trays. One thing about a serious investigation was the inability to cook proper nutritious food. Often Johnny stepped in and did it for her. She always lost weight.

She pulled up her jeans as she went to the kitchen and heard Demi laughing. She knew they'd get on, but Demi and Johnny were the kind of people you could introduce to anyone. It struck her that she'd just introduced the first person from her old life into her new one. The stint in London earlier in the year, when she'd bumped into plenty of ghosts in her forgotten closet, hadn't been the same. This was her home. It was the same with Ted. He was part of her new life and he'd introduced her to his old one through his daughters, June and Amber. It felt good. It was the sort of bond that she hadn't experienced since her father took her hiking every weekend and they shared sandwiches on the top of Wainwrights.

That all changed when she went to college and discovered her wanderlust. The alliances she'd forged along the rocky road of childhood were severed and she never replaced them in London. Most of her friendships had been based around nights out and casual banter. Lately, a solid lump of security had formed somewhere inside her, and it gave her a warmth that hadn't been there before. Connections: she finally got what all the fuss was about. Sure, she'd related to plenty of people in her career, from the lowest to the highest ranks, but in her personal life, it was something she mainly avoided. She'd assumed that all women were like her sister, and all men were like Dave Crawley: desperate to get her wedded and pregnant. She'd almost said yes when he proposed fifteen years ago. Thank God she hadn't. She shivered slightly as she thought of Dave Crawley's new freedom out of HMP Altcourse. It was a part of the job that wasn't advertised widely: the bitter taste of frustration when the law failed. If she examined the British legal system too closely, with its seemingly random habits of jailing an armed burglar for twenty years but a rapist of a child for two, she'd go crazy.

But it did give her an idea.

Thinking about Dave made her think, inevitably, of her sister. She tapped Nikki's number into her phone. She hadn't deleted it; they were still family. Nikki answered quickly and Kelly wasn't ready. She closed the door to the kitchen and took a deep breath.

'Kelly! To what do I owe this pleasure?'

Sarcasm dripped off her sister's tongue, as always. It was her favourite method of communicating, like all people who don't know how else to communicate. Kelly wondered if Nikki ever experienced the reassurance of connection that she'd just discovered, by staying in the Lakes all her life, with her old buddies.

'Hi, Nikki. It's a work call really. How are you?'

'You're asking how I am? You don't speak to me for six months and you call me up to say hello now, you want something?'

Kelly sighed. Her chances of changing Nikki's attitude were about as strong as Brexit going smoothly through parliament. She slammed the oven door and opened the fridge, looking for salad, with her phone under her chin.

'Nikki, you haven't called me or made an effort, either. It's not my job to chase you. You don't even like me, let's be honest here. But I do think about you.'

'Well, thank you, Your Highness.'

'All right, let's cut the bullshit. Carry Tomlin. Did she interview you for that piece in the paper about the police being crap?'

'Why?'

'You must have heard that she was murdered?'

'Of course, it's all anyone is talking about. If you're calling me, it means you haven't caught the bastard yet. Reminds me of something.'

'I'm sorry I didn't find The Teacher sooner. I tried my best. How are the girls?'

Nikki sighed. Kelly thought the change in tone might be a breakthrough.

'Charlie is driving now. Ria's tenth birthday is soon. She wants to go bowling. You can come if you want. She misses Mum.'

'I can understand that. I miss her too. I'd love to come to her birthday, text me the details. I'll be there.'

295

'The journalist found me; I didn't go to her. It was because of The Teacher. I didn't want to talk to her at first but she's persistent. She *was* persistent. Like you. Massive balls.'

'I don't know about that.'

'She said she'd be happy to meet anywhere I wanted to, and that she normally went wherever her sources wanted.'

'And did she mention any others she had coming up?'

'I asked her about the story on all the voodoo crap and she got very excited, saying there were more articles planned and she had plenty of people willing to talk.'

'What was she like?'

'Flaky. Hard-nosed and self-centred. Again, a bit like you.'

'Thanks. Did she mention Mary Hales' death?'

'Yes. She said she reckoned she could find out who did it faster than the police could.'

'That's what I thought.'

'Do you think you know who did it?'

'Not yet, but the investigation is moving along well. Have you ever heard of someone called Kirk Junker or Harry O'Connor?'

She heard Nikki humming. 'O'Connor? That's Irish isn't it? Only the travellers have names like that. I'd watch it if I were you, they're fucking brutal. Wasn't it the O'Connors who were involved in the scraps with police up at Birkett Mire? Years ago, it was. They're always being moved on, fucking pikeys. Never clear up after themselves. It's the poor kids I feel sorry for: never washed or sent to school.'

'Thanks, Nikki. Let me know about Ria's birthday.'

'I will. You still see that old bloke who fancied Mum?'

'Ted?'

'Yeah, that's the one.'

'I do.'

'Why? He's odd.'

'I'll tell you all about it one day.' She hung up.

Birkett Mire again. She prepared a bowl of salad and made a quick dressing in a small jar, and set it on the side. She got the cheese selection, bought from Keswick market by Johnny, out of the fridge and placed it on a board for later. The tarts would take half an hour in the oven. She went back to join Demi and Johnny, and found them laughing together.

'Demi, let's show Johnny the star.'

'The star?' Johnny asked.

'The pentagram I made from spaghetti. Someone at work is much cleverer than me and has made an app to impose it over the Lake District, come on, we'll show you. I need your local knowledge.'

'Kelly tells me that she's quite the artist with a bit of dried pasta. It did make me chuckle at first but I reckon she's on to something.'

'Kelly told me you profile criminals for the police. That must be a brilliant job. All that psycho stuff makes me wish I'd done it. I watch some of the crime programmes on CSI. Kelly hates it, she watches cookery shows instead.'

'I'm not surprised, busman's holiday and all that. Besides, cookery shows are safer.'

They went inside and Kelly powered on her iPad. HOLMES came up on the screen and she quickly read it for any updates. The dynamic reasoning engine was a godsend when her team was tired. Weary human eyes easily missed something, and before the programme had been invented, she reckoned that thousands of criminals must have walked free. Including the most famous of them all, Jack the Ripper himself. The case was every detective's wet dream: to be there in 1888, armed with today's technology... Now that would be something.

'Demi, you know you said the five victims of Jack the Ripper were located in a pentagram? Was that ever used in an investigation?'

'It was seen, by some, as evidence that the Ripper was a Mason; the shape of the compass is traditionally seen as the top and bottom of the pentagram. It's all about precision and craft, that's why they use the symbol; they and hundreds of others like them. The theory was discounted. Now they believe that it wasn't someone educated or of noble birth at all, but of course, the energy that went into those theories at the time probably enabled the real killer to escape. The most logical explanation is that he was a foreign meat handler or barber who scarpered off to New York afterwards.'

'Are you serious about the Jack the Ripper killings being in a pentagram?' Johnny asked.

'It's not something that's been used widely in fiction; the rituals, alleged prostitution and disembowelment have taken more airtime,' said Demi. 'Whatever you're cooking, it smells divine,' she added.

'I'm not saying this is a copycat at all, it's just helpful to have a precedent to compare to, right Demi? Here we go. Look.'

Demi and Johnny watched as Kelly opened Rob's app and imposed a pentacle – the pentagram within a perfect circle – over a map of the northern Lakes.

'OK, so there's Mary's house, and here is where Carry Tomlin was found at Thirlmere. I thought Birkett Mire or Threlkeld Quarry looked promising.' Kelly showed Johnny. 'The other end is Borrowdale Valley.'

'It's like looking for a needle in a haystack,' Johnny said. Demi agreed.

'Do you think it's significant that Castlerigg stone circle is inside the circle?'

They looked at the map. The ancient monument was indeed inside the shape, towards the top, and not too far away from the same longitude as Braithwaite and Threlkeld Quarry.

'The girl who was found is – we think – called Daphne. If we were to find her, then perhaps we'd find her father,' Kelly said.

'But the top of the star is pure rock face,' Johnny said. He pointed to the vast expanse of Lonscale Fell. '*If* your circle is proportioned properly. And it's a massive *if* isn't it? What if the points of the star are different to what you're assuming?' he asked.

'Or upside down?' said Demi.

'Exactly,' said Kelly. 'And there's barely a week left until autumn equinox.'

Chapter 52

Fred O'Reilly was formally brought to Eden House for questioning on the morning of Friday 16 September. He wasn't best pleased, but had waived his right to a lawyer. This made Kelly's life easier. Lawyers had nasty habits of making a suspect clam up in the most unhelpful of ways. She appreciated the need for transparency but she'd seen members of the legal community, too many times, nursing suspects through to lesser sentences for serious crimes. It was something they had to navigate.

It did however, further strengthen Kelly's belief that Fred was innocent of any wrong-doing. Usually, by this point, when formal interview is mentioned, witnesses get nervous. Not so with Fred. Added to which, she had the feeling she always got when she was in his company: it was like a warm blanket. She felt the same with Ted. Maybe all the stuff she'd been reading about was getting to her, but she thought it might be to do with aura, the energy field surrounding every human. From what she'd gathered, Kirk Junker had a rotten one, and she wondered if she'd ever get to meet him, and under what circumstances. Amy Richmond's was different again. The master of disguise, the killer had worked in hospitals all her adult life and not been suspected. Even Kelly hadn't felt any badness in her presence, until she realised who she really was. It's why Nikki had trustingly got into her car.

After the morning brief, and the depressing reality of few extra additions to HOLMES overnight, Kelly went downstairs to the interview rooms, taking DS Will Phillips with her. She found his Ralph Lauren aftershave a familiar source of reassurance. Kelly asked after his wife, and if the long hours just now were being handled well at home. It was something that she kept her eye on at all times. A burned-out officer was no use to her and they weren't machines. She heard on the radio that the Home Secretary had said that the Met should divert resources to tackle knife crime and she'd almost spat her coffee. What resources?

Kelly briefed Will on how the interview would shape up. They wanted to know more about Fred's encounters with Kirk Junker or Harry O'Connor and if there were any other aliases. So far, the O'Reillys and their friends had drip fed the investigation just what had been asked of them; they hadn't been forthcoming with any information on a proactive basis. Except Jock Harris, who still wasn't answering his phone.

'Good morning, Mr O'Reilly.' She kept it formal for the purposes of the recording. Fred confirmed his date of birth and other particulars.

'Before we start, I'm struggling to locate Mr Harris. Do you have any other contact details for him?'

'No, I haven't been able to get him either,' Fred said. 'He was supposed to stay for supper last night, but he said he had to get something done.'

'Did he elaborate?'

'No, and I didn't pry. It's not like him to not return my calls, I thought you might have him.' Fred frowned and Kelly looked at him closer.

'Really? Why would we have him?'

'Well, you seem to think that we're all hiding something, instead of getting out there and finding Mary's killer, you seem to think that I – or one of my friends – have all the answers.'

'I think you might do, Fred. Jock told us about a hotel that Kirk Junker took Edna Beverley to. It was a long time ago. It was around the time her son went missing.'

'I already told you that was before we met.'

'But, given the villainous reputation of Kirk Junker, are you telling me that no one ever talked about him? Or Edna? Or Mary's relationship with him? I find that difficult to believe.'

Fred shuffled in his seat.

'You see, my problem with you is that you're only giving me what you think you can get away with. You're holding back, Fred. Even though your beloved friend was butchered in her own home, and her animals tortured and burned to death, you still won't offer me something.'

Fred squirmed at the mention of the nature of Mary's suffering.

'Recognise this?'

Fred recoiled. 'Is that...?'

'What's the symbol, Fred?'

'The Moon Goddess, I told you before.'

'Not usually drawn in blood though? And this?' The first picture she'd shown him was the one Ted had spotted next to Mary's body, with the corpse blanked out. The second was the crude tattoo gouged into Carry's neck. Fred looked at it in panic.

'On the journalist. I don't think he used sterile equipment, what do you think?'

She felt sorry for the man in front of her, but he needed to start talking and stop prevaricating. No one liked coppers anyway, she wasn't here to be friends.

'Why the Moon Goddess? Is it because it's nearly Mabon? What's so important about her?'

'She's the light!' Fred shouted, and Kelly noticed the veins throbbing in his neck. Fred looked at DS Phillips frantically, as if asking for help. Will didn't change his expression.

'Fred!' Kelly shouted back at him. 'The light begins to die at Mabon, doesn't it? Who do you think is supposed to die? His daughter? Is she going to die? She's beautiful, isn't she? Your friend Joe Spencer saw it. I saw it with my own eyes for Christ's sake. She was like a goddess! He raised a goddess to kill her when the time was right? Is that it?'

Fred looked feverishly between the two officers.

'Fred, I'm not interested in your lifestyle. My only concern is finding the killers of Mary and Carry, and making sure he doesn't do it again. Mabon is next week. There are four elements, or five if you count spirit. He's not even halfway done!' She banged her hand on the table.

'What concerns me most is not what you've told me but what you haven't told me. You spent time with this man. You understand how his mind worked. In fact, you fathomed just how dangerous he was way before the others, didn't you? You figured it out, you rumbled him. Because of your affection for Mary, you wanted to protect her. Not even Jock sussed it, did he? Why did Daphne keep a picture of herself with Jock in her wallet?'

Fred wrung his hands and Kelly saw tears in his eyes.

'You can't save Mary now, but you could save someone else. These types of killers don't stop, Fred. Our profiler has seen it a thousand times before, all over the world: they're sick. They think what they're doing is normal, justice even.'

Fred nodded.

'We know Kirk Junker isn't his real name. We had to pry that out of your group and I know there's more not being shared. Tell me about him!' She raised her voice again and Fred put his hands to his face and began to weep. Kelly looked at Will, who raised his brow. An officer came into the room and passed Kelly a note. Jock Harris was not at home, and his newspaper was still on his porch from yesterday.

Kelly felt a sinking feeling in her stomach.

'We all thought he was abusing his daughter,' Fred said. His shoulders heaved after he'd got the burden off his chest.

'Daphne?'

'Yes.'

She thought about what The Teacher had said and recalled the notes from the Penrith and Lakes they'd found on the system. A girl was brought in and examined but disappeared shortly after with her mother. It had been just when The Teacher said, 2013. The same year of the High Rigg animal cruelty case. It gave her an idea. If this family was constantly on the move, then chances were they'd gone not just from campsite to campsite, but from county to county. She turned to DS Phillips.

'Can you get someone to send out a notice to all forces across England and Wales for history of unsolved animal cruelty cases or child disappearances linked to the travelling community? Put out the photofit again, and the picture of the girl with Jock Harris in view.'

Appeals such as these were first handled locally. Appealing nationally cost money and it had to be justified. They'd received nothing back from Essex Police regarding Jock's statement that Kirk had originated from there. Will left the room.

'Are you worried about Jock?' she asked Fred. She could see in his eyes that he was. Her voice was gentler now and she felt wretched for shouting at the gentle man before her, but someone needed to wake him the hell up. She radioed the duty desk and registered a missing person alert for Jock Harris. 'Go local with it now,' she said. She detailed the request for the tape recorder.

'Daphne was closer to Jock and Mary than anyone else.'

'But they didn't challenge her father? They allowed him to continue. Kirk is tidying up loose ends. We don't know about Jock. Let's hope he's off fishing somewhere.'

'He doesn't fish.'

'Fred, why do you think that Kirk is so angry? This rage that is necessary to do acts like this: where does it come from?'

'He was a sadist. He filmed himself sacrificing wrens on a bonfire, this was way back in 2010. There's a whole web of people who watch this stuff. That's why we protect ourselves.'

'But you said this was all before your time, did you see the video tape?'

'Jock told me.'

'Is that why you're so secretive? To protect Jock? Don't you realise that, at some point, someone has got to tell the truth, else all this stealth is dangerous?'

He nodded.

'I understand, but there are lives at stake here. Possibly Jock's. Is there anywhere you can think of that Kirk used to stay? Anywhere, Fred, we're desperate. He needs to have a bolt hole somewhere. Daphne might still be OK.'

Fred looked up.

'Yes. He boasted about a grand house left to his wife by an old relative.'

'Harry O'Connor?'

'Harry? Yes.'

'And you didn't think of telling us this before? You thought you might sit on the other information you have and we might just go away and leave you alone?'

Fred nodded.

'Tell me everything, and I mean everything.'

'Kirk was what we call a black spirit. He's a Leo: a fire sign. He lusts after destroying things and people.'

'And animals?'

Fred nodded.

'Why didn't anyone report him to the police?'

Fred laughed. It took over his tears and he couldn't stop. Kelly felt a mixture of fury and shame because she knew exactly why people like Fred didn't trust the police. She reddened and Fred gathered himself.

'What would you have done?' he raised his voice to her. 'No one cares for abused children. No one cares for hurt animals. All anyone cares about is money and glamour, and the vile things that make us all ill. Society is sick! Every last one of us. We're dying of greed, rage and lust.'

Kelly watched as spittle gathered at the corners of Fred's mouth. He was on a rant and she allowed him to continue, in the hope that he'd let something out that she could finally fucking work with. It was refreshing and she wanted to egg him on further. She sat back and watched the show. It was his turn to bang his fists on the table. The uniform tasked with chaperoning the detectives moved forward, but Kelly motioned to him that everything was all right. Will came back in the room. Fred glared at him.

'We're rotten to the core! Politics, police, doctors, banks! All of you! Money, money, money! Me, me, me! Fake, fake, fake! All of it! There was no helping poor Daphne, no more than we could have stopped him butchering Mary. For all we know, he took Edna's William and abused him too.'

'He wasn't the only one, Fred. There are thousands of missing children in this country. Have you heard of Kevin Good? And the animals he tortured? Did you know about that? It wasn't just a wren bonfire he liked. Dogs, cats, sheep, livestock? High Rigg? Birkett Mire?'

Fred's pained face changed in a moment.

'Birkett Mire? He talked about that place all the time. He raved about it, how the land was sacred and no one should be able to claim it. He said that the alignment from Castlerigg at Mabon was the most important of all: even more than the solstice at Stonehenge.'

'*Now* you remember what he talked about? This is better, Fred, come on, tell me.'

'Y-yes. I know. I—'

'So Threlkeld is special because of the alignment? But what is special to him? How does he regard a special place such as that? Does he *live* there? *Pray* there? *Kill* there? We sent a car to have a look round and they've reported nothing. What about this place he boasted about, was that Threlkeld? Wait a minute. Was it anywhere near Thirlmere? Off the Great How turning to Raven Crag?'

'He stayed wherever he could in what he could. A stolen campervan would do.'

'A campervan? What model?'

'I never said he still had it…'

'What model?'

'Fiat.'

'When was the last time you saw Jock?'

'Yesterday morning.'

Chapter 53

Josie rolled her eyes as Johnny hummed along to a song on the radio. Callum smiled from the back seat. He thought that Josie's dad was cool. Anyone who worked for the mountain rescue and was ex-army had to be cool. It was just one of those things that was obvious. But Josie was embarrassed of him, he could tell. Callum wasn't embarrassed of his dad any more. There'd been a time, when he guessed he was immature and hormonal, that he'd thought he'd die if his parents came within ten feet of him in public. That was a few years ago, and he observed Connor going through the same thing when he was a similar age. Now he just thought that his dad was a decent person: kind, thoughtful, honest and hardworking. Too hardworking, in fact. He didn't earn enough to work the hours he did, though neither of his parents knew that their eldest son had seen their pay slips. His mother earned more at the hospital. When he was their age, he wanted to be earning more than both of them combined.

That's why he wanted to be an accountant, and he figured that moving to London would set him up for life. He'd read that the CEO of every major company in the capital had studied accountancy. It was the backbone of every firm, and he could work anywhere, for anyone, and eventually himself. He'd taken GCSE business studies and economics, and he intended to take them further to A level. His plan was straight, simple and clean, muddied only by his equal need to disappear in a Fiat campervan around Greece.

'Don't get married, then,' his father had said when he told him about his intentions. 'If you fall for a girl too soon, she'll spend all of your money and force you to have kids. End game, mate. Stay focused.'

It had been half tongue in cheek, because his mother had been listening to their conversation, and pretended indignation at her husband's advice, however, he knew that it was a good point. The problem was that he really liked Josie. She wasn't like other girls: prissy, precious and fake. She talked about real stuff, she smiled widely without stopping to take selfies, and she wasn't on her phone constantly. She was sexy too.

He'd stopped thinking about the girl from the stone circle. What a disaster that trip had been! His dad had been so passionate about it and his history-mad brother had taken tons of photos on his phone, but it had ended with the odd girl and ambulances. He'd looked at her naked breasts, as she cowered behind the rock, and they were tiny. Not like some girls at school. Some of them had huge ones. Josie's were just right. Not too big and not too small.

'So, are we ready?' Johnny asked. They were driving behind the minibus taking their climbing group to Woden's Face in the Borrowdale Valley. They were nervous and Callum knew that Josie's dad was simply trying to make conversation to ease their fears.

'I've known Kev for years. He's a pro. Anyway, you smashed the rehearsal at Blencathra.' Johnny tapped his hand on the wheel as he drove. As they left the southern shore of Derwent Water, the valley opened up before them. It wasn't a wide road, and it was slow going, but the view was spectacular.

'Give it a few months and you'll be begging me to drive you up here for a climb. I used to do all the faces round here.'

'You climbed?' Josie seemed shocked.

'He'd have to, to be qualified in the mountain rescue,' Callum said.

'Thanks, Callum, at least someone knows my worth. How do you think I know Kev? And he's letting me help out today.'

Josie shrugged her shoulders. 'So, what have you climbed, then?'

'Matterhorn, a few cheeky faces in Scotland. The best one was in the Himalayas though, not because it was hard but because of the view. I could see Everest from where we were. I'd never do that, though. Only idiots go that far up into the death zone.'

'Dad!' Josie exclaimed.

'Cool!' Callum couldn't help himself.

'Parents have a life before kids, you know.'

Callum enjoyed the banter from the back seat and thought Johnny even more on point now. In fact, Josie was becoming slightly irritating for her constant tutting at her father, but then she was only fifteen still.

'This is a great place for a swim in summer,' Johnny said, pointing towards the jaws of Borrowdale: a network of gorges and gigantic rock formations forming hidden pools and places to cool off, if one knew where to look.

'The best is Argen's Pool,' said Callum.

'I agree! I took Kelly there last summer!'

Callum knew that Kelly was Johnny's girlfriend. He also knew that she was the policewoman in charge of the murder cases. He also knew that she was fit.

'Argen was supposedly a giant who destroyed Celtic tribes and stole their women. The clansmen sought their revenge by calling on an old hag who was a witch to cast a spell on him and she did, turning him into a gigantic stone.'

'Isn't the same said of Castlerigg?' Callum asked from the back seat.

'I think that story is about the Druids.'

'Who are the Druids?' Josie asked.

'Don't they teach you anything in school?' Johnny asked, toying with her. Callum smiled and replied to her question.

'They were ancient wise people, like priests, who were really respected until the Romans came and destroyed their Pagan lifestyle. Legend says that each of the huge stones is a Druid, and they're holding a religious ceremony, like they would have five thousand years ago. They turned to stone in disgust when Caesar had their king executed.'

'If the stones are five thousand years old, the Romans couldn't have been involved. They only came to Britain two thousand years ago,' Josie contributed at last.

'So, you do listen!' Johnny said. 'It's all hearsay anyway, like all myths. Who knows how they came to get there, but one thing is for sure – they're Borrowdale stones from here,' he said and swept his hand about the valley.

'How did they move them?' Josie asked.

'No idea, rollers made of logs probably,' Callum said.

'You like your history, Callum?' Johnny asked.

'Not really, I prefer maths, but my dad tells us all this stuff.'

'He sounds like an interesting person to know, I'd like to meet him. Will he be in later when I drop you home?'

'We were going to go into Keswick, Dad,' Josie said.

'I know, but I don't want you out late at the moment.'

'Don't worry, no one's doing spells over me and butchering me in rituals.'

'So, that's the gossip is it?'

'Of course, everyone knows that there are more coming, too. That girl who was found on Castlerigg, you know it was Callum and his dad who found her? She probably met the same fate, maybe she's buried right there in the middle of the circle!'

'It's not funny, Josie,' Callum said.

'I know, I'm sorry. I'm nervous about the climb. I didn't mean to...'

'It's OK. What's the hardest climb you've done, Johnny?' Callum changed the subject. He didn't want to think about the girl with the blue eyes who might very well be buried in the middle of Castlerigg. He'd dreamt of the terror behind her eyes and had already pondered what sort of experiences could do that to a person. She seemed ethereal, like a goddess, a fantasy figure from another world begging him to rescue her.

But he hadn't. He'd let them take her and now she was gone. He bit his lip and stared out of the window, barely listening to Johnny's answer. He told them about a climb he'd done in France, on Mont Blanc, in Chamonix, where three climbers had fallen to their deaths.

'They were attempting a trad climb – where there were no anchors in place – but with little experience between them. Several of their camming devices were placed in rock too soft to hold when the lead climber fell, and they all went with him. It was a devastating day for climbing.'

'Thanks, Dad.'

'On a lighter note, I'll take you to the Cochamo Valley in Chile one day, and we'll camp overnight on slings hanging off the face.'

'Woah, that sounds amazing!' Callum said.

'I think we have an adrenaline junkie in the back, Josie.'

'Have you done it?'

'Yeah, it's as incredible as it sounds. There's good climbing to be had in Argentina as well, right next door. Yosemite Park is another good one.'

'I didn't know this about you, Dad.'

'Well I don't go around announcing it. Why would I? We're almost there now. Kev's a great climber, and he's done much more than I have.'

Callum envisioned himself lead climbing in the Andes, hanging off a face, placing cams in tiny cracks, followed by Josie, in tight shorts, peering up at him, depending on him to choose the correct placing. His dream ended when Johnny stopped the car abruptly and announced they had arrived at the Bowderstone car park. The Bowderstone was a popular tourist destination and was simply a gigantic rock, six times the height of a tall man, balanced improbably on one edge, looking like it might topple at any moment. Visitors could climb up a ladder to take photos. No one knew if it was dumped there by deglaciation, or if it broke away from the crag above. Perhaps a wizard placed it there.

Woden's Face was a fifteen-minute walk from the car park and Kev got everybody together to check equipment. The main face was thirty metres tall and had been used to nurture keen enthusiastic young climbers for decades. Callum's stomach knotted as they carried the equipment through the trees to the base of the walk. Training and examining on the face was so popular now that slots were booked. The base was worn away from years of climbing group use, and was clear of vegetation and trees, but looking up, it looked like a vast jungle overhead, with ropes running up and down.

'I was here this morning checking the route, conditions are perfect,' Kev said to Johnny as they walked.

'The next generation of climbers right here,' Johnny replied. 'Do you still do the Spanish trip? I think you've got a future Adam Ondra back there next to my daughter.'

Kev looked back. 'Callum? He's strong, seems keen.'

'Perfect day. Remember the Isle of Skye?'

'Jesus! Best view from the island? Fucking white out.'

'And it was summer.'

They dumped their stuff on the ground and gave the group a minute or two to catch up and gaze up to the top of the thirty-metre face. It always silenced a group of beginners but once they reached the top, the euphoria was epic. They'd all climbed tougher routes up the wall inside the centre. And that was the point – to feel rock and earth as it had stood for millions of years. There was nothing like it. Kev would demonstrate first, and they'd take it slowly, with Johnny belaying at the bottom. A thrum of excitement travelled round the small group and they huddled together, fastening harnesses, checking the stickiness of their shoes, counting carabiners and fiddling with ropes.

Kev got them together and made his typical speech about respect, patience and weight transference.

'Remember what we've discussed about Tai Chi and always having your weight in your waist, even if you do look like a crab hanging there. *Do not climb with your arms!*' he bellowed. The group laughed. He'd drummed this into them a thousand times.

'Climbing is about your feet and your position. Don't get tired, there's no need. Rest and use your whole body. Right, I'm going up first to show you the route. Watch my placings, it'll do you a favour. Remember your body position over a stretch. Here we go.'

He patted the face and Johnny nodded to him. Kev fastened his helmet and began the ascent.

'You *may* fall, but remember you *will* stop. I will place the cams as the lead climber, you're following my route. All you have to do is feed the rope through your biner if it sticks; it should flow through nicely on its own. Belaying, which is what Johnny here has so kindly stepped in to do today, is another course and you're all capable of it.'

Johnny got into position and they all watched as Kev set off. Callum was in awe of the way he moved from hold to hold, pushing in cams, as if he'd been born and raised on the face. His belt rattled with biners and cams, as well as bags of nuts and wires, and Callum imagined himself in a few years' time with Kev's skill. The method of choosing body position and grip, depending on the face, had come quite naturally to him and Kev dished out plenty of encouragement, which was another reason he was enjoying the sport so much.

Kev talked at every grip, about why he'd chosen to place a hand or foot there. The ropes dangled through his carabiners, and every now and again, he'd pull on his belay to demonstrate how strong it was, nodding to warn Johnny first.

Callum peered up and down, between the lead and the belay. He heard Johnny's phone ring from his pocket and Kev admonished his friend in front of the group.

'There's always one.' They all laughed. Johnny had no hands free and so Josie fished his phone out of his pocket and switched it on to silent. Kev carried on.

'I'll now demonstrate a fall and show you that I have complete faith in the belay system and my mate.'

Johnny prepared himself.

There were gasps as Kev fell off the face from about ten metres up, but he soon came to a stop and dangled in the air above them. It didn't require much effort to get his footing on the face again and he straightened up, thanking Johnny.

The group expressed awe and nodded to one another. Callum couldn't wait to get up there. Josie stood next to him and they smiled with pure excitement. He heard Johnny's phone buzz again.

Kev was almost at the top now and the kids became increasingly animated at the prospect of showing off their own skills. Some of them discussed sticking points and tricky grips, others watched in wonder, gazing at their instructor, who made it look so easy.

No one understood what happened next.

Kids chatted to one another about who should go in what order. Callum offered to go first. All they heard was Johnny shouting like a maniac and the swish of air as Kev's body fell away from the face and did not stop. He cried out and everyone knew that he wasn't pissing around (not that he ever would). He was in danger and whatever was happening was not planned.

For some reason that he couldn't explain later, Callum ran towards Johnny. It must have been some instinctive response to help, but no one could have done anything. The shriek that came from their instructor made everyone look up and Callum reached Johnny in time to watch as Kev slammed into the ground, head first. Only the sound of Johnny trying to stop his friend by pulling on the belay, and his biners clanking, could be heard. Kev didn't even groan.

Someone screamed. Someone gasped. Time stood still and everything blurred. Callum felt his legs start to wobble. He heard Johnny's phone buzz again.

A vision replayed in Callum's head and it wouldn't stop: the crack of Kev's helmet hitting the ground and the puff of earth as he slammed into the earth, as the dust underneath his body wafted away in a cloud.

Still, Kev didn't make a sound. A girl began screaming. Callum's head throbbed. He looked at Johnny, who sprang into action, going to Kev and turning his body. He put his head in his hands and simply repeated, 'No, no, no, no…'

There was no chance that Kev was still alive.

Like when he was at Castlerigg, Callum couldn't help but stare at what was in front of him. Kev's neck was twisted at a weird angle and stuff leaked out of his helmet: it was like mush. His arms and legs lay limp and blood began spreading outwards from his body. More girls screamed and someone threw up. Johnny shoed them away and directed them to a place away from the body. Callum felt someone take his hand and he looked down at Josie, whose face was ashen. He shielded her and helped Johnny turn the others away.

The noise attracted tourists and other groups of climbers, and the place turned to chaos, but not before Callum noticed that, when he landed, Kev wasn't attached to a rope at all.

Chapter 54

Kelly answered her phone brightly. It was Johnny, but his voice wasn't right.

'Johnny?' she asked.

'There's been a terrible accident.' His voice cracked and Kelly felt a creeping ache spread from under her ribs.

'What? Are you OK? Is Josie OK?' Her throat constricted. It was bad. She could tell from the sound of his desperate attempt not to break down.

'Kev. The climbing instructor. I don't know... the belay... the rope... I just don't know what happened. He fell right in front of Josie and Callum. It was horrendous.' He sniffed and breathed out.

'Is he all right? Jesus, where are the kids?'

'He's dead, Kelly. He fell twenty-odd metres, head first. The kids saw everything.'

'Where are you?'

'We're at Callum's. His dad is here. The kids are in shock.'

'And you are too. I'm coming. I know his address.'

She rushed from her desk, imparting a garbled message to DS Umshaw, telling her where she was going and why. Kate stood up and followed her to the lift.

'Find out from the emergency services what the hell happened,' Kelly said. As she reached the elevator, a call came in to her phone: it was the control desk downstairs. She tucked the device under her chin and took the stairs instead, so she could listen without the signal being cut off. Kate went after her.

'Guv. We've just had a call from a pod in Keswick: they dealt with a fallen climber in Borrowdale. The emergency services are still there and the first responders have reported suspected foul play.'

Kelly stopped mid-stairway, Kate almost bumped into her. 'The climbing instructor who died? Another one?'

'No, guv, just one that I know about. Today at least. I've been on all day.'

'Can you run the details by me, I think it might be my mistake.'

The controller told Kelly about the location of the accident, the casualty and the witnesses. The main statement had been given by Johnny Frietze. She closed her eyes.

'Foul play, how?' Her skin went cold.

'All I've got is something about a cut rope. They've got some professional climbers there who were preparing to climb, and that's the opinion among them.'

'Thanks. Get me the first responder's squad car number and I'll have them contacted.'

They hung up. Kelly sprinted back up the stairs. Kate rolled her eyes, wishing she was as fit as her boss, and began going back up to the office.

'Kate,' Kelly said over her shoulder.

'Guv?' Kate responded breathlessly.

'I need you to get down to Borrowdale. Where's Rob?'

'No idea, I'll find him, don't worry. Give me the details.' Her steps were laboured as she tried to catch up to Kelly.

'I have to go and make sure that Josie is all right. Let me know when you're there.' She walked away and turned again. 'Make sure the perimeter is secure, get a photographer and a CSI team.'

'On it, boss,' said Kate.

Kelly ran to the stairs for the second time and this time made it to the bottom. She thought about calling Johnny back, but wanted to know more details first before she jumped to conclusions. The last thing he needed to hear right now was that Kev was potentially set up and killed.

Borrowdale. Borrowdale. No. No. No.

Air.

She called Rob.

'Where are you?'

'Getting a jacket potato.'

'Eat it quick. A new case has come in, it's a climbing accident that might not be an accident. An instructor is dead.'

'Where?'

'Borrowdale. Kate's going and I suggested you go with her, unless you've got something else on?'

'No, that's fine, I can go. Where in Borrowdale?'

'Woden's Face, do you know it?'

'Yeah, it's not what it was – overused by students – but they've got to start somewhere. What happened?'

'Well, I don't know all the details yet, but he fell about twenty metres. He was the instructor on an examined climb, he was guiding a group of teenagers, they saw the whole thing. I'm hearing reports that his rope might have been cut.'

'Really? Where? I mean, where exactly was the rope cut? It'd be pretty impossible to pre-cut a modern climbing rope.'

'Are you telling me that it could have been done in real time?' Kelly had imagined a scenario like the movies, where the half-cut rope rubbed itself on sharp rock, thus snapping at the right moment: when too much force was applied.

'I can't say for sure, I'd have to look at it.'

'That's why I want you down there.'

Kelly ended the call as she reached her car. She input Callum's address and pulled away.

It was only minutes later that Rob called her back and she answered on hands-free.

'Guv. I ran Woden's Face through my app. It was you who said Borrowdale might be an option. I've been playing around with all sorts of locations and shapes of stars. Woden's Face fits the model. It's the third point, and if the shape is linear and remains the way I've set it, then Threlkeld Quarry fits too. It's a traditional pentagram.'

'A fall from height,' Kelly said aloud.

'Air,' they said together.

Chapter 55

Callum's family lived on a remote farm off the A66, and the drive up to it was long and desolate. She parked outside and Johnny came out. They embraced and she looked into his eyes: she'd seen the look before, it was the same one he had when he told her snippets about Afghanistan.

'Josie's in bits. Callum is very quiet. I've met his parents. They're good people.'

'What did they see?'

'Everything. His head basically snapped almost clean off and his chest caved in. He just ripped open right in front of us all. He was demonstrating and his belay didn't stop him. I've never heard of it not these days anyway. I was belaying.'

'Oh, Johnny. It wasn't the belay.'

'What?'

'We've got some experts on site and they're saying the rope was cut.'

'What? How the hell could that be? There was no one up there, and Kev had checked the ropes already.'

'What if you didn't see them up there? What if it was planned?'

'Why? Who would do that?'

'Can I see Josie?' She didn't want to mention the star, because he was personally involved now. She felt the burden of guilt: she should have known, she should have worked it out. She'd said Borrowdale was a possibility but completely failed to register the threat when the kids said that was the location of their examined climb. She felt sick with disappointment in herself. When Johnny's shock subsided, he'd work it out for himself. He'd listened to Demi and seen her crude model made with dried spaghetti. He knew that Borrowdale fitted. In his traumatised brain, he just hadn't remembered yet.

They went inside and Kelly shook Joe Spencer's hand, but this time as a fellow concerned parental figure, not a police officer. His face was grey and it matched his son's. She went to Josie and sat next to her, opening her arms. Josie fell into them and began to sob.

She held her for a long time and Joe offered her tea.

'We'll get someone over for you to speak to, maybe not yet, but this type of thing will catch you out before you realise it. You've had a terrible shock. There are specially trained officers to guide you through it. You might not think you need it but it's something to try.'

'I can't get it out of my head. I just keep seeing his face as he fell. He looked at me and I watched him just crash into the floor,' Josie spoke manically, but that was a good sign; it was the quiet ones who didn't let it out who were more of a worry.

'Callum? How are you doing?' Kelly asked.

'I feel sick,' he said. Joe went to his son and sat next to him, after putting a cup of tea on a table next to Kelly.

'No one should have to witness that, son, there's no shame in not knowing how to deal with the vision of it,' Joe said.

'Your dad's right. You wanting to be sick is normal. No one should have to see that.'

'He was such a nice man,' Josie started crying again. 'He was so...' she couldn't find the words.

'Josie, I need to speak to your dad. Mr Spencer—'

'Joe, please,'

'Joe. Could Josie stay here for a little while? Is that all right with you, Josie? Where would you rather be?'

'I'd like to stay, if that's OK?' she said. She looked tiny and innocent, sat on the couch, with her swollen red eyes and massive jumper that had clearly been given to her by Callum.

'Of course she can stay, I'll stay here,' Joe said.

'Thank you. I'll let you know when we're on our way back.'

Johnny went to his daughter and hugged her. 'We won't be long. I need to tell Kelly all about it so it can be investigated properly.'

'Did the rope snap? I don't think I want to do it any more,' Josie said.

Kelly looked at Johnny, who replied. 'We're not sure,' he said. 'There might have been a misunderstanding with the bindings at the top of the climb, we just don't know, but modern ropes don't just snap, Josie, it's a safe sport, but I understand if you don't want to think about it right now. I don't want to leave you,' he added.

'It's all right, Dad. His family deserve to know what happened.'

'I'll look after her, Mr Frietze,' Callum said.

'Call me Johnny.'

They left and got into Kelly's car.

'I'm taking you back to Borrowdale. I have a CSI team on the way, look at this.' She handed Johnny her phone, with the email from Rob sent minutes ago. Rob and Kate were on site and he'd attached photos of the rope. Kelly had checked in advance: there were none of the body. Johnny had a strong stomach but Kev was a pal.

'You are fucking kidding me. Why would Kev be a target?'

'Rage/no rage.'

'What?'

She started the car and pulled away. She figured it was time now to spell it out and she told him about her conversations with Demi and The Teacher, about balance, control, and, again, about the significance of the pentagram. Johnny sat in silence.

'The next one will be full of rage,' Kelly said.

'You're expecting five? How do you do this? It doesn't matter how many people you put away, there's always more out there.'

'That's why I do it.'

She called Kate and Rob on hands-free to find out where they were, and tell them she was on her way.

'Look for the air symbol. It could be anywhere: on the ground, on the rock, in the trees, on the body.' She winced and checked herself, aware of Johnny sat beside her. She altered her voice to a whisper and put her left hand on Johnny's lap. He held it and nodded. He knew it was necessary.

'Has the body been moved yet?' she asked quietly.

'Yes, it was taken by the emergency services. No one thought that it could be anything else but an accident.'

'Fuck.' She swore under her breath. 'Where's he been taken?'

'Penrith and Lakes.'

'Call them and make sure no one touches him, and call the coroner: Ted Wallis. No one else.'

'Right, boss. I spoke to the first responder and they're still on the scene, making sure no one gets anywhere near. CSI is on route from Cockermouth and they're bringing a forensic officer with them. The three climbers who gave statements about the rope are still there.'

'Good.'

After the call, Kelly glanced at Johnny.

'Tell me what happened,' she asked. He began slowly, trying to remember every last detail. She took it in, and tried to picture the scene. He spoke quietly and mechanically. Kelly tried to concentrate on the road, but what she really wanted to do was pull over and hold him, and tell him that it was all right to cry, or scream, or kick something. She felt the burden of his pain. He outlined what he'd seen.

'So, no one was at the top of the rock face. Isn't that unusual?'

'Kev would have been, as the lead climber. It's a training face, nothing should have presented a problem for him. He said he'd already checked the ropes and the route up. He was no amateur. If he said those ropes were sound, then they were.'

'What other ways are there up to the top apart from climbing?'

'You'd have to walk through the trees on the other side.'

'Would you need a vehicle? Where would you park?'

'It'd depend on where you came from. There's plenty of bothies and cottages around about. If you drove, I suppose it'd be Watendlath, but that's a long walk.'

'Not for someone not in a hurry.'

'Fleeing a murder scene?'

'Yes, but they'd know that emergency services would be called, and that would take time. By the time anyone checked the ropes at the top, after such a dramatic scene at the base – and in front of children – they could be easily back to Watendlath to pick up their car. It's a National Trust car park, they might have CCTV. I'm looking for quite a distinctive Fiat campervan.'

'What?' Johnny looked at her oddly. 'The other night, when I collected Callum and Josie from climbing, they both admired an old Fiat campervan. It was definitely the model, they're so distinctive, and smaller than the VWs.'

'That's how they knew about today's climb. Jesus. Maybe they even joined the club.' On the road, she asked Johnny to get the number for the climbing centre and then give it to Eden House to request the member list from the centre and also to ask if their car park had CCTV.

It did.

Usually a drive to Borrowdale would be a pleasurable and relaxing experience: one of those life-affirming days where one is close to nature and thus connecting with Mother Earth. Not today. They remained in silence and Kelly knew that Johnny was hurting. Kev wasn't just a friend. They'd climbed together all over the world, they made rescues together when Kev volunteered for mountain rescue, and they shared a love for the outdoors. It was like a drug – climbers and pursuers of similar sports were like addicts, existing in close tribes, swapping their highs and sharing their stories. But it was about Josie too. The sort of thing that she and Callum had witnessed today wasn't something that anyone – adult or child – should ever see.

Everybody saw it in the movies but in person it was different. It could derail a young life forever. Johnny should know; he'd seen it with plenty of teenaged soldiers.

Looking at shit like that was Kelly's job and she'd trained for it, become hardened to it in some ways, but even for her, it never got easier. Seeing what can be done to a human body to make it stop working was traumatic, and the experience of Kev's death wouldn't leave them anytime soon. Josie had said he'd looked at her as he fell, and Kelly reckoned that in her experience, that sort of thing was worse than seeing flesh and blood come apart. It was the sort of look that could haunt dreams. She knew a child sex abuse specialist officer who looked at, and graded, indecent images of children all day, every day. She said that the image that woke her up in the night wasn't about what was done to the kids; it was the look on their faces.

They reached the National Trust car park at the Bowderstone and Kelly was reminded of a school trip, years ago. They'd all taken it in turns to climb the stone and pose for a picture. She must have been twelve.

'How are you doing?' Kelly asked. Johnny turned to look at her and undid his seat belt.

'I'm all right. It's Josie I'm worried about. And Kev's family. I still don't understand.'

'You don't have to do this now.'

'I do. It's the only opportunity to walk you through it step by step, while it's still fresh.'

'Come on.' They got out and Johnny took Kelly along the path that he'd walked only hours before with his daughter and her boyfriend.

'I can't believe I did this today with Kev.'

'Did you see anyone on your way to the face?'

'No.'

'Were you aware of anyone up top?'

'No.'

They reached the scene and it was busy with officers being directed here and there, someone in a plastic suit, and a CSI mapping out the area, and Rob approached them. Police tape was tied up across trees and Kelly gave Johnny some plastic covers for his shoes.

'DS Umshaw is up there,' Rob said, and he shook Johnny's hand. 'Sorry, mate.'

'How the hell did she get up there?' Kelly asked. They all glanced overhead.

'Some pulley system, guv. The climbers put it together. She was adamant about going up there, I did offer,' he said. 'You know how stubborn she is, guv.'

Kelly looked at the ground beneath them and her eyes were drawn to the earth directly underneath the rock face, which was stained dark red. She stood in front of Johnny's line of sight. Already, several plastic evidence number markers had been placed in various spots. Kelly chatted to the first responding officer, who'd been here for about two hours now. She looked up and saw that there was a small gathering of people at the top of the face, and they communicated by radio to the first responder who'd taken charge. He showed Kelly a plastic bag containing a rope.

'Can you see the cut?'

Kelly beckoned Johnny to take a look.

'Jesus. That's unequivocal,' Johnny said. He bent down and rested on the backs of his legs, holding his head in his hands.

'Any tracks up there leading away?' Kelly asked.

'None obvious, but your colleague up there has found what you were looking for carved into a tree.'

She stepped away and called Kate. 'Guv?'

'I'm here, but I'm not getting hoisted up to where you are. Why didn't you send Rob up? He does this kind of thing all the time. What have you got for me?'

'The air symbol. Much clearer and more precise than the rocks at Thirlmere or the blood at Braithwaite. This took some carving. I'll send a picture.'

'So, they were up there for a quite a while. It has to be someone connected to the climbing club. Not many people

327

would know about the exam unless you attended the club regularly. Plus a Fiat campervan was sighted there.'

Kelly's phone pinged and she opened the text from DS Umshaw. The air symbol was like the others: a triangle. The difference was that it had a line drawn through it, and it reminded Kelly of a child's drawing of a snow-capped mountain.

'Bastard. It's all just a game to him.'

'What?' Johnny asked. She showed him the symbol. 'Fucking psycho. For what? Kev's family destroyed for this? What does it mean?'

'It means there are two elements left: earth and spirit.'

She called the control desk and asked for an update on the patrols checking Threlkeld Quarry. One hadn't been there at all today so Kelly ordered one now. She'd prevent the fourth victim's fate if she had to have officers camp at the fucking quarry all week.

It might not be a perfect pentacle. That might be the last joke.

The voice taunted her, and it was the voice of The Teacher.

Chapter 56

'Guv, we've had a call come in from a Tesco delivery van saying that he reckons the photofits released match a family he saw at a farmhouse near Raven Crag. It's called Great Raven Farm. We already sent a car there but they drew a blank. Do you want another sent?'

She and Johnny were returning to her car at the Bowder-stone car park. Great Raven Farm was the abandoned pile registered to Harry O'Conner. But it was supposed to be empty.

'What did the Tesco driver say? Could he have mixed up the address?'

'He said that he's delivered there a few times and it sticks in his mind because the family is, in his words, very odd. They're unwilling to engage in conversation, barely open the door, demand he leaves the shopping outside and he said they wear unusual clothes.'

'What does that mean?'

'He said that the younger woman wears very large jumpers and it's as if she's disguising herself.'

'Is he positive about the ID?'

'He was pretty convincing. I've checked, guv; there are no other properties close.'

'Does Tesco have the record of the deliveries?'

'Yes, it's the correct address.'

'So why did our squad car report that the place is derelict and empty?'

'Didn't they say that some vehicles were locked in garages, it's possible they're squatters.'

'I'll request a warrant. Tesco would have a record if that food wasn't taken in by someone. Somebody is in there.'

'He said he saw three people.'

'Over what period?'

'About the last four weeks.'

All Kelly could think was that if this was Kirk Junker and his family, the girl might still be alive.

'Good news?' Johnny asked. She turned to him. He'd lost his lustre. Something had gone, she could tell. She reached to take his hand.

'I'm hoping that I might finally have a break.' She stopped walking and made a call to Eden House to process the warrant; they had enough to get a magistrate to turn it around quickly. It was a quick call.

'What makes someone so fucked up that they go round killing strangers for kicks?' Johnny asked, as they set off again. They were alone on the track and could speak freely. Kelly had left Kate and Rob in charge, happy that the scene was secure and as sterile as possible. Forensics were combing the area on hands and knees. She could tell that Johnny was moving into an angry phase of processing what had happened. It was necessary.

'Where do I start? Childhood trauma? Abuse? Growing up thinking that hurting people and animals is normal.' She thought about what she just said and realised that something Demi told her made sense. Serial murderers often hurt animals in their early years, often starting as children. They then seemed to travel a path of gruesome graduation to human beings: sometimes random, sometimes loved ones. It was a mirror image of The Teacher's childhood. She thought about Jock Harris. There was still no sign of him.

'Will you come on a short detour with me to Raven Crag?'

'What for?'

'That's where the address is.'

'Am I supposed to accompany you?'

'You're an important witness, and valuable to the case. More importantly, it's an opportunity being over this side of the National Park. Apparently there were some vehicles in garages and I want to know if one of them is a Fiat camper. You can identify it for me. I feel safer when you're around,' she added. He stopped and turned to her. They embraced and she let the tension leave her body. She desperately wanted to distract him.

'I've been thinking about our holiday,' he said.

'Really?'

'I'm not sure if we should go and leave Josie, now.'

They started to walk again.

'I understand. Why don't we wait and see? It'd be good for her to spend time with Ted. He has a calm and secure way about him that rubs off on those around him. He's like therapy, or at least he is for me.'

'Josie really loves him.'

'I know she does, and he spoils her rotten.'

He smiled and nodded. 'Maybe it's me, I don't want to risk leaving her, rather than it being to protect her.'

'You're bound to be even more protective of her now. It's natural.'

They reached the car and set off back north, travelling through the valley and around Derwent Water in silence. They had so many cheerful memories of this lake, and the many others, that it was difficult to marry the vision out of the car window with their current brief. When they turned off the Keswick roundabout and headed south, down the A591, Kelly began to get butterflies in her stomach. DC Emma Hide called from Eden House and informed her that the CCTV cameras at the climbing centre had picked up a Fiat campervan several times over the last couple of weeks. She'd checked the times and they coincided with when Johnny's daughter had her lessons.

Kelly felt sick. 'Are the plates visible?'

'Yes, and I've run it through the ANPR. It's not registered or insured, but there are several hits of it travelling around the

Lake District. I've got a few grainy images but the ID of the driver is unclear. It has been picked up on the A66 both ways several times, and one was the Friday ninth of September.'

'Mary's murder.'

'As well as north and south on the A591 on Tuesday thirteenth.'

'Carry's murder.'

'There was a hit this morning on the Keswick roundabout, but we don't know which exit it took. Then again at four thirty p.m., east on the A66.'

'That is excellent work, Emma. Thanks.'

She felt Johnny's glance. 'Things are moving. I need that campervan to be at this address.'

'What if it is? Are you prepared?'

The news from Emma about the CCTV was compelling. She made the decision to request an armed response vehicle to attend the farmhouse, and it was granted. The squad car was to wait at the gates, and the ARV would approach the property first. They'd rendezvous at the entrance. The team in Penrith was available.

When they turned off the road which led to Great Raven Farm, Kelly noticed two things. Fresh tyre tracks in the mud, and the fact that the gates were wide open. The ARV team was moments behind and pulled up silently. Introductions were made hastily and the mission discussed. Kelly laid out her objectives and what she knew of the suspected residents of the property, as well as the fact that there was potentially a fourth victim inside. She described Jock Harris. She took care to describe Kirk Junker and showed them his photofit, along with the photo of Daphne and Jock.

'If the suspect is inside the property then he needs to be apprehended straight away. In all honesty, I don't know what we'll find. You'll need forced entry equipment. A squad car has already checked the property before and got no response from any potential occupants. However, they did report several locked barns.'

The team of four armed men acknowledged her caution and checked in with their strategic firearms commander. They had their own chain of command, for accountability. The worst scenario in any situation such as this one was that a weapon would be fired. The best outcome was always that the building was secured and cleared for entry by unarmed officers and detectives. Kelly hated the waiting around, but knew that it was a fundamental aspect of searching a property.

Adrenaline always pumped in situations like this. The team wore armour and helmets and checked their weapons, speaking in their own language, it seemed: in code and firearm speak. They were like a wing of the police force rather than inside the body, and everyone respected them and the risks they took. Kelly shook their hands.

One nodded over to her vehicle and to Johnny.

'Crucial witness,' she said. The officer nodded and briefed his men. He was in charge. They advanced towards the property.

Kirk Junker could have easily moved his family elsewhere, spooked by the last squad car visit.

Kelly went back to her car to listen to events unfold on the radio. Johnny remained quiet and distant. It pained her to see him so lacking in spirit or life. She'd seen it before: parents whose innate mission is to protect their kids from the madness of the world, failing – in their eyes – to have fulfilled their duty.

In the distance, Kelly heard dogs. A shot of stress hormone hit her stomach and she thought of Carry Tomlin's bite wounds. The noise was acknowledged by radio, and the four-man response team approached the property with caution. They reported every visual, and Kelly felt with them, part of the team. The unarmed squad car waited alongside. They'd be second to go in.

The wait was tense.

The radio crackled and they heard shouting as they heard the team move around, checking entrances and locks. A decision was made to force their way in through a wooden door that looked as though it would break easiest. They were right. It didn't take them long to get in. Kelly listened to the radio as room by room was declared cleared and secure. The temptation to approach the building was intense and almost too much. Kelly paced up and down outside her car. Even Johnny got out.

'Oh my God,' they heard over the radio.

Johnny and Kelly looked at one another.

'That's the whole property clear. DI Porter, you need to come and see this.'

Chapter 57

Kelly looked across at Johnny. 'I think you should wait here.'

She expected him to complain, to disagree, or to insist he support her, but he didn't. He accepted her opinion and stayed in the car. She almost regretted suggesting it but knew it was the right thing to do. Rarely did police officers hardened to crime exclaim in such a manner, as the firearms officer had. Whatever they'd seen was serious. She hoped it wasn't the bodies of Daphne and Gloria Junker. Or Jock Harris.

She was joined by the three uniforms from the squad car. They approached the farmhouse.

'Has someone called a medic?' she asked the AR team.

'Yes, but I don't think there's any rush, ma'am.'

Her stomach sank. She followed the officers inside, stepping through the broken doorway. The place stank: that was her first impression. It was also cold and dark. They walked into a kitchen, and heard from the other room that someone was pacifying the dogs.

'How many dogs are there?'

'Three. They're friendly enough.'

The kitchen was filthy and Tesco bags were hung off the back of chairs, full of rubbish. Unwashed pots were everywhere. Flies flew up in groups like birds, when disturbed. She daren't touch anything, and screwed up her nose.

She recognised the smell. It was worse than the mortuary.

Thoughts of being too late plagued her mind and she braced herself for finding Jock and the girl in the next room, completing the five. Would this be the rage to balance the random? But it didn't fit the pentacle. It was the final joke after all. And still they didn't know who Kirk Junker was. This was the house that had once been owned by Harry O'Connor. Did Kirk Junker go around stealing people's names and moving into dead people's homes?

Her heart raced.

When she walked through the door, nothing could have prepared her for what she saw, and she was glad she'd suggested Johnny stay in the car.

The bodies were stiff and discoloured, partly rotted, partly disfigured. They were tied to two chairs: one each. They looked as though they'd been propped up there to watch a soap opera on TV. A thousand scenarios dive-bombed into her head, exploding every theory she'd toyed with for the last two weeks.

She heard a siren in the distance and looked at one of the uniforms. Another gagged next to her and she suggested he wait outside.

'Please don't touch anything. How close did you get to the bodies?' She asked one of the AR team members who'd got in here first. He stroked the dogs. They wagged their tails, disinterested in the corpses. She peered towards the two bodies, looking for the different stages of insect activity.

'Just to make sure they were dead, ma'am.'

'I'm sure they're dead,' she said. 'And, by the look of them, I'd say in my limited experience, without the coroner, that they've been like this for some time.'

He nodded.

'I think the dogs might have had a go,' she said, noticing one of the hands looked chewed. She glanced back at the dogs and their snouts looked stained. The officer patting them recoiled and another came in with some rope to tether them and lead them out. They'd probably be destroyed, given their apparent taste for human flesh. She guessed these were the same animals that terrorised Carry Tomlin, here in this hovel: the vision was repulsive. They whined and looked up at her as they passed, guided by the officer. She felt a pang of sympathy for them: it wasn't their fault.

Flashing lights whirred outside and, shortly after, a medic came into the room.

'Fucking hell. Hi, Kelly.' Kelly was familiar with most of the forensic staff called upon to help the police in Cumbria.

'It's the rocky horror show.'

It was true, the two victims looked as though they were painted for the stage, in some macabre production.

'My guess is they've been dead for over a week, what's yours?' she asked.

He got closer. 'Maybe more. It's nice and cold in here, but there are large larvae in there,' he said, going closer to the body. 'There's a lot of thermal heat being generated inside.' He gently moved a piece of clothing, revealing a mass of crawling insects having a banquet. Kelly looked away.

'Do you know who they are?'

'I think I do. He was my main suspect right there.' Kelly pointed to the male victim. He appeared to be staring straight ahead, at her, waiting for her to sit down and start chatting. She'd seen his face dozens of times, as described in such detail by Fred O'Reilly, and so well painted by the police artist.

She was staring into the face of Kirk Junker, and she'd bet her last dollar that the woman next to him was his wife, Gloria.

The question was, where were Jock Harris and the girl?

But her most disturbing realisation was, if the bodies in front of her had been rotting for more than a week, then Kirk Junker couldn't be her killer.

Chapter 58

'Guv, we've got a situation at the Threlkeld Quarry.' Kelly's radio crackled and beeped.

'When the patrol car got here, they disturbed someone inside one of the containers. The suspect scarpered, seemingly over the lip of the old quarry, and despite a thorough search on foot, they seem to have disappeared. There's a man in a wheelchair here, bound and in rough shape. He was about to have three tons of slag and earth dropped on him inside an old storage unit.'

'Is he alive?'

'Barely. He's got some pretty horrible injuries but he's breathing.'

'Is he able to tell you his name?'

'It's Jock. That's all we got out of him. We've got an ambulance on the way.'

Kelly looked at her phone and brought up the email of the pentacle. She entered the last two locations: Woden's Face and Threlkeld Quarry. They fit perfectly and she shook her head, annoyed with herself for not pinpointing them. But it was an impossible task and no one could have done it. There was only one point missing: the top of the pentagram. And that was somewhere on Lonscale Fell.

She left the farmhouse and went out into the fresh air. More vehicles arrived and a CSI team greeted her. They'd process the whole lot and, judging by the amount of crap inside, it'd take them days. She asked for a pair of shoe covers and gloves and went back inside. The house was simply laid out, or the rooms that were in use. As she wandered around, taking in the scene, she noticed three pairs of wellington boots slung beside a door. She turned them upside down and one of them was a size eight.

Someone shouted from outside. A Fiat campervan had been discovered inside one of the garages, as well as Carry Tomlin's silver Ford Mondeo. Whoever did this was messy, and she was confident that if Carry was killed in here before being dumped at Thirlmere, there'd be DNA evidence. They would also examine the jaws and bite shapes of the three dogs before they were destroyed, though Kelly was pretty confident that they'd match Carry Tomlin's wounds. She walked through the room where the bodies were being photographed, and came out into a hall. The ARV team confirmed that no other persons were inside the house, so she knew she was safe. She found a bathroom and recoiled at the conditions. Had Kirk Junker really made his family live here? Was Daphne safe or was finding her now even more unlikely?

The bath was relatively clean, though there were some cleaning products. Maybe this was where Carry was bathed and drowned. A lab could test the molecular structure of the products present and compare them to what Ted had collected from Carry's lungs. She left the room and tried another. It was fairly tidy and even homely. A couch looked inviting and a table was laid with candles and trinkets. It wasn't until she went closer that she recognised the layout and knew that she was staring at an altar.

But something about this particular arrangement disturbed Kelly. It wasn't like Fred and Mary's in the sense that it invoked a sense of honour and worship. It looked sinister and confused. In the middle was a ceremonial knife exactly the same as Fred had described Mary's. She picked it up with her gloved hand and handled it. It was truly beautiful. She checked her phone and satisfied herself that this was almost an exact match. She turned it over and held it to the little light inside the squalid room. She saw a fingerprint on the hilt. Also on the table were little metal models of figures that reminded her of the monsters and demons of scary children's programmes. There was a vial of liquid and what looked like a wand.

Then she saw the pentacle. It was on a piece of leather, and it was about two inches across. A book lay closed next to it. She picked it up and opened it. She didn't really understand what she was reading, but they appeared to her like chants, songs or poems. They were accompanied by ghastly drawings of violence and destruction, formed by a deranged mind. She sighed and went back out of the room to inform the photographer of what to log and tag. She took off her plastic covers and gloves and went back outside. She'd need an army of forensics here and she called HQ to plead her case. She got what she wanted and spoke to the CSI to make sure they concurred about exactly how to process the site. It could be vital later in court.

She went back to her car to find Johnny sat in the same position, staring towards the fields.

'I need to get a team up Lonscale Fell. You know it like the back of your hand, Johnny.'

'I want to get back to Josie.'

'I understand. Could you recommend someone as good as you?'

'Only the whole team. I'll see who's on duty.'

Kelly noticed that the anger she'd seen earlier was wearing off and he was distant and lethargic.

'Can I drop you at Callum's?'

'Yeah, that's where my car is. Are you any nearer to catching this bastard?'

'The person who I've been chasing is dead inside that farmhouse. It's back to square one for us, but now we know, the leads will pour in. It won't be long.'

'What? Suicide?'

'Definitely not, and I think they've taken his daughter. It's a mess, these people don't want to be found and they don't live like we do: they don't leave paper trails, internet footprints, bank details or...' she thought of something.

'What?'

'The Tesco shop must have been paid for online.'

She started the engine. The drive back to the A66 wasn't far and she took Johnny to Callum's house and left him there, watching him walk up to the door, his shoulders lower than usual. It pained her to leave but she was more useful trying to do her job. She carried on to Eden House, where a mountain rescue team had gathered, along with at least ten uniformed police. Lonscale Fell was a bleak younger brother of Skiddaw. The Jenkin Hill approach was about as dull a walk as could be found, but it was great for dogs and children.

The last element was spirit, if indeed the intended torture of Jock had been meant to be earth. He wasn't strong enough to be interviewed, but the Penrith and Lakes was doing its best to care for him. The squad car that had disturbed the person about to crush him hadn't got a good look at the person who ran away, but they did notice that he wore a baseball cap and was as fast as lightning. He was small and fit.

Rob and Kate were back from Borrowdale and they gathered in the incident room. Kelly took a deep breath and prepared to bring them up to date. It was as much for her benefit as theirs; her head was spinning with the events of the last couple of hours, and they still had a missing minor.

Searching Lonscale Fell was a hunch. They might find nothing, but it fitted the top of their pentagram model. It would have to be an extensive search. They'd start at the Ormathwaite car park and walk in a single row up the fell, looking for any sign of walkers or something out of the ordinary. There were no live cases of missing persons but she had an idea of what they were looking for. She brought up a picture of the girl.

'This is Daphne Junker. She's the daughter of who was our prime suspect, who is now dead, and has apparently been for over a week. Her life is in critical danger, and I have reason to suspect that she might have been brought here, to Lonscale Fell.' She pointed to the map and superimposed the pentacle.

The murmur around the room was incredulous and electric. She now had her five points.

No symbolism had been found yet at the Great Raven Farm, except the altar. There were no obvious signs of anything indicating an element or the Moon Goddess. There was also no symbol found at Threlkeld Quarry, where Jock Harris had been threatened with his end. But the perp was disturbed.

'I've gone live again with the public appeal for the girl,' Kelly said. 'We need to get a move on before we run out of light.'

Chapter 59

They drove in five squad cars and three vans, and people in the streets stopped and stared at them as they passed. It took under twenty minutes to get to the base of the Skiddaw walk and they filed out of their vehicles quietly. A helicopter flew overhead but it was unlikely it'd be able to get near the rock face today in the dangerously high winds. It provided backup instead. Lonscale Fell sat silent and serene above them. It was a straightforward walk and it wouldn't be too challenging staying in formation. As well as the mountain rescue team put together by Johnny, Rob and Emma accompanied Kelly, and they put on walking jackets to start the search. The hardest part was walking vertically uphill, and not on the paths. They had to search every piece of landscape.

They crossed White Beck and trudged on in silence. No one made a sound. And nobody indicated that they'd spotted anything at all that was extraordinary. The wind howled around them with menacing force and, if they weren't careful, it threatened to whip them off the hillside to the crags below. Kelly's mind began to wander and she thought about Josie. Then she thought about Ted, and knew that he'd have been informed about the double homicide at the farm. He'd also know that Kelly would be assigned the case. Her pondering turned to Carry Tomlin and how terrified she must have been inside that house of horrors. Did she see the bodies? Did she know what awaited her? Did she recognise the smell of death?

Their biggest trump card was Jock Harris. He'd apparently spent time with their killer, and as soon as he was strong enough, and fairly lucid, they'd talk to him. Jock was an intelligent man and he remembered details well. She was confident they'd nail the bastard and get them put away for life.

They neared halfway and still no one flagged anything up. Occasionally, they'd all stop for a breather. It was tough going, even for seasoned mountain rescuers and police. The wind picked up even more aggressively, but it didn't spoil the incredibly beautiful view, which was clear over the whole of the Derwent area. The lake sparkled in the distance and Kelly thought about Johnny's boat, the *Wendy*, bobbing up and down and chugging between islands and pub stops. Skiddaw was clear at the top and Kelly could see plenty of coloured dots scaling the summit. Grisedale Pike in the distance looked moody and dominating, as always, half covered in trees, residing above the mighty Whinlatter Forest.

Finally, they reached the top and stopped. Everybody looked at Kelly and she didn't know what to say.

'Take a break everybody,' she said. She walked away from the group and over the lip of the summit. It wasn't a high peak by any stretch of the imagination. It was modest, at about two thousand feet. But it was a taxing walk nonetheless and her chest heaved. She'd tell them to spread out and search the summit, exploring hidden edges and scrubland that was hidden from view. She felt foolish and almost called off the whole thing. She walked away from the main group and faced Keswick. The cars and trees looked like little models and she wanted to cup them in her hand and sort through them looking for answers: it would be a whole lot easier than picking through a theory on a mountainside and coming up with nothing. A senior mountain ranger approached her, he was a pal of Kev and Johnny's.

'Can I call you Kelly in front of this lot?'

'Of course you can.' She smiled at him and she saw the grief and anger in his face. They'd shared plenty of pints over the last few years together, sharing Johnny's stories and appreciating the fells.

'If I were to take shelter for any length of time up here, it'd be behind a pile of Cairn stones just over that lip, facing Blencathra. Gossip at the rescue centre is that whoever took out Kev had recently joined the climbing club. He did a practice walk with the same group over on Blencathra. If your man was stalking them, he'd know these hills like the back of his hand. That's where I'd be.'

Kelly nodded her thanks and he offered her a sip of sweet tea. It was welcome and she took it. It refreshed her and armed her to face the group and share what she'd been told. They'd spread out, making their way in ever-increasing contour lines, as they made their way below the summit line.

The land wasn't littered with features like some hills were. There was little foliage, few boulders or sheer drops and no bothies or shelters for farmers. It was the oldest range in the Lake District and was fairly round and worn and bleak. The fact should help them, Kelly thought. She delivered her instructions and prepared to move off, descending in all the directions of the compass. Kelly faced directly east, towards Blencathra. She'd walked and slipped down only a few metres when the voice of the others disappeared and she was by herself. Only their radios crackled and whistled in the wind.

A small rock caught her foot and she stumbled but kept upright. She wouldn't have thought much of it, except that she was a clumsy idiot, if she hadn't had seen the whip of hair flapping beneath the rock. In a second, she could have missed it. But, as she stared at the vision longer, she realised that she was not mistaken: the blonde hair caught on the breeze again, wafting gently here and there, behind the shelter of the mountainside. Kelly peered over the rock she'd tripped on and held her breath.

Daphne had long blonde hair.

In the moment, she envisaged another gruesome find. One more to add to the list: the fifth and final sacrifice. Spirit. Daphne's spirit. The Moon Goddess. Her heart pounded in her chest and she reached for her radio. Her hands shook.

Looking over the edge of the boulder, which was much larger than she originally thought, she saw a body hunched over. It was sat up and naked.

'Daphne?' Kelly whispered. She realised that the girl wouldn't hear her over even the kindest of winds and she raised her voice.

'Daphne?' She was more emphatic.

The girl turned around and Kelly relaxed a little as she confirmed that she seemed to be lucid and unharmed. But she must also be freezing.

'Thank God!' Kelly went to her, taking off her sweater and reaching into her rucksack for another layer. The girl began rocking back and forth, and Kelly covered her and soothed her.

'You poor thing! How long have you been up here?' Kelly felt her skin and it was icy cold. The girl shouldn't be alive. She spoke into her radio, not wanting to traumatise the girl further. A cheer went up over the radio and within what felt like seconds, two mountain rescue volunteers raced over the lip to the boulder and scrambled down the lip.

Both had medical equipment with them. The medic in their party was on her way; she'd taken the south route down and had a bit of work on hand and knee to get back up and over to where they were. She was there within minutes and Daphne was laid on her side, wrapped in layers, given hot tea, and checked for signs of hypothermia, or worse. The girl didn't say a word, but she did look at Kelly, who smiled reassuringly back to her.

The feeling couldn't be matched. Saving one life, amongst all of the horror she'd witnessed this week, was something that didn't come with a price. The relief overtook Kelly's body and she breathed deeply, holding Daphne's hand.

'Is your name Daphne?' she asked. The girl nodded. Kelly experienced elated joy when Daphne communicated with her. It showed trust, but most of all, it probably indicated that Daphne was all right.

'Are you harmed in any way?' Kelly asked.

Daphne shook her head.

'How did you get here?'

'I can't remember.' A voice, finally. Kelly smiled at her and squeezed her hand.

The medic concluded that Daphne was strong enough to move and she was strapped to a soft-shell portable stretcher. Two mountain rescue volunteers held her securely and Kelly held on to her hand and spoke to her all the way down; partly to keep her awake and partly to cultivate the seed of trust sown on the mountainside.

Kelly smiled at her and was rewarded with a warm grin back. It was the first time that she'd witnessed the girl as anything other than a photographic or mute statistic.

Chapter 60

With Daphne safely admitted to a ward at the Penrith and Lakes Hospital, Kelly paced up and down the lobby area with a coffee, and called Johnny.

'She's alive.'

'That's brilliant, well done. I didn't expect that at all. I thought you'd be calling to say the opposite.'

'Me too. How are Josie and Callum?'

'Not good.'

'I'm sorry.'

'I know.'

Kelly looked about the café area, as if it would provide a solution to her predicament. Johnny sounded as though he spoke with an edge to his voice. She worried that it had sunk in that she should have figured out the Borrowdale connection. After all, Josie, or indeed Callum, could have been the ones climbing when the rope was cut. It could have been his daughter, not just his friend, who he'd seen fall to their deaths. The realisation worried her but irritated her too. She wasn't a machine.

'Johnny, I didn't see it. I didn't expect it.'

She got a flashback of reassuring her sister the same thing when she'd failed to protect her from The Teacher. She was the detective. It was her job to spot stuff like this: make links, join dots, and prevent crime. Josie had been put in danger and it was her fault. Now, Johnny's trust had been tested and stretched beyond its limit, and she was to blame.

'I know.'

It wasn't like him to be so terse. She expected petulance from her sister but not from her lover, who she trusted with her life. It was the beginning of a seed of betrayal and she didn't like it. His faith in her was shaken and she felt the bitter taste of injustice. Never in the three short years here in Cumbria had she once doubted his loyalty and his support. But now she did and it made her feel very alone.

'I told you it was like looking for a needle in a haystack. It was an impossible task to predict. It's about as sure as fortune telling. I was using spaghetti, for God's sake.'

'It's not about the spaghetti. Rob's amazing app should have thrown up something.'

There, it was out. He blamed her. He blamed her team. Her gut turned over and she felt abandoned in the cavern of the place she hated most of all: the damn hospital where her mother died and where The Teacher had played her almost to her own death.

'I'll call you later.'

Johnny hung up without saying goodbye. Kelly felt sick.

DS Kate Umshaw called her and it saved her from wallowing in any more self-pity. She took a deep breath.

'Kate?'

'Boss. We've had some news. The blood on Carla Rigg's – I mean Daphne's – clothes wasn't hers. There's no match. It was somebody else's blood.'

'OK. I'm sure whoever has been threatening her, and was responsible for the death of her parents, could have transferred blood from a victim.'

'The blood samples from her parents have been submitted but they'll take time. The lab did say that the blood on the clothes was from a close family member.'

'I wonder if Daphne saw her parents killed, then. She may have been closer than we think. She's been through so much.'

'Also, guv. There was a laptop seized as part of the forensic search of Great Raven Farm.'

'Really? That's an unexpected result.' The presence of a laptop in Kirk Junker's residence was jarring: she didn't think him the sort of person to bother with modern technology. 'Has it been processed?'

'Yes, guv, and it didn't take long because there were no security measures applied to the machine. It was all there to trawl through on the desktop icons. The log history shows little use, but when it was used it was mainly to an IP address of another independent laptop or iPad.'

'So, they communicated with somebody. Good job, Kate, well done. Do we know where the IP address is registered?'

'Yes, guv.'

'Well, come on then, I need to go and visit Jock Harris and see if he's able to give a statement yet. What's the problem? Something's not right, I can hear it in your voice.'

'It's registered to Broadmoor, guv.'

Chapter 61

Kelly chatted with the ward sister in charge of caring for Jock Harris. A uniformed police officer guarded his room for his safety. The person who had threatened his life was still at large, and he was a key witness.

Kelly followed the nurse inside and Jock stirred. He looked pale and twenty years older than the last time she saw him.

'Hi, Jock. How are you holding up?'

'I've had better days.'

At least he was lucid. And he hadn't lost his sense of humour, despite being moments away from a very horrible and slow death. He must have known for long minutes what his attacker was going to do. She was disappointed that it wasn't tidy, and that all leads brought them to Kirk Junker, but it was just another challenge to overcome and work out.

'We found the bodies of Kirk Junker and, we think, his wife, at a property registered to Harry O'Conner this afternoon, Jock.'

'I know. I was there.'

'What?'

'Daphne called me. She told me where they were. I went to see her.'

'Without informing us? That was reckless!'

'Thanks for letting me know, it was none of your business. It was personal. I went to see Kirk to set a few things straight.'

'Knowing he was our prime suspect! That's perverting the course of justice and withholding key information. Wait a minute, you went there? So, you saw Kirk?'

351

'Yes.'

'Dead?'

'Yes.'

'Do you know who killed him?'

'Yes.'

'Who?'

'His daughter.'

Kelly laughed. 'Daphne? Don't be ridiculous!'

Jock held her gaze and a creeping feeling settled in the back of her throat.

'She tried to kill me too, and I was about to let her. Her plan to punish me was interrupted.'

'The young man with the baseball cap?'

'That was Daphne.'

'Jock, you're over two hundred and twenty pounds at my best guess, Daphne is barely a hundred.'

'It doesn't matter. Kirk was getting old. I am old. Gloria wouldn't say boo to a goose. And the others, well, all you need is some brains and the element of surprise.'

'The others?'

'Haven't you worked it out yet?'

Kelly stared at Jock and images, bodies, details, plans, weapons, and ceremonies jumped into her mind. This girl had been raised around Pagan rituals all her life: sacrifice, punishment, good, evil, dark, and light. She remembered what Kate had told her about the laptop.

It dawned on Kelly that Daphne had likely been talking to The Teacher all this time. She was a protégé. A vulnerable, innocent, perfect protégé, full of anger, hatred and rage. Perfect to be manipulated and moulded. The pentagram was complete after all: Daphne's spirit was the last point of the star: it was her own sacrifice.

Her brain whirred and she worked out that if Kirk and his wife had been dead for a little over a week, then it was feasible that Daphne had taken herself to Castlerigg to cleanse herself the evening she killed her parents. *If* she killed her parents. She was getting ahead of herself and losing the precariously tiny shaft of delineation between fact and fantasy. She had no direct evidence, just Jock's testimony.

'Why should I believe you?'

'You don't have to. I don't really mind if you do or not, I'm just telling you what I know. When I saw Kirk in that chair, full of flies and stinking the place out, I knew she'd done it. She's deranged beyond anything you'll ever see, detective. She's lost to us all. He got what he deserved, though I was cheated.'

'You *wanted* to die?'

'No. I deserved to die. I could have protected her and I didn't. I knew what Kirk was doing to her, and letting others do to her. But I was too scared to do anything about it.'

'Why were you all so scared of him?'

'Because we know what he was capable of. I've seen him conjure demons, detective. Believe me or not, it matters nothing to me.'

The word demons jarred Kelly and she thought about Mary's diary. *There are demons among us and they look like people.*

'I find it impossible to believe that she killed Mary. I've seen her afraid and cowering. I held her hand. She thanked me...'

'Beware then. If you've touched skin then she's halfway to owning you already.'

'Oh, for God's sake, Jock! Stop it, please.' Her emphasis was lost inside the four walls of the hospital room and it fell hollow on the floor. She swallowed. Jock stared at her.

Kelly remembered where she was and what her job was, and sprang into action, batting away any entertainment of what Jock was implying. Ghouls and ghosts, or whatever they believed in, had no place in her world. But she couldn't think straight. She had to get out of the room. She backed away and tried to remember which room Daphne was in.

The uniform outside the room moved aside for her and she told him not to let the man inside out of the room under any circumstances. He nodded.

353

She went to call Johnny but decided not to. Instead she called Rob Shawcross and briefly garbled what she'd just been told.

'Guv, we've had more from the sterile lab examining the laptop from Great Raven Farm. It's been used seven times since the estimated time of death of Kirk Junker and his wife. So unless somebody else was in the farmhouse, and there's no evidence of that so far, Daphne was the one making contact with Broadmoor. I've been in touch with them already – I knew you'd ask – and they've confiscated all electronic equipment from the cell of Amy Richmond. They found an iPad that shouldn't have been there.'

'How quickly can you get to the hospital? I'm calling a squad car in too. What about armed response?'

She was dithering. Asking a junior officer such questions was ludicrous. 'Sorry, Rob. Ignore me, it's been a long bloody day.' Questions assaulted her, as well as the nightmare logistical task of storming a hospital room, with hundreds of innocent civilians close by: half unable to escape if they needed to.

'No worries, guv. What can I do?'

'Call HQ and request armed backup at the Penrith and Lakes. If I need them I'll notify the team. I'm going up to the female ward. There are two uniforms on the door. I'll wait for the squad car before I go in and I'll call the ward to find out exactly where Daphne is. If she's on walkabout around the hospital I'll abandon plan A and wait for backup. Got it?'

'Yes, boss.'

'Get someone to contact security here at the hospital and check all CCTV cameras.'

'Guv.'

Rob was efficient and timely and, in under five minutes, she had confirmation that backup was on its way, and a squad car redirected from an estate in Penrith was three minutes out. Just enough time to get the lift to the eleventh floor to where Daphne was recuperating.

She realised that she hadn't eaten all day and it was beginning to have an effect on her mood. Her conversation with Johnny was forefront on her mind and she was having a hard time pushing it away. She called the ward sister looking after Daphne and tactfully acquired the girl's whereabouts. Sister said she was in her room and hadn't moved since she'd been brought in. She hadn't eaten but was hooked up to a drip and various electrolytes, and was apparently asleep.

Perfect.

The squad car radioed in and announced its arrival, as did Rob. Kelly waited by the lifts and tried to look insignificant. Nobody took any notice of her: she looked like an agitated relative, nothing more. Rob and the uniforms arrived together and they waited for a lift. They squeezed into one carrying a wheelchair, a drip and three children, all crying to their mother that they were hungry. The journey to the eleventh floor was tedious, but at least Kelly knew that there was no jumping out of this window.

When they arrived at the floor, they politely moved around the other passengers and filed out, looking for the correct entry to the ward. The sister was waiting for them.

No circumstances had changed. It was the best news they could have.

Kelly touched base with the armed response team waiting downstairs on standby. They were set to go. The sister took them to the room and left them, as Kelly instructed, and made herself scarce.

Kelly looked at Rob and the two uniforms who'd come in the nearest squad car.

They went inside.

The room was empty but the bathroom door was closed.

'Daphne?' Kelly shouted. 'Daphne, it's me, Kelly, I've come to see how you are.'

There was no response. Kelly whispered into her radio for the armed response team to proceed up the fire exit to the rear of the wing, and approach the eleventh floor on standby.

Kelly tried the door, it was open. Rob nodded and indicated that he was ready.

Beyond the door was merely a patient, unarmed and probably very scared.

She went in.

The bathroom was empty.

They sighed a mixture of relief and frustration. Where the hell could she be? They'd questioned the ward sister who swore that Daphne hadn't left the room.

Out in the corridor, Kelly contemplated her next move and DS Umshaw called once more from Eden House.

'Guv, we've got the governor of Broadmoor on the phone. An inmate wants to speak to the Cumbria Police, but she'll only speak to you.'

'Don't tell me.' Kelly closed her eyes.

'It's Amy Richmond, guv.'

Chapter 62

It was HQ's decision to send Kelly back to Broadmoor. She was being used and she knew it. There was absolutely nothing she could do about it. Daphne was missing and Amy Richmond was hoping for a reduced sentence for helping the police. They had lawyers researching the legal limitations of bargaining pleas. If an inmate could make a plea, then they had to be sane: ergo, Amy Richmond's conviction was unsafe and a retrial would have to be pursued. The psychopath was on shaky ground because she could end up with a heftier term, not a reduced one. Kelly was staggered that a personal audience, face to face with her, was more important than the terms of her incarceration. It made her queasy. Without Johnny to speak to, or her mother, she turned to Ted.

He'd offered to go with her, and despite her better judgement to decline his support, her emotional need triumphed and she accepted. They boarded a plane at the newly opened Carlisle airport bound for Heathrow at seven p.m. A car was ready to meet them in an hour and whisk them down the M4, using blues to get through the traffic. They should be in front of The Teacher by nine p.m. if all ran smoothly.

In the initial phone call that Kelly was forced to take by HQ, Amy Richmond told her that she knew, unequivocally, where to find Daphne.

'Why would you betray your apprentice?' Kelly asked her. Amy didn't answer. The hunt for Daphne had begun and DS Umshaw was left in charge.

Kelly longed to talk to Johnny but Josie needed him even more now. Any distraction from her about her job would be crass and selfish. She realised how heavily she relied on his wisdom, his calm, and his logic. But then she chided herself and gave herself a stern reminder of her status before the man now in her life. She had this. She could get the result she wanted on her own. Affirmation, confidence and encouragement were all very nice if you could get it, but they were luxuries. She was the detective, and this was her job.

Ted looked smart in a suit as he strode across the tarmac, accompanied by airport staff. Carlisle was still in sunlight, though low cloud limited visibility. Heathrow basked in thirty degrees and she missed the southern Indian summers enjoyed down there. She smiled at him and he hugged her. They boarded and final flight checks were already in full swing. The British Airways crew had been briefed and they were given front row seats.

Since the airport opened earlier in the year, Kelly hadn't used it, but now, when they took off, she stared out of her window, at the National Park below them, in awe. She couldn't think of a finer view. It stilled her nerves.

Forty minutes later they were on the ground and escorted off the plane, minutes after it came to a stop. A detective introduced himself and a colleague and they climbed into an unmarked BMW. Blues were only occasionally necessary, as they approached the Bracknell junction and crossed between the M4 and M3 into countryside and towards the huge hospital, famed for its lethal inmates. It was fully dark now and Kelly couldn't make out the building until it loomed large between the trees, lit faintly by security lights. She could have been approaching a grand, remote hotel if it weren't for the barbed wire and lookout towers.

Ted squeezed her hand. They hadn't talked much the whole way. Ted had seen Amy's work himself: he didn't need reminding. Having him there was a source of reassurance and he soothed her just by being next to her. The last time she'd seen Amy, she'd sworn she'd never go back. This was duty. For some screwed up reason, Amy Richmond had developed some kind of obsession and would talk to no one else. It was perverse, but Kelly pushed it from her mind. She had work to do.

They went through the familiar security checks and found themselves at the end of the lit corridor, where The Teacher waited for them. Kelly went in alone. Ted offered to go with her but Kelly was adamant. She had to face this unchaperoned. Her trainers squeaked on the polished floor and she pushed her hair off her face, wishing she'd tied it back. She was weary and sweaty from a long day but inside she was ready. She reached the window and remained standing, though a chair had been provided, like the last time.

Amy Richmond smiled at her.

Kelly didn't change her expression, but just stared back at the killer.

'What do you want, Amy?'

'I bet you're so mad! You want to be up there in your precious fells, don't you? Looking for Daphne with your team. But the senior men in HQ sent you to me.'

'Yep, you got that right. I don't want to be here.'

'I like your edge. Fallen out with hubby?'

Kelly began walking away.

'OK! Come on! I'll tell you where she is. I just wanted to see you again, Kelly. No one gets me in here. It's lonely.'

Kelly stopped and went back to Amy's window.

'Amy, I am not, and never will be, your friend.'

'I know. I just like being in the company of intelligent people like me, rather than the monkeys in here.'

'Some light relief?'

'Yes.'

'I'm waiting.'

'Don't you want to know why she did it?'

'I think I can work that one out myself: child abuse, ritual brainwashing, a broken mind, blah blah.'

'So nonchalant. Maybe you're burned out. You should take a holiday. Still looking at Florida?'

Kelly's mouth opened but no sound came out.

'You should be more careful with your security settings. It's all out there, if you know where to look.'

'You're stalking me? That could extend your sentence.'

'It'd be worth it.'

A chill suddenly made Kelly shiver.

'I still have properties in the Lakes. They're under lots of different names, obviously. Daphne is in a caravan near Birkett Mire. Close to where she watched her father torture animals and her mother forced her to sacrifice herself by moonlight.'

'You wear it like a badge, or a medal: knowing so many nasty, warped individuals, no wonder you're in here. Maybe you are crazy. Daphne definitely is; I've looked into her eyes.'

'Close up? I hope you didn't touch her.'

Kelly was reminded of Jock's warning to this effect, but she pushed it away.

'Is the caravan on a site or by itself?'

'It's on its own, next to the St John's Beck, I bought the land years ago and refuse to sell it. It's mine under an ancient lease that the National Trust can't dispute, though they've tried.'

'I still don't understand why you'd betray her. You taught her, nurtured her, and encouraged her. I've seen the log of your Facetimes and Skype calls. You two are close.'

Amy laughed. 'No, there you've got it wrong, detective. She's a fucking fruitcake! I am looking forward to spending some time with her in here, though.'

'Ah, that's why. I get it now. You want some company.' Kelly shook her head. 'Well, you'll get it.' She dialled Kate Umshaw's number and communicated the information, hoping it wasn't another trick.

'You still can't work it out, can you? How she did it. I mean, with me, it was straightforward: I'm stocky, muscular – more than any man – and older. But, a child? Wispy, weak and goddess-like?'

'You're right.' Kelly folded her arms.

'Maybe she had help?'

Kelly waited.

'But not the kind of help you're thinking of. Nothing that can be quantified by dimension, space and natural laws. Something ethereal, other-worldly and unnatural.'

'Now we're into hocus pocus too? You do need some company.'

'Part of you believes though, doesn't it? You don't want to, but you've seen enough to sow a seed of doubt.'

Kelly squirmed inside. She was desperate for the search to be over, and for Kate to call her, giving her the green light to get the hell out of this place and get back on a plane. But there were no more flights to Carlisle tonight. It didn't matter, she'd agreed with HQ that if they found Daphne tonight, she could justify the cab fare. Failing that, she'd pay for it herself just to get the hell out of this place. She didn't care how much it cost.

'Are you missing your computer?' she asked.

'Of course, but I'll be given it back.'

'You know there's no reduced sentence on offer?'

'It was worth it just to see you. Besides, my appeal is already filed and this will help. I've been very obliging.'

'You've also been very obstructive. You could have told us what you knew weeks ago and prevented three murders. That won't look good.'

Amy smiled.

'I never wanted to look good.'

Kelly glanced at her watch. Twenty minutes had passed. She couldn't wait any longer, she had to get out of there.

'You'll be seen as an accessory. You groomed and guided Daphne. You'll die in here.' Kelly bit her lip, regretting the threat. If Daphne wasn't in a caravan along the St John's Beck, then she could have just compromised the investigation. She damned her own pride.

Her mobile ringing made her jump. It was Kate.

'Guv, a helicopter located a caravan on its own, along the St John's Beck. We're going in. ETA about three minutes.'

Kelly knew that Kate would be receiving information in real time from the squads on site. She hung up and held the phone to her chest. Slowly, she turned towards the door at the end of the corridor and began walking.

'Enjoy Florida, Kelly. I know I'll see you again.'

Kelly turned to her once more. She approached the glass and stared into Amy's eyes and held her gaze. For a tiny moment, the killer lost her swagger. It was a minute fraction of a second, but it happened, and Kelly turned again and walked along the corridor, shutting out anything else the maniac said. She went through the door and breathed deeply. Ted hugged her and she allowed him to hold her.

Her mobile rang again.

Daphne was in police custody.

Chapter 63

Two months later...

The *Wendy* bobbed on the wake of a passenger steamer on Derwent Water. Josie and Callum paddle boarded about a hundred feet away and they could hear their squeals and protests, goading one another and threatening to push the other in.

Johnny flicked through his sailing log and Kelly handed him a glass of wine. In three days they'd fly to Miami and pick up a Dodge Ram, for their epic road trip to Key West. There, they'd sail a rented yacht – a Westerly – northeast, stopping off at whichever tropical island they fancied along the hundred-and-twenty-mile stretch. Big Pine, Duck, Marathon... Seafood tacos, Key Lime pie, chowder, shrimp, coconut...

They both hoped that distance from the Lakes in miles might, if they were lucky, translate to detachment from the place in thought. They knew that chances were slim and the scars were still raw. Johnny looked up appreciatively and took his wine and placed his hand on Kelly's rear. She'd just taken off her short wetsuit, which she'd had on to kayak, and she was wrapped in a small towel. He felt underneath it and squeezed her bottom approvingly.

Kelly had passed her skipper course and Johnny gained his International Certificate of Competence. It had been tricky fitting in all the hours but, without it, they'd have to hire a crew. Conditions in the Florida Bay were pleasant and they wouldn't stray too far from the shore.

Even on the water, where space and time were oftentimes suspended, Kelly still heard voices and saw visions that were unwelcome. Maybe halfway around the world it'd be different.

Perhaps they should have booked a holiday that would assault them and bombard them with noise, distraction and entertainment, thereby pushing away anything else looming in their heads: Vegas neon, Ibiza rave, or even New York traffic might have been wiser, to ward off cognisant intruders. The peace and tranquillity of sailing in a beautiful location, with one companion, and losing any sense of urgency or pressure, might turn out to be their biggest mistake.

They had healed their differences to an extent, but it wasn't the same. Johnny put Josie first and Kelly took a step back and spent more time with Ted, June and Amber. She went to her niece's birthday party alone.

The first person she'd told when a handwritten letter arrived from a Berkshire postcode had been Demi, not Johnny. Demi was writing a new book entitled *The Devil's Apprentice*. Her home address had been blocked, and arrangements had been made for her mail to be delivered to work and sorted there, as approved by HQ, and implemented by the National Offender Management Service.

The letter had been sent on the eve of Samhain, or Halloween. And it was written, as expected, by The Teacher. Kelly hadn't read it but she had glanced over it to confirm the sender and spotted the words 'thank you' and 'Daphne'. She couldn't help it.

She'd testified twice at the trial of Daphne Junker. Although the young woman existed on no national register, that's what they called her. It was held at Carlisle Crown Court and lasted two weeks. The prosecution pleaded sound mind but the defence won with their insanity plea and Daphne was sent to Broadmoor.

Kelly never wanted to interview her. The case was passed to a SIO from Lancashire Police and the trial was prepared by them. She toyed with a sabbatical. She questioned why she did her job. She doubted herself and had moments of anxiety.

It was Ted who helped her see that none of the events could be controlled by her or anyone else.

'Everyone has choices. Yours is to protect and seek justice; The Teacher's is to cause harm. It's that simple. Don't choose to be a victim. Choose to be proud.'

They'd been sitting at the Peaks Bay hotel, in the small garden, looking over Ullswater, where she'd taken Mum to lunch shortly before her last trip into hospital. It was where the ashes of the man she'd known as her father, John Porter, were scattered, incognito, without any of the hotel staff knowing, near a rhododendron bush. The flowers on that particular plant were still bigger than on any other each summer.

Kelly's team did what they did best. They worked the evidence for the appointed SIO, and put in the hours. Together. Both times Kelly went to court, she saw Daphne sitting meek and innocent in the dock. They held a momentary stare the first time and Kelly thought she saw the face of a devil. Occasionally she felt a tingle on her skin where she'd held Daphne's hand and spoken to her, so close that she could smell her hair. But she pushed aside the sensations and brushed the feeling off.

The *Wendy* steadied and Kelly pulled on a sweater. Autumn was on the wane.

She unwrapped some artisan cheese from Keswick market to go with the grapes and chutney set out on a small chopping board. She'd sliced a fresh rye loaf and set it between them with two plates. Goose bumps covered her legs and she wrapped the towel tighter. They sipped wine in between mouthfuls of food and watched as the last of the sun sank lower over the hills to the west. Cat Bells was framed in the darkening sky, and Kelly closed her eyes.

She'd set her out-of-office that afternoon and said farewell to her team for the coming three weeks.

And before that, she'd got a technician to alter her security settings.

Acknowledgments

I would like to thank the following people for their invaluable input into this book and the whole Kelly Porter series.

My agent, Peter Buckman, for his faith, encouragement and loyalty.

Louise, Fran and the whole team at Canelo. I couldn't wish to work with more passionate or professional people.

Inspector Paul Redfearn (Met Police) for cups of tea and golden nuggets of information.

DI Rob Burns (Beds Police) for always being on hand.

Dave Part, my old friend and legendary Jack the Ripper tour guide. I know Barb would have loved the books.

Steve Greenwell for some amazing climbing tips, and Auntie Sarah for introducing us.

The Lemons, Limes and Pips for the love and support.

Finally, Mike, Tilly and Freddie, my biggest fans and constant source of strength and inspiration. I love you.

ⓒ **CANELO**CRIME

Do you love crime fiction and are always on the lookout for brilliant authors?

Canelo Crime is home to some of the most exciting novels around. Thousands of readers are already enjoying our compulsive stories. Are you ready to find your new favourite writer?

Find out more and sign up to our newsletter at canelocrime.com